Praise for the work of

WENDY CORSI STAUB

three-time finalist for the Mary Higgins Clark Award

"A twisting, turning, wholly absorbing thrill ride from one of my favorite writers, *The Butcher's Daughter* had me obsessed the whole way through. A gratifying finale to a terrific trilogy, it als[illegible]nds up on its own. It's suspense [illegible]t."

—Alison Gaylin, Ed[illegible]g author [illegible]

"Wend[illegible]phs in *The Butche*[illegible]ving readers an enthralling[illegible]ng, and above all satisfying fina[illegible] to a superb trilogy."

—Hallie Ephron, *New York Times* bestselling author of *Careful What You Wish For*

By Wendy Corsi Staub

The Foundlings series
The Butcher's Daughter
Dead Silence
Little Girl Lost

Mundy's Landing series
Bone White
Blue Moon
Blood Red

Stand-alone Novels
The Black Widow
The Perfect Stranger
The Good Sister
Shadowkiller
Sleepwalker
Nightwatcher
Hell to Pay
Scared to Death
Live to Tell

WENDY CORSI STAUB

THE BUTCHER'S DAUGHTER

A FOUNDLINGS NOVEL

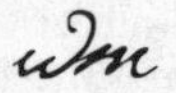

WILLIAM MORROW
An Imprint of HarperCollins*Publishers*

This is a work of fiction. Names, characters, places, and incidents are products of the author's imagination or are used fictitiously and are not to be construed as real. Any resemblance to actual events, locales, organizations, or persons, living or dead, is entirely coincidental.

First William Morrow premium printing: September 2020

Print Edition ISBN: 978-0-06-274209-4
Digital Edition ISBN: 978-0-06-274210-0

Cover design by Amy Halperin
Cover photographs © fotosmile777/Adobe Stock (woman); © Dawna Moore /Alamy Stock Photo (house); © Daniela Duncan/Getty Images (path); © Dawna Moore Photography (trees)
Author photograph by Brody Staub

FIRST EDITION

20 21 22 23 24 QGM 10 9 8 7 6 5 4 3 2 1

For my son Brody,
our newly minted Ithaca College graduate;
For my son Morgan,
my favorite Low Country research trip partner;
For my husband, Mark,
who patiently supported me through every page;
And in loving memory of my dear friends
John Guzzey, Joanie Mackowiak, Pauline Rose,
Paul Schober, and Ron Tausek.

With gratitude to Laura Blake Peterson,
Holly Frederick, and the team at Curtis Brown;
to Lucia Macro, Asanté Simons, Amy Halperin,
and the team at William Morrow;
to meticulous Gina Macedo,
triple crown Foundlings copyeditor;
to Carol Fitzgerald and the team at Bookreporter; to
John Fedyszyn, Tom Murphy, and David Prince
for sharing difficult wartime memories;
to Mark Staub, Lenny Staub, and Tommy Staub
for sharing the good old Bronx days; to Veronica Taglia;
to my family and friends, especially Alison Gaylin
and Suzanne Schmidt, who had my back along the way;
and as always, to booksellers, librarians, and readers
who sustain my creativity and make it all worthwhile.

If oonuh ent kno weh oonuh dah gwine,
oonuh should kno weh oonuh come f'um.

Translation:
If you don't know where you're going,
you should know where you come from.

—Gullah Proverb

Part I

2017

Chapter One

Sunday, January 1, 2017
Upper West Side

The silence gets her.

Strange. It's not as though Aaron ever went banging around the apartment or spoke in a booming voice. These last few months, he'd hardly spoken at all.

Yet on this morning, six weeks into his absence, stillness hangs in the Upper West Side apartment. Even the streets far below their—*her*—bedroom window are oddly quiet. The city that never sleeps seems to be snoozing right through the dawn of the New Year.

Amelia Crenshaw Haines had intended to do the same, having lain awake long after watching the ball drop in Times Square. On television, not the real thing forty-odd blocks down Broadway. But this isn't going to be one of those easy, lazy mornings. Might as well get up and get moving, like she has someplace to go, something to do.

Child, it's Sunday, and you can just get yourself to church, her mother's voice drawls in her head.

Bettina Crenshaw had never missed a service at Harlem's Park Baptist. How tickled she'd have been to see her grown-up daughter sing there in the gospel choir every other Sunday. But Amelia's been on hiatus since November. You can't resonate uplifting spirit when it's been depleted from your own life.

In the sleek, just remodeled bathroom, she plucks the lone toothbrush from the holder and finds perverse pleasure in breaking one of Aaron's rules: squeezing a tube of Crest in the middle. When she turns on the faucet, the new pipes don't creak like the old ones did, and when she turns it off, it no longer continues to drip.

She brews coffee in the sleek, also-just-remodeled kitchen. True to his word, the contractor had finished it just in time for Thanksgiving. But Amelia had spent the holiday at her friend Jessie's boisterous Ithaca household; Aaron had been in New Jersey with his family.

He'd moved out the week in mid-November. Nobody had an affair. There was no dramatic argument. They'd tried couples counseling. It confirmed that they'd simply grown apart.

In the living room, Amelia opens the shades to a towering skyline. The overcast sky is patched with blue, the same shade as the tiny dress mounted in a shadow box across the room. The dress and the tightly woven sweetgrass basket on an adjacent shelf are precious tangible links to whomever she'd been before she became Amelia Crenshaw on Mother's Day 1968.

Amelia was eighteen when she discovered, at Bettina's deathbed, that she wasn't her parents' biological daughter. Her father—Calvin Crenshaw, the man she'd grown up *believing* was her father—told her she'd been abandoned as a newborn in Park Baptist Church. He said he'd discovered her in the basket, wearing the dress and a little gold sapphire-studded signet ring, which she'd lost years ago.

She settles on the couch and makes room for her coffee mug amid remnants of a solo New Year's Eve—protein bar wrapper, empty wineglass, half-empty bottle of Cabernet. Not half-full. Not today.

She'd welcomed the prospect of quietly winding down the season after a rollicking Ithaca Christmas, but New Year's is about nostalgia for auld lang syne and resolution for the year ahead. Her own future—and yes, her past, too—couldn't be more uncertain.

A recent surge in autosomal testing has made her job easier as lab results are processed and loaded into online databases. And a few months ago, she'd finally received a genetic hit on her own bloodline. The long-awaited biological match hadn't resolved the mystery, though. Far from it.

Her DNA test had linked her to a woman in Bettina Crenshaw's tiny Southern hometown—right back to Bettina's own family tree.

If Bettina was Amelia's biological mother, had Calvin been her biological father? Why would he have made up a crazy story about finding her in a church?

Bettina's Georgia kin have been no help. Her closest cousin claimed she knew nothing about the Crenshaws taking in an abandoned baby. Yet when Amelia pressed her with the details, she said, *"I don't know about any initial rings for babies . . ."*

Amelia had never mentioned that it was an initial ring, specifically—engraved with a little blue enamel *C*.

Why the lie? Could Bettina's Southern relatives have been part of a cover-up?

Or am I just paranoid?

Amelia channel surfs past political news and bickering pundits as the media ramps up for the upcoming

Trump inauguration. She also skips images of cozy flannel-clad couples and merry multigenerational gatherings, having almost made it through this season of homey, twinkle-light-lit commercials that remind her of happier holidays.

Clicking along, she spies a familiar face. Not her own, though she appears later in this episode of Black historian Nelson Roger Cartwright's *The Roots and Branches Project.* She's been working for a few years now as an on-air genealogy consultant for the program. With Nelson's new book on bestseller lists, the cable network is airing a holiday weekend marathon to attract his readers and the hundreds of thousands of people who received DNA test kits this Christmas.

Amelia turns the channel to a local newscast and swaps the remote for her steaming coffee mug, waiting for a weather report. If today is nice, she'll kick off 2017 with a long run in the park. If not, she supposes she'll watch the Sugar Bowl—though it won't be much fun without Aaron.

The anchorman returns her bleak gaze. "In Bedford-Stuyvesant, where the violent crime rate continued to drop last year, a double homicide at the Marcy Houses yesterday left a mother and daughter dead and neighbors looking for answers."

The scene shifts to an elderly man standing on a Brooklyn street, with a yellow-crime-scene-taped brick doorway behind him. "Don't know why anyone would do something like that to decent people," he says, shaking his bald head. "They didn't bother anybody, and they didn't have anything worth stealin'."

The screen fills with a pair of close-up photographs of the victims. The older woman is vaguely familiar; the younger is . . .

"The bodies of fifty-three-year-old Alma Harrison and her thirty-one-year-old daughter, Brandy . . ."

Amelia gasps, sloshing hot coffee over her hand.

". . . were discovered late yesterday in their apartment by out-of-state relatives who grew concerned when they failed to show up at a family gathering. Police are seeking information and have ruled out robbery as a motive for the brutal slayings, believed to have taken place early yesterday morning."

Brandy Harrison?

No. Amelia would know that face anywhere.

The dead young woman's name—at least, when Amelia had met her a few months ago when she'd shown up in Amelia's office with her long-lost baby ring—had been Lily Tucker.

Not only that, but . . .

Alma Harrison.

She hurries into the bedroom to find her phone.

Newark Airport

THREE DECADES SINCE she's seen the Manhattan skyline, and she's on the wrong side of the aisle. When the plane pops out beneath a swirly gray swath, her view is of New Jersey sprawl. Still, she presses her forehead to the window, feigning fascination, back turned to her seatmate.

He'd slipped off his wedding ring as he'd boarded back in Punta Cana, leaving a white band etched on his sunburnt finger. She'd pretended that she didn't speak English. Undaunted, he dusted off his clumsy, American-accented Spanish, claiming his name is Reed and that he lives on the Upper East Side. With his dingy teeth and paunch, he doesn't look like a cosmopolitan "Reed." He looks like a Monty from the boroughs—which is exactly who he is, according to the luggage tag she'd glimpsed on his worn nylon carryon.

One duplicitous turn deserves another. She'd introduced herself as Jadzia Hernandez. That's the name on the expertly forged passport that had been delivered to her suite last night, along with a laptop, and a bouquet of white ginger lilies.

She'd slept on crisp hotel linens and boarded her flight long before dawn. Subjected to the Monty monologue, she'd attempted to read the airline magazine, but the type was blurred even when she held it at arm's length. Her once perfect vision has changed. The *world* has changed, beyond the secluded tropical haven where she's spent the last three decades. These days, everyone is plugged into something, lost and insulated.

Not Monty. He has much to say and questions to ask, like whether she's coming to New York on business, or pleasure.

"Ninguno de los dos," she tells him. Neither one.

He waggles bushy eyebrows and says that he can give her pleasure. She shrugs as if the innuendo went right over her head and resumes staring down at ribbons of gray highway winding through gray hills dotted with gray buildings. She remembers a place with turquoise water and verdant mountains and rainbow-hued homes, and knows she'll never see it again, never see—

"Ladies and gentlemen, we have begun our final

descent. Please be sure that your seatbelts are securely fastened . . ."

Monty taps her shoulder and informs her in clumsy Spanish that someone who doesn't speak English won't be able to navigate ground transportation, and she can share his cab to the city.

"*Mucho más barato para compartir,*" he adds.

Much cheaper to share it? So he's not even offering to pay her way?

"*No, gracias,*" she says with a smile and fantasizes about killing him with her bare hands.

When the plane's wheels bump and race the runway, she turns on her phone and tilts the screen away from her nosy seatmate as her messages load, type magnified to compensate for her farsightedness.

Welcome home.

She smiles.

"*Feliz Año,*" Monty says as they part ways in the terminal, pronouncing the second word without the tilde and thus unwittingly transforming the intended "Happy New Year" into "Be happy, asshole."

"Be happy, asshole," she returns in flawless English, waiting long enough to see Monty's jaw drop before disappearing into the crowd.

Central Park West

Stockton Barnes gets off the subway at Eighty-Sixth Street and reaches into his overcoat pocket for his cigarettes before remembering he'd kicked his pack-a-day habit more than three years ago. Damn. If ever there was a time he could use a calming smoke, this is it.

Outside, across the street, every bench along the low stone wall is vacant; the park beyond splotched with glowing lampposts and fringed by tall, bare limbs. He hears a shout from the playground tucked back in there. Not a child, not at this hour, though when Barnes was growing up in Harlem, his father sometimes brought him to the park after dark.

"Don't tell your mother, son. She'll say it's dangerous. That woman thinks everything's dangerous."

Nothing bad ever happened to Barnes on a midnight playground, and his father met his untimely death at home. Keeled over at the breakfast table. Heart attack.

Striding north, Barnes sucks deep breaths of chilly night air into lungs that are growing healthier and pinker by the minute.

Pedestrians are few—a dog-walking matron wearing more fur than her Pomeranian, a jogger in a headlamp, a pair of teenaged girls in identical thousand-dollar black down parkas with red arm patches. The jackets had been designed for arctic explorers but are all the rage in Manhattan's toniest neighborhoods. Barnes's own, a hundred blocks north, isn't one of them.

He turns left onto West Eighty-Seventh Street. New Year's Day is just winding down, and already he counts more bedraggled Christmas trees tossed at the curb than are lit in brownstone windows.

For many, the holidays are steeped in loneliness, depression, and stress: overspending, overtiredness, overindulgence; fighting off the flu or still fighting with family over the November election results; coping with weather woes and travel snafus. None of those scenarios apply to Barnes, but this isn't the merriest of seasons for him, either. A longtime detective with the NYPD Missing Persons Squad, he'd just spent December chasing down people who weren't where they should be, or where their families expected them to be.

'Tis the season for reflecting on the year behind, assessing the one ahead—and for some, resolving to make significant changes that don't involve significant others. Precious few disappearances at this time of year—at any time of year—involve foul play, though it does happen.

Turning right onto Broadway, he spots his destination. He's eaten at most of the all-night diners in the city, this one included. It's not an old-school greasy spoon like some, or one that caters to hipsters or tourists. Just your basic counter-booths-and-tables joint: pie behind glass, ketchup bottles on the tables, and a thick, laminated menu offering everything from hash browns to seared mahi-mahi.

Forty minutes late when he steps over the threshold, he figures she must have given up on him. There aren't many customers at this hour, and he doesn't see her. There's just one Black woman here, way back in a corner booth, intent on her cell phone. That's not her . . .

Wait, yes, it is.

He's seen Amelia Crenshaw Haines on television many times and met her in person twice. She'd always worn business attire, fully made-up, her sleek hair falling to her shoulders. Tonight, she has on a navy hoodie emblazoned with gold letters. Her hair is tucked under a Yankees baseball cap, and her face, when she looks up, bears no evidence of cosmetics.

She puts her phone away as he slides into the booth. "Trying not to be recognized?"

"Recognized?"

"You're a celebrity. On TV, and all. People must bother you when you're out in public."

"Oh, yeah. Me, Halle, Taraji, Beyoncé . . . pesky fans stalk gals like us, you know?"

"Sorry I'm late."

"What happened? Get hung up watching the big Rose Bowl comeback?"

"What comeback?"

"Penn State scored twenty-eight points in the third quarter. USC tied up the fourth with a minute left and won with a forty-six-yard field goal."

Ah, a fellow football fan—and even prettier without all the trimmings. She's precisely the kind of woman who might have convinced this longtime ladies' man to give monogamy another try . . .

If their paths had crossed in another time and place.

If she didn't already have a husband.

And *if* Barnes, who'd been briefly, reluctantly married and long divorced, hadn't promised himself that he'll never go down that road again.

"Unfortunately, I missed the game," he says. "I got held up by a case."

"It's fine. I have nowhere to go, except bed."

Barnes doesn't want to picture her there. No, he does not.

Nor does he want to wonder why she needed to meet with him at this hour on a holiday, though he suspects he knows the answer.

"Every living creature is equipped with natural instinct, Stockton," his friend Wash had once told him. *"Listen to yours."*

Yeah, his instincts tell him to stall whatever's coming. "How was your New Year's Eve?"

"Oh, uh . . . fantastic, if you think watching TV is fantastic. I did catch a glimpse of your pal Rob at the Billboard Hollywood Party."

"Right, one of his artists was performing."

Barnes had met Rob Owens, founder and CEO of Rucker Park Records, in the waiting room of a Brooklyn maternity ward in 1987. That night, Rob's wife, Paulette, delivered their firstborn son, Kurtis, and a woman named Delia Montague delivered the child Barnes had fathered in a one-night stand.

Last summer, after his own ancestral story was featured on an episode of *The Roots and Branches Project*, Rob had told Barnes about Amelia. "This woman is an investigative genealogist who specializes in reuniting long-lost family members. You should hire her to find your daughter."

"I've made a living for thirty years now finding missing people."

"Well, you haven't found her."

"Who says I want to? Or that she wants to be found?"

That was before their autumn trip to Cuba, where Barnes had a shocking encounter he'd never shared with a soul, including Rob. He'd flown home and hired Amelia to help him find the daughter he hasn't seen since she was born in October 1987.

His DNA test results aren't even back—yet Amelia has something to tell him, at this hour on a holiday?

A skinny young waiter sets a plate and a wineglass in front of her and asks Barnes, "Need a menu, or know what you want?"

"No menu. I'll just have the same thing she's having, so, uh . . ."

"Cabernet and cheese fries," she says.

Oh, yes. A woman like Amelia could have gotten a man like Barnes into all sorts of trouble under different circumstances.

"Cabernet and cheese fries. Perfect. Thanks."

The waiter walks away. Amelia tilts the stemmed glass and swirls the maroon liquid before taking a thoughtful sip, as if they're at a Napa vineyard. The lady has class.

"How is it?"

"Not bad, for diner cab." She sets down the glass and looks up at him. "Stock—"

"Just call me Barnes. Nobody but my mother calls me Stockton."

Not anymore.

"All right. Barnes . . ." She rests her hands on the table and leans forward. "Delia's old roommate, Alma Harrison, is dead."

Hardly the bombshell he'd expected. "I'm sorry to hear that, but—"

"Alma's daughter was murdered, too."

"Murdered?"

"Yes. Turns out I knew her—the daughter. She was a client. She came to me in September, and she had my gold baby ring, only she didn't use her real name, and—"

"What?"

"She used an alias. I didn't realize she was Alma's—"

"No, I mean . . . she had *what?*"

"My baby ring," she says slowly.

"Did it have a blue initial *C* and two tiny sapphires?"

Her gasp answers his question.

"There's something I need to tell you," he says, and takes a deep breath.

CONCEALED JUST BEYOND the light spilling from the diner's plate glass window, she watches the couple in the back booth. They're in profile, facing each other. The conversation is serious. She can guess what it's about, having seen surveillance screenshots of their earlier text exchange.

Can you please meet me today?

Did you find her?

I need to update you in person.

Ok, on a case now but I can meet you tonight.

Keeping an eye on the couple, she smokes an American cigarette—unfiltered, yet bland compared to pungent Cuban tobacco. She'd given up the habit years ago. This is merely a prop to ensure that passersby won't give her a second glance. These days, smokers perch solo and in groups outside restaurants and bars all over the city, relegated by law to the sidewalks.

That isn't the only thing that's changed about New York since she'd left in 1987. In the limo from the airport, she'd caught her first glimpse of the altered Manhattan skyline, aglow in late afternoon winter sunshine. New skyscrapers have sprung up everywhere, the tallest of all on the downtown site now conspicuously missing two promontories.

"Excuse me . . ."

Startled by a voice behind her, she whirls to see an emaciated stranger dressed in rags, blond hair matted around a face that was probably once handsome. He throws up his filthy hands. "Hey, don't worry. I was just going to ask for a smoke."

She exhales a stream through her nostrils, regarding him for a moment before taking the pack out of her bag. She removes a single cigarette.

"Thanks," he says. "Been trying to score a smoke for an hour, you know? People look right through me like I'm not even—"

He breaks off as she puts the cigarette into her own mouth.

"Yeah, never mind," he mutters, and turns away.

She grabs his arm.

He spins. "What the hell, lady?"

She holds out the pack of cigarettes, along with a couple of hundred-dollar bills from her pocket.

"You remind me of someone I haven't seen in a while."

Blue eyes wide, he says, "Bless you. You're an angel."

She smiles, lighting the new cigarette with the old. Most people would call her the exact opposite . . . with good reason.

"What in the world is going on, Barnes?" Amelia asks. "How do you know about my ring?"

"I found one just like it, and I gave it to Delia for Charisse."

"Where?"

"At the hospital, when I was visiting a good friend who was—"

"Which hospital?"

"Morningside Memorial. March 7, 1987."

That's precisely where and when Amelia had lost hers . . . the night her mother was dying. *Died.*

Death records are easy enough to find, if you know where to look. A detective would know where to look. So would a con artist conspiring to get the hefty reward Amelia had offered on the Lost and Foundlings website for information about her biological parents.

The ad mentioned the ring she'd been wearing when Calvin found her in 1968—but not that she'd later lost it.

"My friend Wash was a father to me after I lost mine," Barnes goes on. "When I went to the hospital that night, I thought he had pneumonia, or bronchitis. He wouldn't tell me what was wrong, but then, when I saw him . . . I knew. He was dying. The ring I found had a *C* on it, and my father was Charles. Maybe I thought it was a sign from him that Wash was going to be okay."

Amelia's reward notice hadn't specified which letter was engraved on her own ring. She'd shared that information with only three people. Jessie hadn't told. Aaron wouldn't tell. Silas Moss—long confined to a nursing home, his brilliant mind corroded by dementia—can't tell.

Her thoughts spin back to the Brandy Harrison connection.

In September, she'd come to Amelia posing as Lily Tucker, a fellow foundling searching for her roots.

She showed Amelia a tiny signet ring she said she'd been wearing when she'd been abandoned in a Connecticut shopping mall in 1990. It was identical to the one Amelia had on when Calvin found her in 1968.

Amelia never got a chance to ask her about it. Lily was a no-show for her next appointment, and unresponsive when Amelia tried to reschedule with her. That isn't unusual in this business. She warns new clients that not all cases end in happy family reunions, and that they shouldn't embark on a search unless they're braced for possible heartbreak. Many people step back to digest that information and pop up months later ready to proceed with finding their lost loved ones. She'd hoped Lily Tucker would be one of them.

Now it turns out she wasn't Lily Tucker, and she's been murdered, along with her mother.

"Look, Amelia, I was planning on turning the ring in to the hospital's lost and found, but I was upset about Wash that night, and I forgot about it. Lousy, I know." Barnes slumps back in his seat as if crushed beneath three decades of guilt.

But he didn't *steal* the ring. People find, and keep, far more significant things without a hint of remorse. Calvin Crenshaw had scooped up a baby from the church pew like a dropped handkerchief or loose change—assuming what he'd told Amelia was even true.

"That night, right after I left the hospital, I met Delia. It was just a one-night stand," Barnes adds, as if Amelia's opinion of his promiscuity matters. "She got pregnant. I moved. By the time she tracked me down, the baby was about to be born. When I found out what Delia had named her, I couldn't believe it. *Charisse.* She didn't know my father was *Charles.* Listen, I'm a detective, and I'm not supposed to believe in coincidences, but . . ."

"Life is full of them, and I've seen bigger."

"So have I, Amelia. So have I."

"Like your finding my ring?"

"I obviously didn't know it was your ring, so—"

"Then why not mention it from the start? I request full disclosure from my clients, and if that was the one thing you gave your daughter, then it's important."

"It isn't."

"No detail is too trivial when I'm searching for someone's—"

"I don't mean it's not *important.* I mean it's not the *only* thing I gave Delia for Charisse. Look, I—"

"Here you go." The waiter sets Cabernet and cheese fries in front of Barnes and glances at Amelia's food, untouched, cheese goo congealing. "Everything okay here?"

Barnes waves him away. "Everything's *fine.*"

The waiter moves on to clear an adjoining table. A few booths away, a middle-aged woman is finishing a sandwich. The place is otherwise empty.

Barnes resumes his account in a low voice. "My daughter was born prematurely. When I saw her, tiny and fragile and helpless, I wanted nothing but the best for her. In my mind, that meant that I would not—could not—be a part of her life."

He'd told Amelia all of this when they'd met—that he wasn't cut out to be a family man, and certainly not the kind of father his little girl deserved. That if he tried, there'd come a day when she'd need him and he wouldn't be there—because of the job, or because he couldn't get along with her mother, or any number of reasons fathers break their children's hearts. He'd decided she was better off without him, and he'd walked away.

Amelia may not have agreed with his logic, but she accepted his story. She's heard it hundreds, thousands of times.

"I knew I'd do everything in my power to protect that little girl. I couldn't be there with her, but I figured my dad could. That's why I left the ring. But guardian angels can't cover expensive medical care, and neither could her mother and I. Delia was divorced. Unemployed and homeless. I was broke. I was also young and stupid, and I did a stupid thing."

He avoids her gaze, stamping wet interlocking rings on his paper place mat with his water glass as he goes on. "Ever hear of Perry Wayland?"

"Sounds familiar."

"He was a hedge fund millionaire—or billionaire, if you believed the tabloids. He disappeared in October '87, a few days after the stock market crash. His Mercedes was found on the GW Bridge—staged suicide. And . . . this doesn't go any further, okay? Strictly confidential."

"Got it."

"My partner Stef and I tracked Wayland to . . . it doesn't matter where. I didn't see him myself, but Stef did. Wayland said he'd run off with his mistress, and he bribed Stef to look the other way. Stef knew my daughter was fighting for her life in the ICU. He handed me a wad of cash." Barnes looks Amelia in the eye. "I didn't hand it back. I gave it to Delia, and the ring, too, and then I walked away. Wayland left the country with his mistress, and I never told a soul."

Ah, no wonder. He isn't just harboring guilt about the ring. All these years, he's been hiding something much bigger . . . *if* his story is true.

"You told me you looked for Charisse, a few years after she was born. And you met Alma."

He nods. "I went out to where they'd been living, in the Marcy Projects. Alma was still there, and she had a little daughter of her own."

"Brandy Harrison. So that's how she got the ring."

"Probably. Alma said Delia had taken off with Charisse, and she hadn't heard from her. I hoped they'd found a better place. The projects were dangerous back then."

"And dangerous now. I mean . . . they were murdered."

"Yeah."

He looks around for eavesdroppers. The waiter has disappeared. The middle-aged female customer is in earshot, but appears to be lost in her own thoughts.

Barnes leans forward, voice dropping to a whisper. "A few months ago, when I was on vacation in Cuba with Rob and Kurtis, I ran into Perry Wayland. I guess he thought I'd come looking for him—like after all these years, his case mattered to the NYPD. Anyway, he made some threats, and . . ." He heaves a deep breath. "That's why I hired you to find my daughter. Wayland said he already had."

"And you think he got to Alma and Delia?"

"I don't know what to think. But there's one more thing. Do you remember—"

He breaks off, pulls his phone from his pocket, and holds up a forefinger, indicating he has to take the call. "Yeah, Barnes here . . . yeah . . . yeah, I'm on my way."

He hangs up, stands up, throws some cash on the table, and pulls on his coat. "Sorry. I've got to go. It's the job."

"But you said there was one more thing."

"Yeah, not important."

She frowns, watching him walk away as the waiter approaches.

"Can I get you anything else?"

"Just the check, please. And I'll take hers as well." Amelia points to the woman, who reminds her of Bettina Crenshaw, with world-weary posture and tired brown eyes.

"Should I tell her you—"

"No, I'd rather be anonymous. Someone once did the same thing for me."

Nineteen years old, she'd just stepped off a bus in Ithaca, determined to meet the famed Cornell University molecular biology professor Silas Moss. He'd been on television the night before, talking about his pioneering autosomal DNA research project.

She'd walked into Moosewood Restaurant, ordered a meal she couldn't afford, and the waitress told her an anonymous stranger had paid her bill.

"Someday," she'd told an incredulous Amelia, *"when you come across someone who looks like they need a friend, or a favor, you'll do the same for them."*

She's since done just that, more times than she can count.

But she's not so certain her own benefactor that day at Moosewood had been a stranger.

She could have sworn she'd glimpsed a Harlem neighbor in Ithaca—and not just any neighbor. Like

Bettina, the enigmatic Marceline LeBlanc was from somewhere down south.

After Bettina's death, Marceline had come to pay her respects and befriended Amelia. All that summer and into the fall, she'd been almost . . .

A guardian angel.

Like Barnes had wanted for his daughter. Only Marceline had been very much alive, and she was no angel, with a sharp tongue and sharper eyes. Bettina, and Calvin, too, had always warned Amelia to stay away from her—because they were devout Baptists, and she was rumored to practice voodoo? Or because they were afraid she'd tell Amelia something they didn't want her to know?

Marceline said she'd seen Calvin leave Park Baptist with a bundle—Amelia—on that predawn Mother's Day in 1968. But had she also seen whoever left the baby?

Amelia never had a chance to pry it out of her. She left New York for good, headed back home, down south, she said.

Looking back, Amelia understands that Marceline's departure had felt like something of an abandonment. If she hadn't left, Amelia might never have found her way to Ithaca.

Surely, it had been wishful thinking that Marceline had followed her upstate and yes, paid for her lunch. Surely, she hadn't really been there.

But if she had . . . why?

Smoking her last cigarette in the cold night air, the woman leans closer to the diner window to block the reflected glare. She'd forgotten that New York nights are never truly dark.

She misses the balmy black Cuban sky glittering with stars. Here, they're dimmed by streetlights and floodlights, blocked by skyscrapers.

Every time she looks at the new skyline, she expects to see the twin towers. She'd been thirteen hundred miles away in Baracoa, Cuba, when terrorists destroyed them. Monitoring the media hysteria, she believed Judgment Day was nigh, as foretold by her father, via Revelations.

"Alas, alas, that great city, wherein were made rich all that had ships in the sea by reason of her costliness! for in one hour is she made desolate."

The September 11 attacks had been a false alarm. Not the first, nor the last, nor the most notable in her own life.

In October 1987, the Black Monday stock market crash instigated her escape from New York; this past October 2016, Hurricane Matthew triggered her return. Neither catastrophe brought biblical Armageddon, but both are monumental bookends in her personal history, marking the end of the world as *she* knew it.

And in both incidents, the man in the diner had played a pivotal role.

Shifting her position, she notices that his dining companion is now alone at the table.

She whirls just in time to see him step through the glass door onto the sidewalk, flipping up the collar on his woolen coat. He turns in her direction, looking right at her, but doesn't see her.

Focused on the traffic stopped just beyond the red

light on Broadway, he steps to the curb and raises an arm to hail a taxi. The light changes, a yellow cab pulls up, and he's gone.

He's sneaky like that, Stockton Barnes. She'll have to keep a closer eye on him.

She exhales a stream of smoke and returns her gaze to the woman in the diner.

Anyone who's ever lived in New York City knows that it can be an extraordinarily small world. She supposes it was inevitable that Amelia Crenshaw Haines and Stockton Barnes would eventually cross paths. If a missing persons detective wants to find the daughter he'd abandoned in infancy, he's going to turn to an investigative genealogist. Amelia is one of the country's most high-profile experts. *And* they have a mutual acquaintance, Rob Owens.

The Hudson River unfurls a bitter wind. The cigarette has burned to a nub. Isaiah's prophecy rings in her head as she takes a long last drag.

"Woe to the wicked! It will go badly with him, For what he deserves will be done to him."

Her phone buzzes in her pocket, a reminder that someone is waiting for her.

Gypsy Colt crushes the butt on the sidewalk with her black boot and slips away into the night.

Chapter Two

Monday, January 2

Despite a sleepless night, morning-after clarity has left Barnes grateful that his NYPD-issued phone had cut short his diner meeting with Amelia. He'd been about to ask her if she remembered Oran Matthews, the Brooklyn Butcher, and tell her that Wayland's mistress was—*is*—the Butcher's daughter, Gypsy Colt.

As Barnes completes paperwork for a missing persons case after a sleepless night, his body begs him to go home to bed, but his brain is fixated on the damned ring, and the Harrisons' double murder. He makes a couple of calls, asks a couple of questions, and discovers that his old friend Sumaira El Idrissi is working the Harrison case.

One more phone call, this time directly to her.

"Hey, Barnes, what's up?"

"I've got a lead on the Bed-Stuy murders."

"Yeah? What—"

"I need to tell you in person. Are you at the scene?"

"Where else?"

"I'll be there within the hour."

He makes it in forty-five minutes, including a stop at the halal deli and a pause to greet the uniformed cops at the entrance to Alma Harrison's building.

Sumaira is in the hallway outside the apartment, talking to another detective. Seeing Barnes, she excuses herself and strides toward him, phone in hand and a navy wool coat draped over her shoulders like a cape.

Decades ago, Barnes had sworn off dating fellow cops after a brief, disastrous marriage to one, but he regrets it whenever he connects with Sumaira, an attractive brunette in her early forties. Her black pantsuit is unrumpled, her hair looks freshly brushed, and if she has circles under her eyes, they're masked by makeup.

"How are the knuckles holding up?" he asks.

"Exactly how you'd think."

Yeah. Working a case in an impoverished building without interior security cameras to capture criminal activity, detectives have to knock on a lot of doors, and the search for witnesses and information can be grueling and fruitless. Regardless of what neighbors know and their willingness to share, they're understandably wary of unexpected visitors calling "Police!"

"For you." He hands Sumaira a large black coffee and white paper bag from the deli.

She peers inside. "My favorite! Thank you. Let's talk inside," she says around an enormous bite of black-and-white cookie, and leads him past crime scene tape and uniformed cops into Alma Harrison's apartment. A forensics guy is on his phone in a corner of the kitchenette, and another packs up equipment.

If Barnes had never been here before, he might attribute the disarray to crime scene aftermath. But other than fingerprint dust, he's guessing this is what it looked like before the murders, if not what it had smelled like. The corpses are gone, but the stench of death remains despite windows wide-open to the cold morning wind.

Sumaira points to a large dark stain on the floor beneath a string of Christmas lights taped to a blood-spattered living room wall. "Daughter was there. Mother was in the bathroom."

"Same time frame?"

"No. Probably a few hours apart, the mother first." She gestures at a couch littered with food wrappers, a pizza box, and laundry that isn't likely clean. "You want to sit?"

"I don't even want to breathe. How are you eating in here?"

"Starvation and desensitization." She swallows the last of her cookie, crumples the empty bag, and balances it on top of a heap of garbage in a kitchen can. Then she takes a small notebook out of her coat pocket, clicks a pen, and looks at Barnes. "Tell me what you've got."

"I knew them."

"The Harrisons?"

"Not well. But you're never going to believe this . . ."

She jots notes and asks questions as he fills her in. For now, he leaves out Perry Wayland, Cuba, Stef, and the dirty money—not for his own sake, but for his daughter's. Reopening the Wayland cold case would be a complex, expensive bureaucratic task and most certainly stall the investigation. It might also bring his own ugly secret to light, sidelining him with complications and repercussions.

He can't let that happen. His priority is to locate Charisse and find out who'd murdered those two women. Common sense would indicate that Wayland and Gypsy Colt have nothing to do with this.

"But what is your gut telling you, Stockton?" Wash asks in his head.

The exact opposite.

"*Tawafuq*," Sumaira comments.

"Excuse me?"

"In my faith, that's what we call synchronicity others might consider coincidence. Your finding a ring in 1987, giving it to your baby mama, and then thirty years later, her friend's daughter returns it to the original owner . . . *tawafuq*."

"Two things about that. One, she didn't *return* it to Amelia. She just showed it to her."

"Really? I wonder where it is, then? We didn't find anything but costume jewelry here, and believe me, we looked, because the daughter was wearing an expensive necklace and bracelet. What's the second thing?"

"Please don't call Delia my 'baby mama.' I haven't seen her since 1987. Two strangers, one drunken night. That's all it was."

"What about Amelia?"

"She never met her."

"No, I mean, you said she's single. Are you two—"

"I *said* her marriage fell apart over the last few months."

"Isn't that the same thing? Are you seeing her?"

"No, and no." He scowls. "How is this relevant?"

"You're ornery today."

"Sorry." Barnes rubs the burning spot between his shoulder blades. "I haven't eaten or slept in—"

"I get it. Believe me. Anyway . . . *tawafuq*. Every

incident has meaning. You and Amelia were meant to come together."

His phone vibrates. Ah, *tawafuq* sparing them both his ornery reply.

Or is it?

Amelia is asking him to give her a call when he gets up.

Gets up?

What is that woman thinking? Does she know anything about police work?

No, she does not. Because she isn't a cop. But that doesn't mean he wants to date her, or that her texting him in this particular moment has some kind of cosmic significance.

Ignoring the text, he thrusts the phone back into his pocket, apologizes to Sumaira, and asks her what happened to the Harrisons.

"Close range double taps, back of the head."

Double taps—two bullets, rapid fired to get the job done with maximum efficiency.

"No signs of forced entry, robbery, a struggle," she continues. "No known enemies."

"So we're looking at premeditated, execution-style?"

"Yes."

"Who found them?"

"Relatives from Connecticut. The victims were due up there Friday for a family party, but they didn't get off the bus and no one could get ahold of them. Saturday, a cousin came to check on them and found them. No evidence so far of drugs, gangs, organized crime. But the cousin said the daughter had a new boyfriend. Older, and with big bucks. We're following that lead."

"It would tie in with the fancy jewelry."

"Yes, and something else. Here, I'll show you."

She opens the door to a tiny bedroom, and he smells a familiar floral perfume wafting with squalor and death.

Sumaira points to a nightstand. A large etched crystal vase rises above the clutter. It's filled with delicate white blooms. "From a florist, and not cheap. They're lilies."

Not just any lilies, Barnes knows.

White ginger mariposa—the national flower of Cuba.

GYPSY TAKES AN unsatisfying sip of coffee and plunks the cup back on the room service tray beside half-eaten toast and grapefruit. Measly American substitutes for *café con leche*, ripe guava, and thick, butter-slathered Cuban bread.

But New York City does many things better—bagels, pizza, cloaks of anonymity. Here, no one cares who or what she is.

Almost no one.

Stockton Barnes had been assigned to investigate Perry Wayland's disappearance back in 1987. The tabloids had a field day speculating about the suicidal tycoon until that story was eclipsed by a copycat killer who'd nearly succeeded in finishing off the four females who'd survived the Brooklyn Butcher back in 1968.

Gypsy and Perry left the country to await Judgment Day in Baracoa, one of the most remote places on earth. Nearly three decades later, they were still waiting when Barnes showed up in their tiny island community. A coincidence, he claimed. But her father always told her that coincidences are signs. She'd been so caught up in interpreting that one that she'd overlooked something more significant.

A storm of biblical proportion was barreling toward their island paradise, precisely as foretold in Isaiah 28:2: *"A destroying storm, as a flood of mighty waters overflowing . . ."*

Having spent the days leading up to Hurricane Matthew fixated on the detective's presence, she belatedly herded her followers to her mountainside retreat as opposed to the government-ordered shelters. There was no decision to be made. She was not their dictator, but their leader, their savior.

Feverishly flipping through her Bible as the storm blew in, she'd settled on Kings 19:11. *"Go forth, and stand upon the mount."*

If only—

Someone knocks on the suite door.

The housekeeping staff starts at nine, but they wouldn't ignore the Do Not Disturb sign. Nude, she climbs out of bed, ignoring the plush white robe and slippers. Her feet are cold on the marble floor, but she'll be back in bed momentarily, and this time, not alone.

Unless . . .

"Who is it?" she calls through the door, thinking of the detective who'd turned up on that remote New England coastal island and a far more remote Cuban one.

"Who do you think?"

"Just making sure." She flips the security lock, greets her visitor with a passionate kiss, and leads him to the bedroom.

THE CITY THAT had snoozed well past dawn on New Year's yesterday has resumed humming with hyperactivity. Amelia shoulders her way off a rush-hour subway wearing last night's hoodie, jeans, and sneakers under a puffy parka. Unpresentable, yes, but she has no client appointments until this afternoon, and can dash home to shower and change at lunchtime. Right now she's on a mission so pressing that she skips her morning latte, barely breaking stride to buy mucky coffee-cart brew as she hurries toward her office.

At the turn of the last century, the brick tenement was overcrowded with European immigrants and the neighborhood rampant with slums. By the turn of this one, Allen Street's historic medians were decaying and the building was a rat-infested ruin. Now it houses professional offices on a charming block overlooking a restored, landscaped pedestrian mall.

She climbs the creaky wooden stairway to a door bearing a brass plate that reads AMELIA CRENSHAW HAINES, INVESTIGATIVE GENEALOGIST. Every time she sees it, wistfulness taints the surge of pride. No longer just because Bettina, Calvin, and her beloved mentor Silas Moss can't bear witness to her thriving career, but because the husband who'd proudly put up the placard is no longer in her life.

"Who knows? We might find out we can't live without each other, either," Aaron had said, zipping his suitcase on the chilly November morning before walking out the door for the last time.

"I hope so."

"Do you, Amelia?"

She couldn't answer the question then for the fierce lump in her throat.

She can't now, because she's not sure.

Her life has gone on much the same way it always

has. Aaron had traveled more than he was home ever since he'd made partner at his corporate law firm years ago, so she's long accustomed to being on her own. In fact, her loneliest moments had unfolded when they were together.

Her kitten, Clancy, is affectionate company, her work keeps her busier than ever, and her social life is unchanged. Childless by choice, Amelia and Aaron hadn't hung out with fellow couples in years. He'd cultivated his circle of pals and colleagues and she has hers, though her longtime friendship with his sister has grown strained.

"You're part of the family. My parents still want you to come for Thanksgiving," Karyn had said back in November.

"I don't think that's a good idea."

"Oh, Aaron is fine with it. He knows we all love you. He loves you, too. I'm sure you guys will work things out. He can be difficult, but he'll come around."

"It's not just him, Karyn. I have some stuff of my own to work out, too."

"You mean, the thing with your mother?"

The thing with your mother—as if it's some innocuous to-do list detail that needs tending. As if Amelia hadn't finally clawed her way out of a gaping crater, scarred and dazed, only to be hit again by that unexpected DNA match to Bettina.

She's hoping to find some answers at last on Martin Luther King weekend, when she and her friend Jessie fly to Bettina's hometown. The plane tickets had been Jessie's Christmas gift to Amelia.

"We're going to figure this out together, Mimi, on location!"

Jessie is the only one who calls her by that nickname, and as a fellow foundling, the only one who understands what it's like to have been abandoned as a newborn. Well, besides Clancy, who'd been found on the street and brought to a kill shelter, where Amelia had rescued him.

She unlocks the door and steps into an office that had once felt spacious, with high tin ceilings and tall windows. Now it's cluttered with stacks of bankers boxes containing files that long ago overflowed the cabinets, courtesy of predigitalization-era research.

The building is chilly every Monday morning, but she's earlier than usual today, and the place had been vacant through the holiday week. A cold wind rattles the windowpane and a smattering of snowflakes swirl beyond. Still bundled in her coat, she settles on the couch with her client records for the woman she now knows was Brandy Harrison.

Last night as she was drifting off to sleep, she remembered something. Brandy might have lied about her name, but she'd given Amelia a folder filled with newspaper accounts about a Black toddler abandoned at a Connecticut shopping mall in 1990. Why?

Skimming the thick sheaf in the manila folder, Amelia is struck anew by two details.

There's no mention in any press account of a later adoption or charmed life the foundling had supposedly gone on to lead as Lily Tucker.

And the articles Brandy had given her weren't printed off the internet, as they would be if the story had been accessed in online archives. These are photocopies of actual clippings, mostly torn, not cut, from newspapers. Either they'd been collected at the time the story was unfolding, or someone had gone to a lot of trouble and expense to hunt down copies of vintage papers to make the file look authentic.

The Connecticut child was discovered at downtown New Haven's Chapel Square Mall just after the place opened. Unlike Amelia, she'd have been old enough to comprehend that she was alone in the world and surrounded by strangers.

The media accounts detail how she'd been found in a dim corner of the cavernous mall, sound asleep in a cheap folding stroller. The accompanying photos show a strikingly pretty little girl. Her chin is down, upturned gaze wide-eyed and frightened. Amelia studies her features. Her mouth is a delicate rosebud mouth; her enormous eyes fringed by long, thick lashes. There's something familiar about her.

She uses her phone to snap photos of the child in the clippings, then grabs another client's file and snaps a few more. Flipping back through the articles, she makes notes on a pad.

The child is described as unkempt, dressed in grungy pink corduroy overalls and a jacket that was two sizes too big for her, and a season shy of the weather. No mention is made of a little gold ring on a chain.

That doesn't mean there hadn't been one. But why would the authorities withhold it from the press? There was no reward offer to protect, and it wasn't a criminal case.

Her phone dings with a text.

It's from Jessie. Last night, Amelia had called to tell her about her meeting with Barnes. Of course Jessie immediately wanted to know if he was single and hot.

"Both, but that's not why I'm calling," Amelia said.

She told Jessie about the Brooklyn murders and the gold ring, leaving out Perry Wayland and the bribe, having promised Barnes she'd keep it to herself.

Any updates? Jessie asks now.

Amelia writes back, Can you talk?

Her phone rings a moment later.

"Mimi? Everything okay?"

"Yes—it's just a lot to type. Are you on your way to work?" Jessie is a therapist with an enormous caseload.

"Not yet. I just got Theodore to school and now I'm doing laundry. Chip's ski boot socks stink to high heaven and Petty thinks everything that's not a towel should be washed by itself on delicate and hung to dry."

"Can't they do their own?" she asks, aware that Jessie's oldest son and daughter are home from college on winter break.

"They can, if you don't mind having the laundry room tied up for days. I *mind*. Anyway, I was talking to Billy this morning—when we were still on speaking terms, which was before he tried to help me lug two tons of dirty clothes to the basement . . ."

"That's a switch." Jessie's husband is recuperating from a heart attack.

"Yeah, I told him to hold that thought, because the second the cardiologist gives him the all clear, I'm taking a bubble bath while he does the laundry *and* scrubs the toilet."

How Amelia envies the steadfast Jessie and Billy, affectionately—and sometimes not—squabbling through twenty-five years of never having enough time or money, but more than enough love to sustain each other and a kid-filled, pet-filled old house.

"Mimi, I know this Barnes guy is all that—"

"I never said—"

"I heard what you were saying *between* the words."

Amelia sighs. Yes, Barnes is handsome and cool, rugged yet refined—so okay, maybe he is *all that*—but it's beside the point.

"Your perspective is thrown off because he's sweet-talking you. You need to be careful."

"Jessie, if you think any man can sweet-talk me after what I've been through, you're crazy. I'm nowhere near ready to date yet."

"Uh, Mimi? I meant be careful because I'm not sure he's on the up-and-up about your ring. But if—"

"I know what you meant. I was joking! Obviously!"

"Obviously."

Amelia imagines Jessie's wry smile.

"And he is on the up-and-up about the ring," she adds.

"I hope so, because I was telling Billy about this, and he did some sniffing around, and the good news is that Barnes really is an NYPD missing persons detective."

"Of course he is." Though Amelia, too, had done some searching online last night, just to be certain. "What's the bad news?"

"It doesn't mean he wasn't working with Lily Tucker, or whoever she is, to scam you. There are plenty of dirty cops around."

"Barnes isn't one of them."

"I hope you're right."

"I'm always right."

"That's *my* line. So listen, Billy also googled a description of your ring. You know what pops up first? That ad you placed looking for your parents, with a twenty-five-thousand-dollar reward. I bet Brandy tried to look up the ring's value because she needed money, stumbled across your ad, and realized it was worth a lot more than any pawnshop would give her. So she came to you posing as a client."

"But why the little girl who was abandoned in Connecticut in 1990?"

"Because she knew being a foundling would strike a chord with you, just like it did between you and me. Instant bond. Instant trust."

"No, I know, but why that particular foundling?"

"Probably random."

"I don't think so. Hang on. I'm going to send you something." She lowers her phone, finds two photos she snapped, and texts them to Jessie's phone. As she explains her hunch, her friend gasps.

"If you're right, Mimi, then you need to report this."

"I will," she assures her friend.

But not until she's told Stockton Barnes.

GYPSY ROLLS OVER in bed and opens her eyes.

The suite's bedroom is cast in shadow now. A fat pigeon waddles on the sill outside the window. Beyond, storm clouds hang low along the geometric skyline.

Why had she been so homesick for New York City when she'd first arrived in Cuba thirty years ago? It's nothing but gray—buildings, weather, the damned bird, even the modern suite's décor.

She'd give anything to be back in Baracoa, where architecture, wildlife, and natural landscape are drenched in vibrant color.

A fingertip trails along her shoulder like a spider, and she flinches.

"Good morning."

She turns her head. His face is inches from hers. "It's afternoon."

He glances at his watch. He'd pretended to love it, because it was a gift from her. It's a Breitling. Old-school, to replace his smart watch. Distractions are dangerous.

"So? We don't have to be anyplace." He yawns, stretches for the remote on the nightstand, and turns on the television.

Donald Trump, the president elect, is standing at a podium, talking.

"He's the devil."

Gypsy sighs. "No, he isn't."

"Trust me. I've met him."

"So have I." *And I've met the devil, too, and he wasn't Donald Trump.*

She points at the TV. "He's King Cyrus. Winning the election was a preordained miracle. Biblical prophecy told us that God would anoint him to subdue nations, and—I've already explained this to you. Signs are everywhere. Only the chosen ones recognize them."

"Quoting your father again?"

"My father has nothing to do with this. You've read Isaiah *45*." She gestures at the television. "He's the *forty-fifth* president. A sign. Judgment Day is coming. But we don't need to hear Cyrus rant. Turn it off."

"I'll just turn the channel."

"I *said* turn it *off*." She snatches the remote from him, aims, and the screen goes black.

"Hey!" He reaches for it, and she throws it across the room. Grinning as if it's a game, he reaches for her instead.

She evades him, sitting up and pulling on her robe. "You already had your pleasure, my friend. Time for business."

"I'd say we both had our pleasure."

"Well, you know what they say. All play and no work makes Jack a dull—"

"I'm not Jack, and that's not what they say. It's all *work* and no play."

"That's not what *I* say. And you should know by now that what *I* say, *goes*."

He sits up, stoops to snatch his black tee shirt from the floor, and yanks it over his head, then catches her staring at him. He goes still, uncertainty in his eyes, the shirt cowled around his neck.

"Sometimes I wonder just how committed you are," she says.

"To you? One hundred percent! You know that I—"

"To me, and to our destiny. We've got important work to do, and I wonder if you—"

"I'm with you, baby. All the way. You know that."

She knots the robe around her waist and walks to the window. From here, she can see the Park Avenue penthouse where Perry once lived with his wife and daughters. There are potted trees on the little terrace now, a valiant, verdant patch in the bleak cityscape.

Mary, Mary, quite contrary . . .

Gypsy hasn't thought of her in years—the little old lady who'd lived in a small house across from her Bronx high school. Her name might have been Mary, or maybe it was just what everyone called her. Mary, Mary—out there rain or shine, tending her doormat-sized flower patch. Chrysanthemums grew there in the fall, and crocuses in the spring . . .

Gypsy winces, pushing away the memory of a boy who'd once said her eyes were the same shade.

"I need you to find someone," she says, her back still to the man in the bed.

"Someone *else*?"

"Yes. Her name is Margaret Costello."

"Isn't she—"

"Yes. She is."

"But that was a long time ago. I thought we were—"

"If you're not willing, I'm perfectly capable of doing it myself."

"You sure about that?"

"I'm sure about *everything* I do." She turns to regard him through narrowed eyes, irked to see his phone in his hand.

He's always checking the damned thing, even in mid conversation. She's told him how she feels about that, and he's reminded her that technology is crucial to their plan.

He's right, of course. From surveillance software to online records, everything they need is quite literally at their fingertips. It's quite remarkable.

Yet much has been sacrificed.

She thinks of all those years in Cuba. Of Perry's eyes, Perry's whole being, focused only on Gypsy. Not just Perry—an army of followers.

She walks over to the full-length mirror. She takes off the robe, letting it pool at her feet. She reaches for a brush on the vanity and runs it in languid strokes through her long hair.

"Oh, man, baby. What are you trying to do to me?" The man reflected behind her in the bed is now fixated on Gypsy, as he should be.

She looks damned magnificent, not just for her years. In this light, there's no hint of the faint fine lines around her full mouth and violet eyes. Her body is firm and trim, long legged and sun bronzed without tan lines. A small horse is inked above her left breast.

Every time she sees it, she thinks of Oran's favorite scripture. John 8:44.

"Ye are of your father the devil, and the lusts of your father ye will do."

But she has no interest in leading disciples to an eternal reward. There can be just one true prophet in paradise.

And there will be, as long as Margaret Costello and her child are found, and eliminated.

THERE WAS A time when a stroll down Barnes's Washington Heights block felt like Russian roulette. Now there's a community garden adjacent to his building, and a new jungle gym in the courtyard.

As he climbs four flights of stairs to his apartment, he passes a father and son who live on the top floor. They're hand in hand, the child bundled up, bouncing down one step at a time, and whining.

"Because I said so," the man is saying, with a weary headshake and smile for Barnes.

He thinks of his own dad. After a grueling double shift, Charles Barnes would detour on the way home to conceal a copper coin on the slide, swings, or teeter-totter. Then, instead of collapsing into bed, he'd rouse Barnes from his and they'd sneak out into the night to play "Penny on the Playground."

"You're getting colder!" he'd call as Barnes ran around

trying to find the coin. *"Ooooh, now you're warm. Warmer! Son, you are burning* hot*!"*

Not in *this* moment. Stepping over the threshold, Barnes shivers out of his cashmere overcoat and wool suit jacket. Throughout December, his apartment had been so overheated he'd had the windows wide-open on ten-degree nights. A maintenance man had tinkered with the vents. Ever since, the place has felt like a meat locker, but he keeps forgetting to call the super about it.

He locks the dead bolt and puts his badge, keys, wallet, and leather gloves on an adjacent table beside ten days' worth of unopened mail. Mostly bills, catalogs, and junk mail. But there are larger envelopes, too, some red or green. Every January, when he opens the final batch of holiday cards from friends and family, he resolves to send out his own next December. It never happens.

Sitting on the couch to untie his shoes, he eyes the photo cards he'd opened early in December and displayed on a shelf. Some feature smiling kids and babies, others entire families. His friend Rob's card is, as always, the largest and most spectacular of all. He and his wife, Paulette, and their five kids are posed in front of their brick mansion beside a decorated towering pine that rivals the one in Rockefeller Plaza.

The house is as picture-perfect inside as it is out. The family, beyond the facade . . . not so much. Rob swears his rock-solid marriage isn't faltering, but he and Paulette are increasingly at odds about the kids. Their oldest son is pushing thirty, unemployed, and perpetually at odds with his father. Their middle daughter is on academic probation, and their youngest had her driver's license suspended for speeding a few weeks after she got it.

Whenever Rob updates Barnes on the household conflict, Barnes usually feels like he dodged a bullet when he opted out of marriage and fatherhood. Still, even troubled families love each other.

Don't you go feeling sorry for your lonely self, Stockton. You want someone to love, you go find someone to love.

Wash, haunting him as usual.

In the living room, Barnes notices that the coffee table poinsettia has gone limp, and the Douglas fir's branches have withered beneath the ornaments. He's been too busy to water them and now he's too tired and too cold, and anyway, the holidays are over.

Uh-huh, Ebenezer, you just go right ahead and let them die, chides the Ghost of Christmas Past, Present, and Future, all rolled into one. Barnes sighs and returns to the kitchen, dumping this morning's cold coffee from the pot and filling it at the sink.

Petals drop as he waters the plant, and when he reaches for the tree's holder, dry needles rain over a small stack of wrapped gifts. They're from him, waiting for the woman who already has everything and can afford none of it.

His mother is away on a cruise—her Christmas gift to herself, along with a boatload of costume jewelry courtesy of a home shopping program.

"They're from Jennifer Lopez's new line," she'd said at the pier, showing off her shiny earrings and bangles. *"What do you think?"*

I think you're no J. Lo, and you should have put the money toward your insane credit card bills, or the rent.

But he'd long given up trying to curtail his mother's

impulse buys and untangle her finances. She'd given him a heap of Christmas presents he can't wear, use, or fit into his apartment. He'd thanked her and then returned everything, crediting her account, well aware she'll never realize.

He gave himself the only gift that matters this year, revisiting the neighborhood tattoo parlor that had long ago inked his father's initials, and later Wash's, on his right bicep. Now his daughter's name is on his left, scrolled across a heart.

"You make a choice, Stockton, and someday you're either going to regret it, or congratulate yourself that it was the right one," Wash had said the night Barnes confessed he'd gotten a stranger pregnant during a one-night stand.

"There is no choice. I'm not going to help raise a kid, period. It'll be better off without me."

"Were you better off without your father?"

"Hell, no. It's the same thing, whether you drop dead, or take off because the stock market crashed, or because their mother is a pain in the ass, or because you're not cut out for being a dad and you never wanted kids in the first place. The kid gets hurt in the end."

"So it's better to hurt them in the beginning, is that what you're saying?"

It was exactly what Barnes had been saying. Charisse couldn't miss or grieve or hate a man she'd never known.

Now that *someday* is here, is he looking back congratulating himself that he'd made the right choice?

"I still don't know, Wash," he mutters. "How can I know if I regret it until I see how her life turned out?"

He takes a long, hot shower that warms him, leaving him drowsy and craving bed. In the chilly bedroom, he sets the alarm for 3 p.m., and plugs his work phone into the bedside charger.

His personal phone contains a couple of texts. He opens the first as he shoves his bare feet between cold sheets and pulls the quilts up to his chin. It's a video snippet from Rob aboard a private jet with an iconic jazz musician who says, "Hey, Barnes, I hear you're a fan of mine. Happy new year, brother. I hope to see you at Rob's party MLK weekend."

Barnes smiles and sends a return thumbs-up.

The other message—*messages*—are from Amelia. He heaves a weary sigh. She'll have to wait. He puts the phone on the bedside table, turns off the light, and closes his eyes.

Those damned white lilies chase him as he drifts toward sleep. The moment he'd realized what they were, he'd suspected Perry Wayland and Gypsy Colt were involved in the Bed-Stuy murders.

It's too late to save the Harrisons, but his own daughter may be in danger. No one is better equipped—or more determined—to protect her than Barnes himself. And Amelia, who can help him find her.

Wide-awake, he grabs his phone and calls her.

She answers immediately. "Where have you been?"

"Sorry. I was on a case all night and then I went to the Marcy Projects to look into the murders. No witnesses, no suspect, no apparent motive. Someone wanted to take them out."

"Do you think it has anything to do with—"

"It could. You haven't mentioned what I told you to anyone, have you?"

"No, but I—"

"Good. Please don't. And you need to be careful, Amelia."

A pause. "Where are you right now?"

"Home, about to sleep for a few hours. Why?"

"I was going to ask you to come to my office so that I can show you something. Here, I'll send it to you. Can you put me on speaker?"

He obliges, hearing a whoosh on her end, and an incoming text alert on his.

There are two photos. At a glance, he can see that the first is a toddler portrait of Barnes himself. He'd given it to her at their first appointment.

The other is a little girl.

He clicks and waits for it to enlarge as Amelia says, "This child was found in New Haven, Connecticut, twenty-six years ago."

"Brandy and Alma Harrison have family in New Haven. What do you mean by *found*?"

"Just like me, but . . . see any resemblance?"

"To you?"

"No! Barnes, I think she's—"

He gasps as the enlarged photo loads on his phone's screen, and he utters just one word, with wonder and conviction.

"Charisse."

Part II

1968

Chapter Three

Friday, February 2, 1968
Jacksonville, Florida

Before last summer had even unfolded, the newspapers were calling it the "summer of love." For Melody Hunter, it had turned out that way for reasons that had nothing to do with the counterculture convergence on San Francisco's Haight-Ashbury, or her own newlywed status.

"All righty, then, Mrs. Hunter, let's have a look-see."

She can't see the man sitting on a stool between her legs and the stirrups, but she can feel his gloved hands probing inside her. Her face is hot with embarrassment, though he's a physician and she's a grown married woman.

Last Wednesday had been her first visit to this low stucco bungalow that smells of mildew and orange peels. He'd collected a urine sample and sent her home. This morning, he called her in for the verdict.

The nine days between have been hell.

"Well, congratulations, Mrs. Hunter."

"Am I pregnant?"

"You are indeed. First baby is something special. I'm sure you're tickled pink."

"Oh, I am." Melody isn't accustomed to lying to a doctor—lying to anyone, for that matter.

Better get used to it.

"How . . . pregnant?"

"Almost six months along, Mrs. Hunter. I've been in this business a long time, and you're the first married lady I've met who didn't know it until this late stage."

"Well, I, um . . . I've always been irregular . . ."

A lie: her cycles have been clockwork ever since she got her first period at twelve. For a decade, until September, that time of the month has come *precisely* at that time of the month.

"No morning sickness, then? Fainting spells, cramping . . ."

"Not really. I didn't realize I might be expecting till my stomach . . . popped."

Another lie.

All those steamy late summer nights, lying awake on her side of the empty double bed, worrying—sensing—that a fragile new life had taken hold inside her.

By September's end, her period had been MIA. She'd spent autumn mornings vomiting into the toilet, afternoons too drowsy to leave the couch, sleepless nights in denial.

Weren't pregnant women supposed to gain weight? Melody had dropped a dress size.

Didn't pregnant women have strange cravings and ferocious appetites? Melody felt queasy at the slightest whiff of frying food and couldn't find anything remotely appealing on the Thanksgiving table.

Pregnant women couldn't wait to share the news with their families, their friends . . . their husbands. Melody's brain had tiptoed around the truth even when her appetite came raging back and her waistbands became tourniquets. Yet she didn't dare see Doc Krebbs, the obstetrician who'd delivered Melody and her younger sister into the world.

Last year around this time, just before her wedding, her mother had enrolled her as a patient in his practice, and—in typical Honeybee Abernathy fashion—informed Melody after the fact.

"It's time you saw a woman's physician, poppet," she'd drawled, folding linen napkins for her bridge club luncheon. *"Doc Krebbs will answer any questions you might have about y'all's wedding night."*

Melody's face had burned, a blushing bride.

It's burning now, too, but . . .

"Almost done with the pelvic exam, Mrs. Hunter. Take some deep breaths . . . In . . . out . . . Yes, that's it."

Breathe . . . In . . . Out . . . In . . .

"Ouch!"

"I am surely sorry about this," he says. "Just try to relax."

She'd chosen him from the yellow pages because his name is Stevens, like Elizabeth Montgomery's character Samantha on *Bewitched*. People are always telling Melody she looks like her.

If only she could work a magic spell that would make this pregnancy disappear. But there is no magic in real life. Only the underground network she'd heard about back in high school, when a group of girls were gossiping about a classmate's rumored pregnancy.

"There's a place up near Macon where a girl can go to get it taken care of," her friend Charlene had whispered. "You just show up at this church, and they whisk you away and take care of it."

"Take care of it? You mean . . ."

"Shh!"

Melody had asked Charlene the specifics out of curiosity and not necessity. *She* would never find herself in that situation. *She* was a good girl, preserving her virginity for her wedding night.

And so she had. A good girl, a good wife . . .

She stares at a poster taped to the wall—an advertisement for clomiphene, a new fertility drug. It shows a happy woman encircled from behind in the arms of a happy man. Her head is leaning against his chest, his chin on her shoulder. They're wearing dreamy smiles and wedding rings.

Melody and Travis were married last February. His draft notice was waiting when they returned from their honeymoon. After two months of basic training and two more of advanced infantry training, he was allowed a short leave to visit her and then transported to Vietnam. And then . . .

"Ouch!"

"I do apologize, Mrs. Hunter. But the more tense you are, the more uncomfortable it is."

"I'm not tense."

"Then you're the first pregnant newlywed woman I've ever met who is not." Another chuckle, back there beyond the draped cloth over her bent knees, from a man who suspects nothing more than new mom nerves.

"Exactly when . . . I mean, am I due in April?"

"'Bout mid-May. Hold still if you can."

"Sorry. I'm trying."

Mid-May. God help her.

"Your husband is in the army, Mrs. Hunter?"

"Yes."

"Have you had word from him recently? Since . . . ?"

"No, I haven't heard from him . . . since."

Two days ago, the Viet Cong had launched a violent offensive to coincide with the Tet lunar new year.

"I'm sure he's just fine," Dr. Stevens says as though he knows, and Melody nods as though she agrees.

"When he does get in touch, you'll have big news to share with him, won't you?"

"Yes. I surely will."

At last the doctor rolls back and stands, methodically plucking his splayed fingertips to remove one glove, and then the other. He looks like the Kentucky Fried Chicken guy—elderly, with a goatee, horn-rimmed glasses, and a black string tie beneath his white coat.

"No man ever forgets the day he finds out he's going to become a daddy. Got the news from my wife back in '28, right before the Okeechobee Hurricane made landfall. I don't know which one hit harder." A smile curves his lips, but his eyes pity her, a pregnant young wife whose husband might never return.

He makes an appointment to see her next month and hands her a bottle of prenatal vitamins. "All righty, then. You can go ahead and get dressed. Oh, and, Mrs. Hunter?" He turns back in the doorway. "I'll keep your husband in my prayers."

"Thank you."

Travis's well-being should be Melody's only concern right now. She should be at home watching the news, or in church praying.

Six months along . . .

Six months.

The baby had been conceived in late August, early September.

Travis had deployed in July.

The Bronx, New York

HER BIRTH CERTIFICATE says Linda Lucille Miller.

She was named after her mother, plain old Linda Miller, and her mother's favorite comedienne, Lucille Ball. It's hard to imagine that a woman who'd never smiled or shown interest in television, or anything really, would have had a favorite comedienne. It's even harder to imagine that she herself has anything in common with plain old Linda Miller, but her biology teacher says that a person's parents leave a genetic imprint in every cell. She doesn't like to think about that, or about her mother, who always called her Linda Lou.

Everyone else calls her Linda, except her father. To him, she's "Gypsy," the name he'd privately bestowed when she'd come into this world. The name he says everyone else will know when they leave it—en masse, according to his prophecy, and anytime now.

Gypsy Colt Matthews would have been her legal name if he'd had any say in the matter, but he hadn't been around the night she'd been born.

"Hospitals aren't my scene," he'd told her with a shrug.

Her mother hadn't been his *scene*, either. And though he's mentioned the family and friends—*followers*—he'd once had, now there is only his daughter.

"You and me, we're the chosen ones, Gypsy, baby. No one else matters. They'll be gone, just like that, when Judgment Day comes," he says, snapping his fingers. "And it's coming, man. Anytime now. We have to be ready."

When she isn't in the mood for Bible study or reading newspapers in search of signs that the apocalypse is imminent, she claims to be bogged down in homework.

Most of the time, he buys that excuse, especially now that she's in high school. But for her, academics have always been a breeze.

The other day, her biology teacher, Mr. Dixon, asked her if she'd started thinking about college yet.

"Oh, I can't afford that."

"Keep up your studies, and the finest universities in this country will be offering you scholarships."

"Do you really think so?"

"Of course. But you'll have to work hard."

A scholarship . . . college . . . a ticket out of this declining neighborhood and vermin-infested apartment, with windows too warped to open and a bathtub in the kitchen.

Sitting in front of the television news on this Friday evening, she works algebra problems as Walter Cronkite gravely reports the ongoing Tet Offensive in Vietnam and Eddie Adams's graphic photograph yesterday capturing a Viet Cong prisoner's execution. Then he announces the birth of Elvis Presley's daughter.

The war is bad enough, but now her girlhood idol, the world's greatest sex symbol, has become a dad?

Yeah, the world's coming to an end, all right.

She turns off the TV and goes to the icebox to scrounge up some supper. Oran had left a note this morning saying he's working late tonight.

So smart, putting it in writing rather than mentioning it in person before she'd gone off to school. She might have read something into his voice, or seen a glimmer in his eyes.

She can always tell when he's lying, though it usually isn't to her. Often he prefaces a lie with the phrase, "Very truly I tell you," lifted from the gospel according to John, one of his favorite books in the Bible. Fascinated by scholarly theories about John's identity, Oran occasionally claims to have written the book himself, along with Revelation. Gypsy has seen him convince rapt crowds of it, dispatching the naysayers with his breathless, brilliant dissertation.

Yes, he's smart, Oran.

But Gypsy is smarter.

Back in Travis's poppy-red Camaro, Melody puts the top down despite the cool day. She's suffocating. She needs air.

This is going to happen. There's no way out. Not anymore.

Melody's old friend Charlene still lives in town. After going through school together, they'd been bridesmaids in each other's weddings, and had looked forward to sharing married life as couples. But as Travis prepared to deploy, Charlene's husband, Gary, was burning his draft card and marching on Washington.

"He's the devil. You stay away from him," Travis had told Melody. "Stay away from both of them."

"She's my friend."

"You heard the scripture at their wedding, same as at ours. 'And the two become one flesh.' He's the devil, and she's his wife. That makes her the devil, too. You got that?"

"But—"

"You vowed to love, honor, and obey me, Melody. I'm ordering you to stay away from those people. You got *that*?"

I don't take orders from anyone!

It's what she should have said. Instead, she'd cried, and he'd softened.

"Baby, I'm going to war to fight for this country. I'm a patriot, putting my life on the line for your freedom. How do you think I feel when I see these long-haired whining hippies who don't respect me? Can you blame me for wanting to keep you away from them? I'm trying to protect you."

"I know you are, Travis, and I love you for it. I promise I'll stay away from Charlene."

It's far from the only promise she's broken since Travis had left.

Around Thanksgiving, Melody had called Charlene to ask her about the underground network that helped pregnant young women. But the moment she picked up the phone, Charlene announced that she and Gary were expecting their first child. Melody stammered a congratulations and hung up.

On a grim December day she'd finally found her way, on her own, to the so-called way station: a small white clapboard church in a backwater Georgia town up near Macon.

Otis Redding's hometown. The musician had been killed in a plane crash days earlier. Melody had wept as if she'd known him personally. She hadn't, but . . .

"I have kin up Macon way. They introduced me to their old pal Otis . . ."

That voice, rich as pecan pie, had still oozed into her mind even then. Even now.

She closes her eyes and sees dolphin fins dancing in pink light arced across a glittering blue sea. She remembers leaning against a strong chest, encircled in the arms of a man who wasn't wearing a wedding ring.

"That's the most beautiful sunrise I've ever seen," she'd murmured, and he'd told her that in his world, they refer to dawn as *dayclean.*

She'd loved that. *Dayclean*: a fresh start, with yesterday left behind.

Ah, it really had been a summer of love, hadn't it? If not in the beginning, then certainly when it had drawn to a close. Love, and many other things—not all splendored, as the song goes.

Here on the southern Atlantic coast, summer gives way to hurricane season.

Melody starts the engine.

The radio disk jockey is in mid-announcement: Priscilla Presley delivered a baby girl yesterday.

"That's right, all y'all. Elvis is a daddy. Let's celebrate that with his latest hit."

Melody turns off the radio amid the opening notes of "Just Call Me Lonesome."

The doctor's words echo in the silence.

"No man ever forgets the day he finds out he's going to become a daddy."

There are no hurricanes in the forecast today. The

winter sky is a brilliant blue as she heads northeast toward Barrow Island off the coast of Georgia to deliver the news in person.

Brooklyn

"MATTHEWS! YOU'RE STILL HERE?"

Oran looks up from his stack of files. The clinic's obstetrician, Harold Brooks, has exchanged his white lab coat for a tweed overcoat.

"Not for long," he says. "I have to finish this paperwork."

"Take care getting home. It's sleeting out there." Brooks puts on his hat, black galoshes squeaking as he heads for the door. "Be sure to lock up. There was an armed robbery the other night at the pharmacy around the corner—a masked man with a gun. Sign of the times."

End times, Oran wants to say, and then elaborate—oh, how passionately he can elaborate on that topic. But this isn't the right time or place. Or person. This man will never be one of the chosen few.

"Have a good night, Doctor."

"You, too. See you tomorrow." Brooks disappears into the blustery February evening.

The receptionist, Carla, is long gone, as are the nurses. Ordinarily, Oran, too, would have left after the day's final patient departed. For what they're paying him, the paperwork can wait.

He'd been anxious, sitting there at his desk in the reception area, waiting for the doctor to split. If she'd shown up while he was here . . .

She hadn't. But she's coming soon.

He locks the door and goes to the darkened patient examination room with a window facing the subway entrance. He watches Brooks pause to light a cigarette, shielding the flame from the precipitation.

Get moving, man! Go!

Slush appears to be freezing on the steps to the elevated subway platform. The doctor ascends with great care and disappears from view above.

Oran watches the stairway until the next Manhattan-bound train rumbles away with Brooks on board. Carla had confided that the doctor—married with five children at home in Oyster Bay—is having an affair with one of the nurses. *Not* the stacked blonde one, she'd added, as though that were the shame of it all. No, he's sleeping with the quiet, middle-aged brunette who lives alone in the Village.

Carla, a stacked blonde herself, enjoys office gossip. That's served Oran well. He's turned on the charm with her, too, volunteering to cover the phones during her extra-long lunch breaks—a key part of his plan.

Oran grabs Dr. Brooks's white lab coat hanging on a hook behind the door. It smells of cigarettes and Brut aftershave. He slips into it. The sleeves are a little short. The other girls hadn't seemed to notice. Such a trivial detail in such a monumental moment in their young lives.

He drapes the stethoscope around his neck. Spotting the doctor's thick reading glasses on his desk, Oran tries them on and checks the mirror. A blurry man with a brown crew cut gazes back at him, blue eyes masked behind the thick horn-rims.

Square and stodgy. Nice. He practices Dr. Brooks's

commanding stride and mutters to himself, getting into character.

With the first girl, he'd accidentally dropped a "far out" into the conversation. It might have given her pause, though only for a moment, and then he reeled her back in.

Oran has a way with women. With *people.* Always has.

"That's my handsome, charming boy. He knows how to wrap everyone around his little finger," his mother, Pamela, used to say.

He isn't just good-looking, quick-witted, and charismatic. He's smart. Genius IQ, just like his Gypsy. Like his mother, Pamela, too, his grandmother claimed, but that was hard to believe. Pamela had been spectacularly stupid, throwing away opportunities just as she'd thrown away her parents, and her son.

He opens a file cabinet's bottom drawer and reaches way into the back, retrieving a new patient chart hidden inside a long-dead elderly patient's folder. Pushing the glasses down his nose, he skims the details she'd provided over the phone when she called looking for an appointment while Carla was out to lunch.

She'd given her name, address, and date of birth. When he'd asked which school she attends, she'd asked, "Why do you want to know?"

"Routine question."

"That seems awfully personal."

"This is a medical office, ma'am. We hold your information in strictest confidence."

He'd smiled when she named one of the borough's Catholic high schools, clinching her place in his plan.

She'd faltered again when he'd gone on to more

intimate questions about her menstrual cycles, regularity, and date of her last period, but complied just as the others had. Catholic schoolgirls are trained to comply with authority. They're also aware that contraception and premarital sex go against the teachings of the church, but shame doesn't keep them from breaking the rules. God forgives their sins, just as Oran does.

Hearing a knock, he takes off the glasses. He needs to be able to see her. See into her soul to confirm that she's worthy.

They're lining up nicely, his girls. She'll be the third. If all goes as planned, he'll need just one more.

He pastes on a benevolent smile and opens the door to a petite young woman.

"You must be Margaret Costello."

Chapter Four

Melody doesn't pass another car as she covers the last few miles of the mainland's palmetto-lined backroad, dotted with fishing shacks and the occasional heap of rubble Hurricane Dora had left back in '64.

Midway across the low, rickety bridge to Barrow, a pair of nearly identical young Negro boys look up from their fishing lines and gape. She isn't imagining the scrutiny, but it's not because they know her terrible secret. It's not even because of Travis's flashy sports car.

She's white—*buckruh*, as the island's Gullah population would say. She doesn't belong out here.

The sun sets as she bumps along the island's only thoroughfare. It's unpaved and bisects dense maritime forest. Twice, she passes the unmarked turnoff and has to turn the car around, a painstaking maneuver in the dark on the narrow road. At last, she finds her way to a low antebellum cottage framed by live oaks dripping silvery Spanish moss. Beside the bright blue front door, upended blue bottles adorn a crepe myrtle's branches.

The house is dark, and she hears barking inside.

"It's okay, Otis, it's only me," she calls, and the dog grows frenzied at the sound of her voice.

No one answers her knock. She tries the door. It's unlocked. "Hello? Anyone—"

Oof. The pup bursts through the door to joyfully paw and lick her.

"All right, boy, you need to go back inside."

He sits looking at her, tail thumping the porch floor, expression stating that he's not going without her. She won't go in uninvited. So she settles into a creaky wooden rocking chair on the low porch with Otis contentedly at her feet, waiting for the man they both love.

A creamy moon sliver rides amid more stars than Melody ever sees at home a few miles down the coast, across the state line. Out here there's no ambient light to dim them, just a smattering of sleeping households scattered in acres of marshland.

Listening for footsteps to crunch up the lane, she hears nothing but insects whirring in the dense undergrowth, and every so often a soft equine nickering.

Barrow Island is populated by more wild horses than people. The few families that live here go back at least a hundred years, their collective roots entangled like a mangrove. A good number work in the paper mill, or as domestic staff on the mainland. Some are tradespeople, some unemployed, some enlisted and fighting in Vietnam.

One man is none of those things.

He's a poet, a writer, a reader, a historian, a free thinker, an activist, and for a fleeting time in that summer of love, he was *everything*—her everything.

Staring at a bare, unruly wisteria vine tangling up the porch post and crawling along the slatted blue ceiling, she thinks of the one her mother has spent years diligently pruning and training over an arbor, infuriated by its refusal to flower.

"The garden club president told me I've done everything right!" she'd told Melody last spring when the wisteria burst forth with sturdy green leaves and not a hint of delicate blossom.

"Maybe you should just give up on it, Mother."

"Never!" snapped Honeybee Abernathy—born Hannah Beauregard, descended from the confederate general known as the Little Napoleon.

Otis lifts his head expectantly, ears twitching. Melody expects to hear a car, but he's looking in the wrong direction. Moments later, there's a thrash-splash in the gator-infested marsh beyond the trees. She shudders, and the dog rests his head on his paws once again.

A damp gust slinks through the live oaks, giving the gnarled moss a good shake. The February night is cool and breezy, scented by the sea and the occasional waft of noxious fumes from a mainland paper mill. She wishes she were wearing a warmer coat, a head scarf, gloves.

She remembers a sweltering late August afternoon back home when everything in the world was stifling and still, except the ocean and her own rage. She couldn't bear to remain in the house where she'd just opened a drawer to look for something and found . . .

Something else. Something so terrible she was certain her eyes had deceived her. But it was real, and she'd fled.

She'd covered two miles from her house near the Intracoastal Amelia River across town to Main Beach, where the Atlantic Ocean lay sparkling blue. She'd left her shoes in the dunes beside a sea turtle's nest and wandered out to the beach. The tide was going out. She walked south, ten miles all the way down to American Beach, established on Amelia's south end as a "Negro Ocean Playground" three decades before the Civil Rights Act began allowing Black people on public beaches.

She walked without realizing where she was or that hours had passed, and the sunbathers, swimmers, and even the surfers had disappeared. A late afternoon storm exploded like a vengeful sea monster rising from the depths. She ran for cover toward the nearest building beyond the dunes, a small cottage painted bright blue.

"Come on, now," a tall, shirtless Black man called in a rich baritone, holding the door open. Seeing the shaggy black Lab bounding around and yapping beside him, she'd thought he was talking to the dog—but no, he was waving Melody forward. "Come on inside, ma'am. Hurry! This is a nasty one!"

She ran right through that door and into the house. Just one sparsely furnished room, spotless and homey, but far from modern. In one corner, a wall-mounted sink, an icebox, and a battle-scarred stove on spindly legs.

It wasn't his home, he said, closing the door after her, shutting out the wet wind. He was just staying at a traveling friend's place for a few days, keeping an eye on things. There'd been some ugliness and vandalism in the area.

As he pulled on a chambray shirt, she noticed his lean muscles and that he was wearing a gold necklace. Not hippie beads or a peace sign pendant, yet unusual, she thought, for someone so clean-cut.

A violent gust extinguished the lightbulbs before

she could get a closer look at the necklace. As he went around holding matches to candles, the dog wagged its tail at Melody and settled at her feet, nuzzling her hand.

"Now, Otis, you just let her be. Don't go slobbering all over our guest."

"Oh, I don't mind. I like dogs. His name is Otis? After Otis Redding?"

"Yes, ma'am." He looked pleased.

"His version of 'Try a Little Tenderness' is one of my favorite songs. You must really like his music, too, if you named your dog after him."

"He's one of the finest men I've ever known."

"You *know* him?"

"Not well, but I have kin up Macon way. They introduced me to Otis a time or two, before he hit the big time."

Well, that had broken the ice. They'd talked about Otis Redding and Otis the pup.

"You have a dog?" he asked.

"No, but . . . No."

Her sister had always longed for one, begged for one, but Honeybee didn't want muddy paws traipsing through the house. Melody didn't tell him that, though. About her mother, or Ellie. Not that first day.

They talked about music, and books. About Dr. King and the war and LBJ.

"Sounds like you don't trust the president much."

"No, ma'am, I surely do not."

"Please don't call me ma'am. I'm only twenty-one and it makes me feel like somebody's mother."

"Well, then, what's your name?"

"Melody."

"Melody. No wonder you know so much about music. Your name is like a song."

She'd felt a shiver in the heat. "While my mother was waiting for my father to come back from the war so that they could get married, she was studying to be a singer. She has a wonderful voice."

"How about you?"

"My voice? It's all right, but . . ."

"No, I mean what did you want to be before you got married?"

She'd followed his gaze to her ring and hid it in a fist.

She'd been a music major at the University of Florida, pursuing the career that had eluded her mother. But she met Travis during Christmas break sophomore year. When she returned to Gainesville, he visited her every weekend, and when she came home that summer, he'd proposed.

She was hoping to finish her education. No reason to rush, as President Johnson had already rescinded the draft exemption for married men. But Travis wanted her to drop out, and Travis wanted a Valentine's Day wedding, and whatever Travis wants . . .

Otis's ears perk up again, and Melody hears a car's approach with a distinctly clattering engine.

She takes a deep breath, preparing herself to face Cyril LeBlanc with the news that she's expecting his child.

MARGARET COSTELLO HAS a pronounced widow's peak above fine features and intense blue eyes. Her dark hair is teased and sprayed into a fashionable flip, protected by a lime-green scarf knotted under her chin. It matches her gloves and vinyl go-go boots. Even wrapped in that bulky brown plaid wool coat, Oran can see that her figure is slender, though not *too* slender for his purposes.

She's nervous, spilling too many words into too little space.

"Sorry I'm late, but it's getting nasty out and I had to come all the way from Bensonhurst, and this place was hard to find, and then when I did I walked by a few times because I wasn't sure . . ." She tilts her head at the sign taped to the window. "Aren't you closed? It says that the hours are—"

"I keep telling the receptionist to update that. We take late appointments on Fridays now."

"You have a receptionist?"

"She sits right over there." He points at Carla's desk.

"But you're the one who answered the phone when I called."

Hmm. None of the others had noted that, nor questioned the hours. Smart, feisty little thing. Reminds him of his Gypsy.

"Around here, when it's busy, we all pitch in wherever we're needed. Now, let's get you into an exam room."

"But . . . don't you have a nurse or something?"

"I sent them all home for the evening. You're late, and the weather is nasty, and you're the last appointment tonight."

Still she hesitates, just inside the door, as though she wants to jerk it open behind her and flee into the night. His own fingers itch to reach behind her and lock it, but he doesn't dare scare her. Not when they're so close, and she's so perfect, so very much like his own little girl.

A vision flashes in his mind—a prophecy. Margaret will have a daughter who looks like her, a sweet sister for his Gypsy.

"I, uh . . ."

He blinks and sees that she's watching him just as Gypsy does, as though she can see right through him.

"I have to go. I, um, changed my mind about—"

"There's a twenty-five-dollar fee for last-minute cancellations."

"Twenty-five dollars? But . . . it's a free clinic."

"Free for our *patients*. Do you know how many girls make appointments, show up, and then are too scared to go through with it?"

Something flashes in her blue eyes. *I'm no coward*, she's thinking.

Oran unspools words like a rescuer dropping a lifeline to a child who's toddled to the edge of a precipice.

"Most of these young women are very much like yourself—they've taken a big risk just by calling us, let alone coming here. They're defying society, their parents, the Catholic Church . . . even the law, as of two years ago!"

A well-placed reminder that family planning services and birth control distribution had been illegal until the 1965 Supreme Court ruling. It's all so new, and she's so young—how would Margaret have any idea how any of it works? Few people do.

"Just think about all those people who claim to have a young woman's best interests in mind—" He breaks off, raises his voice to an annoying intonation, "'It's for your own good, we're only trying to protect you,' they say, don't they? And you are so obedient, such a good, perfect girl. Until you fall in love. They don't like that, do they? They don't trust him to protect you the way they do, but they don't know him, do they? They don't know how it is with you two. And when you decide to protect *yourself* against unwanted pregnancy . . ."

She's looking down now, at the lime-green plastic boots that reveal so much more than mere fashion sense. Only a spirited, carefree soul would wear boots like that on a night like this.

"So yes, we understand how it is with these young women who make appointments. But we have to protect ourselves, too, and our patients. We can't afford to waste our time and resources on girls who aren't mature enough, strong enough, to go through with it. That's why we have the cancellation fee." Mythical, but she wouldn't suspect that.

Her chin trembles. She lifts it.

"I know it's not easy, but the hardest part of this is over," he says. "You're here. Now all you need is a quick exam, I'll give you your birth control prescription, and you'll be on your way."

Ah, yes. She wants the magic Pill. But does she want it badly enough to ignore her gut instincts and follow him into the exam room?

Yes, she does.

He ushers her inside, tells her to get undressed, put on a gown, lie on the table with feet in the stirrups. He turns his back while she does so, pulling on sterile gloves and laying out instruments on the countertop the way he's seen Dr. Brooks do, watching the proceedings through a crack in the door.

When he turns back, there she is, dutifully lying on

the table, shivering in the chilly room, eyes squeezed closed. She's at his mercy, and they both know it.

"All right, now, Margaret. Just try to relax. This won't hurt a bit."

He walks toward her.

Five minutes later, she emerges from the examination room, fully clothed and looking relieved. Oran is waiting for her.

"There now, see? I told you it wouldn't be so bad, didn't I?"

"It wasn't. Not at all."

He hands her a little brown bag. "Here you go."

She peers inside. "That's it? That's the Pill? I thought it came in a packet, not a bottle."

"Some do, some don't. Be sure you take it every time you menstruate, on days three through seven."

She narrows her eyes. "I thought you take it every day."

"That's a lot for a girl to remember, isn't it? One slip and"—he snaps his fingers—"you're pregnant. So they've developed these new pills that are just as effective and you don't have to take them as often. I've given you enough to last through three cycles. I'll call you to see how you're—"

"Call me?" She shakes her head. "No! Please don't call. My parents can't . . . please."

"I see. Discretion is in order, then?"

"Yes. I . . . I don't want anyone to know about this."

"Of course." He nods, assured that what happened here will remain private.

That's why he's chosen only teenaged girls, always so tentative and vaguely ashamed. He suspects, though, that even the more experienced grown women and wives who visit the clinic keep the details to themselves.

Margaret has no idea that her cursory internal exam—a finger poke, a couple of belly pats—wasn't the norm. He knew she just wanted to get it over with, and he felt the same way. Now isn't the time for anything more intimate.

That time will come, though.

May 10. He'd done the math after she'd called and given him the details of her menstrual cycle.

He opens the appointment book waiting on the receptionist's desk. The real one is tucked in a drawer for the time being. This one is identical, but belongs only to him.

They schedule her next visit for early May, an evening, of course.

"Have a good evening, Margaret, and get home safely."

"I will, Doctor. Thank you."

Oran locks the door after her and watches from the window as those go-go boots ascend the slick subway stairs. Once, she slips and nearly falls, but steadies herself and continues doggedly on up.

Attagirl. You're doing just fine. And I'll see you in May, on the night when you'll be most fertile.

Back in the reception area, he takes the official appointment book out of the drawer and opens it on the desk.

He looks down at his own, smiling. A few days ago, he'd had Christina Myers in for her second visit to make sure that she's been taking her "birth control pills" precisely as he'd directed and avoiding intercourse until they "become effective." She'd thanked him profusely and he'd given her another three months' worth. Placebos this time. Why hand out more clomiphene than he had to? He needs it for the others.

His pulse quickens when he sees the bold black circle around next Tuesday, February 13, along with the initials *CM*. Not another appointment for Christina, but a rendezvous on the night she'll be most fertile.

Melody sits beside Cyril staring into the darkness beyond the porch. Both their rocking chairs are motionless as is Otis lying on the plank floor between them, nose on his paws, eyes alert as though he, too, is absorbing the news that Melody is pregnant.

Cyril LeBlanc is not the kind of man to blurt a reaction.

He's the kind of man whose first question tonight, after months apart with no communication, had been pure selflessness.

"Did you get news about your husband?"

He knows she wouldn't pop up unexpectedly for coffee and casual conversation. Everyone is well aware of what's happening in Southeast Asia this week. The grim headlines are pervasive. People are dying. Hundreds, thousands of people. Civilians, the enemy, American soldiers.

"No. No word yet."

"Bloodbath over there."

"That's what the news is saying, but the president thinks the offensive will be over soon. He says we're way more powerful than—"

"You really believe that, Melody? You need to wake up!"

"What?"

"Not just you—Americans! We need to wake up. This is not our war to be fighting. We have our own war right here. Dr. King says . . . never mind. I'm sorry. All I wanted to know was whether you'd heard from your husband, and here I am on my damned soapbox again."

"It's all right. And thank you for asking."

It speaks volumes about Cyril's character, given what he's been through and what she's told him about Travis.

What does it say about your own that you're still married to him?

But how do you divorce your husband when he's under siege overseas?

How do you pray for his safe return, knowing what you know?

Her fingers toy with the etched metal buttons on the cardigan he'd taken off and draped around her shoulders when he'd spotted her here in the February chill. She presses her nose into the soft wool, breathing him in, sneaking a glance at him.

He's thinner since she'd last seen him, and his textured hair is longer—not a full afro, but shaggy and tousled, like Jimi Hendrix.

Twilight shadows don't mask the long scars on his face.

Surgical incisions, he'd told her last summer when she'd first noticed them. He'd been injured when he and a group of fellow NAACP Youth Council demonstrators had been attacked by a mob of two hundred white men armed with makeshift clubs outside a luncheonette. His jaw had been broken; a second blow had shattered his foot and left him with a lifelong limp.

Where had her husband been on that day, Jacksonville's now-infamous Axe Handle Saturday?

August 1960 . . .

Travis would have been sixteen years old, cruising the streets, riding the waves, watching Hitchcock's *Psycho* at the drive-in with girls who wore red lipstick. Girls like Amy Connors and Debbie Mason; prissy, pretty girls who'd made Melody's little sister's junior high school days miserable.

Born just eighteen months apart, Melody and Eleanor had been inseparable. Melly and Ellie, everyone called them. In the summer of 1960, Melody had been fourteen; Ellie thirteen, and ill, and dying, and lying in a casket with her hands clasped across the pale pink silk bodice Honeybee had chosen.

Her sister would have hated spending eternity in that childish dress that didn't do a thing for her scrawny figure. She'd have hated that the undertaker had curled her long black hair into unnatural corkscrews, and the lipstick . . .

Before Ellie got sick, she and Melody had futilely begged their mother to let them wear red lipstick, like Marilyn Monroe. This lipstick was as sickly pink as the unnatural color on Ellie's cheeks, freckles hidden behind pale makeup. She could have been a stranger lying there, but it was Ellie in a death mask.

Amy and Debbie had been the first to arrive, crying into lace handkerchiefs, seeking macabre dibs on the loss. People who'd never known Ellie had wept as if they had, touching her hand as they filed past, talking about what a wonderful girl she'd been.

Ellie would have hated it, all of it. She didn't like attention. That's why she never sang for anyone but the family, even though her voice was every bit as lovely as Honeybee's and better, back then, than Melody's.

Daddy stood between the casket and Melody, nodding and shaking hands. Honeybee wailed and moaned and sometimes fainted dead away. Not just there, at the funeral home, but for weeks afterward. Months.

Melody's own grief had been devastating, but her parents' sorrow was unbearable. Even their longtime housekeeper, Raelene, was shattered. Some days, the household adults were hypervigilant with Melody, as though she, too, might succumb if they turned their backs for an instant. Other days they barely seemed to notice her, and she could escape to the beach. She'd walk for hours, finding some strange measure of reassurance in predictable tidal rhythms, scooping up the occasional gleaming black shark's tooth deposited amid shell shards in her path, remembering a time when there'd been two sets of barefoot prints along the scalloped edge of hard-packed, glistening sand.

"Melody . . ." Cyril's voice drags Melody back to the present. He reaches for her hand. Travis's wedding band glitters in the starlight before his fingers close over it. "I don't know what to do. You and me, we can't be together. Not just because you're married. Not even just because of who you're married to."

"Well, what if I give the baby up for adoption?"

Until this moment, she hadn't even considered the idea. But now that it's out there, it holds terrible, heartbreaking logic.

"You think people are likely to adopt a biracial baby?"

She nods.

"*Decent* people?" Her heart sinks as he goes on, "And you think a married woman can give up a baby for adoption without her husband's consent?"

"Well, then, what if . . ." She takes a deep breath and utters the awful sentence that's been eating away at her for months now, but especially the last few days, since the Tet began. "What if Travis doesn't come home?"

He stiffens and releases her hand. "Don't say that."

"He's a soldier in combat. If he doesn't make it . . ."

"That wouldn't change a thing for you and me."

"But I'd be a widow, not—"

"A *white* widow. And I would still be—I will *always* be—a Black man. Marriage between us is against the law."

"Laws are changing."

"Not around these parts. Not anytime soon."

He's right. No Southern state has yet repealed its law against interracial marriage, despite last summer's Supreme Court unanimous unconstitutionality ruling.

"Don't you see? Nothing that happens, nothing we can say, nothing *we can do*, will ever change anything," he tells her. "We are who we are. We are *where* we are."

She's silent, resting her right hand on her belly, feeling a quickening within. It's probably just her imagination, anxiety, hunger pains. But maybe not. Maybe the child—Cyril's child—wants to make itself known.

Or maybe Travis's child is issuing a warning.

"Then what are we going to do?" she asks.

Cyril stands. "We need to think on it. But you best be getting home now. It's late."

"I don't want to go back there."

"You have to."

"I'm so sick of all my life, doing what I have to do, what I'm supposed to do, pretending to feel the way I'm supposed to feel."

"It's what we all do. That's just how it is."

"Not out here. You don't understand. Things are different here."

"Things are different everywhere."

She'd expected more from him than oppositional platitudes. But maybe that's what he's hearing from her. She needs to explain so that he'll understand.

"My mother . . . she's impossible."

"Impossible? Now, I don't think that's—"

"She wants me to join her bridge club!"

"Bridge club! Well, now, it's no wonder you're getting all worked up!" He shakes his head in mock dismay. "You might as well march off to 'Nam."

"I'm serious! Please don't be like them—like everyone else. Please listen to me!"

"I'm sorry." He sits down beside her again. "I'm listening."

"My mother just . . . she wants me to be excited about buying venetian blinds. She wants me to be more ladylike." She struggles to put her frustration into words that will make him grasp what her life will be like if she goes back there. "She wants me to be . . . just like her."

"Isn't that what every mother wants?"

"I don't want my daughter to be anything like me. I

want her to be whoever she wants to be and feel whatever she feels."

"Daughter?"

Melody closes her eyes and sees pink yarn, tiny sleeves. Sees blood dripped on leather pumps. December, up Macon way . . .

Her eyes snap open. "She's going to be a fine human being, Cyril."

"She."

"Yes. She's a girl." She shrugs. "I know I don't *know* it, but I do."

"Maternal instinct," he says softly, and she nods.

A little girl. Maybe she'll have Melody's high cheekbones, and Cyril's warm brown eyes.

Not Travis's icy blue ones. She would never have been able to love Travis's child the way she'll love Cyril's.

Cyril is a good man.

Travis, she'd discovered after she'd married him and he'd flown away to Vietnam, is a hateful, cold-blooded killer whose parting words still ring in her ears.

"He's the devil, and she's his wife. That makes her the devil, too."

Chapter Five

Tuesday, February 13, 1968
The Bronx

According to the printed school lunch menu posted outside the cafeteria, it's Italian Spaghetti Day. Gypsy would have guessed that based on the line for food that stretches out the door, and the mouthwatering smell of garlic and tomatoes permeating the corridors.

Famished, she pushes past everyone. She can't afford to buy the hot lunch, or the cold lunch, or the little carton of milk, for that matter.

Every day, she brings a brown bag and eats alone wherever she can find a table that hasn't already been staked out, territory marked by stacks of textbooks and purses and sweaters draped over empty chairs.

Often, as today, she winds up at the end of a table adjacent to the big trash can that's already full of ripening garbage from the earlier lunch periods. She always does her best not to let the smell get to her, trying to lose herself in a textbook, or sometimes doing her homework between bites of whatever she'd scrounged up from home.

Today, it's two stale slices of Wonder Bread smeared with as much peanut butter as she could scrape from a jar most people would have considered empty after the last use. But her father's payday is a week away, and there's rarely much left over for groceries. She'd shoplifted the peanut butter in January, and bought the bread with a quarter she'd found on the sidewalk.

Though her eyes are trained on her open notebook, her ears are focused on the conversation at a nearby table. A wide pillar blocks the occupants from her view, but she recognizes the voices—Sharon Walker and Connie Barbero. She usually manages to tune out their chatter, but today one of them mentioned Greg Martinez.

He's in her last period class, and sits in the back row with a posse of popular boys. She'd dismissed him along with the others before she'd noticed his name on the first quarter honor roll right above her own. Ever since then, she's had her eye on him. He lives in her neighborhood, on a block that's not much better than her own, though she doesn't know which building is his.

Whenever she sees him on the street, or in the hallway, he always smiles and says hello, unlike his friends.

Unlike anyone else, really, in this school.

When she was younger, she'd had friends. Not the kind who go to each other's houses after school and share sleepovers, because Gypsy never had a mother, or a father she'd want anyone to meet. But back at PS 77, the other girls used to talk to her, and eat lunch with her, and invite her to skip rope and play jacks at recess.

Even then, she'd been aware of her own poverty, but she was far from the only poor girl at school. Being one of the smartest and prettiest balanced things out.

That had changed in junior high. There were more kids, some significantly better off, with scorn for the impoverished. Confidence shaken, she'd retreated, dwelling on the shabbiness of her clothes, that her apartment was a dump, that her father was . . .

"A psycho lunatic," she'd overheard Carol-Ann Ellis telling Sharon and Connie one day over a smoke in the girls' bathroom. All three had been unaware that Gypsy was there, washing her hands at the sink. At first, she hadn't realized that her former friends were even talking about Oran. But apparently, Carol-Ann had run into him on the street as he was preaching one of his sidewalk sermons.

Sometimes, he does it in street clothes. But occasionally, depending on the audience he wants to attract, he'll wear a priest's collar, or a robe, or some other religious garment.

That day, he must have been wearing a turban. The others giggled as Carol-Ann imitated him, striding around with a towel wrapped around her head.

"Repent, ye sinners, for the end is nigh . . ."

Looking into the mirror, Gypsy had seen tears spring to her eyes and red-hot shame flame her face, and in the background, filmy with tobacco haze, the other girls were seeing her. Wide-eyed, Carol-Ann had clapped a hand over her own mouth, but a snort of laughter escaped on a puff of smoke. Gypsy turned and walked past their little coven without a word, head held high, tears held back.

As soon as she stepped out into the hall, she heard raucous laughter erupt in the bathroom.

Junior high had been lonely, but that was all right.

Gypsy didn't need girlfriends. Nor did she need boyfriends.

Not then, anyway. Now she thinks about Greg Martinez a lot, and she wonders what it would be like to kiss him. Judging by the wistful way she's caught him gazing at her, she's suspected that he's been wondering the same thing.

Today's cafeteria conversation seems to confirm it. The girls are saying that he's going to ask someone in his biology class to the Valentine's dance. They're filled with disdain over his choice, so it *has* to be Gypsy. There are only half a dozen girls in the class, and one is Carol-Ann Ellis. Sharon and Connie certainly don't hate her. Of the other girls, two are already going steady, and two are nowhere near pretty enough for Greg, who looks like a movie star with black hair, soft eyes, and a sensitive mouth.

"If he was really going to ask, he already would have," Connie is telling Sharon. "The dance is Friday night!"

"But Valentine's Day's tomorrow, and he wants to do it then. He's going to bring a red rose to class and ask her."

"How do you know?"

"Vinnie! How else?" Sharon's steady is one of Greg's best friends.

"That's so romantic! Like a marriage proposal. I hate her, don't you?"

"Of course! Who doesn't?"

That clinches it for Gypsy. They're definitely talking about her. But this time, their words don't sting.

Who cares how they feel about her? Greg is going to ask her out.

"She doesn't deserve him. Why her?"

"Well, I heard he's kind of shy," Connie says, "and he figured out she has a crush on him."

"Like you have on Ricky Pflueger?"

"At least I'm not obvious like she is, the way she goes around fawning and mooning and—"

"Shh! Here she comes!"

It isn't me. I'm not the one.

Gypsy peers around the pillar to see who it is, sandwich clogging her mouth like a wet sock when she sees Carol-Ann Ellis joining Sharon and Connie.

Her family isn't well-off by any stretch. She, too, lives in Gypsy's neighborhood. But Mr. Ellis works at Alexander's and Mrs. Ellis works in a beauty parlor. Carol-Ann reaps the benefits. She's wearing a wide-belted, patch-pocketed pastel minidress and white go-go boots. Her honey-colored hair is newly cut short with long bangs. Beneath the sleek side part, plucked brows and false lashes make her blue eyes look enormous.

Carol-Ann's so-called friends welcome her to the table, and the three of them put their heads together. What would happen if Gypsy walked over there and told Carol-Ann what the others had been saying about her?

You think she'd believe you?

Greg has made his choice. He prefers a girl who looks like—and has the personality and IQ of—a department store mannequin. Good for him. Good for her.

Good for me, too.

Still hungry, she realizes that she'd shoved what was left of her sandwich into the brown paper bag, now wadded into a ball and clenched in her fist. She turns, takes aim at the garbage can, and tosses. It goes right in. She leaves the cafeteria without a backward glance.

Her father isn't crazy. Judgment Day is coming, and when it does, they'll all have to answer for their sins. Not Gypsy, though. The chosen ones—chosen by God, and not by Greg Martinez—will be in paradise. Then, her father says, none of this will matter.

If only it didn't matter so much now.

Fernandina Beach, Florida

MELODY HAD WRITTEN to Travis over the weekend, words catapulting out of her onto three sheets of paper in a pastel stationery pad. She told him she'd fallen in love with someone else, and that she's expecting his child. She told him what she'd found in his drawer, that she can't stay married to a hate-filled man, that she wants a divorce.

She addressed an envelope to his APO and stamped it. But she couldn't quite bring herself to tear off the pages and send them overseas.

Honeybee had telephoned a couple of hours ago. "Any word on Travis?"

"Now, don't you think I'd have called you if there was?" she'd snapped, then said, "Oh, Mother, I'm sorry. But I can't stand the phone ringing. Every time I hear it, I think . . ."

"They wouldn't call you if something had happened. They'd show up in person, like they did across the street when the Bradys' son—"

"For heaven's sake!"

"I'm sorry, all I meant was—"

"I know. I'm sorry, too. I didn't mean to snap."

"Well, of course you're on edge, what with all the waitin' and worryin'. You'll come for supper tonight, won't you? Raelene made chicken and dumplings."

There's no food in the house. She's supposed to be eating for two, but she's barely eaten for one. Still, she'd hesitated. Honeybee asks too many questions, gossips about everyone, notices everything.

Melody has lived all her life in this quiet, lamplit neighborhood of old houses and small businesses, tall foliage and tropical fronds lining streets with alphabetical botanical names. Walking to her parents' house for supper, she crosses Date Street, Cedar, Beech, and Ash, where she makes a left turn toward the river.

The moon is full and the weather unseasonably balmy, but she senses a storm brewing out at sea. Or maybe it's just inside her.

Her parents had spent a long weekend visiting old friends, but had called her long-distance daily to check in about Travis and reassure her that no news is good news.

Her in-laws, Bob and Doris Hunter, had also called. They live here on Amelia Island, in a new split-level over by their country club and Bob's car dealership. They aren't the warmest people in the world. She isn't particularly fond of them, and vice versa, she supposes.

Still, they'd all made efforts to bond after Travis's departure. It was evident that the awkward visits were as much a chore for the Hunters as they were for Melody, so she'd tapered off even before she'd made the awful discovery about their son. After that, she'd seen them only at Thanksgiving and Christmas. Her mother insisted on inviting them because *"They're family now,"* though Honeybee doesn't care for the Hunters, either.

"Y'all were barely married before Travis left," she told Melody after a painfully stilted, perfunctory visit. *"When he's back home, it'll be different, you'll see. And my goodness, just wait until you give them a grandbaby. Those two will be doting just like your daddy and me."*

A car's headlights swing past Melody, and then the brake lights go on. The driver leans out and drawls, "Well, if it ain't Mrs. Hunter."

Rodney Lee Midget had gone through school with Travis, a few years ahead of Melody. Rodney Lee has always been tall and beefy, with a florid complexion and double chins, earning recess taunts about his paradoxical last name. Rodney Lee Giant, kids called him. Children can be cruel, but Melody recalls the victim as something of a schoolyard bully himself.

"Hi, there, Rodney Lee."

"Any word about Travis? Been thinking about him over there fighting for our country."

"Nothing yet, and I wouldn't say he's fighting for our country. It's not like we were attacked, like Pearl Harbor."

"*Attacked?* Now, don't you worry none. President Johnson says victory is within our grasp, so—"

"President Johnson doesn't know what he's talking about!" Seeing his jaw drop, she adds, "Martin Luther King says, 'Every time we drop our bombs in North Vietnam, President Johnson talks eloquently about peace.' That make sense to you, Rodney Lee?"

"Martin Luther King? No, he don't make a lick of sense to me."

"That's not what I meant. It's—"

"Guess someone's been putting crazy ideas into that pretty little head of yours. Unpatriotic ideas."

"What did I say that's unpatriotic?"

"You said the president's a damned fool."

"I didn't say that."

"That's what I heard."

"Yes, well . . . 'people generally see what they look for, and hear what they listen for,'" she mutters.

"What's that?"

"A quote from a book."

"Martin Luther King write it?"

"No, Harper Lee did."

"Who's he? Another one of those Negroes tryin' to start trouble?"

She takes a deep breath, but thinks better of engaging. "Never mind. Forget it. I have to go. I'm heading over to have supper with my mother and daddy."

"Did you smash up Travis's Camaro?"

"What?" Something twitches in her gut, and this time, it isn't a tiny karate foot.

"I could'a sworn I've seen you drivin' it all over creation since he's been gone, but now here you are, walkin' the streets at night all by your lonesome."

"The car's just fine, Rodney Lee. I just like to walk when I'm here in town. It's nice to get fresh air."

"Is that so." His expression and inflection are exactly the same as before, but she notes a slight shift in his tone. "Ain't safe for a woman to be alone out here in the night."

"In Fernandina?" She laughs and looks around at the empty streets. "Don't be silly."

"Ain't safe anywhere these days, what with all the hippies and Negroes runnin' amuck. Hop in and I'll give you a ride."

She stiffens, shaking her head firmly. "No, thank you. It's just a little ways down. You have a good evening, Rodney Lee. Bye now."

"You, too, ma'am. You be careful." Rodney Lee guns his engine.

She walks on toward her parents' house, uneasiness dogging her steps as she watches the turquoise Impala disappear into the night, taillights gleaming like the devil's eyes.

Barrow Island, Georgia

CYRIL KNOWS EVERY turn and rut in the wide sandy road that runs the length of the island. His feet scatter long pine needles and shell fragments that gleam beneath glittering stars and a fat full moon. He left Otis home tonight, but grabbed a flashlight—not in case the gleaming night sky suddenly goes pitch-dark, but because it's heavy enough to serve as a blunt force weapon.

He isn't worried about the island's natural predators. Even the gators leave you alone unless you're fool enough to wade into the surrounding swamps. But in this modern world, human predators are plentiful. A Black man never knows when or where he might run into trouble.

His friend Jimmy Davis has twin sons who spend

every afternoon fishing on the bridge. Jimmy said they've seen a couple of mainland good ol' boys on the island lately, cruising around in a blue sedan. Jimmy hadn't believed them at first because they'd also told him they'd seen a beautiful blonde driving over in a sports car. Cyril hadn't let on about Melody, but told Jimmy he thought folks should be on the lookout for trouble.

A few days later, Jimmy's brother Tommy had seen the same blue sedan. The young men weren't vandalizing anything or threatening anyone—yet. But a lot of local folks have been sticking close to home at night, with shotguns close at hand, just in case someone decides to stir things up.

Cyril's not the kind of man to sleep with a gun or hide himself away behind locked doors. Nor is he the kind to go running to his mama for reassurance in troubled times. But she lives just down the road from him and tonight, that's where he's headed. He needs advice, and Marceline LeBlanc is the only person in the world he can trust with a secret this weighty.

His mother's home, like his own, had once been one of the outbuildings on a large rice plantation. The main house sits a quarter mile down the road, long abandoned and boarded up, vines snaking around the stately white pillars like gnarled fingers grasping from the marshland's murky depths. It's haunted by old island souls, according to his mother. Of course, she says the same about her own place, though there, it's primarily his dead father's spirit drifting in and out, bothering her with advice and admonishment.

"Your daddy was boddun' me all night long," she'd told

Cyril a few days ago. *"That man doesn't know the meanin' of rest in peace."*

Cyril tends to dismiss his mother's talk of spirits, though even before Melody had come to him with her plight, he'd had his own share of sleepless nights. Not because ghosts have been boddun' him, but because of increasing conflict between Black and white folks.

He's heard sketchy reports that the South Carolina Highway Patrol had opened fire on a campus where Black college kids were protesting a segregated bowling alley. Three students were killed, a couple of dozen injured.

He'd also heard that the Klan had lynched a Black teenager somewhere on the Gulf coast, then dumped his body into the bayou. A week later, it has yet to turn up, and likely never will if the gators reduced him to chum.

Maybe it didn't happen at all. Maybe it wouldn't happen here. Or now.

As always, the island's peaceable kingdom ignores his presence. Night birds chatter in overhead branches, and stealthy creatures rustle bordering fronds. Half a dozen wild horses graze in a clearing. One of Marceline's many cats, a sleek, well-fed black fellow with lime-colored eyes, strolls across his path without glancing in his direction.

He wonders whether the animals would react differently to mainland interlopers, sensing danger. He wants to think he'd be capable of the same response. He wonders if the Black teenager in the bayou had sensed his executioners in his midst, and then he wonders whether the boy might be a myth—fodder to fuel the racial tension.

He turns up the lane that leads to Marceline's place. It's larger than his own two-room abode, framed by mossy live oaks and resurrection fern. Her front door is also blue, and her crepe myrtle tree covered in blue bottles.

You'd be hard-pressed to find a yard on Barrow Island without a bottle tree, or a door painted any color other than haint blue, both to ward off evil spirits. The Gullah culture is alive here. Virtually every islander is of West African descent, their ancestors transported to America by wealthy Southern planters. A century ago, after the Civil War, freed slaves had populated Barrow and several other Sea Islands along the southern Atlantic coast. Some have since moved on. Marceline's family had largely left the island to find work during the Great Depression and most had settled on the Georgia mainland. Three of her four sisters are still there, along with various extended relatives.

But Marceline plans to live out her days on this insular island, steeped in low country tradition and lore, language and food.

The windows are closed against the chill, and his footsteps are muffled in the grass, yet the front door opens before he reaches the house. If he asks, she'll say she didn't hear him coming.

"I can always feeeeeel you," she's told him all his life, and taps her heart. *"Right there."*

In her world, maternal instinct is more powerful than any of the five senses.

By day, she wears bright dresses and turbans, earrings jangling like wind chimes. Tonight, she's barefoot in a simple white nightgown, her thick cornrows hanging long and loose.

"'*S'mattuh?*" she calls from the porch—Gullah shorthand for "What's the matter?"

"I brought you some ham hocks from the store," he says, holding up the package wrapped in brown paper and twine. By day, most days, he mans the counter at a small mainland butcher shop.

She thanks him with a cursory "T'engky"—and asks again what's wrong, why he's here.

She really does seem to *feeeeel* him. But will she understand him, and will she empathize? He suspects the answer is no. His mother isn't just intuitive, brilliant, and resourceful—she's fiercely opinionated.

No turning back now. He takes a deep breath. "I need to talk to you about something."

"You in trouble?"

"Yes."

Marceline holds the door open wide. "Come."

He crosses the threshold into a wide little house with low beadboard ceilings, pocked wide-planked floors, and whitewashed walls.

He'd entered this world in the back bedroom in 1938, three decades almost to the day after Marceline had been delivered in the same room, same bed. Her father, too, had been born here back in the late nineteenth century. *His* father, born into slavery, had expanded the place from shanty to home.

Cyril thinks of his great-grandparents whenever he gets to fretting that Negro lives will never evolve in the South. They may have a long way to go, but they've come a long way in the last hundred years. Oh, how he longs to stay alive for the better part of the next hundred to witness Dr. King's dream become reality.

A plank propped across a pair of sawhorses holds a row of sweetgrass baskets Marceline weaves and sells to mainland vendors. She'd always hoped to get a real worktable, but could never afford it, struggling to keep a roof over their heads and food on the table and figure out a way to further his education.

How proud Marceline had been when he'd earned his high school diploma, hanging it in a frame on the wall above the sofa.

At eighteen, he'd worked three jobs—as a shrimp boat fisherman, busboy, and meat cutter at a processing plant. He'd put aside his dream of enrolling at Bethune-Cookman University down in Daytona. There was no money for that, and he couldn't leave her alone on Barrow. But he'd spent every spare moment at the Wilder Park Negro Library in Jacksonville's Sugar Hill neighborhood. There, he rubbed shoulders with successful, educated people and got to know the fine woman who'd led him into activism. Mrs. Willye F. Dennis was the branch librarian and a driving force in the burgeoning civil rights movement.

Predictably, his mama hadn't approved. *"Why's that woman runnin' around protestin' all over creation when she got a husband and two children at home?"*

Cyril suspected that she was just jealous of his relationship with any female who wasn't her, and that she was worried for his safety. She'd surely been beside herself eight years ago, when he and a group of fellow NAACP Youth Council demonstrators had been attacked by a mob of two hundred white men armed with makeshift clubs.

Not just fearful, though. Outraged, and proud that he'd taken a stand. She never said as much, but he could tell. And she no longer pitches fits about his activism.

She leads him to the kitchen. A savory supper scents the air hours after she washed the pans and plates on the drainboard.

She turns on the overhead light, turns, and looks him up and down. "You wasting away, son. When was the last time you had supshun? I got frogmore."

Supshun is nutritious food; *frogmore*, a stew of shrimp and smoked meat, potatoes, and corn.

Cyril shakes his head. He can't recall the last time he sat down for a meal, but he can't choke food into an anxiety-churned stomach.

She fills two jelly glasses with sweet tea and sets them on the table. It's pushed into a corner, with the pair of ladderback chairs that have been here all his life. Marceline takes her seat, closest to the stove. As Cyril sinks into his, his body remembers to distribute his weight to make up for the wobble due to one wooden leg being a hair shorter.

Now he's got a permanent wobble of his own, due to his broken ankle. He supposes he should be grateful that the Axe Handle Saturday injury had kept him out of 'Nam—he'd been declared 4-F when they'd tried to draft him a few years back. Though he won't see active combat in a foreign jungle, he's engaged in an ongoing, escalating battle just the same.

Marceline sips her tea and gives him an expectant look. "Well?"

"There's a woman . . ."

She nods. "There is *aaaalways* a woman. You runnin' round with that crookety Glenda again?"

Crookety—the Gullah insult she reserves for his

on-again, off-again childhood sweetheart. Sometimes he thinks she wouldn't like any woman in his life. The oldest of five sisters, she'd told him from an early age never to take a female at face value.

"See, womenfolk, they always thinkin' and plottin' and schemin' to outsmart you, Cyril."

"You are?"

"Not *me.* I'm your mama. But the rest of them . . . you be careful."

Now her eyes are narrowed as always when Glenda enters a conversation.

"Come on, Mama. She's married now, and she lives in Savannah. I haven't even seen her in years."

"So? She's settlin' for second best. If she comes around here again lookin' for you—"

"She hasn't. And she won't."

"Then who is this crookety woman?"

"She's not crookety, and you don't know her."

"I know everyone." She gestures around as if the room is crowded with people.

"She doesn't live on Barrow. And she's buckruh."

"Buckruh!" She leans back in her chair, arms folded, eyes closed as if in prayer. "Why you go lookin' for trouble, son?"

"I didn't. We met by chance, just like you and Daddy."

His father had come to Barrow on a shrimp boat one day with a storm bearing down.

"That man took one look at me and was smitten," Marceline has always said. *"When the storm passed, he stayed behind. There we were, arm in arm on the beach, just smilin' and wavin' and the boat sailed away without him. I said, 'What you gonna do now?' And he said, 'Marry you.' And*

I said, 'I don't think so.' Your daddy just laughed and said, 'Wait and see.'"

It had been perhaps the only time in her life that Marceline LeBlanc had changed her mind about something. Once she gets an idea in her head, it roots and grows like a big old oak.

"Buckruh." Marceline shakes her head.

"I haven't even seen her since last summer, Mama. We only went out a couple of times."

Went out—as though they'd dated, in public, like any other couple. As though their skin matched, and one of them wasn't married to someone else; as though it was legal for them to love each other.

"Mmm-hmm. Why you got trouble with her?"

"She's going to have a baby."

She digests the news like a bad oyster and says, "Well, she can't be aimin' for a shotgun wedding, seein' as that's illegal."

Anti-miscegenation laws, ruled unconstitutional last summer, are still being fully enforced south of the Mason-Dixon Line.

"She's already got a husband."

"Crookety!"

"It isn't like that."

"Sounds that way to me, if she didn't tell you she's already married—"

"I knew it all along. She never lied about anything."

Marceline's jaw sets. "I raised you to be an honorable man."

"I am, and she's an honorable woman. Young, from a good family over in Fernandina, married last February. Her husband is in Vietnam, and—"

She slaps both hands on the table. "The husband is fighting for his *country*? And the wife is goin' around—"

"It isn't like that. The husband is no hero, Mama."

"You watch your tongue! I know how you feel about this war, but you got no say in whether we're fightin' it, or about soldiers in combat!"

He should have known her temper would flare at the mention of Travis Hunter's service.

His own daddy had been killed in action during World War II, serving with the 761st Tank Battalion. Cyril has no memory of Cyril LeBlanc, Sr., though he wears his father's military dog tags and tiny gold baby ring on a chain around his neck.

Whenever Marceline speaks of him, she makes it sound like he'd outshone the baseball great and outranked General Patton himself.

But his battalion wasn't just fighting the Nazis. They'd faced opposition from fellow American soldiers—buckruh, including Patton, who doubted the Negro soldiers' competency. The general had eventually relied upon them during the Battle of the Bulge, but where had that gotten Cyril's father? Killed in action, buried amid a sea of white crosses in Belgium, segregated from the buckruh even in death.

"You got no right to condemn any brave soldier doin' his patriotic duty, son!"

"Travis Hunter is a bad man, Mama."

"Jealousy is the work of the devil."

"I'm not jealous. And Hunter *is* the devil. She told me—"

"Cyril, your brain is too smart for sweetmout' talk."

"My *brain* didn't get me into this."

"Well, your damned heart's not going to get you out. What does she want from you? Money?"

"No."

"Good, 'cause you got none to spare."

"Can you just . . ." He clears his throat, but his voice is hoarse. "A child's life is at stake, Mama."

She's silent for a moment. "You sure it's *your* child?"

"Yes."

"Well, then, she can give it up for adoption. Plenty of folks just waitin' for the good Lord to bless them, and some been blessed and lost their babies, and for some of those, it ain't ever goin' to happen again the natural way, like your cousin up there in New—"

"A married woman can't put a child up for adoption. And she can't raise it with her husband."

"Maybe he won't be able to tell."

"She's a green-eyed blonde, and he's fair, too, with blue eyes." Cyril's never met the man, but he'd seen his damned picture, and the expression in those frosty eyes had made his blood run cold. "If he ever figures out that her baby has a Black man's blood running through its veins, he'll destroy it, and her."

"What kind of man—"

"Look at this!" He pulls a crumpled newspaper clipping from his pocket.

Marceline leans forward to take it in—the caption, the context, the grainy image.

A group of men stand shoulder to shoulder, wearing robes emblazoned with a familiar cross-shaped crest, their triangular hoods raised to reveal their faces. The photo is sepia-toned, but his mother will know at a glance that the hoods and robes are white and the crest red, the splotch in the middle symbolizing a drop of blood.

"This here is a Klan rally."

"July of '66, up in Raleigh. They were protesting Dr. King's appearance at Reynolds Coliseum."

"You were there that day." In her rich patois, the word *there* is interchangeable with *day*. "You rode all the way up to Carolina with those NAACP friends of yours. That where you got that newspaper?"

"No. Melody found it in her husband's belongings after he left."

"Why was she goin' through his things? And just 'cause he had a piece o' paper doesn't mean—"

"She found his damned costume, too."

He sees her mulling it over, not wanting to bend.

"Mama! Wake up! You see this right here?" He jabs at a sickening, unabashed grin beneath a conical cap. "That's Travis Hunter."

Chapter Six

The Bronx, New York

On his way home from work, Oran stops at John's Bargain Store to pick up a heart-shaped box of Brach's chocolates for the only woman in his life. Then he swings by the White Castle on Bruckner Boulevard to get a sack of her favorite little hamburgers. To his dismay, the price has gone up from twelve cents each to fourteen since his last visit months ago. Worth it, though, because they'll make Gypsy happy. And tonight, he needs her to be happy.

He unlocks the door and steps from a dingy hall to a dingier apartment—two small rooms plus a smaller kitchen. The tub is there; the toilet is in an adjacent cubicle.

Gypsy is sprawled on the mattress that serves as her bed and the sofa, doing her homework.

He holds out the box of chocolates.

"Valentine's Day isn't until tomorrow," she tells him.

"So? I'm giving it to you early."

"Why?" She peers up at him like someone trying to pinpoint a stranger's face, and for a moment, he thinks she knows what's going on. Everything.

Then she looks down at the grease-splotched paper bag in his hand. "What's that?"

"Sliders."

"Why?"

"Because it's dinnertime, man, and we have to eat!"

"I know, but why are you buying White Castle and candy when we don't have any money? That's what you're always saying, isn't it? That's why we have to live in this disgusting dump instead of—"

He hurtles the bag and box at her. That shuts her up, but she glares at him.

He turns away from the intense violet eyes that can reach right into his soul like predator talons clawing for a kill. He's been preaching his own omniscience all her life, but his daughter's is becoming impossible to ignore.

Storming into the bedroom, he slams the door, breathing hard, and stares into the mirror hanging on the back. A wild-eyed demon meets his gaze.

This isn't how it's supposed to be, how *Oran* is supposed to be. He's savior, not destructor. But sometimes, people get under his skin, man. Even his daughter, whenever he looks at her and catches a hint of Linda.

It's not often. Gypsy, unlike her mother, unlike womankind, is strong.

She knocks on the bedroom door. "Hey, come and eat dinner with me."

The man in the mirror raises his eyebrows. "What for?"

"It's dinnertime, man, and we have to eat."

Her echo of his own words is such a perfect imitation that he sees his scowl give way to—not a grin, exactly. But the creases at the bridge of his nose smooth out, and his jaw unclenches.

He opens the door. There's his girl, the only one he's ever loved.

She holds up the sack of sliders. "I already ate one. And two pieces of candy."

"Two?"

"Sorry. I can save the rest for tomorrow."

"You don't have to. Did you stick your finger in 'em already?"

Of course she did. She always does.

"Yeah. I like to see what the fillings are before I choose."

"And you like to make sure your old man doesn't eat any."

"You can have the maple."

"I hate maple."

He makes a face, and she laughs.

"I'll take the cherry, though," he adds, picking up the box and opening it.

"Sorry. That's my favorite."

Yeah, no kidding.

He tells her to clear the clutter from the small table so that they can sit down.

The dome-shaped cherry one is right in the center, surrounded by nine other chocolates and two empty black fluted wrappers.

When she turns her back, he slips a tiny packet out of his pocket. It holds one small pill.

He lifts the cherry. Viscous pink filling oozes from the hole she'd poked in its underside. He pushes the white tablet into it, puts the candy back into the box, and is closing the lid when Gypsy turns back. Her eyes narrow.

"Hey! Did you steal one?"

"Nope."

"Give it here." She holds out her hand, and he puts the box into it, pulse racing.

Gypsy lifts the lid and takes inventory. She plucks the cherry from the box and pops it into her mouth. "I don't trust you," she says, and he sees the slick of goo on her tongue.

They sit and gobble down the food. He keeps an eye on her, waiting for the yawning to begin. As expected, it doesn't take long.

Powerful stuff. It won't hurt her—he'd never hurt his beautiful girl—but she'll sleep soon, and soundly.

AIN'T SAFE ANYWHERE these days, what with all the hippies and Negroes runnin' amuck . . .

Rodney Lee's comment is nothing Melody hasn't heard before, from just about everyone in these parts. She assures herself that she shouldn't be feeling so uneasy, looking over her shoulder, making sure Rodney Lee didn't come back around again to trail her up the street, on foot or in his car.

When she replays the conversation, trying to put her finger on what else is bothering her, she settles on his comments about LBJ and MLK, and being "unpatriotic."

Plenty of Americans aren't fans of Dr. King, she reminds herself, and not all are members of the so-called Invisible Empire.

Forget about it, she thinks as her parents' house draws her like a beacon, windows aglow with lamplight and vintage gas fixtures flickering on the upper and lower verandahs. Both porch ceilings are painted haint blue, a fact she never noticed before she met Cyril.

Honeybee, gracious Southern hostess that she is, seems to have invited last-minute supper guests. An unfamiliar gold Cadillac DeVille sits parked at the curb.

Melody mounts the wide, curved brick steps and opens the front door. Ah, home. The front hall is warmly lit by a graceful nineteenth-century pendant light, and a Johnny Mercer instrumental plays on the parlor hi-fi. The air is fragranced with Raelene's pineapple upside-down cake, a sure sign that the visitors aren't close friends. Her mother only serves it for company or celebrations.

Melody hangs her jacket on the carved antique coat tree beside a man's topcoat and hat and a woman's double-breasted jacket, familiar perfume wafting from the nubby pear-colored fabric. She can't place the scent, but it triggers something unpleasant. One of her mother's bridge club friends? A disapproving maiden aunt?

"Someone's been putting crazy ideas into that pretty little head of yours."

Have people been talking behind her back? Could someone have seen her with Cyril last summer, and come here to confront her and her parents about it?

But where? Certainly not in American Beach, or on Barrow. The locals would have no more business out there than . . .

Than you do?

She turns and catches sight of herself in the full-length mirror. Oh, dear. She's wearing dungarees, a wrinkled white blouse, and scuffed flats. No lipstick or powder. Her blond hair is parted in the middle, flipped above her shoulders and caught in a black headband. She hasn't brushed it since this morning.

Honeybee's voice sails in from the dining room, beyond French doors. "Is that you, poppet?"

It's what her parents have called her ever since her sister's death, because there can be no "Melly" without Ellie.

"Yes, I'll be right there!"

She heads for the kitchen. It runs the width of the house, with beamed ceilings, whitewashed walls, and tall windows overlooking Honeybee's spot-lit perennial gardens and the wooden arbor with its barren wisteria vine.

Plump, apron-clad Raelene bustles from the Frigidaire to the sink and back again. Wisps of gray hair escape her bun, and her fair, freckled complexion is flushed with exertion.

Raelene has been with the Abernathy family since Melody's parents were newlyweds—born into the position, she likes to say. Her own mother had worked for the Beauregard family for decades, and Raelene and Honeybee are the same age—childhood playmates turned employer and employee. Honeybee often comments by way of praise that Raelene knows her place. Yet she understands Honeybee perhaps better than Melody and her father do.

She flashes a warm smile. "Evenin', Mrs. Hunter."

"I hate it when you call me *Mrs. Hunter*, Raelene. That's my miserable mother-in-law's name, and I—"

"Oh, hush, now! You'll get used to bein' a Mrs. just like the rest of us."

Melody sighs. Maybe if her husband were a wonderful man like Raelene's Elmer. They'd married young, raised four children and now have more than a dozen grandchildren. They'd waltzed like young lovers at her wedding last February. At the time, Melody had fancied that she and Travis would be the same way, still head over heels thirty, forty years into the future.

"You'd best get to the table so that I can serve up the supper," Raelene tells her. "Your Mama's been frettin'."

"Why? Who's joining us, Princess Margaret and Lord Snowdon?"

"I guess they'd be a lot more down-to-earth than . . ."

"Than who?"

Raelene shakes her head, lips sealed.

Melody heads for the dining room and stops just outside the door, eavesdropping. Andy Williams is singing "Charade" and her mother is going on about the weekend trip.

"And then Wayne and Donna showed us some land where Walt Disney's going to build a new theme park, and—"

"In *Orlando*?" a familiar female voice asks.

"Isn't Walt Disney dead?" a familiar male chimes in.

No. Oh, no. Mother, what have you done?

"He passed away a year or two ago," Melody's father is saying. "I'll tell you what, there's nothing on that land but grass and cows right now, but Wayne said it's going to be bigger and better than Disneyland."

"I'll believe *that* when I see it. We were out in California with Travis when Disneyland opened back in '55. A hundred degrees in Anaheim. Miserable. Just miserable."

"Melody! My goodness, where are you?" Honeybee calls as though she's miles away, and tells the guests, "I'm so sorry, I'm sure she'll be—"

"I'm right here." She plunges into the wallpapered,

candlelit room like a child who can barely swim stepping off the high-dive.

The oval table is set with bone china, silver, and crystal. Her father is at the head, her father-in-law at the foot, her mother and mother-in-law seated opposite each other. All four are smoking cigarettes and drinking gimlets. Both women are attractive blondes and wearing green. But Honeybee's sprayed bouffant, pastel mint cashmere sweater and pearls look dated beside the other woman's smooth coif and citron geometric-patterned shift accessorized with a chunky Bakelite pendant.

"Look who's here, Melody!" Honeybee's smile is strained, her tone too bright. "I thought it would be a nice surprise for you. I know you're missing Travis and so worried."

"We *all* are," his mother says.

"How nice to see you," Melody manages. "I was wondering who was . . . um, did you get a new car?"

Her father-in-law nods. "Just a few days ago. A beaut, isn't she?"

So sneaky of them. She would never have come inside had she realized they were here.

"Sit right down, sugar. Supper's been ready for a while." Honeybee points to the vacant chair and place setting between Travis's parents—her designated spot, as if she's one of them. "Raelene? You can serve now!"

As Melody moves toward her place, the baby kicks sharply in protest. She gasps and presses a hand to her belly. One of the buttons across her midsection has popped right off. Looking up, she sees her parents and her in-laws gawking at the telltale gap.

Her mother claps her hands and jumps to her feet. "Melody! You're expecting!"

"I'm . . ." She shakes her head, helpless. There's no denying it.

"Well, I declare! Isn't this the most magnificent news ever?" Honeybee embraces her, beaming. "Wait until I see that rascal Doc Krebbs. I was in for my checkup just last week, and he never said a word. When are you due?"

"April. April . . . 4."

"Why, that's Travis's birthday!" His mother smiles at Melody for the first time in . . .

Ever, she realizes. That same crazy, irrational part of her is pleased, as if she's an ordinary daughter-in-law seeking approval from the mother of the man she loves. As if the baby inside of her is a part of him. As if everyone in this room is one big happy family.

"Now, can all y'all think of a more divine birthday gift for Travis than becoming a daddy?" Honeybee crows.

"Sit down, poppet. You look a little pale." Her father pulls out her chair and gives her shoulder a squeeze when she lowers herself into it.

"You do look pale, dear. Too much excitement. Relax. Here, calm your nerves." Honeybee thrusts her gold-plated cigarette case and lighter into her daughter's hands, and calls into the kitchen, "Raelene? Can you please bring a gimlet for Melody?"

"I'll have another myself," Travis's father says. He isn't smiling, but he doesn't look quite as stern as usual.

"Another round, Raelene!" Honeybee calls. "We *must* toast this marvelous news. If only Travis was here. I'm sure he was just tickled when you wrote to tell him, Melody."

She says nothing, and feels her mother-in-law's gaze.

"Melody?" Doris asks, a freshly lit Pall Mall poised in its opera-length silver holder against her pursed red lips. "You did tell him?"

"Not yet," she says. "I wanted to . . . be sure."

"*Sure?* Bless your heart. Your due date is two months away! How much more sure do you think you're going to be?" Honeybee pats her shoulder and offers Doris a bemused mother-to-mother smile.

Doris doesn't return it, focused on Melody. "Don't you think you should have told my son before you went around telling the rest of the world?"

Ah, there's the disapproving mother-in-law.

Melody glares right back at her, not in the mood to play nice with the woman who spawned the likes of Travis Hunter.

"Raelene?" Honeybee shouts, before she can reply. "The gimlets!"

"Coming, Mrs. Abernathy!"

"I'm sure Melody hasn't gone around telling anyone," her father says firmly. "Have you, poppet."

It isn't a question. Nor is her response a lie.

"I think the father should always be the first to know, but Travis isn't here. I was hoping he'd call so that I could tell him on the phone, but since he hasn't, I have a letter all set to mail him," she says, mostly to Doris, feeling sweat beading along her hairline. She puts down the cigarette case and lighter and pulls a lace handkerchief from her pocket to dab her forehead.

She'd like nothing better than to toss back the gimlet Raelene serves from a silver tray, but her stomach recoils at the first sip. She pokes at her meal, and the pineapple cake might as well be sand on her tongue. Honeybee notices, of course, and chalks it up to pregnancy nausea.

"I could not even look at rich food the whole nine months I was expecting you and your sister. Cake, pastries, ice cream—just mention pralines, and I'd just . . ." She sighs an almost gleeful little sigh, bent on making up for months of shared pregnancy tales. "But then, my goodness, out of nowhere, I developed an uncontrollable craving for lemon icebox pie. I just couldn't get enough of it! Remember, darling?"

Melody's father shrugs. "Poppet's never been fond of dessert. She'll be just fine."

"Of course she will! This is the grandest time in a woman's life. I'm so happy for you, Melody. I can hardly wait for April."

Acid bubbles into her throat. She swallows it back as Andy Williams sings about fate pulling the strings.

Her in-laws insist on driving her home in their new car. Her father-in-law walks her to the door, a hand under her elbow.

"You should leave a light on when you go out at night, Melody."

"I thought I had," she murmurs, fitting the key into the lock.

"You're just like Doris," he says with a rare grin.

Never, she thinks, turning the key.

"She was forgetful, too, when she was expecting," Bob goes on. "Sometimes I thought she might be losing her doggone mind. Oh, well. You have a good night."

"Thank you. And thank you for the ride."

"No problem. Family, you know . . ." He tips his hat

and heads down the walk to the car, and her mother-in-law.

Doris leans out the window. "Melody? See that you send that letter to Travis first thing in the morning."

"Oh, I will."

She locks the door and leans against it, exhaling at last.

"What am I going to do?" she asks the dark, empty room.

She turns on the lamp she could have sworn she'd left burning, and goes into the kitchen to find the letter she'd written Travis over the weekend.

Now that the family knows about the baby, there will be no keeping it from Travis. She'll have to rewrite her letter, only telling him that news. The rest can wait.

She sighs, opens a drawer, and finds a pen, her mind already arranging and rearranging the words she'll write to Travis. She turns and grabs the pad of paper, wondering if she should destroy the confession she'd written and start fresh in a few days, or weeks, whenever she gets word that he's safe. Or that he is not, in which case there will be no need—

Melody gasps.

"What in the world . . . ?" she whispers, gaping at the paper in her hand. *Blank.*

She whirls back to the counter. Maybe she'd torn off the pages she'd written after all, sealed them into the envelope. But the envelope is gone.

You're just like Doris.

"Never!" She must have put the letter away for safekeeping. She checks the kitchen drawers, the desk in the living room, her nightstand, and the dog-eared pages of *To Kill a Mockingbird.*

She goes through the entire house again room by room, and once more inch by inch. Even that doesn't take very long.

There's no sign of the letter.

"She was forgetful, too, when she was expecting."

Could she have mailed it and forgotten?

Had she imagined writing it in the first place?

"Sometimes, I thought she might be losing her doggone mind."

She doesn't feel as though she's gone insane. But insane people probably never do.

Back in the kitchen, she stares down at the blank page and sees faint indentations. When she holds it up to the light, she can make out several of the words she'd written, superimposed over others.

The letter had been real.

What on earth could have happened to it?

AROUND MIDNIGHT, MARCELINE walks her son to the door.

"You want some biscuits to take with you? You barely touched your victuals."

"I told you I wasn't hungry."

She'd insisted on heating frogmore for him anyway. It gave her something to do, standing at the stove, stirring bubbling stew in the cast-iron pot. Anything was better than just sitting there across the table, facing those big brown eyes of his.

Boddun' eyes, her mama would've called them.

Botherin' about what's going to become of them—not just this baby, and the buckruh woman, but all of them. The whole world's gone crazy—people fighting, hating, killing colored people.

"All right, then, Cyril, you get along home. Day-clean be here before you know it."

He opens the door. "Well, look who's here. Good evening, Ms. Maisie."

Marceline's fat orange-and-white tabby sits on the mat wearing an indignant scowl as though she'd been knocking for hours. She strolls over the threshold and nudges her furry head against Cyril's ankles.

From the time he was a young'un, he's had a way with God's creatures. Marceline has seen dolphins flank him in the sea like bodyguards, and butterflies bypass a patch of blooming clover to alight on her boy's shoulder.

He steps outside, then turns back. "T'engky, Mama."

"What for?"

"For letting me talk. For not judging me."

"Only one can judge you is the good Lord above, Cyril. You going to talk, what am I going to do but listen?"

"Tell me what to do."

She shrugs. "Ain't up to me now, is it. Or you. You ain't the one growing a child in your belly."

"Well, what do you think Melody should do?"

"Nothing she *can* do, is there, 'cept wait for the baby to be born come May. You best hope Travis Hunter won't be back home by then."

"I hope he's not home by then, or soon after, or ev—"

"Shush, boy. Don't you stand in your daddy's house wishin' a soldier dead."

"It's your house, Mama. You're the one who was born here. And this man . . . he's not a hero. This isn't even a war our country should be fighting."

"You the *prezzydent?*" she asks, sounding like her

own Grammy. "Get on home now, son. You be safe." She hesitates, then reaches out and gives his shoulder a little pat.

He raises an eyebrow but says nothing, just turns and walks out into the night.

She isn't much for expressing her feelings or showing affection. When he was a baby, yes, and into his toddler years, but . . .

Not in a long time. Not since she'd lost her husband. A woman can't just go on with life the way it used to be. A woman—a widow—can't be who she used to be, how she used to be. Everything is different after your husband is killed.

In the early days after Cyril, Sr., had shipped out overseas, she'd longed to feel his arms around her again. After the telegram, when she knew she never would, the ache became unbearable. She'd decided that it's easier to just keep your distance from folks, even the ones you care about. Even your own son. Raising a child on hugs and kisses and sweet promises seemed as foolhardy as raising him on cookies and pies.

She feels unsettled, standing in the doorway watching her son cross the yard in the moonlight. He reminds her not of his father, but of her own father, who'd taught himself how to read and wanted her to get a good education. But he'd died of the Spanish influenza when Marceline was ten, leaving her mother with five daughters to raise. Firstborn Marceline left school to take care of the others, and she didn't need anyone takin' care of her. She came of age determined to be a spinster. No man was man enough for her, and she'd had her fill of running a household.

That's what she'd told Cyril, Sr., when they met.

He'd thrown back his head and laughed, and asked her where she'd been all his life.

"Right here on Barrow Island, and I ain't fixing to leave, either."

Neither was he. When that longline shrimp boat headed south two days later without him, Marceline and Cyril, Sr., stood arm in arm on the beach, watching it until it disappeared. She was in her late twenties then, and head over heels in love.

She locks up the house and goes through the rooms extinguishing lights, pausing to gaze at the large red leather satchel that sits on a bench at the foot of her bed because there's nowhere else to store it. It's packed full of all the things Cyril, Sr., had left behind when he'd up and enlisted the day after Pearl Harbor was attacked. Clothes, mostly, and some books and a few precious family photographs.

Back in the parlor, she sits on the davenport where she'd finally accepted her husband's marriage proposal thirty-five years ago, listening for his voice amid droning marsh bugs and a hooting owl in a distant perch.

He's been gone decades more than the few years they were married, but the dead are always around and can speak to you if you're open to their presence. Other people's ears don't hear, and sometimes she's not even sure her own ears are hearing him, but her heart surely does.

"I don't like this either," she whispers, shaking her head, her long braids swishing and swaying over her shoulders. "Anyone finds out about that woman and her baby, and our boy is going to face a world of trouble. Worse than before. Way worse."

She shudders, remembering what had happened

when he and his NAACP Youth Council friends had staged a peaceful protest at a whites-only lunch counter. They'd been attacked by a white mob that swelled and rioted through the streets attacking all people of color.

"Buckruh been comin' around here, last couple'a weeks or so," she goes on. "Checkin' things out, I s'pose. Folks are scared. Not me."

"I'm the one goin' off to war," he'd said, all those years ago. *"If I ain't scared, then you can't be scared."*

That was the last conversation they'd ever had when they were both on this earthly plane.

"You ain't gotta do anything but wait for me to come home, woman. So what are you boddun' about?"

He'd made it sound so easy. The waiting, and the going off to war.

It would have been hell even if there had just been one war to fight, with Cyril, Sr., and his fellow Black soldiers fighting alongside the buckruh troops. But it hadn't happened that way.

Marceline doesn't know exactly what her husband endured over there, and he'd never had a chance to tell her. But she's heard stories, and she has her suspicions, and though that war is long over, some battles wage on.

Travis Hunter isn't the only violent, hate-filled *buckruh* around these parts. A carful of troublemakers has been spotted on the island lately. They didn't say anything to anyone, or trespass on private property, but they shouldn't be out joyriding around in a fancy blue car in these parts.

"Heard tell it's not haint blue, but more turquoise-like," she tells her dead husband. "Up to no good. And if they find out about what that boy's been doin', and this baby . . . You need to protect him, and so does the good Lord above."

Marceline sighs, stands, and goes to the bedroom, bracing for another sleepless night.

Oran takes a last look at Gypsy before leaving home. Deep in slumber, she's serene, an angel. She'll never know he's gone. He'll be back before sunrise.

He takes the subway to Sheepshead Bay. Perched at the southern edge of Brooklyn, the neighborhood lies within the perimeter of America's largest metropolis, but it feels like a small seaside village.

As a child, Oran had spent a lot of time here, never with his mother. Still in her teens when he'd started school, Pamela always had better things to do. Whenever her parents forced him on her, she'd take him to the movies, or to ride the rides at Coney Island. The carnival atmosphere was more her speed.

Oran's grandparents, however, had loved Sheepshead Bay. It reminded them of the coastal Connecticut town they'd visited after his grandfather got back from fighting in the trenches during the First World War.

Sometimes, when Pamela was in a rare teasing mood, she'd remind her parents that she'd been born nine months later, and ask them whether she'd been conceived in Connecticut. Her father would turn red and retreat, and her mother would purse her lips and tell her daughter not to say such things.

"What things?" Pamela would ask, a gleam in her eye. "It's not like you hadn't already been married forever by then. It's not like you were me, having a baby with any old—"

"Shush!"

Any old worthless piece of trash. Yeah, Oran knew. He'd found his father soon after his mother had managed to attach herself to an equally worthless piece of trash.

Eddie was in prison, last Oran knew. Maybe his mother is, too, or maybe she's dead. If not, he hopes she thinks of him, of how she failed him, every day for the rest of her miserable life.

At least Pamela's parents, while strict and old-fashioned, had been good to Oran. Sometimes, after church on a beautiful summer Sunday afternoon, they'd pack up a picnic lunch and ride the bus down to Sheepshead Bay. Out there, by the shimmery blue, boat-bobbing water, his grandparents didn't fret about money, work, Pamela's behavior, Oran's future. They were relaxed, laughing and reminiscing about that long-ago vacation in Connecticut.

Oran's never been to New England. He has, however, seen plenty of movies about charming towns where neighbors chat over white picket fences.

Like *Shadow of a Doubt*, an Alfred Hitchcock thriller he'd seen on a cold winter night very much like this one. Pamela had paid for his ticket with the money his grandfather had given her, and then gone off for a rendezvous, leaving Oran in the theater to watch the feature alone. It was set in an idyllic, peaceful community where life is just about perfect . . . until an outsider shows up, and bad things—terrible, deadly things—begin to happen.

As a child, in broad daylight, Oran had felt a sense of belonging here in Sheepshead Bay. On this cold February night, he is without a doubt an outsider. But he's not alone.

His heart pounds faster than his feet along the pavement, and he summons Deuteronomy to calm himself.

"And shall say unto them, Hear, O Israel, ye approach this day unto battle against your enemies: let not your hearts faint, fear not, and do not tremble, neither be ye terrified because of them; For the Lord your God is He that goeth with you, to fight for you against your enemies, to save you."

He presses on, past Italian pizzerias long closed for the night and Irish pubs going strong at this hour on a weeknight. The moon is fat and full, riding high above the steepled bell tower at Saint Paul's redbrick Catholic church. Two days ago, from an alley across the street, he'd watched Christina climb the steps with her parents and younger sister for mass. In the days ahead, she'll trail their wooden coffins down the stone steps.

The block is lined with tall trees, parked cars, row houses with darkened windows, a smattering of shuttered shops. His footsteps slow, and his pulse picks up as he reaches the beige brick duplex.

The Myers family lives on the first floor.

Oran turns to scan the street, making sure there are no witnesses. Then he makes his way around the house to the back, pulling on a hand-knit balaclava to cover most of his face. He deftly jimmies open a window he's practiced on several times since he'd met Christina.

Once, he'd even climbed inside and crept through the house, memorizing the layout, figuring out who sleeps where. The two daughters, Christina and Allison, share a bedroom across from their parents. Twin beds in both rooms.

Both doors are closed.

He opens the door to the master bedroom, slips over the threshold, and closes it behind him.

"When thou comest nigh unto a city to fight against it, then proclaim peace unto it."

He stands just inside the door, waiting for his eyes to acclimate, listening to deep, rhythmic breathing and gentle snoring. Christina's parents are asleep. Moonlight filters through the lace curtains. Clothing hangs on the bedpost—an orange shirt and striped bell bottoms he'd seen the father wearing. Oran approaches the closer bed, gloved hand clutching the meat cleaver he'd borrowed from the kitchen.

He leans over and whispers close to the father's ear. "Hey, man . . ."

A little sighing sound from the bed. The room is bright enough for Oran to see him open drowsy eyes.

"Shhh. I'm here for Christina. I need her to come with me, you dig?"

The man's gaze widens. He opens his mouth. Oran clamps his hand over it, muffling his cry. The wife stirs.

"Shhh," Oran says again, so close to the man's ear that his lips brush the flesh. "All I need to know is if you're cool with Christina coming with me."

"And it shall be, if it make thee answer of peace, and open unto thee, then it shall be, that all the people that is found therein shall be tributaries unto thee, and they shall serve thee."

"You with me, man? If you're not going to give me any trouble with this, just nod, and then I can just—"

The man shifts violently, trying to wrench himself upward.

"And if it will make no peace with thee, but will make war against thee, then thou shalt besiege it."

Oran plunges the knife into his throat.

MELODY DRIVES TO Barrow Island just before dawn, moments stringing along in her memory like twinkle lights.

Cyril showing her how to feed wild horses from her hand. Cyril lying in a patch of shady grass, reading aloud. Cyril floating beside her in the warm sea as fat white fish jumped and splashed around them and dolphins breached out past the break. Cyril on the beach, eyes closed, as she sang "At Last," his favorite song. Cyril pulling her down beside him, saying, "Baby, you sing it better than Etta James herself." Melody laughing, protesting. Cyril silencing her with a kiss.

Oh, how they'd tried not to let it happen. But Melody has always been *"persistent as a bloodthirsty skeeter,"* as her daddy likes to say.

Later—not that first night, but soon after—he'd claimed that he had indeed been waiting for her. For the idea of her. For a woman who'd spark hope in his soul in this miserable, hate and war-ridden world, he'd explained as she traced his bare chest with the hand that wasn't wearing a gold band.

He, however, was wearing one on the chain around his neck. Not a wedding ring, but a baby ring she'd discovered had belonged to his late father, as had the dog tags hanging alongside it.

She sees it now, as Cyril answers the door barefoot in dungarees, pulling a tee shirt over his bare chest. Otis bounds out, yapping in excitement.

"What are you doing here at this hour? Is everything okay?"

Melody just looks at him as she pats the dog's head, and Cyril nods. Of course not. Nothing is okay.

"Come in and sit down. I can make coffee? Or I have sweet tea . . ."

"Just sit with me, Cyril. We need to talk."

"You're right. We do."

The house is tiny, and modestly furnished. No sofa and no dining table, no record player or rugs or framed photos . . .

Back in September, she'd brought her Kodak Brownie to Barrow to photograph the wild horses and dancing dolphins. The creatures had evaded her lens that day, but she'd captured Cyril. When she later showed him the prints, he told her that no one had taken a picture of him since he was a child. She gave it to him. Tangible keepsakes would be dangerous for her.

"Have a seat," Cyril says, gesturing at the one ancient upholstered chair, and pulling up a wooden one across from it. The dog's wet nose nudges her bare knees.

"Otis! Stop that! Sit!"

"It's okay. He's happy to see me."

"Well, so am I."

Buoyed by his faint smile, she leans in to embrace him and for a moment, her world is righted. Then she remembers the missing letter, and that her parents and in-laws know about the baby. She tells Cyril, and the news scrapes the light from his face.

"Maybe no one ever needs to know it isn't Travis's child. Maybe she'll be the spitting image of her mama."

"First of all, I don't want that. I want her to look like *you*. And second—"

"You're a damned *fool*! That child looking like me wouldn't be good for anyone, and you know it!"

"Don't talk to me that way!"

"Don't be so stubborn! It's risky for you to even be here!"

"Risky for *you*," she says slowly, as the light dawns.

"Risky for both of us."

"I'm sorry. I just—I needed you. Please, Cyril. Please don't turn your back on me. On us—me and the baby."

He looks at the ceiling, and she sees his jaw working. When he meets her eyes again, his voice is hoarse. "I will never turn my back! *Never*. I'll give you all the money I have to take care of this child. It isn't much, but—"

"I don't want your money. I want you. I want your love."

"I love you. All right? I love you. It isn't enough. It isn't anything."

Air whooshes out of her as if someone pushed her to the ground and stomped a boot into her gut.

"It's everything," she whispers. "To me, it's everything."

"Melody—"

"Times are changing, Cyril. Laws are changing, people are changing, the whole world is changing. Everything's changing, except my mind. I don't care who this baby looks like. I'm not raising her with Travis. *You're* her father. I'm raising her with you."

"If you're sure about this—"

"I've never been more sure about anything in my life."

"Then we'll find a way. But we can't go rushing into anything."

"It's a little late for that, don't you think?" She flashes a wry smile.

"I'll save every cent I can, and I'll figure out where we can go when the baby comes. My mother has family up north. Maybe we can stay with them awhile. I don't even know them, really, but family's family."

Yes. How can she leave hers, after all her parents have been through?

Yet how can she stay? What will happen to her parents when people find out their daughter left her husband to have another man's baby?

Not just any man. A Black man.

Either way, their hearts will be broken. Reverend King and the Supreme Court and civil rights activists are making progress, but true change will be a long time coming.

Cyril pulls a clean red bandana from his back pocket and hands it to her. "There now. Wipe your eyes. I have to get to work, and you best get on home."

"What about Travis, though? Do you think I should write and tell him?"

"What I think doesn't matter. I've got no say in this."

"You have a right to an opinion, considering it's your child."

"You think that gives me rights? You think I got any rights at all in this world?" Catching sight of her expression, he softens. "I'm sorry. I didn't mean to snap at you. But I don't know what to tell you, except what we already know. Travis Hunter is dangerous."

"The baby's not due for a few more months. I'll wait a little longer, until we have a plan."

He walks her out to her car and opens the driver's side door for her.

"Listen now, just in case . . . if anything goes wrong, I want you to tell her about me. That I was a good man, in here." He taps his chest, just left of the gold chain dangling with the baby ring and military tags.

"What are you talking about?"

"If it turns out we can't be together, tell her that I loved her, and you, more than—"

"But she'll know that. Because you'll be there to tell her."

"I hope so. I just hope and pray the world is different for her."

"She'll do whatever it takes to make it better, just like her daddy." Sitting behind the wheel, she smiles up at him.

He leans in and kisses her forehead.

"And she's going to grow up to be a brave, strong woman just like her mama."

Part III

2017

Chapter seven

Tuesday, January 3, 2017
New Haven, Connecticut

On this gray Tuesday morning, the seventy-five-mile drive from Upper Manhattan has taken nearly four hours in rush hour traffic on rain-slicked Interstate 95. Barnes is at the wheel, Amelia in the passenger's seat. She clutches Lily Tucker's case file and fields texts from Jessie, who'd reacted to today's trip as if it were an abduction. Amelia had promised to keep in touch, though she hadn't meant every minute. Thankfully, Jessie's first therapy client arrives just as they exit the interstate, allowing Amelia to sign off for a while.

"All good?" Barnes asks. She'd told him she was dealing with a client.

"All good."

"We're almost there. I just hope . . ." He thrums the top of the steering wheel, shaking his head.

"I know."

She can offer no reassurance that they're about to find his daughter, or a clue to what's become of her. Even if they do, it may not be positive news. But with luck, they'll be closer to untangling the past—his, hers, and the mysterious ring that links them.

Noticing a street sign, she tells him that the Chapel

Square Mall, where Charisse was found, was located nearby. "If she *was* Charisse," she adds belatedly.

"She was. Those huge eyes . . . she looks so much like Delia. And maybe a little like me, too."

Amelia doesn't disagree. But when you're looking for a lost biological relative, the mind's eye sometimes sees what it wants to see.

"Anyway," she goes on, "the mall closed years ago."

"In 2002. I looked it up yesterday. Looks like every bus in New Haven stopped there back in the day. If someone came up from the city and was looking for a convenient, busy public place to dump an innocent kid, that was it."

He's right. She, too, had done her homework.

Built in 1967, the mall was intended to become an urban crown jewel, but it had deteriorated through the '70s and '80s. By the time the little girl was found, the place had a seedy and dangerous reputation.

She recognizes the broad, boxy structure, now an upscale apartment building. It's located just across from the historic town green lined with local government and Yale University buildings. She sees Barnes watch it disappear in the rearview mirror as they drive on.

All these years, he thought he'd provided a better life for his daughter by giving Delia that money and walking away. Now he's learned the little girl was endangered and abandoned soon afterward. He isn't just curious, but furious.

She breaks the moody silence as they cruise on through the city, past stately brick university buildings. "Pretty fancy around here."

"Welcome to the Ivy League."

"Reminds me of Cornell."

"You went to Cornell?"

"Ithaca College."

"IC. The sweatshirt you were wearing at the diner the other night."

"Good memory."

"Yeah, well . . . I'm a detective. I pay attention to details . . ."

She senses an unspoken *and*.

Another silence follows, this one awkward, at least for her. He seems to be pondering something, but says nothing.

The Ivy League buildings give way to close-set wood-frame houses, crumbling pavement, and shuttered industrial properties. Pockets of redevelopment and rehabilitation bloom amid poverty and blight. Church steeples poke the stormy sky above revitalized storefronts and seedy bars. Abandoned slums and vacant lots share blocks with renovated Victorians. Some residents push strollers or stride with backpacks; others loiter on corners, looking for trouble.

Barnes slows in front of a two-story house that looks freshly painted in a creamy green with maroon trim. There's a fat wreath on the front door, and the windows twinkle Christmas lights in January morning gloom.

He squeezes the car into the lineup parked at the curb. "Looks like they've got company. Not surprising at a time like this."

They get out of the car and Amelia follows him up the walk to the doorstep. "Wait, are we going to say we're . . . you know, on official business?"

"Just follow my lead." He rings the bell, jaw clenched.

A portly bald Black man opens the door. Neatly

dressed in a blue cardigan and tan corduroys, he has a trimmed gray mustache and wary gaze.

"James Harrison?"

"Yes. Can I help you?"

"I'm Detective Stockton Barnes, and this is Investigator Amelia Crenshaw Haines. We're so sorry for your loss. We just drove up from New York, following up on a few things."

It's all true, though he doesn't show his badge. Nor does the man ask for it before opening the door and inviting them into a wallpapered foyer with a Christmas garland trailing up the wooden staircase and a shrub-like red poinsettia at its base. In adjoining rooms, a television is tuned to a children's show, adult voices chatter, dishes clatter, a sink tap runs. The air is fragrant with bacon.

"The family's all still here," Harrison says. "They came for the holidays, and . . . well, they stayed, now that Alma and Brandy are . . ."

"We understand, and we apologize for interrupting," Barnes tells him. "I know you've already spoken with detectives, but if we could just ask some additional questions . . . we're following up a couple of leads."

"Anything I can do to help."

"Thank you. I understand you were expecting the victims here for a family party."

"That's right. When they didn't show, we sent a cousin and her husband over to check on them, and they found . . ." He sighs, head bowed.

"Are they here today, by chance?"

"Kendra and Jeremy? No, they live in New York."

"Jimmy?" a female voice calls from the other room. "Who's here?"

"NYPD!" he calls back.

Though Barnes never said that, specifically, he doesn't correct the assumption that they're part of the homicide team. Uncomfortable, Amelia looks at the floor, spots a couple of stray plastic Lego blocks, and feels even worse.

A woman appears in the doorway, attractive and sharp-eyed, drying her hands on a dish towel. James introduces her as his wife, Regina, and their visitors as New York detectives.

"I'm actually . . . an investigator," Amelia clarifies.

Barnes tenses beside her, but the Harrisons nod. It makes no difference to them.

Anyway, Amelia reminds herself, she and Barnes are here to help these people—and maybe, yes, themselves in the process. It's not as if she's never bent the rules on a client-related quest—even broken a few to wheedle her way into private or sealed records.

Barnes takes out a notebook. "And how are you related to the victims, Mr. and Mrs. Harrison?"

"Alma is—uh, *was* my niece," James says, and his wife pats his shoulder.

Barnes asks him about his past, and he proudly tells them that his mother wanted her children to get good educations and build careers. He'd studied accounting at CUNY; his sister pursued law enforcement at John Jay.

"Now you're an accountant. Is your sister a police officer?"

"She didn't finish school, but she married a cop, and her son Hiram's a lawyer," he adds proudly.

Barnes asks if they're here today, probably thinking that they'll know criminal case procedures and will likely ask to see their credentials. But James says his sister, now widowed, lives in Florida and his nephew is tied up on a case in New York, where he practices.

A little boy comes into the room, calling Regina "Grammy" and showing her a picture he colored.

"Who all is here?" Barnes asks James as his wife admires her grandson's artwork.

He writes down the names as the Harrisons mention them—their daughter and her fiancé; their son, daughter-in-law, and their three children; Regina's brother and nephew; Jimmy's sister . . .

"Not the one in Florida? With the lawyer son? Hiram, you said?"

"Right. Hiram Trimble."

Barnes frowns as if that rings a bell, and he jots it down. "He would have been Alma's cousin?"

"Right. But he doesn't practice criminal law," he adds, as if that might be why Barnes is asking.

Why *is* he asking, Amelia wonders, when he'd been asking about the guests who are currently in the house.

He looks up from his pad. "And Alma's parents are . . ."

"My brother and sister-in-law. They died years ago."

"Any siblings?"

"Only one, but she passed away back in . . . when was it, Regina—'90, or '92?"

"What's that?" she asks, still crouched on the floor beside her grandson. She looks up at them as though she'd lost track of the conversation, but Amelia has been keeping an eye on her, and she's been following it.

"What year did Charisse die?"

Upper East Side

GYPSY AWAKENS ALONE in the suite, the top of her skull gripped in a crown of pain. It's the kind of headache that doesn't abate with food, coffee, water, a hot shower, fresh air; the kind of headache that has struck before, and never stopped her. She doesn't allow herself to wallow in pain any more than she'd wallow in self-pity or grief.

Standing at the curb trying to hail a cab as the traffic flies past her, close enough to touch, makes her think of Carol-Ann Ellis. She seldom has, in all the years since she left New York, and it isn't a memory she welcomes, so she heads for the IRT subway at West Seventy-Second Street.

On the median that separates Broadway and Amsterdam Avenue, the street-level station is just as she remembers it, with wrought iron pillars and windows. The system map, too, remains intact. But the turnstile slots for tokens have given way to card readers.

A man sees her pondering the ticket machine, mistakes her for a tourist, and helps her buy a MetroCard. Then he offers to show her around the city later and hands her his business card. The type is bold and large enough for her to see that he works for a hedge fund.

She turns away, pitches the card into a trash can right there in front of him, and descends the steps to the tracks. She thinks of Perry. He, too, had worked for a hedge fund, had also been clean-cut, worn custom-made suits, and carried a briefcase. But Perry drove his Mercedes to his lower Manhattan office every day. He wouldn't have dreamed of setting a Ferragamo wing tip on the subway back then. But the Perry who'd since lived in Cuba for twenty-nine years had done many things that would have made his younger self shudder.

Gypsy marveled at the well-lit platforms, electronic signs predicting arrivals to the minute, and sleek, graffiti-free train that whisked her to Fulton Street in eighteen minutes.

The financial district is more crowded than it had been in her day, and not just with Wall Street types. Midtown offices in various industries have moved downtown over the last fifteen years, bringing hordes of commuters and endless construction. Chain stores, hotels, and restaurants now line the maze of narrow streets.

Her first stop is a drugstore, where she buys a plastic rain poncho, small folding umbrella, ibuprofen, a bottle of water, and—an afterthought, because she can't read the label—a pair of readers. The recommended dose is two capsules. She downs four.

Next stop: 195 Broadway, the building where Perry's hedge fund career had unfolded. She steps into the cavernous lobby, planning to visit the floor where he'd worked. But the elevator banks now lie beyond a security desk, and the guards won't let her through.

Back out on the street, she heads for the site where the twin towers had begun their fateful climb to the sky in 1968. She remembers thinking then that stone and steel were indestructible compared to the world that came crashing down in that tumultuous year of war and racial tension, assassinations . . . murder.

The notorious Brooklyn Butcher had slaughtered four families, orphaning and raping and impregnating teenaged survivors Tara Sheeran, Christina Myers,

Margaret Costello, and Bernadette DiMeo. The first three later gave birth to their rapist's babies; the fourth didn't carry her pregnancy to term. The media coverage was relentless.

Gypsy was fourteen years old, and her name had been kept out of the press, but her father's made every headline.

Oran Matthews was the Brooklyn Butcher.

After his arrest, Gypsy had been placed in the foster system. There, she could mask her true identity and become anyone she wanted to be. She could seduce damaged lost souls, like her friend, Red. She could forget the past, or she could use it to mold the future. She could learn from her father's mistakes, and reinterpret the lessons he'd taught her. When memories overtook her, she could lose herself in her academic studies. She could earn a scholarship to a fine college where she could seduce wealthy, privileged lost souls like Perry Wayland, who would die for her.

In 1987, an incarcerated Oran had concluded that the long anticipated biblical Armageddon was imminent. He'd ordered Gypsy to assemble Tara Sheeran, Christina Myers, Margaret Costello, and Bernadette DiMeo, along with their offspring, and await the Rapture.

That's not how it was supposed to be. All those years in prison had warped her father's mind and memory.

"You and me, we're the chosen ones, Gypsy, baby. No one else matters. They'll be gone, just like that, when Judgment Day comes . . ."

There was no room in eternal paradise for her so-called sisters and brothers. Gypsy had summoned

Red, who'd eliminated all but two in a spree the papers had dubbed copycat killings.

By the time it was over, Gypsy and Perry were bound for a fresh start in Cuba. Judgment Day no longer seemed imminent, and her unfinished business—Margaret, and possibly a daughter, left alive—lost significance with every mile that separated her from the US, and faded with every year that passed.

Now, though, the urgency has returned. Now everything has changed.

Everything.

Anticipating a post-apocalyptic wasteland, she finds the World Trade Center site crawling with tourists and hawkers selling 9/11 souvenirs. At the vast fountain memorial where the North Tower had stood, Gypsy lowers her umbrella to gaze at the empty sky. Her head throbs, and she remembers a perfect September night at Windows on the World, the elegant restaurant 107 stories above the city.

It was there, over a bottle of Dom Pérignon, that she and Perry had formulated the plan that had led them to Baracoa. Donald Trump and his glamorous wife Ivana had stopped by their table to say hello. Tycoon to tycoon, he'd winked at the married Perry when he'd introduced Gypsy as a colleague.

Thirty years later, the towers and Baracoa have been decimated, Trump is on his third wife, about to be inaugurated as president of the United States, and Perry—

Her cell phone rings.

She checks the Caller ID, as though it might be anyone other than the one person who'd call her on this number. But it's him. Of course it is. He's the only person who'd call her now, period; the only one in the world who knows, or even cares, that she's alive.

"Where are you?" he asks.

"I had to run an errand." She watches rain patter into walls of water cascading along the North Tower's footprint, a symbolic rectangular bottomless pit at its center.

"Get back to the hotel as soon as you can. I have something to show you. You don't have to worry about Margaret Costello anymore."

"You found her?"

"I found her obituary."

WHAT YEAR DID Charisse die?

James Harrison's question hangs in the air, and Barnes grabs the hall table to steady himself.

Charisse . . . *died?*

"Hey, there, are you all right?" Harrison asks and he nods, unable to speak.

Amelia looks equally stricken, murmuring, "How sad. What happened?"

"Drowned with another teenager in a riptide off Coney Island about twenty, twenty-five years ago, and it put poor Esther in an early grave."

"Esther?"

"My brother's wife. Charisse's mother. And if that tragedy hadn't killed her, this one would have. Alma and Brandy. Oh, Lord."

"Why don't you go make Grammy another pretty picture," Regina tells her grandson, shooing him back into the next room and grunting as she straightens again. "I don't like to talk about any of this in front of the little ones. Anyway, Jimmy, it was more than thirty years ago. Charisse died in August '87, right before Hiram's engagement party, and Esther was gone, too, before the wedding the following summer."

Barnes exhales at last, grasping details that had escaped him.

Their Charisse's mother had been Esther, not Delia, and the girl had drowned in August '87 . . .

His own Charisse hadn't even been born yet.

Now he recalls Delia mentioning that she'd named their daughter after Alma's late sister. But for Barnes, the name was a link to his father, Charles, in some mysterious cosmic coincidence . . .

Or not.

Tawafuq.

Hiram Trimble had been the attorney who'd tracked him down in 1987 when Delia was pregnant and threatening a paternity suit.

"Forget the lawyer. Talk to her," Wash had advised. *"This isn't about paper. It's about people. And about perspective. Ask yourself who you are, Stockton. Better yet, who you want to be."*

I'm trying, Wash. Man, am I trying.

He looks at Jimmy. "According to the case file, there was another Charisse in Alma's life. Her friend Delia's daughter, born in October 1987. The two of them lived with Alma and Brandy for a few years. Do you remember them?"

Jimmy and Regina exchange a glance so fleeting he isn't sure he caught it.

"Not really," Jimmy says, picking invisible lint off his sweater.

"Meaning . . ."

"Alma had a lot of friends," Regina speaks up, "and we never saw much of her."

"They did visit you here in Connecticut, though—Alma, and Brandy?"

"Sometimes."

"With Delia and her daughter?" When Regina doesn't answer, Barnes turns to Jimmy, who shrugs.

"This house has always been full of people coming and going. Family, friends . . . Just like today."

"But today, you know exactly who's here." He waves his pad, where he'd written the list of relatives' names. "Look, we're trying to find out who killed your niece and her daughter, and keep you and your other loved ones safe. So I need straight answers. Where are Delia and Charisse now?"

"I have no idea," Jimmy says. "Do you, Regina?"

"None."

"And when was the last time you saw them, Mr. Harrison?"

"A long time ago."

"Five years? Ten?"

He shrugs. "Longer."

"Fifteen? Twenty?"

"Regina?" He looks to the wife, who seems to have the more accurate sense of time.

"Oh, it's been at least . . . let's see, twenty-five, thirty years. Delia's Charisse was just a little thing, and she was about the same age as Bobby's other—"

"About thirty years, then," Jimmy cuts in, as if that settles it.

"About thirty years. That's right."

"And Delia's daughter was the same age as . . ." Barnes prompts.

"Bobby's."

"Bobby's . . ."

"Right." She turns toward the kitchen. "I need to go and check the—"

"The same age as Bobby's other . . . what?"

"Daughter! Now can I please—"

"Just a second." He jots a note, thinking back to the few conversations he ever had with, and about, Delia.

"Who's Bobby?"

"He's my nephew," Regina tells him. "My oldest brother's son."

It's a common name, and one that had also belonged to Delia's ex-husband. Unless they're the same person, and she'd been a part of this family at one time?

"Tell me about Bobby and his daughter," Barnes says. "Or is it *daughters*?"

Jimmy toys with a new snag on his sweater sleeve, undoubtedly courtesy of having plucked at nonexistent lint.

Regina speaks up. "Monica is twenty-nine. She's in the service—special ops."

"She must be a tough cookie," Amelia comments, as Barnes writes it down.

"She had to be, with—"

"With . . . ?"

"Bobby had a lot of problems, but he's straightened out now, and—"

"Aunt Regina? What's going on?" A man steps into the room. He's about Barnes's age, lanky, casually dressed in running pants, high-tops with the laces dragging, and a Brooklyn Nets tee shirt.

"These detectives are from New York. They're trying to find out what happened in Bed-Stuy."

"You must be Bobby," Barnes says.

The man nods, stepping closer, and Barnes sees

that he has a long slash of scar alongside his mouth. "How come you were talking about me?"

"It's all good, son. We were just saying that Delia's Charisse was about the same age as Monica," Jimmy tells him.

"What does that have to do with Alma and Brandy getting killed?"

"They were asking about it."

"About me and my ex?"

So he *is* Delia's no-good former husband.

"Let's back up. What's your full name? No worries, sir, it's routine," Barnes adds, seeing his wary expression.

"Bobby—Robert—Montague. No middle name."

Barnes writes that down, along with other basics. Bobby lives alone in nearby Bridgeport, and he works at a harbor freight company. His daughter Monica is stationed somewhere overseas—he isn't sure where.

"Backing up . . . you and Delia got married . . . when?"

"In 1986."

"And you were divorced a few years later?"

"We never got divorced."

"Then . . . you're still married?"

"Who knows? I haven't seen her since Thanksgiving Day in 1990."

"Where is she now?"

"Probably dead by now."

"Bobby!"

"I'm not the only one who thinks that, Aunt Regina! Ask anyone in the family. Right, Uncle Jimmy?"

"Drugs'll kill you. I wouldn't be surprised. But we

don't know for sure. Alma said she up and left one day, and that's all we know."

Barnes turns back to Bobby. "What happened that Thanksgiving?"

"Delia showed up at my place out of the blue. She said she wanted to have turkey with me and Cynthia."

"Cynthia?"

"Monica's mother. I moved in with her when I left Delia, because she was pregnant. The next thing you know, Delia is pregnant, too." He smirks. "So that Thanksgiving, Cynthia went nuts, screaming at Delia, and Delia, you know, she's whacked out of her mind, so she starts laughing like a maniac, and the girls are crying hysterically, and one of the neighbors called the cops, so now there's sirens wailing, too, and—"

"Hold on, back up . . . which girls were crying?"

"Monica and Charisse."

"Delia brought Charisse?"

"Yeah, they took the bus up to Bridgeport from the city. It was pouring, I remember, and they were drenched, and Delia had this pie she probably picked out of the garbage. It was soggy with pieces missing, and she kept trying to give it to Cynthia. Man, I thought Cynthia was gonna shove it into her face. But the cops got there in the nick of time."

Barnes scrawls the facts, wondering where he'd been that Thanksgiving, when his daughter was crying in the rain? Wash was gone by then, and so was his *abuela*. His mother had given up cooking when his father died. Most likely, Barnes had been working that holiday. Or maybe he'd been at Rob's, where every holiday is a sprawling extravaganza.

One thing is certain—wherever he'd spent that

day, Charisse had been on his mind, same as she is every day.

He asks Bobby what else had happened, but he'd been high at the time, and the details aren't clear. All he knows for sure is that Cynthia kicked out Delia, gave him an ultimatum, and he checked himself into rehab the next day.

"Saved myself. Too bad Delia didn't do the same thing."

"Maybe that's why she ran off."

"No way. We'd talked about it a few times—getting clean, you know. But she couldn't do it alone, and she had nowhere to leave the kid."

"What about Alma?"

"She was fed up. She wanted them both out. Not that I blame her. Delia was a hot mess, but man, there was something about her that was just . . . irresistible, you know what I'm sayin'?"

Do I ever.

"You know how I got this?" he asks, gesturing at the scar by his mouth. "Street fight. Some guy was harassing her, and I knew he had a blade, but I didn't care. I was willing to die for that woman. Wound up in the hospital. Married her the second I got out. That's how crazy I was about Delia Montague."

"That's pretty crazy."

"Even crazier trying to get away from her a few years later. She kept roping me back in. She couldn't pay the rent on her own, so she lost the apartment, and lost job after job, too. She started talking about moving up here with us."

"With you and your girlfriend?" Amelia asks Bobby as Barnes flips a page, writing notes, trying to keep up.

"Yeah, she thought Cynthia would be cool with it and she wanted me to see if Cynthia could get her hired as a security guard! I said, 'Girl, for one thing, Cynthia hates you, and for another, even I wouldn't hire you to guard my beer while I'm in the bathroom. Forget a whole shopping mall.'"

"Shopping mall?" Amelia echoes, and Barnes jerks his head up.

"Yeah, that's where Cynthia worked back then."

"Which mall?"

"Chapel Square."

Chapter Eight

Still shrouded in her wet plastic poncho, stomach queasy from the excessive painkillers that failed to kill her pain, Gypsy dons her new magnifying glasses and skims the printed page.

Margaret Costello's obituary is dated November 15, 2015. She'd died at sixty-five after a short illness, predeceased by her parents, brother, and grandmother, victims of the Brooklyn Butcher on May 10, 1968.

No mention of the daughter she'd delivered the following winter, Gypsy points out to the rather smug man lounging on the velvet couch in the middle of the suite. He'd handed over the obituary looking like a dutiful toddler expecting praise, or a treat.

"It says she leaves no survivors," he comments.

"But it doesn't say that the daughter predeceased her. It would, if she'd been a part of Margaret's life."

"That doesn't mean she's not dead."

"And it doesn't mean she doesn't exist."

Gypsy paces, boot heels clacking on the marble floor.

Her old friend Red, so proficient and eager to please—Red, who'd gotten into sealed adoption records to locate Christina Myers's son—even the clever, cunning Red had found no trace of Margaret's daughter.

The press had long speculated that the baby, born

to an addicted, traumatized teen, hadn't lived past infancy, perhaps destroyed by her own unstable mother.

All very reassuring, but still . . .

"If there's any chance that girl is still alive . . ."

"That girl—you mean your *sister*?" he asks with maddening emphasis.

"Yes." She glares at him, his face distorted through the lenses.

She takes them off, and the poncho, too, letting it drop like a soggy garbage bag.

"Sorry, Gypsy, but if you're going to . . . I just want you to keep that in mind. In case you . . . forgot."

"I never forget anything. *Never.* Why do you suppose Red went to Ithaca?"

"What are you talking about?"

"The 'copycat killer.'" She inserts the phrase in finger quotations. "In 1987, Red killed Bernadette DiMeo in Manhattan and then drove straight to Ithaca. Cornell University is there, and that's where Bernadette went after her family was murdered. But she was the only one of those four girls who didn't carry my father's baby to term."

"Unless she did?"

"What if Red found out and went to Ithaca to find him, or her?"

"Bernadette isn't the only one who has ties to Ithaca. Amelia Crenshaw Haines went to Ithaca College. She still has friends there, and she just spent the holidays with them."

Gypsy ponders that, circling the couch like a shark, fingertips pressing her temples in a futile effort to ease the throbbing.

"Probably a coincidence," she concludes. "Ithaca's one of the most popular college towns in the country. I need you to find out whether Bernadette DiMeo and Margaret Costello have living offspring."

"What about Connecticut? You wanted me to go back up there tonight. Do you still need me to—"

"Yes. That, too."

She needs him, unfortunately. Needs his money. But only for a little while longer.

After leaving the Harrison home, Amelia and Barnes head for a Starbucks. Not for the caffeination, or the ambiance, but for the Wi-Fi. Located on the green across from the old Chapel Square Mall site, the place is busy even with Yale on winter recess.

Barnes waits to order while Amelia stalks about-to-be-vacated tables. By the time he gets their beverages, she's landed a prime corner spot and is answering a text from Jessie, who's alarmed that she's "disappeared."

Amelia replies with one word, all caps: RELAX!

Jessie's response is immediate. Are you ok?

Amelia sends a thumbs-up and a heart, then puts down her phone and takes a steaming cup from Barnes. "Thanks. Decaf, right?"

"Double caf." At her alarmed expression, he flashes a smile. "Yeah, decaf. But why bother? You might as well have hot chocolate instead."

"I'm not a fan."

"Of hot chocolate?"

"Or any chocolate."

"What is wrong with you, woman?"

"I don't like sweets, and I can't drink caffeine this late in the day."

"Late? It's not even noon. And if I *don't* drink caffeine my brain will be mush."

"Doesn't it keep you up at night?"

"Plenty of things keep me up at night. Coffee isn't one of them."

Charisse.

She'd expected him to tell the Harrisons about the connection, or at least ask what they knew about the child abandoned at Chapel Square Mall. But Barnes hadn't batted an eye when Bobby mentioned that Cynthia had worked there back in 1990, just asked for her contact information.

Bobby claimed he didn't know where to find her. The relationship ended badly and they've been estranged for years.

"What about Monica?"

"Her, too. I wasn't a good father."

"You tried to be," his aunt Regina said.

"Not till it was too late. Damage was done. By the time I changed my ways, she didn't want anything to do with me."

Amelia knew those words had struck a chord with Barnes, though he remained poised and professional, never hinting at a personal connection as he interviewed the other adult relatives.

None had anything to add. No one knew anything about the man Brandy's been dating, other than that he was wealthy.

"Kendra told us about him," Regina said. "She and Brandy are the same age. They saw each other sometimes."

She provided contact information, and Amelia asked Barnes if he wanted her to try calling the cousin during the short drive back to the green.

"Not just yet. She and her husband, Jeremy, are official witnesses, and Homicide will be working with them. Let's wait and see what else we find."

Barnes pushes aside his coffee cup to make room for his notebook on the table as Amelia types details about Cynthia into the search engine. They don't have much to go on, but they try various terms to narrow the search—geographic locations, security guard employment, and her daughter's first name, Bobby's last name, Montague.

"Is it just me," she asks Barnes as they scan a list of dismissible hits, "or do you think the Harrisons are a little off? Maybe . . . hiding something?"

He seems to weigh his reply. "I don't think they're harboring a murderer, or that their family had anything to do with what happened to Alma and Brandy. James and Regina were pretty guarded, but a lot of people are, when they're being questioned by the police."

"I'm not the police," Amelia reminds him.

"They didn't know that."

"Isn't it a crime to impersonate a police officer?"

"Amelia, come on. I said you were an investigator, which you are. They drew their own conclusions. But tell me why you think the Harrisons are hiding something."

"You don't think they are?"

"I'm asking what *you* think."

"Well, a few times, it seemed like Regina almost slipped up and said too much when we were asking about Delia and Charisse."

"Right. And they didn't bother to mention that Delia's ex-husband was in the next room when I first brought her up. They didn't want us asking him about her."

"Or Cynthia, either," Amelia says.

"And she had after-hours access to Chapel Square Mall when Charisse was abandoned. We need to find her."

She nods, typing again, well aware that finding Cynthia might not lead to finding Charisse, or Lily Tucker, if that's who she became. When Barnes asked the Harrisons if they'd ever heard of anyone by the name, everyone denied it—though Amelia had again detected a hint of anxiety in Jimmy and Regina. She mentions it now, and Barnes shrugs.

"Hard to tell. Like I said, even innocent people get nervous when they're being questioned."

"Right, but you'd think Bobby would be the antsy one, considering his history, and he seemed to be telling the truth about—"

"Amelia!" Barnes grabs her arm. "I just remembered something. Bobby said a neighbor called the police the day Delia showed up in Bridgeport."

"You're right!"

"We need to look for domestic disturbance records for that Thanksgiving."

Her fingers fly over the keyboard. Five minutes later, they've got a full name and current address and are back in the car, heading east on 95 toward Bridgeport.

Left alone in the suite, Gypsy opens her laptop, pulls up a map of Ithaca, and studies the location.

Coincidence is irrelevant . . .

But had it been a coincidence?

From Manhattan, the town lies in the opposite direction of Block Island, where Gypsy and Perry had been holed up at a dive motel. Red was supposed to complete the mission and return—although by then, of course, they'd have been gone. Perry, with his sadistic sense of humor, had gotten a kick out of imagining that little scenario—Red, triumphant after ridding the world of false prophets, returning to rejoin the chosen few . . .

"But sorry, you aren't one of us," he'd said in mock disappointment after Red left the Sandy Oyster for the last time. *"See you in paradise. Oh, wait . . ."*

Gypsy, too, had laughed. Not because she found it amusing, but because she needed Perry and his money as much as she needed Red. Both would be dispensable once she got what she wanted.

Maybe Red had figured that out.

Ithaca sits at the foot of Cayuga Lake in central New York State. It's not on any well-traveled major highway a person would follow directly out of New York City if they were heading, say, to the Canadian border after committing the last of five murders in a twenty-four-hour spree. It must have been a deliberate destination. Why?

She closes the map, thinking about Red's final New York encounter with Bernadette DiMeo.

Gypsy had never doubted the public consensus that her pregnancy had been terminated or more likely, miscarried. She was a devout Catholic who'd attended daily mass until the day she died.

But what if she'd revealed to Red, in her last moments on earth, that she'd carried Oran's child to term after all, and the child, now grown, is still in Ithaca?

Gypsy pulls up a series of photos printed in the *Daily News* during Oran's trial. All four of his teenaged rape victims had testified. Three of the girls—Margaret Costello, Tara Sheeran, and Christina Myers—were visibly pregnant that autumn. Even in December, though, Bernadette DiMeo was fashionably—for that era—emaciated.

Gypsy remembers how the girls at school—especially Carol-Ann Ellis—had idolized Twiggy.

This isn't about Carol-Ann, though.

Bernadette . . .

Gypsy focuses on the photo. There's no way a girl as skinny as Bernadette had been that winter was six months pregnant.

It doesn't mean that a misguided, drug-fueled Red hadn't gone to Bernadette's former college town looking for a grown child who'd never been born. But what if there'd been some other motivation?

Opening a new search engine, she types Brooklyn Butcher Copycat Murders, 10/23/87-10/24/87 and Ithaca, bringing up accounts of the murder spree. She magnifies the screen and studies the facts.

Red had been a young child when the original murders had taken place and was later determined to have had no ties to Oran Matthews and acted alone. Case closed for the police, and for the press.

Not for the mastermind behind it.

"What am I missing, Red? Why did you go to Ithaca that night?"

Put yourself in Red's shoes. Why drive two hundred miles to a place that isn't on the way to any conceivable destination?

With police closing in, Red fled Manhattan in a stolen car, got as far as Ithaca, broke into a house, and died after a brief scuffle with the residents. As minors, their identities were kept out of the news.

In article after article, Gypsy finds the same information, until she comes across a speculative gold mine in the comments section of a popular true crime website.

Even postmortem, Oran's had his share of Brooklyn Butcher-obsessed devotees. These people know more about him, and about Red, than Gypsy ever knew, or cares to, and their posts contain well-informed theories regarding unsolved elements of either crime.

One yields a compelling fact.

Red's final showdown and demise occurred in a house located directly next door to famed Cornell molecular biologist Silas Moss, who'd appeared on national television the night before. The general consensus among true crime buffs: the Moss home had been the true destination, and Red had simply gotten the address wrong.

Gypsy skims the commentary.

What do you expect from someone about to kick from methamphetamine OD?

Been there, done that, lived to tell about it, and couldn't have found my way out of a damned bathroom stall.

The dealer should be held accountable for the OD *and* the murder spree.

Gypsy and Perry had warned Red not to take too much, that it might result in a reckless mistake.

"We didn't expect it to kill you, though," she whispers, shaking her head with regret—if only because the truth had died with that moronic, dispensable loser.

Gypsy's search for Silas Moss yields a trove of information on a distinguished career. It makes sense that Red heard about the professor's pioneering work reconnecting biological families and thought he might somehow be enlisted to turn up Margaret Costello's missing daughter via DNA.

DNA that Oran—and thus, Gypsy—would share.

Uneasiness creeps in as she skims the transcript of Barbara Walters's interview with Silas Moss, aired Friday, October 23, 1987.

> DNA is a distinctly patterned chain of genetic material found in every cell of every living organism . . .

> Our blood relatives will have similar markers, sharing ancestral origin, physical traits, predisposition to certain diseases . . .

The information, revolutionary at the time, isn't news now—not even to Gypsy. Not scientifically.

Psychologically, it strikes like an ominous wartime bulletin.

Blood relatives . . .

Every cell . . .

"Oh! I'm sorry!"

Startled by a voice, Gypsy whirls to see a woman wearing a hotel maid's uniform. She's a blue-eyed blonde, middle-aged. The door to the hall is propped open, a cleaning cart framed beyond it.

"Housekeeping—I knocked, but you didn't—"

"There's a Do Not Disturb!"

"I'm sorry. I didn't see . . ." She turns to look. "There is no Do Not Disturb."

Gypsy closes the lid on her laptop. The sofa isn't against a wall, but rather sits in the middle of the suite's living room, back to the entry. Anyone walking in would have a clear view of the screen.

How long had the maid been standing behind her?

She plucks something from the floor and waves it at Gypsy. It's the Do Not Disturb sign. "It's here. Inside, you see? Not on the door. You made a mistake."

"I didn't make the mistake. My friend did."

Damn him.

"But don't you want the maid to make up the room?" he'd asked on his way out, when she'd told him to be sure the sign was in place. "Bed made up with fresh sheets . . . so that we can destroy the bed again later?"

"I want privacy. And you'll be in Connecticut, keeping an eye on her like I told you. Find out everything you can, because when the time comes, we'll need to move fast."

He'd grumbled his way out the door. Had he left the sign off on purpose?

Is the maid really a maid?

Her name tag reads Kasia. Gypsy memorizes it, and her face, and her hairstyle. A short cut with long bangs, parted on the side above her blue eyes. But she could be wearing a wig, and colored contact lenses, faking the Slavic accent. She might not be a maid at all. She might have crept up behind Gypsy and peered over her shoulder and seen what she was doing online.

"I'm sorry. I will leave. I take garbage?" She reaches for the soggy plastic cape lying on the floor behind the couch.

"That's not garbage, it's my raincoat!"

"So sorry, so sorry. Do you want me to leave fresh towels or—"

"Just go."

Kasia fumbles her way out into the hall, closing the door behind her.

Gypsy strides over to it and slides the chain, hand trembling. Turning, she spots a figure across the room, and gasps.

But it's just her reflection in the mirror. She walks over and peers closer, confirming traces of the other woman's features in her own.

We could be related. She could be Margaret's daughter. She found me before I could find her. She wants to destroy me before I can destroy her.

If she's Oran's daughter, she's inherently smart, and dangerous.

So? You're smarter. More dangerous.

She returns to the closed door and leans into the peephole, expecting to find a blue eye looking back at her. She sees only the open door to the suite across from hers, and the edge of the maid's cart alongside it.

She puts her hand on the knob, then pulls it back. There will be security cameras in the hallway.

That's all right. Gypsy is one step ahead of the woman calling herself Kasia—and she'll stay a few steps behind her when she leaves after her shift.

BARNES DRIVES AROUND Cynthia Randall's residential industrial neighborhood looking for a parking spot. Warehouses and shuttered manufacturers share blocks with storefronts and houses that aren't so much historic as they are *old*.

The only people who seem to be out and about can't be considered pedestrians. They're not walking; they're loitering.

Barnes knows the type. He *was* the type, back in his juvenile delinquent days after his father died, before Wash came along one night when Barnes was breaking into cars.

In his troubled youth, his street name had been "Gloss," so smooth and slick that nothing ever stuck. Wash did—his friendship, the legacy of NYPD service, the lessons he taught, his warnings, and his advice—with two noted exceptions.

Barnes has spent his adult life rationalizing his reckless behavior in March and October 1987. When he was younger, he blamed circumstances.

The night Barnes slept with Delia Montague, Wash was hospitalized for the illness that would kill him. The night Barnes accepted the dirty money from Stef and walked away from his newborn daughter, Wash's health was deteriorating, and a close mutual friend of theirs had just been killed in an armed robbery.

Three decades later, Barnes owns his mistakes. Too bad being older and wiser doesn't grant you a time-travel pass to undo the damage and make things right.

Barnes squeezes the car into a spot in front of a church where the signboard letters have been rearranged to spell an obscenity, and baby Jesus is ankle-shackled to the manger in the curbside plaster crèche.

They walk several blocks, long-legged Amelia matching his stride, her boot heels clicking along the sidewalk. They pass a playground, empty swings dangling above muddy trenches.

"Can we go to the park and play Penny on the Playground, Daddy?"

"You're getting warmer, son!"

At Cynthia's address, they find a multifamily house. The peeling paint job isn't quite white and isn't quite beige. A few tufts of grass poke alongside puddles in a tiny yard that's mostly mud. There's a small rutted driveway with space for two cars. A dented Toyota occupies one, with two children's car seats in the back. There are two front doors on the small cinderblock stoop covered by a vinyl awning. One is hung with a tinsel candy cane that appears to have weathered many a nor'easter.

At an adjacent house across the chain-link fence, a large dog is leashed to a stub of a tree. He growls and yaps wildly as they approach.

"Aw, nice doggy," Amelia says. "What's your name, fella?"

"My money's on 'Satan,'" Barnes mutters.

They ascend the steps. The wrought iron railing wobbles in his hand, detached from its concrete anchor. The other railing is a crude, splintery-looking replacement crafted from two-by-fours.

Cynthia Randall lives at 265A, the door on the left. Not the one with the bedraggled candy cane—for better or worse, he's not sure.

He rings the bell, and they wait. Satan barks, trying to launch himself over the fence.

After a minute, Barnes rings again. Still nothing.

He knocks. The candy cane door remains closed, but the other one opens. A young Hispanic woman stands with a baby on her hip and a toddler lurking at her knees.

"Buck! *Cállate la boca!*" she shouts at the dog next door, and to Barnes's shock, the animal obeys. She turns back to Barnes and Amelia, resuming a conversation they haven't yet had. "Hi. Cynthia's at work till . . . What's today, Tuesday?"

"Wednesday."

"Oh, *si.* Wednesday—she'll be home in about half an hour if you want to come back. I would have you come in to wait, but I'm about to put these two down for their naps, and they need a quiet house to sleep. Don't ring the bell or knock when you come back. And don't get Buck going, because that dog, he is *loco.*"

She closes the door.

Barnes and Amelia look at each other, then down at the steps. Dry, thanks to the awning. They sit down to wait.

"It can't possibly be getting dark out yet, can it?" Amelia checks her watch.

"It can. Dead of winter, and the farther east you go, the earlier the sun sets."

"When there *is* sun." She looks from the grim sky to the burned-out house across the street. "You know until today, I assumed New England was all fancy suburbs and picturesque small towns, not gritty cities."

"Eh, I'll take a gritty city any day. Small towns aren't all they're cracked up to be."

"I don't know about that. I was planning to stay in Ithaca after college."

Ithaca.

When she'd mentioned it earlier, he'd almost told her about Gypsy Colt and Perry Wayland and the Brooklyn Butcher copycat who'd died there. But he'd stopped himself, deciding it might not be relevant.

Ithaca isn't exactly a tiny town in the middle of nowhere. It's a small city that draws thirty thousand college students a year. Amelia had been one of them.

Tawafuq?

"Why didn't you stay?" he asks her.

"My husband didn't like it. *Future* husband, back then, and, uh . . . past husband now."

"You're not together anymore?"

"Trial separation, but I keep forgetting, like—you know when something bad happens and you wake up the next morning and everything seems fine but you have this vague feeling that things are off, and then—bam. It hits you again."

"Yeah. I do know."

"Except, it's not exactly the next morning. Aaron left six weeks ago. As I was saying, back when he was my future husband, I decided I loved him more than I loved Ithaca, so I left."

"Do you regret it?"

"No. New York is home. What I regret is not figuring out *why* Aaron wouldn't consider living upstate. It's not because he's such a city person. He grew up in Jersey and he just moved into a condo in Westchester. What he didn't like about Ithaca is that my friends Jessie and Silas live there. She's a fellow foundling, and he's the professor who inspired my career and was one of the first scientists to use DNA to trace biological roots."

"Your husband doesn't like them? Is he jealous?"

"It's not that."

A couple of adolescent boys ride by on cobbled-together bikes, helmetless and smoking cigarettes. The dog next door starts barking again.

"Hey, Buck, will you quiet down?"

The dog ignores Barnes.

"I don't think he speaks English," Amelia says. "Hey, Buck? *Cállate la boca!*"

"You speak Spanish?"

"Fluently, but I don't think Buck cares."

"Oh, well. Tell me about your husband and your friends," Barnes says over the yapping.

"Aaron's always been polite to them, but he never embraced them the way they'd have embraced him, if he'd given them the chance. In therapy, I found out that to him, they're anchors to my unresolved past. To me, they were—they still *are*—lifelines. And family."

"But you left them to marry him."

"And become part of another family—Aaron, and my in-laws. When I met them, I thought they were perfect—just like the Huxtables on *The Cosby Show.*"

"Bill Cosby doesn't exactly live up to that image these days," Barnes reminds her, considering that the man who'd played the lovable patriarch stands accused of molesting women.

"I know, but Aaron's family does. If they weren't so damned wonderful, I probably wouldn't have married him in the first place, or stayed with him for twenty-five years."

"I'm sorry."

"So am I—for telling you all this. I didn't mean to—"

"Oh, hey, it's okay. I get it. I have a broken marriage in my past, too."

"What happened?"

"We were both cops. That never works."

"I know a few who are happily married to each other."

"Well, they probably didn't mistake infatuation for love at an age when most people decide it's time to settle down. That was our other problem."

"One of ours, too. But mostly, Aaron doesn't want to live in the past, and he says I'm fixated on it. I guess when you're always feeling like someone important is missing, you hurt the people who are there."

"Yeah, I can relate to that. Probably one more reason my marriage didn't work out. People like us should probably just stay single, or . . ."

Or have relationships with other people like us.

A Jeep pulls into the driveway. The dog begins to bark.

"Shut the eff up, Buck!" a middle-aged Black woman calls as she gets out of the car, and the dog falls silent.

"Guess it wasn't the language barrier," Barnes mutters to Amelia as they get to their feet. "We were just too polite."

The woman walks toward them, keys in hand. She's sturdy looking, with an attractive face and wearing an unzipped down puffer coat over a dark uniform.

"Cynthia Randall?" he asks and she nods, walking slowly toward them, keys in hand.

He introduces himself and Amelia the same way he had back at the Harrisons', only this time he doesn't mention that they're here from New York.

"We're investigating a case, and we wanted to ask you a couple of questions."

She sighs. "Is this about the break-ins down the block?"

"Sorry, but do you mind if we talk inside?" Amelia asks, bouncing a little as if she's freezing.

"Not if you have ID." She sticks her key into the lock.

Barnes shows her his badge.

"NYPD? What are you doing up here?"

"As I said, we're on a case, and we've had a lead that brought us to Connecticut."

Cynthia takes that in stride, inviting them in. She flips on a light, throws her coat on a hook by the door, takes theirs, and does the same. The place is clean if small and cluttered, with too much furniture in a mishmash of styles. There are a couple of foil-potted poinsettias on the coffee table and a small tabletop Christmas tree. She stoops to plug it in, bathing the room in a colorful glow, as Barnes and Amelia sit on the couch. The bulbs are the old-fashioned pointed oval kind, opaque and deep-hued.

"Nice tree," Barnes comments.

"Fake."

"You don't see lights like that very often. Remind me of when I was a kid."

"Yeah, well, these days everyone has those little twinkly, transparent candy-ass lights."

He checks out several framed photos—Monica, he guesses, in various stages of her life. School photos, a graduation shot, and one in a military uniform.

Cynthia follows his gaze. "My daughter. She's in the military, stationed overseas."

"Guessing she's no candy-ass."

"You got that right."

Cynthia sits in a chair and swaps her black lace-up shoes for Dearfoams. "Sorry, but my feet are killing me. I'm on them all day at the shelter."

"Shelter?"

"For domestic abuse victims—I'm a security guard there, and I figured that's why you— Why *are* you here?"

"Following up on a cold case."

"But you're getting warmer, son . . ."

"Not domestic abuse?"

"Missing persons."

No need to bring up the double murder. While he still believes Gypsy Colt and Perry Wayland are behind the Harrison slayings, Cynthia Randall may be the key to finding Charisse, and he has to tread carefully.

She repositions a throw pillow behind her and settles against it as if her back, too, is aching. "I worked doubles over the holidays. Tough time at the shelter, especially for the poor little kids dragged through their parents' messes."

"That's true. And the case we're investigating involves a child," Barnes tells her, opening the notebook to a clean page. "Her name is Charisse Montague."

Cynthia sits up in her chair, gripping the arms, eyes narrowed.

"You know her, then?"

"She's my stepdaughter."

"Your . . ." Amelia pauses and looks at Barnes.

"Stepdaughter. My ex-husband Bobby's kid from his first marriage."

Something flutters in Barnes's gut—not instinct. Dread.

He stares down at the motionless pen as Amelia does the talking. "When was the last time you saw Charisse?"

"When she was, I don't know, maybe three or four? Bobby's ex was bad news."

"Drugs?"

"Even before that. Aimless, kind of shifty, you know? Looking for a free ride. She'd been arrested, too."

Barnes nods. He'd found her mug shots in the system when he'd gone looking for her years ago. Not just the shoplifting charge, but a couple of other misdemeanors after Charisse was born. And then, after 1990—nothing at all. Meaning she cleaned up her act, or changed her identity, died . . .

"After Bobby told Delia he was leaving her for me because I was pregnant, she got pregnant, too, to trap him."

"So she conceived a baby with someone else? That doesn't seem—"

"No, not with someone else. With Bobby. He had one foot out the door and she got pregnant because she thought she'd be able to hang on to him, and I guess it worked for a while."

"We . . ." Amelia glances at Barnes. "We were under the impression that Delia's daughter was fathered by another man."

"Oh, hell, I wish! Bobby was still with her on and off in January, and the due date was nine months later."

Barnes finds his voice. "The baby wasn't born until later in October, and she was—"

"Overdue. Yeah, I remember. Monica was born in September."

Not overdue! Premature!

That's what Delia had told Barnes.

His daughter had been so tiny and fragile.

His daughter. *His*, not Bobby's.

"So there we were with our own life and our own daughter, and Delia kept bouncing back. Nothing was ever enough for her. Years after they split up and she had his wages garnished, she was looking for more money. It was like she just—"

"Wait, she had his wages garnished?" Barnes cuts in, incredulous.

"Yeah, for child support."

But . . .

But that would take a court order, and establishment of paternity.

He can't speak.

Amelia clears her throat. "So then . . . Charisse was definitely Bobby's daughter?"

"Oh, hell, yes. One hundred percent."

Barnes attempts to take a deep breath and resume the questioning, but the air has been sucked out of the room.

Bobby's daughter.

Not mine.

Chapter Nine

Westport, Connecticut

Plunking the last red plastic storage tub on the attic floor, Liliana Ford hears the unmistakable tinkling of broken glass.

"Damn!"

Please don't let it be one of her mother-in-law's old German mercury baubles, presented, along with vintage colored light strings and an antique treetop angel, as a wedding shower gift last spring.

"They belonged to my grandmother. I know you'll cherish them."

"Oh, I absolutely will."

I absolutely won't shatter an ornament when I take down the tree the moment your son leaves for a business trip.

Liliana doesn't open the box now to investigate. The broken glass can wait until next December, when she and Bryant have another year of marriage under their belts and her relationship with his intimidating mother has solidified.

Liliana returns to the second floor and walks down a short hall lined with a bathroom and three bedrooms, all roughly the same size. No master suite in this small shingled colonial that had been at the top of their budget and the only affordable house in her husband's toney hometown.

Downstairs, the living room looks oddly empty, the tree standing dark and unembellished in its stand. Maybe she should have waited till January 6—the Feast of the Epiphany. Her Catholic parents have always left theirs up till then, and she'd always been disappointed when it came down.

But theirs had been decorated with *white* fairy lights, and they'd know why she isn't comfortable with the colored ones she'd just stashed in the attic. Bryant will not.

"He's your husband now," her mother had said, calling in December from her Florida retirement condo. "You should tell him what's going on."

"I know, and I will . . . when the time is right."

"How about now? It's the anniversary, and—"

"I know what day it is, believe me, but Bry's in Boston, and I'm about to get on a train to Philly."

They have important sales rep jobs, a busy life, and a bright future. No need to dwell on a long-ago night, and a little Christmas tree with bright old-fashioned lights, two women screaming at each other.

She'd been so cold, wet, sleepy, and young . . .

Just three years old. Yet she'd understood what they were saying: both her mother and father were gone, and neither of those women wanted to take care of her.

She doesn't remember much of her life before that night—snippets of gloomy rooms, city streets, strangers. Her mother, miserable. Her father, smacking her. Nor does she remember the six-month aftermath—being abandoned, discovered, turned over to social services, placed in foster care.

Her next retained memory is a happy one—a

summer beach, building sandcastles with a new dad who never lifted a hand to her, as her new mom laughed, holding a camera.

Maybe she only remembers because she's seen those pictures countless times, the first in a childhood photo album that began midway through June 1991—essentially, when her life began. Everything that had come before should be irrelevant. All that should matter is the wonderful life that followed.

She walks over to the tree, reaches into the branches, and clasps her hands around the trunk. Dry needles rain over her new Christmas sweater. Her own mother had sent it from Florida in a boxful of gifts that had included an "Our First Christmas" ornament and a rectangular package labeled with her name and a Post-it that read "Open in Private."

Inside, she found a new book by Nelson Roger Cartwright, who hosts the television program *The Roots and Branches Project.* She's never seen it, but she knows it's about finding biological relatives.

Avid viewers, her parents have always been honest with her about how she came into their lives. It's not as if they could lie. They're white; she's Black. So of course Bryant knows she's adopted. He just doesn't know the circumstances. It's not easy to admit to the man who loves and wants her that there was a time when no one did. When the authorities plastered her face over newspapers and television the way they do children that have gone missing, and she'd gone unrecognized—or at least unclaimed.

She'd hidden the book in her nightstand drawer, alongside the DNA test kit her mother had given her after she got engaged.

"Maybe it will be easier to tell Bryant about your past if you have some answers about where you came from."

"I'm not ready for that."

"Then maybe you're not ready for marriage. Spouses shouldn't keep secrets this big from each other. Don't you think it's time you found out about your birth parents?"

She didn't then.

But she'd changed her mind this fall, after an unsettling incident she's kept to herself.

It was probably nothing. Still, she'd spit into the test tube and mailed the test away. The results should be back any day now.

She has no intention of reuniting with her biological parents, but she wants to know whatever happened to them, for her own peace of mind, and her future children's.

Clumsily maneuvering the tree to the door in its stand, she feels water slop onto the hardwood. It's all right. She'll clean it up. She just wants the damned thing out.

She drags it onto the porch. A foggy evening is pushing in. She shivers in the chill, goose bumps prickling her skin like pine needles poking through her sweater.

It's because she was thinking about her past. She needs to stop. A new year is underway. She's a newlywed, settled in a charming neighborhood filled with large trees and cozy houses populated with young couples and families.

She just needs to get rid of this damned—

Poised to drag the tree down the steps, she sees someone standing just beyond the streetlamp's glow.

She peers at the shadow and it—*he*—watches her in return.

She drops the tree onto the porch, hurries back inside, and closes the door. The dog ambles over.

"It's all right, don't worry. We're safe."

Briana wags her tail. She'd probably wag it at an armed intruder, so grateful is she to have a home and family after having been abandoned by her previous owner.

I know how you feel, sweetie.

Bryant had wanted to buy a purebred, but she'd talked him into a shelter pet. Now he wants to go back to find a male companion for Briana.

"She seems lonely, doesn't she?" he'd asked last night, packing for his business trip as Briana lay watching with her nose on her paws. "We need to save another dog."

"We can't save all the dogs, Bry."

"I know, but . . . just one more. We can call it, uh . . . some other combination of our names."

"Like what? Li-an?"

"For a guy dog? No way. Maybe our last name and your maiden name . . ."

"Ford and Tucker? Yeah, I don't think that's a good idea."

Their laughter echoes in her head now as she stares out into the dusk, wishing her husband were here.

When this happened in the fall, she'd chalked it up to her imagination.

Now Liliana turns the dead bolt with a trembling hand, certain someone is out there watching her . . . again.

Amelia has spent her career warning her clients that the answers they find might not be the ones they'd hoped for or expected. Though her work sometimes leads to happy reunions, it just as often leads to disappointment, or devastation. Sometimes, she senses which it will be even before she starts her research.

That hadn't been the case with Stockton Barnes. Not in the beginning, when he was just another client, and she was caught up in her own personal drama. Not until the photographic resemblance had convinced her she'd found his biological child.

Guess my clients aren't the only ones who see what they want to see.

The revelation that the little girl abandoned at the mall may not have been his biological child changes Barnes's relationship to the case, but they still need to find out what happened to her, and what Cynthia Randall had to do with it.

"When did you last see Bobby's daughter Charisse?" she asks Cynthia, and there's a subtle shift in her demeanor.

"Right after he left for rehab."

"When was that?"

"I don't know . . . late '80s? Why aren't you asking *him* about her? She's his kid, not mine."

Barnes speaks at last. "We did ask him! That's why we're here. Bobby told us you and Delia had a falling-out on Thanksgiving in 1990. Do you remember that?"

"I had a lot of arguments with Delia. She liked to show up here like she was part of the family. She wasn't."

"But her daughter was," Amelia points out. "Did she have regular visitations with her father?"

"One weekend a month until Bobby went to rehab. By the time he got back, Delia had cut him out of her life, and the kid's. Can't say I blame her. I wised up and did the same thing."

"What did he say about the estrangement with Delia and Charisse?" Barnes asks.

"Not a word. I'd told him I didn't ever want to hear her name again, and he never mentioned it. But it wasn't hard to figure out, since I never saw Delia or Charisse again after that Thanksgiving."

"You just said you did."

"Did I?"

Barnes flips back a page in his notebook. "You said you saw her right *after* Bobby left for rehab."

"Then I guess I did. Delia probably showed up to dump her off with me on Bobby's weekend."

"Probably?"

"It's not easy to remember the stuff you spent the last twenty or thirty years trying to forget. I had a lot going on back then, raising my daughter with Bobby out of the picture, and working two jobs."

"Where were you working?"

"I was a teller at the Bank of New England. But they're long gone," she adds, seeing Barnes writing it down. "They went belly-up a year later. Seized by the FDIC in the banking crisis a year later."

"What about your other job?"

"I was a security guard."

"At the shelter?" Amelia asks when she doesn't elaborate.

"Nah, I've worked security at a lot of places."

"Where were you in December 1990?"

"I don't remember."

"Bobby says you were working at the Chapel Square Mall," Barnes informs her. "And while he was gone, Delia and Charisse disappeared."

"What do you mean they disappeared?"

"They moved out of Brooklyn and no one ever heard from them again," Amelia says, though they're not entirely certain that's the case.

"Delia was an addict. If she disappeared, she probably OD'd on some street. That's what Bobby always said was going to happen."

Amelia and Barnes had considered that while driving to Bridgeport. He'd called a colleague back in New York and asked her to pull records for unidentified female DRTs fitting her description in late November and December 1990.

"DRTs?" Amelia had asked, and he'd explained that it's police jargon for dead right there, and that there were plenty of them back in the height of New York's crack epidemic.

"If Delia Montague OD'd, where's her little girl?" Barnes asks Cynthia.

"How would I know if Bobby doesn't? They were living with one of his cousins. You should ask—"

"She's dead, Cynthia."

"Alma?"

"And her daughter, Brandy. They were murdered a few days ago."

Her shock appears genuine. "Who did it?"

"Good question."

"But . . . you said you were here on a missing persons case, not . . ."

"We are." Barnes pulls a folded piece of paper from his notebook and hands it to her.

She stares at the photocopied article about the little girl found at Chapel Square Mall.

"Do you recognize her?"

She says nothing.

"Come on, Cynthia. She's your stepdaughter. We know it, and you know it."

Still nothing. But she looks up and nods, tears in her eyes.

In all her years working with foundlings, and being one, Amelia has met a couple of mothers who abandoned their infants out of fear and confusion. This is the first time she's ever come face-to-face with someone who'd abandoned another woman's child.

"Why didn't you identify her when she was found in the mall?" she asks Cynthia.

"I . . . I would have, if I'd known, but I didn't—"

"Cut the bullshit! It was all over the papers."

"I don't read the papers."

"You were working at that mall when it happened. There is no way, and I mean *no way,* that you didn't know. You kept your mouth shut because you're the one who left her there."

Silence.

Then Barnes says, "Look, Cynthia, we've got evidence."

"Wh—*what?*"

"We know your husband's ex-wife showed up and dumped her on you, and—"

"That's a lie! You don't have evidence."

He pushes on. "We do. We know what happened. Delia showed up, and you—"

"It wasn't Delia!"

"What do you mean?"

She presses a fist to her mouth.

"Cynthia. Tell us."

"Alma brought her! I told her Bobby wasn't even around, but she didn't care. It was late, and she'd taken the bus up from the city with Charisse strapped in the stroller. Poor thing wasn't even bundled up, and she was looking at me with those big sad eyes . . ."

"Keep going," Barnes says, voice flat.

"She told me Delia had taken off a few weeks ago. It wasn't the first time, but she'd had it, and she couldn't take care of her like I could." She chokes a bitter laugh. "That's what she said. And then she just turned around and walked out the door. I was shouting after her, asking what about the rest of the family, you know? She said she'd been asking them, and no one wanted her."

"That's hard to believe. They seem like a close-knit family."

"They are, but . . . not then. Not with Bobby. He treated them like dirt. Stole from them. They kept giving him chances, but he burned every bridge. That's why we were alone here that Thanksgiving. He wasn't welcome there anymore."

"And they didn't want Charisse."

"No one did." Wiping tears from her eyes, she doesn't see Barnes wince.

"Including you. So you took her to a public place, and you abandoned her."

"It seemed like the only thing I could do. If I got the police involved, or social services, she'd just wind up back with Bobby eventually, and . . ."

"And with you."

"Look, I'm not proud of it," she tells him. "But she was better off because of what I did."

He says nothing.

Amelia has to. "How do you know she's better off?"

"Because Bobby's family must have seen those newspaper photos same as anyone else, and they didn't step forward. Not one of them!"

"Are you saying the Harrisons knew the abandoned child was Bobby's daughter?"

"Of course they knew. And I didn't *abandon* her. I was on duty that night. I kept an eye on her until she was found."

"But when she was, you pretended you had nothing to do with it." Amelia bites her lip and tastes blood.

"You must have been questioned, Cynthia," Barnes says. "So you lied?"

"To protect her."

"To protect *yourself*."

"And my daughter, Monica. A mother does what she has to do. A good mother, I mean. Delia wasn't one. And Bobby wasn't a good father."

"And you take the prize for world's worst stepmother," Amelia says.

"You would have done the same thing in my shoes."

"I would *never* do what you did! Leaving an innocent little girl alone in a public place is the most—"

"She wasn't alone! I told you, I—"

"Yeah, you watched her. Terrific."

"You don't understand." She brushes tears from her eyes. "Every year at Christmas, I thought about that little girl and I hoped—I *prayed*—she'd found a good home with parents who loved her, and that she wouldn't remember where she came from."

Maybe she doesn't. And maybe that's for the best. But Amelia knows too well that her original family and home must have left an imprint on her heart. She's likely gone through life instinctively seeking some intangible face or place from the past, a search that can alienate a woman from people who love her in the present.

"I thought when Amelia found out that she really was her parents' biological daughter, she'd finally be able to put this stuff to rest and move on," Aaron had told their therapist during their final counseling session in November. "But she's more obsessed than ever."

"Because I still don't have answers! If Bettina was my birth mother, why would Calvin have told me I was a foundling? Was he lying? Or did he not know the truth himself? Was he my father, or was it someone else?"

Aaron shot the therapist a "See what I mean?" look and then shook his head sadly at Amelia. "You said you were ready to move on. That's why we're here. That's why we're trying—but you're not."

"Of course I am. Whose idea was it to come to counseling? Mine! And if that isn't trying, then I don't know what—"

"No, I mean you're not *moving on.* I don't think you can. I don't think you want to. And I don't think either of us can live like this anymore."

He was right.

And Amelia knows in her heart that no matter what she and Aaron and the therapist have said, this isn't a trial separation.

It's permanent.

In the white marble bathroom, Gypsy steps into a steamy shower for the second time today and leans into the hot spray like a cushion. Somewhere along her evening journey from the hotel to a distant Queens neighborhood, she'd acquired a pounding heart to accompany her pounding head. Neither had let up on the return trip, despite a satisfying, clockwork mission.

She doesn't *do* anxiety.

Yet she hasn't had to do what she'd done in Queens in a long, long time. For years now, decades, she's had an army of devotees at her disposal.

She massages shampoo into her skull. The scented suds won't ease the tension headache, but they'll wash away any traces of Kasia's blood.

There had been surprisingly little spatter. Not a hint of commotion to draw witnesses even though Gypsy killed her right there in public after following her off the subway. They shuffled along in a weary crowd from a well-lit platform to a dimly lit staircase to a shadowy street, thick with honking traffic and shiny with rain. Seasoned New York commuters, they wore earbuds, nearly all of them, and opened umbrellas without missing a step as they ventured into the downpour.

Gypsy held her own umbrella low and close to shield the pistol. Her hand was shaky, but she fired one bullet into Kasia's blond wig and kept on walking, turning into another subway entrance a few yards away. She stripped off the plastic rain cape, shoved it into a garbage can, and pushed through the turnstile as a Manhattan-bound train pulled into the station. This one had vacant seats and only a few passengers, vacant eyed. No one noticed Gypsy. She wondered whether anyone had yet noticed that the woman lying in the street above hadn't tripped or slipped and fallen.

There's no way they'll think this is an accident.

Not like in the Bronx. Mother's Day 1968. It had been raining then, too. Rushing gutters awash with blood.

As the subway carried her back to Manhattan, she imagined Kasia's blood pouring into a puddle, pooling into the gutter, down the storm drain, trailing her through the tunnels.

Now she looks down, expecting to see red swirling into the drain at her feet, but sees only water and suds.

She wraps herself in a thick white towel. Had Kasia herself folded and placed it here earlier?

No, because she's not really a maid. She was just posing as one, to outwit you. But you knew she was your sister.

She doesn't bother to close the drapes before slipping into bed, hair still damp, head still throbbing, heart still racing. Beyond the window, the old Wayland penthouse glows like a constellation.

When at last she falls asleep, Perry—young again, dashing and handsome—is waiting for her. They're sipping champagne at Windows on the World.

"I don't need you," she tells him. "Only your money."

"You're wrong. You need *me*."

"I'm never wrong."

"But you are." He points and the wall of glass is gone. The city far below has become a roaring ocean, the building a windswept cliff.

"See? There she is!" Perry shouts above the gale, waving his arms, trying to show Gypsy something just over the edge.

"I know! I saw her! I killed her!"

"No! You missed her."

"I shot her in the head, just the way Red and I learned at target practice years ago . . ."

"You're wrong, Gypsy!"

"I'm never—"

"You're wrong! She was right there in front of you, and you missed her."

She wakes up, jarred out of the dream by a noise—a door closing, footsteps tapping.

"Perry?" she calls, wide-eyed in the dark. Or . . . *Kasia.*

Footsteps again—not in this suite, she realizes after a moment, but retreating to a distant corner of another. It's just another guest. Not a ghost. The luxurious grand dame of a hotel isn't any more soundproof than it is haunted.

Gypsy turns on the lamp. Her laptop is on the nightstand; Perry's voice in her head.

"She was right there in front of you . . ."

"Shut up, Perry. What do you know? You weren't even there. You aren't even here."

It was just a dream. A nightmare, the ocean raging as it had in the hurricane . . .

Gypsy grabs the laptop. It's still open to the page she'd been reading earlier when the so-called maid barged into the suite.

She scans the text and picks up where she'd left off.

> . . . Silas Moss is credited with mentoring Amelia Crenshaw Haines, one of the nation's foremost investigative genealogists and a regular on Nelson Roger Cartwright's *The Roots and Branches Project* . . .

So there *is* a connection that goes beyond Ithaca being one of the country's foremost college towns. But Amelia would have attended college almost twenty years after Bernadette. She never even met Stockton Barnes until a few months ago, and that was only because he hired her to find his daughter.

Gypsy launches a new search: Amelia Crenshaw Haines, Ithaca.

She begins on Amelia's own website, studying her bio, her career, her photos . . .

One leaps out at her.

There's a young Amelia in a college cap and gown . . .

And she's standing arm in arm with a young Margaret Costello.

How can it be? A miracle. A sign. A prophecy.

Quilt fisted against her mouth, eyes wide, Gypsy reads the caption.

Commencement Day 1990: Amelia with her close friend Jessamine McCall, 21, of Ithaca . . .

All right, then. Of course the girl with the widow's peak and dimples isn't Margaret Costello. In 1990, she'd have been pushing forty. The child she'd conceived with Oran would have been twenty-one.

Perry was right. There it is, right in front of Gypsy. There *she* is.

That blonde maid wasn't Margaret's daughter.

Jessamine McCall is.

Part IV

1968

Chapter Ten

Thursday, April 4, 1968
Fernandina Beach

After the Tet Offensive, Travis had resurfaced in Vietnam. Melody hadn't been home on the February afternoon when he tried to reach her by telephone to tell her he had survived, so he dialed his mother next.

Doris told him about the baby.

Never much of a correspondent, Travis reacted to the news with a barrage of enthusiastic letters to his wife. They were dated through late February, but have since stopped coming.

Melody isn't sure what to make of that.

Surely she'd have heard by now if something had happened to him. Somber word reaches the States with heightened military efficiency these days. The newspapers publish a list of local casualties and POWs on the front page after the families have been informed. But the silence is ominous.

Travis's birthday, and her own fake due date dawns with bright sunshine and phone calls from her mother and mother-in-law, anticipating labor to be punctual as sunrise and high tide.

"Not yet," she says, "but I'll let you know."

Doris accepts that reply, hangs up, and moves on

with her plans to go to the beauty shop, golf all afternoon, and dine at the country club. Becoming a grandmother isn't the highlight of her life, or even her year. She seems pleased, but hardly euphoric.

But the hypervigilant Honeybee shows up in person with a still-steaming batch of Raelene's homemade biscuits for Melody's breakfast, along with the morning paper and a fragrant vaseful of cascading lavender blossoms.

"The wisteria finally bloomed!" Her mother sets the flowers in the middle of the table with a triumphant smile. "When I looked out and saw it this morning, I said to your daddy, that surely is a sign!"

"A sign?"

"That our grandbaby is coming today. How must poor Travis feel, on the other side of the world for the big event?"

"I'm sure he's been through worse, Mother."

"Well, yes, but . . ." Honeybee chatters on. "Daddy got the bassinet out of the attic before he left for work, and Raelene cleaned it up real nice and we set it up in your old room. I bought two new skirts for it. One is pink and the other is blue just in case—"

"Wait, Mother, what are you talking about?"

"The bassinet. The one we had for you and Ellie." A brief, sad flash of smile before she goes on, "I told you I'd have it all set for when you and the baby come to stay."

"No, you told me you'd have it all set for when the baby *comes*."

"To stay."

"I don't think you mentioned that part. I need the bassinet here."

"Don't be silly. You can't come home from the hospital to an empty house. You have no idea the toll childbirth takes on a woman's body, or how demanding it is to care for an infant. I told you I'd help you."

"I thought you meant here!"

Honeybee shakes her head. "Of course not. You'll stay with us for the first few months."

"Months!"

"Weeks, anyway. Eight to twelve at the very least."

Melody unfolds the newspaper and looks for an article to read aloud—anything to change the subject. She skims past war news and lands on an article about LBJ's meeting yesterday with Senator Robert Kennedy to discuss the president's decision not to seek or accept another term in office.

"Oh, it would be marvelous to elect another Kennedy, wouldn't it? Bobby and Ethel are so attractive, and they have that enormous family. Ten children romping in the White House would surely go a long way toward healing this country after what happened to poor JFK!"

"My goodness, Mother. To think that you didn't even approve of the first Kennedy in the White House, back in the day."

"Now, why would you say a thing like that?"

"*You* said it. 'A Roman Catholic running for president? What is this world coming to? Next thing you know, we'll have . . .'"

A colored candidate.

Melody can't bear to utter the remainder of the sentence.

"I never said any such thing," Honeybee says with a brisk, dismissive wave. "I just adored John Kennedy, and Jacqueline and those sweet children. Why, little Caroline looked so much like . . ."

"I know."

During those Camelot years that Ellie hadn't lived to see, the impish yet ladylike First Daughter, with that shy smile and her blond bobbed hair clipped with pretty bows and barrettes, had born a remarkable resemblance to Ellie's childhood portraits.

Honeybee rises abruptly and carries her half-finished plate over to the sink. She stands for a moment, back turned, before turning on the tap and pulling on dish gloves.

She knows her mother hadn't been in her right mind during that election season. Autumn, 1960. She remembers the occasion well because it had been the first time a grieving Honeybee had agreed to socialize. Daddy had talked her into hosting her club, but when the time came, she was in her room, crying. He went up to talk to her while Melody helped Raelene in the kitchen, spreading deviled ham on crackers as the housekeeper separated egg whites for a batch of pink lady cocktails.

"I'm just prayin' your mama can pull herself together before the ladies arrive," Raelene said, adding extra gin to the silver shaker.

When the doorbell rang, Honeybee floated down the stairs on a cloud of Evening in Paris and apricot silk chiffon. Melody had been reassured to hear her playing the charming hostess just as she always had. But as the evening wore on, she'd become uncharacteristically outspoken for a woman who'd taught her daughters that it wasn't polite to discuss religion or politics in a social setting.

"Your mama's just not herself," Raelene said, brewing strong black coffee as Melody sliced pineapple upside down cake, Honeybee's too-raucous laughter filtering in from the dining room. "Going to be a long time before she's back to normal."

Melody had convinced herself that her mother—so proudly descended from the man who'd brought down the Union army at Bull Run—isn't intolerant. Just old-fashioned, with traditional values.

But what about her friends? They'd prayed with the Abernathys through Ellie's illness, brought casseroles after her death, and buoyed and coaxed her throughout the painstaking return to normalcy. But Melody believes there are plenty of people in this small Southern town, those women included, who'd ostracize her parents over a scandalous affair and mixed-race grandbaby.

It's just the way things are, perhaps the way they'll always be. It's why she has to leave.

"Well, I declare! There's not a cloud in the sky," Honeybee chirps over at the sink, pointing with a sudsy finger. "What a glorious spring day for a baby to come into this beautiful world."

The child in Melody's womb offers a sharp kick in response, and Melody fills her mouth with yet another bite of biscuit, though there's barely room in her stomach, what with the two she already ate.

Honeybee just goes on talking as always, keeping up a steady stream of conversation, insisting that Melody stay off her feet as she tidies the kitchen and mops the floor.

When she pours herself a glass of sweet tea and seems to be settling in to spend the day, Melody clears her throat. "Mother, I'm sorry, but I really need some quiet time."

"That sounds lovely. We can sit in the living room and be quiet together."

"Some quiet time *alone*."

"You don't want to be alone when you go into labor," Honeybee says in her "Honeybee knows best" way.

Maybe I do, Melody thinks, and wonders if her mother is ever going to allow her to be alone again.

"I'm not going into labor. Today is just the *due date*, Mother. You always said you went weeks past yours with Ellie and me."

"Weeks? Heavens, no. It was just a few days."

"Well, you can't stay here for a few days."

Honeybee doesn't reply, but her expression says that she can, indeed.

"Mother!"

"I just don't want to miss a moment of the happiest day of my life." At Melody's look she elaborates, "The day I become a grandma!"

"Well, what about the day I was born? And Ellie? And your wedding day? You waited so long for Daddy to come home from the war."

"But I was terrified of being a wife and a mother. I wasn't sure I was capable of any of it."

"I find it hard to believe that you ever doubted yourself, Mother, in anything at all."

"I was young. We all have our insecurities in our youth. I'm afraid I wasted a lot of time fretting back in those days, and singing was the only thing I'd ever done well. Now I get to live vicariously through my beautiful daughter. I want all your dreams to come true, Melody."

"But just last year, you talked me out of taking music courses at Jacksonville University."

"Because . . . why would you ever want to do that?" Honeybee's eyes are wide, as if Melody had suggested that she planned to run off with a rock and roll band.

"To finish my education, and . . . and pursue my dream. Isn't that what you just said you wanted me to do?"

"I meant your dream of having a husband and children . . . a family, a home of your own."

Oh. That dream.

"Melody, I've never regretted giving up my music to marry and raise a family. And I'm sure you'll find that you have more than enough to keep you busy, too."

"It's not about being busy, Mother. It's about doing something that I love to do. My music made me happy. Why did I have to give it up?"

"For Travis! And because it was time to grow up. Other things are more important now. You'll see." She heads for the door. "I'll let you get your rest, but I'm just a hop, skip, and jump away if you need me, you hear?"

"Loud and clear."

"I'll come on back with supper. Raelene is making chicken à la King."

"Well, all right. But not until at least seven o'clock."

"How about five—"

"Seven! And not a moment sooner!"

Melody closes the door after her and waits a few minutes to make sure Honeybee doesn't boomerang. Then she hurries into the bedroom and changes from her dungarees and smock top to a turquoise maternity dress with a white Peter Pan collar and bow.

"You look purty as a picture in that color," Cyril had said when she'd worn it to visit him a few weeks back, the compliment like a rainbow illuminating the gray March day.

His eyes are perpetually glad to see her, yet he never wants her to stay long. Too dangerous for her there, he says. No married, pregnant white woman would have any business visiting a Black man on Barrow.

He's been increasingly grim lately, brooding about the war, wrapped up in the looming presidential election and his crusade to educate and register Black voters, all the while working and saving money for their escape.

It won't be long now, but there are so many details to work out. Cyril hasn't yet told his own mother they're going, or written to ask his cousin if they can stay.

"I don't want word to get out," he told Melody recently. "If it ever got back to Travis Hunter . . ."

"For all we know, he's dead."

Melody grabs her car keys and heads out the door, not wanting to remember what Cyril had said in response.

"Or he's one step ahead of us, plotting revenge."

The Bronx

"MISS MATTHEWS? CAN you tell us?"

Gypsy looks up from the notebook page where she'd been doodling peace signs to see the teacher, Mr. Dixon, wearing the same expression as Wile E. Coyote when he's about to catch the Road Runner.

On the blackboard behind him, a chalk-scrawled timeline depicts genetic milestones leading up to the present day. She notes a series of dusty white dots alongside December 1967, where Dixon had staccato tapped in an effort to rouse an answer from this drowsy last period classroom.

"Stanford professor Arthur Kornberg synthesized deoxyribonucleic acid in a test tube," she says, "and President Johnson congratulated him for unlocking a fundamental secret of life."

She resists the urge to punctuate that with a smug "beep, beep."

Her competent reply crushes Dixon's expectant smile like a cartoon anvil. "Uh . . . that's right. Take notes. This will be on Monday's test."

He turns back to the board, droning on about DNA and genetics as Gypsy jots the Kornberg information in her notebook.

Beneath it, for her own amusement, she writes, "April, 1968: Science teacher Alfred Dixon transforms a fascinating subject into diethyl ether."

She stares at the word *ether.*

Something weighty and frightening nudges her brain, even as the girl behind her taps her shoulder.

She swivels to see a folded piece of notebook paper with her own name on it.

Opening it, she sees a pencil-written note.

Can I walk you home after school? G.M.

She folds the note, shoves it into her textbook, and rests her chin on her fist.

Greg Martinez has been going steady with Carol-Ann Ellis since February. He had, indeed, presented her with a red rose in class on Valentine's Day and asked her to the dance. Gypsy hadn't been there to witness it.

That was the day after her father had surprised her with a heart-shaped box of chocolates. The day she'd slept through her alarm clock. She remembers dragging herself out of bed late that morning to try to get ready for school, feeling as though she was sleepwalking, her head pounding, stomach queasy, mouth dry. She'd crawled back into bed, thinking she must be coming down with something. But when she awakened again midafternoon, the stupor and symptoms had lifted, and she'd forgotten all about it until—

The girl behind her pokes her again, and gestures at Greg when Gypsy glances back. He's sprawled in his usual seat in the back of the room, alongside a couple of his buddies.

He catches her eye, raises his brows and opens his hands palms up in a silent *Well?*

Gypsy shrugs and faces forward again.

One Saturday last month, her father had come home with chocolate cream eggs.

"Easter's almost a month away," she'd protested, "and we don't celebrate it."

Once, she'd asked him why not. Oran's long-winded response about shunning the so-called resurrection of a false prophet had meant little to a child coveting other little girls' frilly dresses and baskets filled with candy.

"These aren't Easter eggs," he'd told her last month, offering her the package. "They're for your birthday."

"That was yesterday." He doesn't believe in celebrating mortal birthdays, either. She'd peered inside. "Where'd you get these? They're all smushed."

"I'll take them back if you don't want them."

"I didn't say that."

She'd eaten them all and fallen into bed soon after. Had it been a school night, she'd probably have slept right through her alarm clock as she had in February.

The girl behind her delivers another note from the back row.

I broke up with Carol-Ann. G.M.

Good for him.

She has other things to ponder right now, like that March Sunday when she'd awakened to find that it was midafternoon, and she felt shrouded in a strange fog once again. Again, she had a headache, upset stomach, parched throat. Again, she wondered if she'd caught some kind of flu bug.

The bell rings.

Gypsy grabs her things and is halfway out the door when Greg catches up to her, touching her arm. "Hey, I thought we could—"

"Sorry, I have to go."

She pulls away and pushes through the throng of students in the corridor, lost in the past and those damned chocolates that *were* Easter eggs no matter what Oran wanted to say about celebrating her birthday.

Ether eggs . . .

Barrow Island

Cyril is in the bedroom stripping off his Morrison's Meat Market uniform when he hears Otis yap out on the porch. He figures a squirrel must have ventured into the yard, or a female dog is out there in the night.

He'd long-ago learned to differentiate between wary barks and excited barks. But commotion escalates into canine jubilation that can only mean one thing.

He rebuttons his trousers and looks around for a clean shirt. Finding none, he goes shirtless into the front room.

Beyond the screen door, Melody is climbing out of her red convertible wearing a short A-line dress the same shade as a summer sea, and he reckons she smells even sweeter than the wisteria blooms tumbling from the gnarled porch vine.

She pauses to steady herself on her feet, resting a hand on the small of her back. Face without a hint of makeup, blond hair unteased and hanging loose, a few inches shorter than usual in white patent leather flats with buckles, she looks younger than her years, and more vulnerable than she is.

After giving Otis an affectionate pat, she straightens and smiles when she sees Cyril watching her.

"You want to come in?" he asks.

"I like it out here, with everything in bloom. It smells heavenly."

"That time of year."

He steps outside and they settle into rockers.

"My mother's wisteria blossomed for the first time," Melody says. "She thinks it's a sign."

"That spring is here?"

"That the baby is about to be, but . . ." She sighs, leaning her head back and staring at the porch ceiling. "She's had that plant forever, and it never flowered. She made it happen through sheer will. She's a force of nature. You never met a woman like my mother."

"She sounds a lot like mine. If Marceline LeBlanc

sets her mind to something, she doesn't let anything get in her way, and she doesn't wait around for someone else to fix things for her. Not many women are like that. She is. You are."

"Me?"

"You. That's how I know you're going to be just fine, no matter what happens."

She digests that comment. He stares at the horses out on the grass, listening to their chairs creaking back and forth and marsh birds singing in the thicket.

"The only thing that's going to happen," she says, "is you and me and our baby and dayclean."

"Dayclean?"

"A fresh start."

He smiles. "Well, our money's adding up, slowly but surely."

"Will it be enough? Because maybe I can ask my parents if—"

"Melody! You can't ask your parents—"

"They love me. I keep thinking maybe if they knew, they could—"

"Put that thought right out of your head. If you tell anyone, our lives will be in jeopardy! Our baby's life!" His tone is hushed, harsh.

He sees her arms go to her stomach, cradling it. He turns to survey the dirt lane leading back out to the road, imagining spies in the verdant shadows at the property's perimeter. Nothing to see but wild horses grazing beneath wooly swirls of Spanish moss, but rumors of white mainland trespassers persist.

"I know," she says softly. "It's just hard."

He turns back to her, brushing a blond strand out

of her eyes. She meets his gaze head-on, and lifts her chin.

No delicate Southern belle, his Melody. Even eight months into her pregnancy, the woman is about as fragile as the ancient live oak throwing shade over half the yard. It's the reason—one of the reasons—he'd been drawn to her. She isn't afraid to think deeply about things, or to challenge what she's always thought, or to feel. She wasn't afraid of anything.

But right now, she should be.

"Don't worry, Cyril. I won't tell a soul and I don't need help from anyone except you."

"Not even your mother? Because in your condition you must be—"

"Not even my mother," she tells him. "I promise."

WAITING AT THE intersection outside the school, Gypsy sees purple crocuses poking up in the tiny garden across the street. The old woman is out there with a watering can.

Mary, Mary, quite contrary . . .

Just the other day, Gypsy had mentioned her to Oran, who'd launched a lengthy tirade about metaphorical religious significance in the nursery rhyme.

Psycho lunatic, she'd thought. But then, in the next breath, he was warning her to be careful crossing streets after school because there'd been a fatal hit and run a few blocks away, on Webster Avenue.

"Was it a student?"

"Nah, some old coot."

"Well, I'm not an old coot," she'd shot back, and he'd laughed.

He'd laughed, too, on that March Sunday when she'd told him that she'd slept most of the day.

"Guess you ate too many sweets last night."

"Chocolate wakes you up. It doesn't put you to sleep."

"Listen to Miss Smarty-Pants."

Troubling thoughts stall in her brain as she skirts around ambling pedestrians: strung out flower children wearing Nehru jackets and headbands, chatty young mothers pushing baby buggies, herds of schoolchildren fluttering Crayola drawings.

Last Halloween, she'd heard about unsuspecting trick-or-treaters getting Halloween candy laced with LSD. Had someone done the same to her Valentine's and Easter chocolate? Where had her father bought it?

At Webster Avenue, she watches traffic zoom past, shifting her weight from one foot to the other, anxiously waiting for a light to change. She needs to get home and tell him what happened, and he has to report it—though the thought of Oran getting involved with "the fuzz" on the right side of the law is laughable.

But acid doesn't knock you out. It makes you feel groovy and happy.

She thinks of her mother, a strung out, rail-thin beauty with long black hair, glazed blue eyes, and a faraway smile.

She hadn't known Linda very well, never lived with her, and wasn't particularly fond of her. She was just someone who'd drifted into their lives from time to time—never on holidays or for Gypsy's birthday, never to attend parent conferences or tend to her when she was ill.

For years, Linda showed up without warning whenever she needed a place to stay for a couple of days, a week or two at most. And then one day—

Someone jostles her; people push past. The light has changed. She crosses the street and moves on down the next block, no longer in a hurry to get home.

She hears her father calling her Miss Smarty-Pants. She sees his mocking grin, sees him turn away, but not before she'd glimpsed something disconcerting in his gaze.

Why would he have drugged her? She's heard of hippie parents smoking grass with their teenagers, but this wasn't like that. This had been sneaky and underhanded, and it had been some kind of powerful knockout drug.

Her mind chases logic down dark alleys as she drags her feet along the sidewalk, trying to make sense of it. You don't incapacitate someone in that way unless they pose some kind of threat—or maybe if you're delusional.

Her father has his moments, but even his most feverish rants are a means to a benevolent end where his daughter is concerned. All he wants is to save her soul and lead her to eternal paradise when the world goes up in flames. He truly believes he's the Messiah.

Does she believe it?

Not as unequivocally as she had when she was younger. She has more questions now. Sometimes he answers them, dispelling her doubts with patience and clarity. Other times, he raves that she's a disbeliever.

At the Grand Concourse she waits shoulder to

shoulder in a crowd of fellow New Yorkers impatient to cross to the subway on the opposite side.

Traffic zips along the busy boulevard, a transit bus speeding past so close it all but grazes the tip of Gypsy's nose. She remembers her father's warning about the hit and run and takes a step backward from the curb. Her gaze falls on a corner newsstand. There's Twiggy on a magazine cover. She shifts her gaze to a stack of newspapers, and a headline engulfs her like a swirling black funnel.

BROOKLYN'S TENSE ANTICIPATION OF BUTCHER'S NEXT STRIKE: FEBRUARY 13, MARCH 23, APRIL . . . ?

Back home, Melody forages the cabinets, famished, and grateful that Honeybee will be here with supper later.

Munching a handful of dry cereal, she eyes the *Betty Crocker's Dinner for Two Cookbook* she'd wedged under the kitchen window to keep it open this morning.

Raelene had given it to her as a wedding gift. "A wife should make supper for her husband. Only way to keep a marriage going strong."

"Really? 'Cause Mother and Daddy just celebrated their twenty-fifth anniversary, and I've never even seen her light a stove burner."

"Believe you me, your mama knows her way around a chicken fried steak. That woman made a mean pan gravy back in the day."

Maybe, but in this one, Honeybee serves sandwiches for supper on Raelene's nights off.

Still, Melody had given it a shot. The first night she'd attempted a homemade meal, Travis had poked at the brown blob on his plate. "Why in tarnation would you make pralines for supper?"

"That's mashed potatoes!"

She'd dissolved into tears that he'd found even more amusing. Later, though, he'd gone out to a drive-in restaurant and come home with burgers and French fries for both of them. The next night, when she'd served up a still-smoking chicken that resembled a heap of coal, he'd suggested they make peanut butter sandwiches.

After the first couple of days, though, he hadn't bothered to humor her. He didn't even invite her along when he left to scrounge a meal.

Before he deployed, he told Melody, "I'm not eating chop suey over there, I'll tell you that much."

"It's Vietnam, not China."

"So what?"

"Chop suey is Chinese food."

"What's the difference? I'll tell you what, I'm not eating whatever those people live on."

"Guess you'll get by just fine on C rations."

He fixed her with a look. "Guess I'll have a hankering for American home cooking when I get back. Since you like to spend all day watching soap operas, you can tune in to Julia Child instead, and learn something."

"Julia Child makes French food."

"How come you're nitpicking about foreigners all of a sudden? Why you giving me sass when I'm going to *fight* for this *country*?"

She figured she'd have plenty of time to learn to cook while he was gone, but who wanted to slave over a hot stove in the heat of a Southern summer? Instead, she'd decided to knit him a sweater to send in a care package, and went looking in his bureau drawer to check his size.

That's when she found his robe and hood, his UKA member card and pendant, copies of *Fiery Cross* magazine, and tucked into the pages of a dog-eared handbook, the damning newspaper clipping he'd so proudly preserved.

Raleigh in late July 1966—they'd been dating a few months by then. He'd claimed he was going on a fishing trip with his buddies, but his story hadn't rung entirely true. She'd spent that steamy weekend agonizing that he'd gone off with another girl, but dismissed her fears when he'd proposed the following weekend.

What a fool she'd been. She might have forgiven him for a last fling, but this? Never.

"Melody! Where are you?"

Honeybee, with supper, though it's nowhere near six o'clock yet, let alone the requested seven. Maybe *her* subconscious maternal mind sensed her daughter's raging hunger.

Yet when she opens the door, Honeybee says, "Oh, thank goodness! I've been trying to call you, and I was worried when you didn't answer."

"I was napping," Melody lies, "and I didn't hear the phone."

"I'll just turn the ringer up." Honeybee goes straight to the kitchen, moves the curly cord aside, and pushes the notched lever on the base all the way to the right.

"There. You won't be able to sleep through that. Now let me show you what I've brought."

In addition to Raelene's chicken à la King and more infant formula and diapers, she has a chocolate cake with *Happy Birthday, Travis* piped in blue frosting.

"But . . . Travis isn't here."

"That doesn't mean we can't celebrate his birthday. I thought it would be nice to invite his parents over later, and Daddy and Raelene. We'll have a nice little party, and—"

"Mother, no! No parties. No company!" Seeing Honeybee's expression, she adds, "Please, I appreciate it, really I do, but all I want is to eat my supper and go to bed. I'm just exhausted."

"You poor thing. Here, get off your feet." She pulls out a chair, and Melody all but collapses into it.

Her mother stands behind her, stroking her head and crooning reassurances.

Honeybee's faults—the pride, the overprotectiveness, the strength—make her a wonderful mother.

A mother who's lost a precious child.

For the first time in her adult life, Melody comprehends Ellie's death with crushing maternal perspective. No wonder Honeybee had wailed and fainted her way through those terrible dark days. Yet for her family's sake, she'd fought her way back.

Melody turns and hugs her hard, whispering, "Thank you."

"For supper? Why, Raelene made it. All I did was—"

"For everything."

It would be such a relief to confess the whole sorrowful situation and cry on her mother's shoulder. But when she takes a deep breath, the wisteria-scented air reminds her of the conversation on Cyril's porch, and she'd promised him she wouldn't tell.

Oh, Mother. I'm so sorry I can't spare you more heartache than anyone deserves in this lifetime.

GYPSY GAZES AT the television just as she had the newspaper's front page this afternoon, seeing it and yet not, like a child watching clouds drift by. Only this time, the innocuous image doesn't whirl without warning into a terrifying storm of speculation.

February 13, March 23.

Those are the dates when Oran had given her candy that could only have been laced with some kind of sedative.

On those same dates, a killer had crept into two households, one in Sheepshead Bay, the other in Bay Ridge, and murdered all but one member of each family.

Gypsy hadn't paid much attention to the first slaying back in February, though she'd read about it in the papers. She always moves past articles that don't tick Oran's apocalyptic list.

The second crime was harder to ignore. The press was whipped into a gruesome frenzy unseen since the Boston Strangler case a few years back. Soon New York's killer earned his own macabre nickname: the Brooklyn Butcher.

Gypsy had overheard Carol-Ann talking about it to her friends at school.

"My parents are wigging out about the psycho killer on the loose! They keep telling me to be careful, and they, like, barge into my room to check on me all night long. They think someone's going to break in and kill us all in our sleep."

"Not *all* of you," Connie Barbero said. "He leaves the teenaged daughter alive."

"Groovy. I wouldn't mind being an orphan."

She'd giggled, and Gypsy had fumed. Carol-Ann didn't know how lucky she was, living her charmed life with two doting parents, her own bedroom, a fashionable wardrobe, and Greg.

Oran hadn't warned Gypsy about the psycho killer, and she'd noticed that he'd been acting cagey from time to time. Does that mean—

No! He's just far more fixated on the looming apocalypse than he is urban crime. As for the skittishness, she'd come up with a theory one day when he'd asked whether she wished she had brothers and sisters.

"What? No! I like it just the two of us."

He'd been silent, staring down at his hands, clasped as if in prayer, and it had occurred to her that he might be seeing a woman. Maybe he thought she wouldn't like that.

He'd be right.

Maybe he's involved with someone, and that's why he's seemed so furtive. But would he drug his own daughter just so that he could sneak out on a date?

On television, a wayward dog snatches a woman's purse.

Oran's voice echoes in Gypsy's head. *"Can't trust anyone these days."*

That's what he'd said not long ago after a sweet-looking little girl had tried to pickpocket him on the subway.

"I'm telling you, man, you have got to be careful out there! Keep an eye out for trouble because you never know who's out to get you."

Yes, and he'd cautioned Gypsy to be careful crossing the street after that deadly hit and run on Webster Avenue. And when she was younger, he'd told her to stay away from the drug dealers who congregate on the corner by their building.

"I don't want you turning into a strung out junkie like your mother."

"Don't worry. I don't want to be like her in any way."

"Just stay away from those freaks and stay strong. Linda is spineless and pathetic."

It's true. Her mother never defended herself when she and Oran argued—rather, when Oran raged at her. She'd just sit there staring into space, sometimes with tears rolling down her cheeks as he spewed scornful Bible passages about weak women.

Gypsy doesn't want to think about Linda right now, or wonder what happened to her.

She tries to lose herself in a televised chase scene as the thieving dog escapes and its owner, caught red-handed with the purse, is jailed. He explains to a fellow inmate that he hasn't always been law-abiding, but this time, he's innocent.

The character's name is Gypsy. A sign?

"Signs are everywhere, man," Oran's voice reminds her. *"But only the chosen ones recognize them. You and me . . . we look, and we see, and we know . . ."*

On-screen, the dog finds its way to Sister Bertrille on a beach with orphans.

Gypsy thinks again of Carol-Ann's callous comment about her parents being murdered.

Again, thoughts of her own mother barge in.

Linda wasn't maternal by any stretch of the imagination. She always seemed glad to see Gypsy, though. And no matter how little attention she paid her daughter, she never left without saying goodbye.

Never, until her final visit. One morning, she was gone. So was their shag rug. Oran had found it in a dumpster, good as new except for a couple of stains and worn spots. Gypsy misses that rug.

On TV, *The Flying Nun* has vanished, a grim news anchorman in its place, interrupting the program with a special bulletin.

The reporter begins, "Tragic news tonight out of Memphis . . ."

Chapter Eleven

Friday, April 5, 1968
Fernandina Beach, Florida

Melody forces herself out of bed and opens the shades, expecting to see a grim gray sky weeping the same tears she'd cried into her pillow last night. It betrays her, deep blue and streaming sunbeams.

She pads into the kitchen and notices the wall phone receiver dangling from its curly cord. Her mother had wanted to spend the night on the davenport, but Melody insisted she go home. Honeybee called, though, twice, to make sure everything was still all right. This time, Melody really was asleep. After the second call, she took the phone off the hook.

Now she replaces the receiver and turns to the fridge. The phone rings before she can open it.

"Melody! I tried to call you last night, and—"

"You did call me last night, Mother. Twice."

"Well, I called again after that, and it kept ringing busy. Gracious, I had half a mind to send Daddy over to check on you, but he said you'd probably taken it off the hook and gone to sleep."

"He was right, and how many times can you call to make sure I'm all right?"

"That's not why I called you the second time. I

wanted to be sure you'd heard about the assassination, and I figured you—"

"*Assassination!* President Johnson?"

"Martin Luther King."

"*What?*"

"Shot dead last night in Memphis. Now, I did think it was disgraceful, the way he was riling people up, but he was a Christian and a man of the cloth and I . . ."

Melody's knees buckle under the weight of tragic shock. The phone's cord won't reach the kitchen chairs. She sinks down onto the linoleum, leans against the cabinets and closes her eyes as Honeybee chatters on.

"Shot dead last night."

April 4. The civil rights movement's most prominent leader, who'd hoped that one day, black and white would no longer matter, had been assassinated on her make-believe due date. All that hope and promise, shattered with an assassin's bullet.

Oh, Lord. Cyril will be devastated.

She cuts into her mother's monologue. "I'm sorry, but I've got to run."

"Are you in labor?"

"I just have to go to the supermarket. There's no food and my grocery list is a mile long."

Wrong thing to say.

Honeybee pounces on it. "I'll come right on over to get the list and then I'll go downtown to Food Fair."

"No, please, Mother. I need to do this on my own."

"Don't be silly! It's the least I can do. See you soon!"

Melody hears a click. She drops the receiver and reaches for a drawer handle to pull herself up. One tug and the drawer slides forward and drops out, narrowly missing her head. Flatware clatters around her. She ignores it, crawling to the locked back door so that she can use the doorknob as leverage. It takes a few wriggling tries.

You are not helpless, not a victim.

A brave, strong, enormously pregnant woman . . .

Only when she's in the car on her way to Barrow does she realize she's still wearing her nightgown, had left the telephone receiver dangling from its cord, and forgot to lock the house. Not only that, but she punctured her knee on fork tines. She blots blood with the hem of her nightgown. Nothing matters but getting to Cyril.

Ordinarily, he'd be behind the counter at Morrison's Meat Market on the mainland at this hour on a weekday, but there's a sign on the window. CLOSED TO HONOR MLK.

Driving on, she sees similar signs on other businesses, not all of them Negro-owned. The world, according to one radio announcer, has shuttered and shattered overnight. He delivers frenzied news bulletins about the Memphis assassin manhunt, rioting in Washington, nationwide despair.

On Barrow, as on the mainland, all is quiet. Driving over the intracoastal bridge, she looks for the young brothers who fish there. They always turn to admire the Camaro, and the last few trips, they'd shyly returned her wave. Today, there's no sign of them, or of another soul as she bumps along the dirt road to Cyril's place.

His beat-up car isn't out front. She pulls up and parks. The engine and radio give way to chirping birds and humming insects, and as she approaches, excited barks from Otis inside the house. She tries the door. Locked.

Shuttered. Shattered.

Otis barks and then whimpers for a while as she waits on the porch, but then quiets. She pictures him on the other side of the door, nose on his paws.

"It's okay, boy. I'm not going anywhere. I'm here."

She settles into the rocking chair with the bloody hem of her nightie draped over the gash in her knee.

She remembers a gray-haired woman with blood-stained white pumps.

December, up Macon way.

The pastor who'd answered her knock that day wasn't at all what she'd been expecting. He reminded her of her grandfather, with a pot belly and a mostly bald head.

"You need a referral, ma'am?"

"I . . . I, um . . ."

"It's all right. You come right around back to my living quarters and I'll get you started and on your way."

He sat her down in a parlor filled with comfortable antiques and books. She tried to eavesdrop on the phone call he placed from the next room, but his voice was muffled.

After a couple of minutes, he reappeared with a glass of sweet tea. "Someone is on the way. I have to be at choir practice in ten minutes, but you can wait right here for her."

His eyes were kind. No judgment. He'd wished her well. "I have a spare room upstairs," he'd added. "In case you need a place to spend the night when . . ."

When it's over.

Oh, how she longed for it to be over.

What-ifs jabbed her as she sat stiffly on the nubby green davenport. She sipped the tea but there was too much sugar for her liking, so she set the glass on a coaster and clasped her hands in her lap.

On the bookshelves, modern novels were sprinkled among dog-eared classics. Sue Kaufman's *Diary of a Mad Housewife* alongside *Uncle Tom's Cabin.*

She thought of Charlene, married to Gary. Gary, burning his draft card. Travis, burning crosses.

Was this the courageous choice, or the cowardly one?

A middle-aged woman showed up to drive her to another town. She had a towering blond beehive and a deeply tanned face, and had called Melody "hun." She'd brought along her knitting, pink yarn poking out of a bag on the front seat between them. They'd made small talk, sharing no personal details—not even names. Unnecessary, the pastor had said. Easier that way. Safer.

They arrived at a little house tucked at the end of a magnolia-bordered lane. Melody thought of the Brothers Grimm, and how the cannibalistic crone had lured Hansel and Gretel, disguising her lair with sweet confections.

Two vehicles were parked out front. One was a pickup truck with Georgia plates. The other had North Carolina plates and was occupied. A redhead, who appeared to be in her early thirties, sat in the driver's seat, smoking a cigarette and reading a movie magazine. Melody sat huddled on the front seat as the two women exchanged longtime acquaintance pleasantries.

"How's that little grandbaby of yours doing?" the redhead asked Beehive.

"Gettin' bigger every day. Already outgrew the sweater I made her, so I'm knittin' a new one for Christmas."

Melody had stared down at the pink yarn and thought about the baby inside her and wondered how far along might be too far along for . . . this.

There were no rules regulating the procedure itself, only laws making it illegal. And she knew nothing about obstetrics, beyond basic birds and bees information.

After some time—twenty minutes, an hour, maybe several—the screen door creaked open. Redhead closed her magazine, propped her cigarette in the dashboard ashtray, and got out of the car.

The woman in the doorway appeared to be in her late forties, maybe early fifties, with a weathered face and an unkempt, lopsided salt-and-pepper bun. She wore a wedding band, a house dress, and white pumps. Her arms were wrapped around her midsection as if she were cold, or in pain, or . . .

Bereft.

"All right, there, Dottie?"

"Always am, ain't I?" the older woman told her escort, as her eyes met Melody's. No tears. No shame. Nothing at all.

Chilled, Melody cast her own gaze downward, and saw that the woman's leather shoes were spattered in blood.

The redhead had helped her into the passenger seat and driven her away.

Melody's driver had turned to her. "You ready to go on in, hun?"

"Does it . . . hurt?"

"There's a lot of things in this old world that hurt a whole lot worse."

"I didn't mean me, I meant . . . does it hurt the baby?"

She saw the woman wince behind her reassuring smile. "It's all over real quick, that's what I know."

Melody closed her eyes, bowed her head and whispered, "I can't."

Inside Cyril's house, Otis whines and scratches the door. Inside Melody's belly, tiny feet and fists hammer as if to break free.

"Come on out," she whispers. "Come now, and when your daddy gets back, he'll take care of us. It's going to be just the three of us, forever."

She rocks the chair, cradling her unborn child and staring at the wisteria blooms dripping over the porch rail, until the sun rides high in a clear sky hung with puffy white clouds. *Haint* blue, Cyril calls it, like his front door and her parents' porch ceiling and Travis's eyes, too.

You couldn't see the shade in the newspaper photo she'd found in his drawer, but their expression was vivid. Those eyes beamed with hatred, and were unashamed for it.

How could she never have seen him for what he truly was? Had she been blinded by . . .

Not *love.*

She'd never loved him, though she'd assumed she had, before she ever grasped what love was.

Travis had slipped so easily into her life that it would never have occurred to her that he didn't belong there. Because women like Melody grow up and date suitable men from good families, with nice looks and perfect manners and enough money to buy a house and support a wife and children. Women like Melody hope that one of those will pick her to be his bride, and when he does, they say yes, just as their mothers and grandmothers had. Generations of women, saying yes . . .

"I want all your dreams to come true, Melody . . . a husband and children . . . a family, a home of your own . . ."

If she hadn't come across the evidence in Travis's drawer, would she have gone years, decades, without sensing it? Would they have raised a family and grown old together? Or would she have looked into those eyes of his one day and seen the truth?

Haint blue doesn't always ward off evil. Sometimes, it harbors it.

Greg Martinez stops Gypsy in the hallway before her first class.

"Hey, there. You got away from me yesterday," he says in his slightly Spanish-accented English, smiling down at her.

"The bell rang. Everyone got away. That's what happens when school is over, you know?"

"Yeah, but most people don't rush out like the devil is chasing them."

"Maybe he was." He crooks a dark brow, and she shrugs. "I just had some stuff to take care of at home."

"What kind of stuff?"

"Homework. Chores."

Trying to figure out whether my father drugged me.

"Did you hear about the assassination?"

"Who didn't?"

"Upsetting, isn't it?"

"It's an assassination. Of course it's upsetting." Not nearly as upsetting as what's going on in her head, though, or at home.

"Bet I can make things better for you."

"I doubt that."

Greg rests a palm on the row of lockers just above her head. She notices his white teeth and sexy dark sideburns.

"Go out with me."

"Why?"

"Why?"

"Why are you asking me out?"

"Because you're foxy."

"There are plenty of foxy girls around here who'd be happy to date you."

"You're the only one who's smart, too."

"Yeah, well . . . I won't argue with that."

He grins. "What do you say? Coke date tonight?"

"I guess. Sure. Why not."

"Outta sight! We can talk about it in class." He flashes another smile and walks away, calling, "Hey, Pflueger, wait up!"

What are you thinking? What are you doing?

She doesn't need any complications right now. She has to take it back.

But Greg has caught up with his friend Ricky Pflueger and disappeared into the crowd.

She turns with a sigh that turns into a gasp. Connie Barbero is behind her. *Right* behind her.

"Saw you talking to Greg. What about?"

"The assassination." Gypsy sidesteps her, hugging her stack of books against her chest as she heads toward her first class.

"Um, excuse me? I'm speaking to you!"

Gypsy ignores her.

"So *rude*!" the girl calls after her.

Connie Barbero is the least of her problems today, and a date with Greg Martinez is no remedy. But maybe she deserves an escape. Maybe, just this once, she can be just like anyone else.

SQUINTING INTO THE sunshine, hair streaming behind her in the warm, briny wind, Melody drives back from Barrow with the top down.

The car radio reports violence spreading in cities across the country. Washington is burning now, as is Chicago. The president has deployed the army and national guard.

Where are you, Cyril?

On the mainland, most restaurants are closed. Passing a seafood shack that isn't, she smells deep fried goodness wafting in the air. If she'd gotten herself dressed this morning, she could pull into the parking lot, march up to the window, and order up the biggest platter they have. Shrimp and oysters, onion rings, hush puppies . . .

But this is a small island. People will talk about the crazy housewife roaming in her nightie.

A little farther up the coastal road, the curb service drive-in is open, though not busy on this somber afternoon. She chooses an intercom-equipped parking space at the back of the lot by the outhouse, scrapes some loose change from the glove compartment and orders as much food as she can pay for. Then she darts into the outhouse. It's wretched, but she has no choice.

Back in the car, Bobby Goldsboro is singing "Honey" on the radio, and she craves a sticky slick of it oozing over a buttery biscuit, even though the song is about a girl. She flips the knob to find a fresh news bulletin.

". . . and at this hour, in Memphis's Negro District, thousands of mourners are gathering at the RS Lewis Funeral Home, where the Reverend King lies in an open bronze casket . . ."

She remembers all those strangers filing past poor pale and pasty pink Ellie.

A carhop walks toward her, bearing a hamburger, French fries, and a chocolate milkshake on a tray. She's young, black, and strikingly pretty, with long legs beneath her short uniform skirt.

"Here you go, ma'am. Enjoy." Her eyes are sad, her voice and her smile faraway.

Watching her retreat toward the building, Melody wants to summon her back and ask how she's doing on this sorrowful day, whether she's okay. Would it be wrong, though, to speak of what happened? Yes—like Amy Connors and Debbie Mason, first in line to weep over a death that isn't hers to mourn. This time, the loss belongs to this young woman . . .

And to Cyril.

She knows, just *knows* that he's gone to Memphis. He'll want to pay his respects to the man who'd had a dream that would have changed countless lives.

The hamburger swims before her eyes and she's

certain she can't possibly force food past the lump in her throat. Yet she manages to swallow the first bite, for the baby's sake.

A carful of teenagers pulls into the parking lot. It, too, is a convertible. The driver and his female passenger are blond and sun-kissed; the three boys in back are perched parade-style atop the seat. Cream's "Sunshine of Your Love" blasts from the speakers. Not a care in the world.

Melody finds Clapton's psychedelic guitar riff on her own radio and gobbles the meal as she drives home. Rounding the corner onto her street, she sees her mother's car parked at the curb. And her father's. Why isn't he behind his desk down at the savings and loan? And . . .

Is that her father-in-law's new gold Caddy? Yes, and Rodney Lee Midget's turquoise Impala, and . . . a police car?

And all those neighbors gathered on the sidewalk out front . . .

It can only mean one thing.

Travis.

Brooklyn

ORAN WATCHES DOOMED actress Sharon Tate stare at herself in the mirror. She knows she's about to die. What is she thinking? Is she frightened?

She's blonde, with hazel eyes, but her delicate features remind him of his Gypsy. That's what had drawn him the first time, back in December. Four months later, it's what makes this particular scene so hard to watch.

This isn't how he'd planned on spending the day. He'd arrived at the clinic on time this morning only to find it closed for the day. Carla had been there, hanging a sign on the window.

"Too dangerous, Dr. Brooks said. Negroes are rioting all over the city. It's not safe to be out on the streets today. Get home safely."

"You, too," Oran had told her.

Passing the movie theater, he'd noticed the marquee: VALLEY OF THE DOLLS–ABSOLUTELY THE LAST CHANCE! 5 MORE DAYS!

It's been playing since before Christmas, and he's seen it, what, ten times? Twelve, now?

Movie theaters have been a haven since he'd been a kid, when his mother would dump him off at Loew's Coney Island for hours. There in the dark, he'd never cared where Pamela had gone, what she was doing, or with whom. He was content to watch the same film back-to-back until he knew the lines and the characters felt like real people, losing himself in a fantasy world where his mother didn't even exist. Later, it had been the same with Linda.

When she went into labor in the spring of '54, Oran split.

Gypsy Colt was playing at Loews. He sat bathed in the big screen's Technicolor glow, erasing Linda, like his mother, from his consciousness. But his child . . .

Oh, his child came alive before his eyes. He envisioned a daughter, a glorious beauty with black hair, a brilliant mind, a passionate soul.

His first true prophecy.

The moment he'd lain eyes on his baby girl, he'd embraced his mission with fresh fervor. He would deliver her—deliver them both—to eternal salvation.

Soon he will.

Last chance . . .

When he'd seen that marquee, he'd walked into the theater and bought a ticket for the first showing. Now, halfway through the second, Oran wishes he hadn't come, or hadn't stayed.

He shifts his weight in his seat as the beautiful Sharon Tate toys with the orange bottle of sleeping pills.

He has a similar bottle at home, stolen in that February "armed robbery" Dr. Brooks had mentioned at that pharmacy around the block from the clinic. Having noted that the place is always deserted around closing time, just the elderly pharmacist there behind the counter, Oran had gone in one stormy night. The whole thing had taken a minute of his time. He'd worn a mask, but he hadn't had a gun, just made it look that way.

Crime is rampant in that neighborhood in these times. Even the press hadn't connected the robbery to the so-called Brooklyn Butcher murders the following week.

Had Gypsy?

She'd seemed suspicious of the chocolate eggs he'd brought her a few weeks ago. But then she'd eaten them and fallen asleep, just like in February with the Valentine candy.

But later, he'd caught her looking at him, wearing a thoughtful expression. As if she knew.

On-screen, Sharon Tate pours a handful of barbiturates into her hand, swallows them, and lies down to die.

Oran closes his eyes in the dark, reminding himself that his Gypsy gets just one pill at a time. She isn't going to die. No, she's going to live forever. And when Judgment Day comes, she'll agree that the sleeping pills he'd given her had been a small price to pay for eternal salvation.

MELODY SEARCHES HER soul for even a hint of shock or sorrow for Travis but feels only relief—and guilt for that. Her foot moves from the brake and the car rolls slowly toward the house where everyone is waiting to comfort the new widow.

"There she is!" someone shouts.

All heads turn, and she hears a collective outcry.

She steels herself for what lies ahead, jangling jitters just like before every musical theater performance back in her school days. Only this time, she's all grown up and she isn't . . .

Aren't you? Isn't that exactly what you're doing? Performing, acting, pretending to be someone else?

The front door flies open. Honeybee hurtles herself through it, arms outstretched, shrieking gratitude to Jesus. Melody's father and her in-laws and Raelene are behind her, trailed by Rodney Lee and two local police officers. She knows them both. The younger one, Scotty Jackson, graduated high school with Travis and Rodney Lee, and had been the valedictorian of their class. The older one, Duke Mason, is Debbie Mason's father and had grown up with Melody's daddy. Both men had been guests at her wedding last year.

Honeybee throws her arms around Melody. "Oh, thank heavens!"

She tries to pull back, but her mother is suffocating her in an embrace, rambling about Melody having gone missing and the kitchen being "ransacked" and "bloody" . . .

One of the cops intervenes. "I'm sorry, Mrs. Abernathy, but we'll need to ask Mrs. Hunter here a few questions."

"Ask away." She strokes Melody's hair back from her face. "I'm sure we all have the same questions. Melody, what happened to you?"

"To *me*?"

"When I got here and saw the kitchen ransacked and bloody . . . why, I called the police right away!"

"They're not here because . . . because something happened to Travis?"

"Oh, you poor thing. Of course not!"

She ventures a look at her in-laws, wishing she hadn't voiced the question. They just stand there, smartly dressed as always, faces stoic beneath their hat brims. Raelene and her father are beside them. Rodney Lee is apart from the others, watching Melody intently, eyes narrowed, lips pressed in a straight line.

"I was just frantic," Honeybee goes on. "I called around, and of course everyone rushed right over."

"You called *Rodney Lee*?"

"No, but when he drove by and saw the fuss, he stopped and he told me—"

"Shush, now, Honeybee, and let's leave this to the law," her father says, with a nod at his old pal Duke Mason.

The man's bushy salt-and-pepper mustache quirks above an all-business smile. "Mrs. Hunter? How 'bout we go inside. That all right with you?"

She nods and turns toward the house. Her mother turns with her, arm still resting on Melody's shoulders.

"If the rest of y'all could just wait out here," Mason adds, "we'd be mighty appreciative."

"But I'm—"

"Come on, Honeybee, let her go, now. She's just fine, see?" Melody's father gently tugs his wife away.

Mason holds the door open for her as though Melody's the visitor here, and Scotty leads her over the threshold, the hand on her elbow more of a clamp than gentlemanly guidance.

Mason closes the door behind them. Melody feels as though he's just locked her into a cell. Irrational, she knows. This is home. It should be a haven. Maybe it had been, right after the honeymoon, but not anymore. It's filled with furniture she and Travis had picked out together, the cabinet with their wedding china, and bare surfaces and wall space where framed photos of the two of them had been displayed. Now they're stashed in a drawer along with their satin-bound wedding album, hidden away just like his Klan regalia.

"Ma'am?"

"Pardon?"

"I *said*, were you harmed in any way?"

"Harmed? I'm fine, I just need a glass of water." She starts toward the kitchen.

"I'll get it for you." Scotty steps into her path.

She's struck by his resemblance to Travis, though the two men share no physical characteristics. Scotty is short and wiry and dark. Yet his smile steers clear of his eyes, like her husband's.

He has the same commanding air. To be expected, she reminds herself, seeing as he's an officer of the law, with above-average intelligence and the confidence—arrogance—to go with it.

He leaves the room. Officer Mason gestures at the davenport. "Why don't you just have a seat right there, ma'am. Try to relax. I've known you all your life. Known your daddy all his, too. Why, I was just down at the bank the other day, signing papers for my new mortgage. So you see, I'm here to help you. Why don't you tell me what's going on?"

"Don't you think that's a question I should be asking, not answering? Since this is my house, and I have no idea what all y'all are doing here?"

"Well, now, ma'am, it's like your mama said—she'd told you she'd be right on over but when she got here, you were gone, even though you were expecting her."

She weighs the wisdom of a quip—*If you knew my mother, you'd have taken off, too.*

But now doesn't seem like a good time to make light of things. And anyway, he does know her mother. Everyone in this town knows everyone else. She lets him go right on talking.

"Honeybee thought, bein' in your . . . condition, you know, that maybe you'd gone into labor and left in a hurry. And when she saw the kitchen—well, like she said, she called us, and everyone else."

"Not Rodney Lee."

"No, Mr. Midget got wind of it and came by, real chivalrous and neighborly like, and . . ."

Scotty's back, pressing a glass of lukewarm water into her hand.

"Here you go, Mrs. Hunter."

She ignores him, prodding Mason. "Mr. Midget came by, and . . ."

"Yes, ma'am, and when he saw the mess in the kitchen, he said—"

"Sorry to interrupt, but you might want to drink some of that water," Scotty advises, pushing the glass into her hand. "You're looking awfully flushed."

"What did Rodney Lee *say*?"

"Said you got real friendly with a Negro from out Barrow way," Mason tells her, "and that he might'a done something awful to you."

"He'd never hurt me!" she screams, plunking the glass onto the end table, and missing. It crashes to the floor and shatters into a storm of glistening daggers.

She hears her mother cry out beyond the window screens, and her father calls, "Everything all right in there, Duke?"

"Just fine, sir," Mason calls back. "Just a little mishap here, is all."

"So there *is* a Negro man? Why didn't you let us know?"

"Let you know what?" she asks Scotty.

"That this no good n—"

"Officer Jackson," Mason cuts him off with a warning look, and turns to Melody. "Mrs. Hunter, if someone's been bothering you, especially while you're pregnant and alone here with your husband away serving our country, we'd want to—"

"No one's been bothering me!" Melody's heart

pounds along in time with the baby's fists. "Where on earth would you get that idea, Officer Mason?"

"Like Rodn—uh, Mr. Midget said, these people have plumb gone crazy, torching and looting every—"

"Do you see any torching and looting here? Do you?"

"Well, now, ma'am, your kitchen sure looks like it's been looted," Mason says, "and there was blood all over the—"

"I cut my knee when the drawer fell! And then I went out!"

"Dressed like that? Without pickin' up all that mess, or at least wipin' up the blood?" Scotty shakes his head.

"Where'd you go, Mrs. Hunter, that you were in such a hurry to get out of here that you couldn't even get dressed?"

"For a walk!"

"You were driving," Mason points out.

The truth would have been so simple.

I heard about the assassination and I went to visit a friend.

"I drove to the beach. I walked on the beach."

Duke says, "Seems to me a woman in your condition shouldn't really be walkin' around on any beach. And in a nightgown."

"Let's get back to the Negro," Scotty suggests. "He put you up to this?"

"Did who put me up to what? I don't know what you're talking about."

"You said *he* wouldn't hurt you—so you do know Cyril LeBlanc?"

The name hits like a razor-sharp shard.

She thinks of Rodney Lee in his car on that February night when she was on her way to her parents' house. *"Someone's been putting crazy ideas into that pretty little head of yours."*

She'd read that dog-eared handbook in Travis's drawer. Read all about sacred duty to the brotherhood, and the oath to protect the sanctity of womanhood, the American home, and patriotism.

"Mrs. Hunter? Do you know Cyril LeBlanc?" Mason gazes at her, forefinger propped on the tip of his mustache. "He works behind the counter over at that colored meat market—Morrison's."

"I don't shop there."

"I wouldn't expect that you do. But you know him?"

"No. Now I'm going to ask you gentlemen to be on your way."

"Ma'am—"

"I'm sure you understand. All this fuss isn't healthy for a woman in my *condition*. So if you'll excuse me . . ."

She sails out of the room, closes the bedroom door behind her and turns the lock. Then she leans back against it, shaken, eyes closed, thinking of the white hood in her husband's drawer and the scars on Cyril's face.

WEARY AFTER A milk delivery shift that had begun in the wee hours and then all the excitement over at Travis's place this afternoon, Rodney Lee pulls up in front of the low stone block house he shares with his mother.

She's not home. On Fridays, she goes from her waitress job at the luncheonette to the bartending job she'd started a few weeks ago. This one is at a joint where Rodney Lee always liked to shoot pool with his buddies. Now that she's behind the bar, he stays away, even on nights when she's not working. No man wants to see, or even hear about, his mother falling all over the patrons, and none are off-limits when Ruth Ann Midget starts sampling as much as she's pouring. He's gotten into more than his share of skirmishes with guys his own age who think it's funny to tell him they'd messed around with his old lady.

Before he throws the first punch, he always says, *"Take it back, or I'll kill you."*

Some do, right away. Others hold out a little longer.

In the end, they all take it back. Even when it's the truth.

He parks the Impala at the curb and goes to the mailbox. A letter from Travis isn't the only thing he's looking for, but the other evaporates from his thoughts the moment he sees an envelope with the familiar red-and-blue-ticked border right there on top of the stack.

He opens the door, and his mother's cat pushes out past him. It brushes against his legs, and he kicks it.

"Whole damned house smells like your piss," he calls after it as it scampers into the weeds and disappears over the chain-link fence.

He slams the door and dumps everything but the letter onto the pile of unopened mail on the hall table. The heap topples, scattering envelopes—mostly overdue bills and collection notices—all over the floor. No draft notice today.

But it's coming. The first week in March, he'd been summoned for his armed forces physical. Stripped down and funneled along with hundreds, maybe thousands of fellow underwear-clad healthy specimens, he wondered how many would be dead in a year's time.

He'd passed the physical examination. And then he passed the mental aptitude tests that had tripped up his pal Buddy when he'd attempted to enlist right out of high school.

"I thought they were looking for soldiers, not geniuses," he'd complained after being deemed mentally unfit for the army. But Buddy has a second chance, now that the Pentagon lowered the recruitment standards. He reports to basic training in a couple of weeks.

Rodney Lee's Statement of Acceptability arrived in the mail before the month was out. It's just a matter of time before he's called up as an infantryman. He'll do his patriotic duty, just like Travis.

"I wouldn't say he's fighting for our country," Melody Hunter had the nerve to tell Rodney Lee the night he'd stopped to offer her a ride. Then she'd gone on to criticize President Johnson.

Until then, Rodney Lee hadn't believed the gossip about her, even though he'd heard she'd been driving Travis's car around Barrow Island last summer. He'd figured there was a logical explanation for that—maybe dropping off a housekeeper, some such thing.

Only she doesn't have a housekeeper, and her mama and daddy's housekeeper is white, and there was rumored to be a man involved.

A man who is not white.

What kind of woman would do such a thing?

The kind of woman who'd badmouth her own soldier husband during wartime, *and* the president of the United States. That's what kind of woman.

Something had clicked in Rodney Lee's brain the

night Melody Hunter had said those terrible things. He couldn't just stand by and let her get away with this.

Knowing she was safely occupied at her parents' house, he'd driven over to her place, parked on a neighboring block, and snuck through yards feeling like a damned burglar. The back door had been locked, but Travis had lived there alone before the wedding, and Rodney Lee knew he had a key hidden out back. That's how Mary Jane Foster used to let herself in while Travis was at work, so's she could have dinner waiting for him.

She sure can cook, Mary Jane. Travis didn't want leftovers around in case Melody came over unexpectedly and opened the fridge, so he always handed them off to Rodney Lee.

"Too bad Mary Jane's not the kind of girl you date out in the open," he'd told Travis over day-old fried Spam and Betty Crocker Scalloped Potatoes. "'Cause if she was, I'd be asking her to come as my guest to your wedding."

The invitations had been out a few weeks by then. Rodney Lee didn't have a steady, couldn't find a willing date, and didn't want to go alone.

"I oughta smack you good for even saying such a thing," Travis had said.

"I just meant, she's a bartender down at the Palace, and a few years older than us and not from a respectable family, is all."

"I know what you meant about *that.* But don't you think it would be a slap in the face to me if you brought my girl to my own wedding?"

"Aw, come on now, I'm just pickin' with you," Rodney

Lee said hastily. You don't cross Travis Hunter when he gets that mean gleam in his eye.

His wife sure has, though. Crossed him, that is. In worse ways than unpatriotic talk.

On that February night, he'd found a letter she'd written to Travis and left lying right there on the kitchen counter.

Turned out the things he'd been hearing were true, and then some.

Shaking with fury, he'd searched that house for more evidence. He hadn't found any, but the letter was incriminating enough. He took it home and wrote a note of his own, explaining the situation to Travis. He'd folded it around Melody's letter and sealed the whole thing into the envelope she'd already stamped and addressed.

Let her wonder what had happened to it. Let her worry about who might have taken it and knows her dirty little secret.

Her letter had been dated a few days before he'd found it. Maybe she'd have eventually sent it to Travis.

But what if she'd decided to burn it and carry her secret to the grave? If Rodney Lee hadn't come along, Travis would have gone on fighting for their country and his life with that woman on his mind and in his heart. A man deserves the truth, in case he never comes home—or in case he does.

He figured Travis would be upset, sure, but more angry than anything else. Furious, and who wouldn't be? He'd married the prettiest girl in town, had given her everything a husband could provide, and how did she repay him?

Rodney Lee skims the letter, then reads it more

carefully. Travis doesn't spell things out, but Rodney Lee knows what he's getting at. As a knight in the Invisible Empire, Rodney Lee bears a sacred duty to defend patriotism, and to protect womanhood and the sanctity of the American home.

Remember what we pledged when we took the oath. "Bear ye one another's burdens." You do what you have to do to make this right, Rodney Lee, just like that time on the Panhandle. I'll be forever grateful.

The Panhandle . . .

Rodney Lee flashes back to '65. They were on their way to visit a pal in Tallahassee that night, whole carload of them: Travis, Clive, Buddy, Hank Roberts, who shipped out to Vietnam a few months before Travis had, and Scotty Jackson, back before he was local law enforcement. If he'd been a cop then, none of it would have gone down the way it had.

Good thing he's a cop now, though, with a solid brain in his head. He'd known just how to handle the situation this morning. The moment he got the call that Melody Hunter had gone missing, he found Rodney Lee and told him to get over there in a hurry.

"Make it look like you're just driving by," he'd cautioned. *"But you're gonna want to be around for this."*

Rodney Lee figured Melody had either run off with Cyril LeBlanc, or been harmed by someone who didn't like what she'd been up to any more than Rodney Lee and the boys do. They'd never lay a hand on Travis's wife, though. That's the difference. You don't harm women; you provide chivalrous protection, even to the ones who stray so far from the fold.

En route to the Panhandle, they'd stopped off for some beers at a roadhouse. There were plenty of loose-looking women hanging around.

"Help Me, Rhonda" was playing on the jukebox as he gravitated over to one who was drinking gin, snapping gum, and smoking a cigarette. Her name happened to be Rhonda, like the song—one heck of a coincidence, he'd said, and she'd laughed. But he thought it was maybe in that "not with you, but at you" way the high school girls used to do with him.

When the song ended, Travis ambled over.

"Hey, Travis, this here's Rhonda."

"Sure, she is, and I'm Mr. Tambourine Man."

The girl returned his sly grin and promptly shifted her interest from Rodney Lee to Travis the way girls always did.

That night at the crowded roadhouse, the war was a dim and distant threat and the boys were carefree, living it up. They pounded a couple of rounds. Travis went to take a leak out back and got into an altercation with some mouthy colored kid working in the kitchen.

"He's bigger'n me," he'd reported back to Rodney Lee, "but not bigger than you."

"I'll take care of it," Rodney Lee said, and rolled up his sleeves.

Ten minutes later, they were back on the road to Tallahassee. Rodney Lee had found the kid more meek than mouthy, but he'd dutifully left him face down, trickling blood into the dusty back parking lot.

He hadn't even considered that he'd killed him till they stopped back into the Roadhouse again on the way home a few days later. "Rhonda" spotted them before they set foot inside.

"The police been around here askin' if anyone's seen all y'all or knows who you are," she warned them. "Unless you want to be questioned about a murder, you best go back to where you come from."

He'd been shaken up, hearing that. But Travis started laughing as soon as they were back in the car, clapping Rodney Lee on the back.

"Guess she really is 'Help Me, Rhonda,' 'cause she sure helped *you*, you big ol' outlaw!"

Rodney Lee's misgivings had transformed into pride, and they'd whooped up and yee-ha'd all the way back to Fernandina.

After that, they all called him Outlaw, the best nickname he'd ever had. A hell of a lot better than Rodney Lee Giant. Travis had come up with that one, too, back on the grade school playground, but he didn't mean no harm. He was a good guy. Everyone liked him—girls, guys, teachers, parents.

Someone like Travis deserves the best things in life. He doesn't deserve to die facedown in a foreign jungle like he's no better than some wiseass colored kid out behind a panhandle roadhouse. And if he does make it home alive, he sure as hell doesn't deserve the shame his fool wife will bring him.

You do what you have to do to make this right . . .

There's only one way Rodney Lee can do that, and this time, it'll take more than fists. It could be dangerous. Deadly, even for an outlaw. But when he joined the Invisible Empire, he'd sworn to protect his brothers' homes, reputations, interests, and families, and he'd meant it.

LeBlanc is tall—not nearly as tall as Rodney Lee, but lean and powerfully built. One on one, unarmed, things might not go in Rodney Lee's favor. He can't afford to mess this up. He'll call on Clive and Buddy to help. And Scotty can help him figure out how to handle this thing—make it look like an accident, or send a message loud and clear.

He folds the letter back into the envelope, puts it into his pocket, and begins picking up the mail that had scattered all over the floor. As expected, today's batch had brought nothing but more bills and collection notices, and . . .

He spots an envelope addressed to him and stares at the words printed in the upper left-hand corner.

Selective Service, Official Business.

On her way to meet Greg, Gypsy convinces herself that the date is a cruel prank. Maybe Connie and Sharon put him up to it, or even Carol-Ann. But when she rounds the corner by the Rexall, he's waiting out front. He looks relaxed, leaning against the plate glass window, hands in his pockets, one shoe propped on the brick storefront. He smiles when he spots her.

"You look pretty," he says, like she's wearing a fancy party dress and not the thrift shop purple plaid jumper and cardigan she wears to school every other day.

He holds the door open for her. The place is crowded with teenagers. She scans for familiar faces as they make their way to a booth near the back, half wishing someone from school will see her with Greg, half hoping nobody does.

The waitress comes over with paper place mats and laminated menus.

"Aren't you going to look at it?" Greg asks when Gypsy pushes hers aside.

"I thought we were having Cokes?"

"Not literally. Coke date—it's just a phrase, you know? Do you want a hamburger? Ice cream?"

"Oh, um . . . Whatever you want."

He smiles as if he hasn't guessed that Gypsy's never been on a Coke date before, or any date, never been here before, never shared a table with a boy. He's treating her as though she's a regular person, like everyone else, for a change.

They get a chocolate egg cream with two straws and share a plate of French fries. At first, Greg does most of the talking. He tells her about his family. His older brother was drafted and is shipping out to Vietnam in a few weeks, and his mother is a night shift nurse at Bronx Municipal Hospital.

"How about you? Tell me about your family."

"It's just . . . my dad. That's it. Not really a family."

"Nice that you have a dad. Mine took off when I was a baby."

She expects him to ask about her mother, but instead, he asks what she thinks about the assassination, and next week's biology test, and what kind of music she likes.

How, she wonders, does he know what to say, and what not to say?

Eventually, she relaxes enough to ask questions rather than just answer them. And she allows herself to lean in and sip from her straw while he's sipping from his, instead of waiting for him to finish. Once, their noses bump and they laugh, and she imagines him kissing her right there, across the table, but he doesn't. The date flies by, over too soon.

On the way out, they pass three steady couples they know from school, jammed into one booth. Greg stops to talk to them, including Gypsy in the conversation as if she belongs, and the others treat her that way. One of the girls compliments her on her outfit, and another notes that her sweater matches her eyes. They seem genuine, and Gypsy says thank you. Just like a regular person. Like one of them.

Out on the sidewalk, Greg says, "I'll walk you home."

"Oh, no, I'm fine."

"It's not safe out here tonight. You hear those sirens?"

"There are sirens every night."

"Not like this. There's rioting all over the city. It's bad."

"I'm not afraid."

"Because you're white?"

"Because I'm just not afraid."

"Of anything?"

She considers the question. "No."

Not of anything you'd ever understand.

Beneath a glowing streetlamp, he leans in and kisses her on the lips. Then he smiles, tells her to get home safely, and walks in the opposite direction, hands in his pockets, whistling.

Gypsy floats back to her building.

"Where have you been, man?" Oran's voice calls in the dark as she steps over the threshold.

"Out." She flips on a light, takes off her sweater, looks around for an empty surface, and resorts to the doorknob. The place is a mess. Even when it's clean, it's dirty. But it hasn't been clean in a long, long time.

Oran appears in the doorway—disheveled, unshaven, barefoot, wearing striped bell bottoms and an orange shirt that are too big for his scrawny frame.

"I've got a surprise for my Gypsy."

She goes still, closes her eyes, and braces herself for more chocolates. This time, she won't eat them, but she won't let on, either. Not until she's certain. She can say that she's full and that she's saving them for later, and then she'll examine them to see if—

"Hey, you're not looking!"

Gypsy opens her eyes.

He's stripped off the shirt, grinning. "Check it out, man."

"What?"

He points at his bony chest, and she leans in. "Is that a *tattoo*?"

"Yep."

"You got a tattoo."

He nods, looking pleased with himself. "It's a horse, you dig?"

"Is that . . . because of me?"

Something flashes in his eyes, as if she might be mistaken, but why else would he have a horse permanently etched on his skin?

"You're my Gypsy Colt. And you'll get one, too. '*Ye are of your father . . .*'"

He's quoting his favorite gospel. John 8:44.

"But I don't want—"

"'*And the lusts of your father ye will do . . .*'"

She wants to remind him that he skipped part of the passage.

"Ye are of your father the devil, *and the lusts of your father ye will do."*

But he isn't the devil. He loves her. It's a gift.

She sighs, eyes closed, face tilted to the heavens, refusing to allow the rest of the Bible verse into her head. "All right."

"Groovy. That way, we'll know that we belong to each other, in case . . ."

"In case what?"

"In case one of us forgets that and loses her way."

Chapter Twelve

Thursday, April 25, 1968
Fernandina Beach

Propped on three pillows to alleviate heartburn, Melody is too weary to heave her swollen body out of bed this morning. She's been up and down to the bathroom all night, courtesy of this boulder of a baby resting on her bladder.

Every time she fell asleep, she drifted right back into the nightmares that have haunted her sleep for weeks. She never remembers the details much past morning, though she's certain Travis and Cyril are in all of them.

She'd read in the paper that a local NAACP delegation had set out for Memphis in the early morning hours after the assassination. They paid their respects as King's body lay in state, then traveled on to Atlanta for the funeral. Governor Maddox, a segregationist who considered King an enemy of the people, had denied him a state funeral. But the somber procession passed the Capitol building from Ebenezer Baptist Church to Morehouse College.

She'd searched television news footage in vain for Cyril's face.

Riots and violence plague cities across the country. This is war, right here on American soil, and Cyril is on the front lines. Something might happen to him, could already have happened, and she'd never know. There will be no official knocking on her door to deliver the news, no outpouring of support, no one to even grasp her grief.

Ten days after the assassination, she'd attended the seaside Easter sunrise service with her parents. Watching pink and orange glaze the horizon out beyond the rustling sea oats and shadowy dunes, she experienced sharp nudges in her womb, as though that tiny person was trying to tell her something.

Yes. Dayclean.

That afternoon, she'd driven out to Barrow for the first time since April 5, keeping an eye on the rearview mirror for the turquoise Impala. She's been looking over her shoulder for Rodney Lee even when she's home alone, but she could no longer stay away from Cyril.

His place was still shuttered with an air of desertion, though, as if he hadn't been back since he'd left for Memphis. Otis was there, barking inside the house, but the doors were locked. She'd scrawled a note on a napkin from the car, left it fluttering beneath the doormat and drove home to wait for him. He hadn't come that night, or the next. He hadn't come at all.

And she's still had no word from Travis in Vietnam, though Doris had mentioned last week that he'd sent a lovely Easter card. She hadn't asked whether he'd been in touch with Melody. Of course she'd assume that he had. Why wouldn't he write to his wife?

Maybe his letters had gotten lost in the mail.

Or maybe Rodney Lee had gotten to him with his suspicions.

The police had followed up a few times, checking in on her, asking if she wanted to file a harassment report against the Negro. She'd pretended she had no idea what—or whom—they were talking about. She'd done the same with her parents.

"The only one who's been tormenting me is Rodney Lee Midget," she'd told her mother.

Honeybee, bless her heart, is the kind of person who can be led to recall things that had never happened, and to answer her own questions with speculation. She'd convinced herself, her husband, Raelene, and very nearly Melody, too, that Rodney Lee had been infatuated with Melody and having lost her to Travis, had decided to stir up trouble with outrageous claims.

Meanwhile, with every day that passes without a contraction, Honeybee has grown more concerned that Melody's "modern" obstetrician has allowed her pregnancy to proceed so far past her due date without intervention.

"He's a quack!" she'd stormed this past weekend at Sunday dinner. "What's his name?"

"Dr. Smith."

"What kind of name is that?"

"Smith? It's the most common name in the country," Melody had said indignantly.

"Well, where is his office located? I'm going to march in there and—"

"Now, Honeybee, why don't you just leave doctoring to the doctor?" her father said.

"He's the wrong doctor. I'm in a mind to get Doc Krebbs to pay Melody a house call just to make sure—"

"Mother, no! It's fine! I'm fine, and the baby's fine, just taking its time, and Dr. Smith says—"

"I don't care what he says! He's wrong!"

"Well, Dr. Spock says—"

"And I surely don't care what *that* man says!"

"You're the one who gave me his book," Melody reminded her.

"That's before I heard about all the unpatriotic rubbish he's been spreading."

"The war has nothing to do with his medical skills." *And it isn't rubbish*, she'd been tempted to add, but knew better. Honeybee wouldn't tolerate her daughter's disapproval of Vietnam any more than she does public opposition, whether from a renowned, Yale-educated pediatrician or long-haired hippies.

Raelene might share Honeybee's political views, but she'd stepped in to offer castor oil and herbal tea, home remedies guaranteed to bring on labor. Melody had promised to try them, and gone back to brooding about the impending birth, Cyril and Travis, her parents, Rodney Lee, and her in-laws.

Tuesday, she'd seen Dr. Stevens for a checkup. He'd listened to the baby's heartbeat and smiled.

"That's a good, strong little person you got in there, Mrs. Hunter."

"When do you think she'll be born?"

"Well, now, I don't know if she's a she . . ."

"She is."

". . . and only the good Lord in heaven above knows when she—or he—will be delivered. Mid-May on, I'd say, but you pay a mind to signs that it's coming sooner."

"If it was sooner—like, say, this week—would everything be all right? A baby this premature could survive?"

"Oh, sure, sure. These days, babies born even two months ahead of their due dates are pulling through just fine, so long as their mamas get to the hospital. Wonders of modern medicine, and all. But your baby's only one month out, so don't you worry none, Mrs. Hunter."

She'd gone home, gulped a hefty dose of castor oil, and made a cup of Raelene's herbal tea. She'd done the same yesterday, several times.

And now—

Out of nowhere, a savage cramp, the kind that seizes her calves sometimes when she's lying in bed, clenches her midsection. She cries out and sits up, doubled over until it passes.

Something's happened to the baby.

Terrified, she gets out of bed and hurries to the phone. Her first instinct is to call her mother. But as she inserts her forefinger into the dial and starts to rotate it, the pain comes again, and she knows.

The baby isn't in peril; she's about to enter the world.

Two weeks have passed since Oran took Gypsy to a tattoo parlor in Greenwich Village to get a horse inked just above her left breast.

"In case one of us forgets and loses her way," he'd said.

Her way. Not *his* way, or *their* way.

She'd been paranoid, at first, that he knew she was suspicious of him. But the more she thought about it all, the more she realized it was ludicrous to think that her father had not only slipped drugs into her chocolate, but is the Brooklyn Butcher. Imagine if Greg found out she'd even considered such a thing?

He'd think she'd lost her mind, and she wouldn't blame him. A couple of random coincidences don't mean that her father is a cold-blooded killer.

She's since put that notion out of her head, and her guilty conscience had allowed Oran to talk her into the tattoo.

"If you do this for me, Gypsy, I'll figure out how to get the bread to move us out of this dump."

"I don't want to move."

"I thought you hate it here."

She had, until Greg Martinez asked her out.

"I don't want to switch schools. I just wish we had a nicer place to live around here. If you can get the bread for that—"

"None of this matters. Paradise is waiting for us, Gypsy."

She put aside her suspicions and focused on her relationship with Greg. He takes her out on weekend nights, and she's pretty sure he's going to ask her to go steady tomorrow night. It's time. They've already gone to third base and he wants to go farther. Plus, he'd asked Carol-Ann to be his steady after taking her out just once—though their first date had been at a big school dance, and not just the drugstore.

There haven't been any dances lately, but if there were, Gypsy knows Greg would take her. And she's sure he'd eat lunch with her every day if she asked him to, instead of sitting with his friends at his usual table while she eats alone in a corner, same as always.

Sometimes, she does feel a little wistful walking into the cafeteria on her own. Today, carrying a bruised apple in a brown bag, she sees Greg waiting in line for the hot lunch. He's busy talking to Ricky

Pflueger and playing solo catch with a wadded piece of paper, so he doesn't see her.

The only empty table is adjacent to the one where Carol-Ann is sitting with Sharon and Connie. They stop talking and stare when Gypsy sits down. She ignores them, opening a textbook and taking a bite of her apple.

A shadow falls over the page. She looks up to see Carol-Ann. She's wearing a bright yellow shift.

Greg's favorite color. He'd mentioned it yesterday as they walked past the old lady's garden patch across the street, daffodils blooming where the crocuses had faded.

"Wow, Linda," Carol-Ann says, "I never would've guessed that *you* read *Vogue*."

"This isn't *Vogue*."

"You're funny. I mean, you obviously read *Vogue*, too." At her blank look, Carol-Ann adds, "Twiggy? This month's cover?"

"What are you talking about?"

"Twiggy! The skinny English model."

"You mean your idol?"

"Mine? No, I'd be famished if I just ate an apple for lunch, but good for you, dieting and all. I bet you'll look just like her in no time."

Gypsy holds her gaze, takes another bite of her apple, and returns to her book. After a moment she turns another page and asks, without looking up, "Why are you still here?"

"Because I'm talking to you."

"Why?"

"Because we're friends, so I thought I'd just—"

"We are *not* friends."

"Wow. Guess you think you're hot stuff now, with a tattoo and all."

How can she possibly know about that? It's hidden beneath Gypsy's blouse and brassiere. She hasn't even changed for PE ever since she got it, feigning period cramps. Greg is the only one who's seen it. He thinks it's far out, but he wouldn't tell Carol-Ann, of all people. He can't stand her, and he'd promised not to tell anyone.

Carol-Ann leans in. "He's just using you, you know."

No, he isn't.

She doesn't say it, though.

"He's seeing how far you'll let him go. That's all he wants."

Gypsy looks up at her. "You know what they say about apples, right?"

"Um, what?"

"They don't fall far from trees. And since my old man's a psycho lunatic . . ." She methodically devours what's left of the apple, core, seeds, and all, eyes glued to Carol-Ann.

She does her best to return the glare, but falters. "See you later, freak," she mutters, and returns to her own table.

Gypsy looks back at her book, the text gibberish as she forces the bristly mess down her throat.

Greg isn't using her. He's crazy about her. He says it all the time.

But how can Carol-Ann know about the tattoo?

Oran must be out there talking about it. Yes, and Carol-Ann ran into him again, preaching one of his sidewalk sermons. That has to be it.

She glances over to see Greg carrying a tray heaped with steaming food to a table filled with popular kids. She tries to catch his eye. If he spots her, he might come over. Not to eat with her. She wouldn't expect him to do that. But he might want to say hi.

Unfortunately, he doesn't see her. He sits in a vacant seat with his back to her.

I trust him, though. Of course I do. He'd never hurt me any more than my father would.

THE SUN IS shining on Sheepshead Bay this afternoon. Oran settles on a bus stop bench across from Holy Father High School, where Christina Myers is a sophomore. School doesn't let out for another ten minutes.

He'd left work early, telling Carla he'd received an emergency phone call from his daughter's school nurse while he was manning the phones during her lunch break.

"I hope everything is all right," she said as he hurried toward the door.

"She hurt her leg in PE. They think it might be broken. I'm going to take her to the doctor for an X-ray."

The windows are open at the school across the street. When the bell rings, he hears it loud and clear.

It doesn't take long for the sidewalks to fill with students. From a distance, dressed in their uniforms—green sweaters, plaid skirts, knee socks, and loafers—the girls look identical to him. Even at a closer glance, they're similarly pretty, with long hair. Some wear it teased at the top, or flipped at the ends, or tied up in ribbons.

He thinks of his Gypsy, trimming her hair every two months with kitchen shears.

"You can't even support me," she'd said once when he'd asked her if she ever wished for siblings. "How would you support other kids? And if I had brothers and sisters, they'd have a mother. I don't want a mother living here. Do you?"

"No! No way, man!"

It was the truth, but he could tell she hadn't believed him, and didn't bother to tell her that she had it all wrong. In time, his reasoning will become clear.

Just when he's certain he'll never find Christina in the crowd, he spots her. It's her slumped posture that gives her away, and the fact that she's alone, while the other girls congregate in pairs or groups.

Oran pulls on his white doctor's coat, crosses the street, and walks toward her with a purposeful stride. Walking slowly with her head down, she doesn't see him coming. He manages to graze her arm just as she passes.

"Sorry," he says and then, turning around, "Christina?"

She whirls, blank, and then . . . "Doctor!"

So, she remembers who he is, but doesn't seem to have connected him to what happened on that February night. He hadn't expected her to. He'd worn a ski mask, and she'd been unconscious after the first few seconds of her ordeal. According to the newspaper accounts of the crimes, she'd told police that the man who'd murdered her family and raped her had been a stranger, and she had little memory of the attack.

"Nice to see you. How have you been?"

"I . . . I've . . . I . . ." She trails off with a forlorn little shake of her head.

All around them, students are chattering and scattering. None give Christina and Oran a second glance, but he sees her glancing around as if to make sure.

"Are you all right, Christina?"

Her mouth opens and closes.

"Did something happen?"

"You don't know?"

Ah, there it is. He manages to contain his glee. "Know what?"

"I . . . my family . . . I lost my family, and . . ."

"Oh, Christina, I'm so sorry to hear that. Was there an accident?"

"No. Not an accident. I can't—I don't really want to talk about it. It's hard."

"I'm sure it is. Are you taking care of yourself? You look so pale, almost as if . . . well, if I didn't know better, I'd think . . ."

"What?"

"No, nothing. You're taking the medication I prescribed, aren't you?"

She looks at the ground. "Why do you ask?"

"If you weren't taking it, I'd suspect you might be . . ."

"What?"

She knows. He can see it on her face. Knows what he's going to say.

He, in turn, knows that it's the truth. He leans forward and whispers, *"Pregnant."*

Her head jerks up as if he'd held a lit match to her chin, and her startled eyes meet his.

"Of course . . ." He rubs his chin. "The Pill isn't foolproof."

She stares at him. He can see her trembling.

"Christina, do you think you're pregnant?"

She hesitates. "I don't know."

"Come to the clinic and I'll do a test for you. Tomorrow night at seven—we'll do an after-hours appointment, like before. If you'd like to bring your boyfriend . . ."

"We broke up."

"I'm sorry to hear that. This must be hard for you, trying to get through this without him, or your parents, your sister . . ."

"It is. It's really . . . it's hard."

"Do you have a guardian who can help you?"

"My aunt, but she's not . . . she won't understand about this."

He nods. "I'm sorry. You can count on me, though, Christina. I'll do whatever I can to help you. I'll see you at the clinic tomorrow night, all right?"

"All right. Thank you."

He touches her arm. "It's going to be just fine. I promise."

She turns to go, then swivels back. "Doctor? How did you know I have—I had—a sister?"

"You mentioned it, when we met at the clinic," he manages without missing a beat.

"Did I?"

"Yes, but you've been through so much . . . it's no wonder you're having trouble remembering. I'll see you tomorrow." He walks away, resisting the urge to look back.

Rodney Lee Midget's previous trips to Barrow Island had often been made in broad daylight, and always in the turquoise Impala accompanied by Buddy and Clive, two of his oldest friends, and fellow knights in the brotherhood.

They'd never cared who saw them; in fact, they wanted to be seen. Send a message, loud and clear.

We're here, and all y'all had best watch your step, know your place.

Tonight, they arrive from the mainland by boat, trolling along the Intracoastal under cover of darkness. Thunder rumbles in the distance as they tie up to a forgotten piling and wade in through the muck, but it'll hold off. Doesn't smell like rain, and there's none in the forecast.

By the time his feet hit solid ground, Rodney Lee has been devoured by mosquitos, though no one else seems bothered by them.

"Guess I'm just naturally sweeter than the rest of y'all," he comments, scratching furiously, and is even more irritated when Clive shushes him. "Ain't no one out here but skeeters and gators."

"Maybe, maybe not. No tellin' what goes on out here when they think no one's keepin' an eye on 'em."

"The gators?" Buddy asks.

"Not the gators! The Negroes!" Clive hisses.

"I'll tell you what one of 'em's been doin'," Rodney Lee says. "But not no more. Not after we're finished with him."

He thinks about the letter he'll be mailing tomorrow morning, letting Travis know that it's done, just like he promised. That man deserves peace of mind.

So do I.

Like Buddy, Rodney Lee has been ordered to report to basic training on Monday. This is their last chance to take care of business on Barrow before shipping out.

"Come on, let's move." Rodney Lee trains a flashlight's beam low on the tangled path leading away from the water. They follow it a quarter of a mile, to the one sandy, rutted road that runs the length of the island, parallel to the Intracoastal and the ocean.

Rodney Lee turns off the flashlight and shifts the can of kerosene to his right hand. Clive carries the lighter. It's a fancy antique one he inherited from his grandpappy, shaped like a pistol. When you press the trigger, a flame pops out of the barrel.

Buddy has a real pistol, and a coil of rope.

They're still not sure how it's going to go down. All depends on how much he fights back, though Rodney Lee can't imagine he would.

The place is dark when they get there, but the junker car is parked in the driveway. They'd spotted it parked at Morrison's Meat Market on the mainland last week, and known he was back from wherever he'd gone off to. Probably looting up in Washington, or maybe even Kansas City, he was gone so long. The riots there had started up almost a week after the assassination, with more than a hundred arrests and a handful of people dead. Or maybe he'd joined the masses of Vietnam protestors.

Shameful, all this public carrying-on and home front violence in a nation at war overseas.

They pull on their robes and hoods and Rodney Lee leads the way toward the house, footsteps softly crushing dry pine needles and magnolia leaves along the path, punctuated by rumbles of a far-off thunderstorm.

Behind him, Clive trips over a jutting live oak root and falls forward into Buddy, who lets out a grunt.

Inside the house, a dog starts yapping.

They freeze.

A deep voice carries through the open window. "Cut that out, Otis! It's just armadillos prowling around out there."

The barking continues.

Rodney Lee hates dogs, having been attacked by a mean one when he was a toddler. He falters, imagining a snarling monster bursting at him out of the darkness.

"We still goin' or what?" Clive whispers behind him. He's the kind of guy who's always itching for a confrontation, despite his small, wiry build. His parents scraped up enough money to send him to college, but he's planning to enlist in the Marine Corps right after he gets his degree and sheds his student exemption next month.

"Hell, yeah, we're still goin'," Rodney Lee snaps, as if there isn't a reluctant bone in his own body.

Outlaws ain't afraid of a stupid mongrel mutt.

Rodney Lee gestures to the others to follow him past the porch, around to the back. The property is thick with sabal palmettos and low-hanging live oak boughs, the air with bugs and humidity. Inside, the dog is still barking like crazy. Rodney Lee looks at Buddy, then gives a meaningful nod toward the window.

"Take care of it," he whispers, "the second we get inside."

"Take care of what?"

"The damned dog!"

"You mean . . . feed it?"

"I mean, kill it," Rodney Lee growls. "Better yet, don't wait till we get inside. If we can get a shot at it through that there window, then—"

"Keep your voice down!" Clive growls, like he's the one in charge of this wrecking crew.

Rodney Lee glares at him, wishing for the first time that he'd come alone tonight, as if this were a personal matter and not an official mission. But he doesn't own a pistol; his old man hadn't hung around long enough to teach him how to shoot one.

He'd taken off so long ago that Rodney Lee can't even recall what he looked like. Nothing to his memory but stale cigarette smoke, a nightly drunken rage, and a wedding band he'd hurtled at his wife the night he'd stormed out for the last time—headed for his mistress's bed, Ruth had told her son. A couple of times, she'd sent him to spy on the woman's house over by the tracks. Rodney Lee never saw his daddy there. But Mama, she'd had a man in her own bed right after he left, and there's been a parade of them ever since.

Two things that would come back to haunt Rodney Lee had occurred on his eighteenth birthday back in '62: he'd registered for the draft, and his mother had given him his father's gold wedding ring.

"You can use it when you get married," she'd said, like it was a symbol of wedded bliss.

He keeps it on his key chain, a reminder of the kind of man he never wants to be.

That's why he's been so torn up about Melody. Ain't right, what she's been doing to Travis.

The dog's barking is getting to him, every yap like a dull knife sawing at his frayed nerves. He creeps toward the window. It's propped open with a holey, rickety-looking wooden screen that looks like it would topple inward with a slight tap. He doesn't even have to get up on his tiptoes to look inside. The curtains are parted to let in humid night air, the room beyond shrouded in shadow. The dog is going crazy in there, and he wonders how the hell anyone can sleep through the commotion.

He turns back to tell Clive to take a shot in the dark, just for the hell of it.

There are no longer two men silhouetted behind him. There are three, and the third figure isn't wearing a hood and robe.

Before he can react, a deep voice says, "Get the hell off this property."

It can't be LeBlanc. No Black man in his right mind would confront three cloaked intruders.

But then lightning illuminates the scene, and he sees that he was wrong about that, and right about something else. Cyril LeBlanc isn't in his right mind. He's gripping an enormous meat cleaver, raised and ready.

He wouldn't dare use it, Rodney Lee assures himself. Black man kills a white man in these parts, in these times, and he might as well just slit his own damned throat.

"I said, get the hell off—"

"Yeah, we heard what you *said*," Rodney Lee tells him, "and we ain't goin' nowhere. We got some business with you."

The man snickers, shaking his head, not wavering one bit.

"What you got to say about Melody Hunter?"

Still LeBlanc holds the blade steady and utters not a word.

Thunder rumbles closer now, and something shifts in the sultry air, as if the temperature has just dropped a notch, and a storm might be rolling in after all.

"We know all about how you two been carrying on, and so does her husband. You're in trouble, so you best lay down your weapon and face it like a man."

LeBlanc doesn't move, but the next flash of lightning reveals eyes that are twin cauldrons of rage. He's not going to go down without a fight.

Jacksonville

"Mrs. Hunter?" Someone calls from far away, across a black void.

The hospital. She's in the hospital, and there's so much pain . . .

She starts to slip back.

"Come on, now, can you wake up for me?"

She doesn't recognize the voice. It isn't Cyril. No, it's a woman, yet she sounds so very much like him.

"Open your eyes, honey. That's it . . ."

Melody blinks up into bright light, bracing herself for the delivery room, and unbearable pain.

But the pain is gone, and she's not in the hospital after all. No bright lights, no Doc Krebbs, no strangers in surgical masks. She sees pale yellow walls, and a framed painting of a white duck floating on a rippling pond with a row of ducklings trailing after her.

"Where . . ." Her throat is too dry to continue.

"In the nursery," the voice tells her in that Creole

dialect, and she turns her head to see sun streaming in a window.

"This . . ." she rasps. "This is the nursery?"

A laugh, and a middle-aged Black woman in a white cap and uniform comes into view. "*This*," she says, turning a crank on Melody's bed, "is your room for the next week, until it's time for you two to go home."

She raises the top half of the bed, and Melody can see now that she is, indeed, in a hospital room. She's vaguely aware of other sounds—footsteps in the corridor, a cart rattling past, a crackly voice on an intercom, a baby wailing in the distance. But the nurse's words are loud and clear.

You two . . .

She looks down at her midsection, tucked beneath a soft beige blanket. It's not flat, but the enormous mound of stomach has disappeared.

"I'm Yvonne," the nurse says. "I'll be taking care of you today. How are you feeling?"

Groggy. Confused.

She thinks back.

She'd been at home, alone, frantic with pain. Had she been thinking clearly, she'd have summoned Dr. Stevens, but when you're helpless and hurting, primal instinct takes over and you call the person who's cared for you all your life.

Honeybee had materialized instantaneously, like Endora on *Bewitched*, and they'd met Doc Krebbs at the hospital. She remembers writhing in agony as they wheeled her into a delivery room, and hearing someone shrieking. Now, with a throat so sore she can barely swallow, she realizes the shrieks may have been her own.

Yvonne leans over the bed. Her eyes are warm and kind. "Mind giving me a wrist so that I can check your pulse?"

She extracts an arm from beneath the blankets, wincing at the effort, and wincing again when Yvonne gently presses her wrist. "T'engky."

Cyril says it that way, too. The first time she'd asked him what it meant, he'd laughed. "It means 'thank you,' and if you think I have an accent, you should hear my mama."

"All righty. Pulse is good."

"Are you . . . your accent. It reminds me of . . . a friend. Where are you from?"

"Live here in Jacksonville now, but I grew up on a little island off the coast of Georgia."

"Barrow?"

"Sapelo."

There are Gullah Geechee communities up and down the coastal low country. She can't assume that everyone with a patois might be connected to Cyril.

"Before, you said something about . . . the nursery?"

"Thought you were asking about the baby. That's where she is."

"She?"

"Yes, indeed." She pours water into a glass. "A little girl. Just perfect. Healthiest preemie I ever did see."

A little girl . . . perfect . . . healthy . . .

Melody's heart inflates.

I just knew it. I just knew I was having a daughter.

But then the word *preemie* hits her like a pin in

a balloon. She remembers the lies, and Travis, and Rodney Lee.

"Does she look . . ."

"Like you?" Yvonne finishes for her when she falters. "That's what every new mama is wanting to know before she lays eyes on her child. I surely did with my daughter, and she's the spitting image of me now that she's all grown up, but wouldn't you know that the first time I saw her, she was whiter than this bedsheet!"

Melody raises her eyebrows, and Yvonne grins.

"You see, I was young and I didn't know back then that it takes some time for Negro babies to get their pigment. Her daddy didn't know that, either, and oh, my, you should'a heard him!" Yvonne chuckles, shaking her head as she swings a tray over Melody's bed and sets the glass on it. "Tell you what, you sip some of this water for me while I go fetch your little girl and you can see her for yourself."

She sails out of the room.

Melody lifts the glass. Her hand is shaking. Water sloshes over the rim, running down her fingers. She puts the glass down.

Is it true? Will her baby be white, at least for a while, regardless of whether Cyril is the daddy? It wouldn't solve her dilemma, but will at least buy her some time to sort things out.

Her gaze settles on a vase of pink tulips. Who brought them? Could Cyril have . . .

But of course not. He wouldn't know she's here, she realizes, feeling more alone than she ever has in her life.

Then the nurse is back, placing a bundle into her arms.

A tiny, pale-skinned girl gazes up at her with enormous eyes the shade of a dusky sea, and Melody realizes that she'll never be alone again.

MARCELINE AWAKENS TO a predawn rain and a familiar, unsettled feeling.

Years ago, when Cyril, Sr., had gone off to war, she'd drift from slumber in sweet anticipation of dayclean, only to open her eyes to the sensation that something was wrong. It always took her a few waking moments to remember that her husband was in danger on overseas battlefields, but once she got used to reality again and the day settled over her, the uneasiness would lift.

"You ain't gotta do anything but wait for me to come home."

"You never did, though, did you?" She climbs out of bed and glances at that old red satchel full of his things.

Oldest story in the world.

A man, he goes and he does. A woman just waits.

But the good Lord alone knows what's going to happen when that buckruh woman's wait is over.

Maybe that's why Marceline's apprehension persists as she stands at the stove, stirring her grits. She can feel her husband's spirit boddun' around her.

"I know, Cyril. I been frettin' about that boy."

She'd heard about the violence unfolding in Memphis and Atlanta, and across the country. He'd turned up back home a few days ago none the worse for his sojourn if somewhat subdued, as though someone had dimmed a lamp behind his eyes.

It's to be expected. He's not the only one mourning the fallen civil rights leader. A tide of grief rolled across Barrow Island when the news broke, and the world beyond is more tumultuous than ever.

"That why you been boddun' me all the time now?" she asks Cyril, Sr. "Or is it something else?"

No reply, just raindrops pattering on the roof, and one of the cats crying on the porch.

She goes to the door to let it in. But when she peers into the wet morning gloom, there's no sign of a feline. And when she returns to the kitchen, she sees that the pot has boiled over, though she'd set it on a low flame.

"You tryin' to tell me something?" she asks her dead husband.

She eats the grits with butter and salt, remembering how Cyril, Sr., used to cover his with a layer of sugar. She never did care for that, and scolded him that their son would pick up the bad habit.

He hadn't, though. He's a good boy. A good man.

A better man than Mrs. Melody Hunter deserves.

Marceline had gone over to Amelia Island a time or two back in February and March, to see what she could see.

Fernandina Beach is a small enough town that everyone knows everyone else—the household help included. Through a series of casual conversations, Marceline had found her way to a young Gullah woman who worked for a woman who was in a weekly bridge club with Melody's mother, Honeybee.

"You ever happen to overhear any she she talk?"

In their shared dialect, *she she talk* is a certain brand of gossip—the kind she imagined a housekeeper might overhear from a gaggle of buckruh women, and she was right.

Honeybee had told the others how newlywed Melody and her husband had moved into a gray bungalow on Elm Street. He was in Vietnam now, and she was expecting their first child.

"That woman, she's all aflutter about her grandbaby," the housekeeper told Marceline.

Her grandbaby . . . and mine.

"Why you want to know all this?"

"I worked for the Abernathys years ago. Just wonderin' how it all turned out."

You got to be a trutemout', you heah me? her dead daddy scolded in her head.

Back in his day, she imagines, it was easy to be someone who always tells the truth. But in hers, when lives are hanging in the balance, sometimes the only way to get at the truth is with a lie.

Marceline had walked along Elm Street looking for the gray bungalow, knowing she'd find it before she crossed Eighth, where the neighborhood transitioned into Southside. There are a few white households in that part of town now, but she'd bet Travis Hunter's isn't one of them.

She'd have known the house by its description, but she'd spotted the red Camaro first. She'd heard about a buckruh woman driving it around Barrow a while back. At the time, she hadn't connected her to Cyril, and why would she?

Oh, son. What have you gotten yourself into?

She hadn't knocked on the door. She'd returned several times, though, just to walk past. And then one day, she'd crossed paths with a pretty, hugely pregnant blonde woman carrying grocery bags that looked too heavy for someone in her condition.

If she were anyone else, Marceline might have stopped and offered her a hand.

When they were close enough, the woman met her gaze with a friendly smile and a pleasant, *"Good morning."*

Marceline returned the greeting, surprised by it and by the sweet susceptibility in those big green eyes. She'd turned her head a few times after they'd passed each other, expecting the young woman to walk right on by the gray house, but no, she was unlocking the front door and going inside.

This, then, was Melody Hunter. Not at all crookety, far as Marceline could tell.

She stands and washes her half-finished bowl of grits down the drain. She never leaves dirty dishes in the sink, but she doesn't want to waste any time getting over to Cyril's. He'll be leaving soon for his job at the mainland meat market, if he isn't already on his way. Her heart races as she pulls on a dress and shoes and hurries out into the rain without an umbrella.

It lets up as she makes her way down to Cyril's place as fast as her legs can carry her along the mucky road lined with live oaks. With all the dry weather lately, the resurrection ferns had been curled and gray as the Spanish moss, but the rain has transformed them into lush, verdant fronds. A good sign, she tells herself.

At the turnoff, a mare and her foal doze beneath a lush canopy of branches. She spots Cyril's car out front and is momentarily reassured to hear Otis barking inside. But the dog isn't offering his usual friendly greeting, nor alerting his master to a visitor. He's distressed.

Marceline knocks. Cyril doesn't come, and it's

locked. When she calls for him, Otis lets out a yelp, recognizing her voice.

"Calm down, boy." She finds the back door unlocked, lets herself in, and the frantic dog hurtles himself at her.

"Shush, now. Shush. Cyril? Cyril! You here?"

The house doesn't smell of the coffee he boils every morning. She notes the pot sitting dry and empty on the stove, supper dishes in the drainboard, key chain hanging on a hook by the door. She tells herself he's merely sleeping, and why wouldn't he be, after all the traveling and such?

But in the bedroom, the bed is unoccupied and unmade. She'd taught him better than that.

"Where's he gone off to all sudden-like?" she asks her dead husband.

The dog whines, nudging her knees with his wet nose, and she looks down into his sad eyes.

Marceline LeBlanc does not cry. She didn't when she lost her husband, and she won't now. She lifts her head and closes her eyes in a quick prayer, then gives Otis a firm pat.

"Bet you need supshun, boy." Opening the icebox, she finds a paper-wrapped packet of bones Cyril brings from the butcher shop. She puts a large one into a bowl and sets it on the floor.

"You stay here and eat your breakfast. I'll be back."

She steps out the back door and stands surveying the property. The rain has let up, mud puddles pooling around the yard and dense foliage dripping. Must have been some storm, she thinks, spotting a broken bough on the vast live oak bordering the marshland path out back. Then milky sun breaks through the overcast sky, and she sees a flash of blue on a low-hanging branch.

Walking toward it, she tells herself that it's a house finch egg gleaming in a nest of Spanish moss, or water droplets catching the light just so.

But she knows better even before she's close enough to see that the branch didn't get torn off in a storm, and that wild horses didn't trample the tall grasses beneath.

Humans did that.

Eyes narrowed, hand trembling, Marceline reaches toward the broken chain snagged on a twig, dog tags and baby ring glinting in the morning sun.

Part V

2017

Chapter Thirteen

Friday, January 13, 2017
Savannah, Georgia

After a bumpy flight courtesy of a nor'easter moving up the mid-Atlantic coast, Amelia and Jessie land in Georgia on a sunny Friday. Heading for the baggage claim, they bypass a local information booth with brochures about the charming Southern city neither of them has ever visited before.

"Jess, I'm sorry you flew us all the way here and you don't even get to—"

"We'll come back someday to sightsee." She links her arm in Amelia's. She's nearly a foot shorter, a widow's peak parting her sleek dark hair above a pert, pretty face. "Friday the thirteenth is going to be your luckiest day ever."

"You're an amazing friend. How am I ever going to repay you?"

"By getting us to Marshboro. I'm still stressed from last night," Jessie says around a yawn. Driving to New York last night, she'd swerved into a ditch after nearly hitting a deer on the winding, snowy highway through the Catskills.

"That was so dangerous, Jessie. I really wish you'd just taken a connecting flight from Ithaca instead of risking your life so that we could fly together."

"I wasn't risking my life. Just the stupid deer's. And don't you remember what we promised each other when we met?"

"That we'd help each other find our biological families?"

"Exactly. I started this journey with you when I was eighteen. Do you think I'm going to miss a minute of the final stretch?" Her friend flashes her dimples.

"I love you, Jessie. And if you ever change your mind and decide you want to look for your birth parents after all—"

"No, I'm good." Jessie had long ago put aside her curiosity about that. But things are different for her. She'd been raised by loving parents who are still alive, and she's happily married with children of her own.

Amelia's life, by contrast, leaves a lot to be desired.

"Remind me to text the owner of the place we're staying before we get to Marshboro," Jessie says, settling back in the passenger's seat as Amelia takes the wheel of the rental car. "She said to let her know when we're ten minutes away so she can let us in."

"I'll wake you up when we get off the highway."

"I'm not going to sleep, Mimi. Don't worry. I'll keep you company."

She's snoring, head thrown back, before they enter southbound Interstate 95.

Amelia thinks back to ten days ago, when she and Stockton Barnes had followed the same highway north from New York to Connecticut. She's spoken to him a few times since—brief conversations about the still-unsolved double murder and the continued search for the grown foundling who hadn't been his daughter after all.

If he was devastated to get the news, he hasn't let on to Amelia—but he's a cop, and cops are expert compartmentalizers. On the other hand, maybe he's relieved. His life will be less complicated if he doesn't have a missing, abandoned daughter with ties to a double murder investigation.

"Hitting me with that paternity claim was obviously just another one of Delia's scams," he'd said flatly on the drive home from Bridgeport. "Her husband left her pregnant and moved in with another woman. So she found some stupid sap to sleep with. Guess she figured she had a better chance of getting financial support out of a New York cop than her loser ex-husband. Man, was she right. Stupid sap."

"You're not a stupid sap."

"I was back then. I believed her. I was losing Wash, and when I first saw that baby, I guess . . . it made the future seem less lonely, thinking I had a daughter. I thought that baby really was a preemie. She was so tiny and fragile, and she had so many problems . . . Now I know it's because her mother was an addict."

"But Bobby said Delia didn't get into all that until after the baby was born."

Barnes just looked at her.

Okay, so Bobby isn't the most credible witness in the world. Cynthia may not be, either. But Amelia has compared Barnes's childhood photo with Charisse's several times since that day. If her mind's eye were seeing only what it wants to, it wouldn't see a resemblance.

But Amelia can't unsee it. Nor can she ignore that Brandy had approached her as a client and shown her the lost baby ring.

Today, however, is about confronting Bettina's

family, and she pokes her passenger back to consciousness as she exits the interstate.

"Hey, we're almost there."

Jessie stretches and looks out the window. The sun is shining, the sky is blue, and they're traveling a straight, narrow east-west highway bordered on both sides by a grassy shoulder, tall Southern pines and utility poles. No houses, no businesses, no other cars on the road. No hotels or motels or even inns in the immediate area, but Jessie had rented what she'd described as a storybook cottage.

"Are you excited, Mimi?"

"*Nervous* is a better word for it, and maybe a little..." She swallows a lump, thinking of Bettina, wondering how many times she'd traveled this same road as a little girl growing up in the area.

Chances are, not many. She'd never learned to drive, and her family had been too poor to own a car. She'd never even been out of Georgia until a church youth group outing took her to Memphis. That's where she'd met Calvin, who was there visiting family. He was a few years older, already living in New York City.

"It was love at first sight, child," Bettina had told Amelia. "Your daddy and me, we just knew we had to be together."

They'd written letters for a year. Calvin had proposed in one of them. He'd only been to Marshboro once, for their wedding. As far as Amelia knows, Bettina had never returned after taking the bus to her new home in New York.

Their life together had been just as impoverished as her childhood had been, but Bettina wasn't one to complain about such things. About anything. That stoic, accepting nature had gotten her through some difficult times, but it had expedited her own demise, as far as Amelia's concerned. Her mother had ignored ominous physical symptoms until it was too late. It had taken Amelia a long time to forgive her for that, for dying—and for not telling Amelia the truth about how she'd come to her and Calvin . . .

Only for *that* truth to become a lie when Amelia's DNA linked her right back to Bettina.

The speed limit drops to 45 mph, and she spots a trooper hidden behind a clump of palmettos just beyond.

A little farther down, it drops to thirty as they pass a painted sign that reads, "Welcome to Marshboro, Georgia, Population 710."

"It's grown since I checked a few months ago. It used to be only 706."

"Wow." Jessie runs a hand through her short dark hair, and it spikes above her widow's peak. "Ithaca is *small*, but this is . . ."

"A post-millennial metropolis. That's what Auntie Birdie predicted back in 1989, when she came up for Daddy's funeral."

"She was a regular Nostradamus." Jessie consults the directions on her phone. "Keep an eye out for Main Street. That's where our cottage is."

They're on it. It's the only road in town. They pass a firehouse, a gas station with a Circle K, and a luncheonette.

"Slow down, Mimi—that's it!" Jessie points at a small structure just ahead.

It's white with a blue-painted door, perched between two churches. She spots a tire swing dangling from magnolia branches in front of one and knows Bettina's family had been congregants there. She'd shared fond memories of that swing.

"In springtime, child, that big old tree was just covered with blooms, and my cousins and I would pump our legs so hard, trying to soar up there and pick one."

As she pulls into the cottage's dirt driveway, Amelia sees that the church is, indeed, Second Baptist, and the sign out front reads "48th Annual MLK Fundraiser—All Are Welcome—9 a.m. to 5 p.m. Saturday, 1/14."

As she and Jessie take their bags from the trunk, an elderly white woman ambles over from across the street. She's wearing bare-toed slippers and a housedress.

"You must be Thelma! I'm Jessie, and this is Mimi."

The woman fumbles in her pockets. "Nice to meet y'all. I've got the keys right here some—" She breaks off, gaping at Amelia, as if seeing her for the first time.

"Are you . . ."

"She's on TV!" Jessie announces.

"You're an actress?"

"No, I'm on a program called *The Roots and Branches Project*."

"Well, bless your heart! I've never seen it. But you do remind me of someone, that's all," Thelma says, looking again at Amelia as she pulls the key from her pocket. "Why don't we go on inside and I'll show you around."

As they follow her toward the door, Amelia looks back over her shoulder, feeling like she's being watched from every window along the street.

Marshboro, Georgia

Seated in a window booth, Gypsy sips her third cup of coffee, craving a cigarette, and stares across the street at the little white house with a blue door.

Years ago, before she and Perry left New York, she'd learned how to cover a paper trail. Leaving an electronic one is a new concern, and the reason she's numb with exhaustion, having just spent seventeen hours driving a thousand miles from New York.

"But you flew here from Cuba, Gypsy," he'd pointed out yesterday afternoon as she was leaving.

"Well, I couldn't have driven, could I?"

"I don't think it's a good idea, a woman on the road alone in the dead of night, dead of winter . . . I'll come with you."

"*What?* You know I need you here to take care of Stockton Barnes and his daughter."

"I thought you were going to hire someone to do that, like the Harrisons," he said, as if they were discussing whether to send shirts out to be laundered.

She'd reminded him, yet again, that this—tomorrow—will be different. It has to be handled precisely according to her plan, and *he* needs to be the one to do it.

"Is everything okay, ma'am?"

She turns away from the window. The restaurant has emptied since she sat down an hour ago, and the waitress stands beside her table. "You haven't touched your fried chicken. I've never had a customer who didn't . . ."

She talks on, just as she had when Gypsy first arrived, ordered coffee, and sat staring at the menu.

She'd blabbed about how the fried chicken is the house specialty, has won awards, people come from all over just to taste it. Gypsy only wanted caffeine, but ordered the meal just to shut her up.

Now she pushes the plate away, knocking into her water glass and sloshing some on the paper place mat. "Sorry—Aunt Beulah, is it?"

"Uh, yes, this is Aunt Beulah's, ma'am."

"But you're not Aunt Beulah?"

"She's, uh, not a real person. It's just a name. I don't know if there ever was a—"

"Then you won't be offended," Gypsy cuts in, "when I tell you that the chicken is lousy."

The woman's eyes widen in dismay.

What are you doing?

Gypsy clamps her mouth shut. She's exhausted, nerves frayed, body still aching from clenching the wheel through Washington, D.C.'s rush hour last night and Savannah's this morning, with a Carolina ice storm in between. Exhausted, and steeped in the hot fury that had ignited ten days ago, when she'd discovered that Margaret Costello's daughter is alive after all.

"Why don't I just leave this here so that you can be on your way. Have a good day." The waitress tears a green check off her pad, drops it by Gypsy's plate, and scurries back toward the kitchen, ignoring the tip and dirty dishes on a newly vacated table in her path.

Gypsy hasn't had a good day since she'd impulsively risked everything—*everything*—to execute a woman who *wasn't* Margaret Costello's daughter.

"But, Gypsy! Why did you think the maid was—"

"Because she looked like her! Like me!"

Like Carol-Ann Ellis!

He thrust a newspaper in front of her. Staring at Kasia's photo beneath the tabloid headline THE KILLER NOBODY SAW, Gypsy could no longer see a resemblance to Carol-Ann. Nor to herself, or Margaret. But by then, she'd already discovered Margaret's daughter.

Jessamine had been abandoned as an infant in the Ithaca gorge not far from Cornell University, on the eve of the new semester in January 1969. That's precisely when Bernadette returned to campus from New York after her winter break and Oran's sentencing.

Had Margaret Costello accompanied her? Or had Margaret persuaded Bernadette to take her child?

The details no longer matter. One of them had left her there, in the gorge, on a frigid night she likely wasn't meant to survive.

After a well-publicized, futile search for the infant's parents or a clue to her identity, she was adopted by a local couple who lived on North Cayuga Street. Their neighbor Professor Silas Moss later said that the foundling next door sparked his interest in using DNA to connect long-lost biological relatives.

For Gypsy, the missing pieces fell into place. Red's final confrontation with Bernadette must have revealed that Margaret's daughter was alive in Ithaca.

You were there that night to kill her, weren't you, Red? And you were so close . . . if only you hadn't made such stupid, reckless mistakes.

But going to the wrong address wasn't one of them. Jessamine McCall lived in the house Red visited on that night in October 1987. Now she lives adjacent, in Professor Moss's former residence, with her police officer husband and their three children. But she isn't there today. She's here on Marshboro's Main Street with her old friend Amelia, settling into the white cottage with the blue door.

Gypsy leaves cash on the table with her check, exits the luncheonette, and pauses on the sidewalk to light a cigarette.

Across the way, the rental car is still parked in the driveway.

Gypsy had already known about the trip, courtesy of Amelia's texts with Stockton Barnes. She hadn't paid much attention, though, until she grasped Jessie's true identity.

"Are you sure she's your sister, Gypsy?" he'd asked.

"Stop calling her my sister. She's Margaret's daughter."

"And your father's daughter, so that makes her your—"

"I know what that makes her!"

She'd clenched her phone against her ear, gazing out the window at the former Wayland penthouse, breathing in and out. She knows what happens when a person gets reckless. Oran's misstep resulted in arrest; Red's in death. Mere mortals, both, in the end.

For Gypsy, immortality awaits. She won't allow Jessamine Hanson and Amelia Crenshaw Haines and Stockton Barnes to claim it for themselves.

She won't let that happen. But the conspirators aren't meant to die today on a sunny street. No, they'll meet their fate tomorrow, as foretold in Revelations, in the sea of glass glowing with fire.

Saddle River, New Jersey

"HERE WE ARE, sir," the debonair British driver announces from the front seat of the Porsche SUV.

Barnes looks up from the text he'd been typing, asking a colleague for an update on a search he'd requested over a week ago.

They've arrived at Rob's pillared redbrick mansion—white pillars, red brick, and a lineup of vehicles on the circular driveway awaiting the valet attendants. The fundraiser, held annually on Martin Luther King weekend, is a catered affair with live jazz music and two hundred glitzy guests, many of whom are in the entertainment industry. Barnes usually enjoys putting on one of his own well-cut suits, rubbing shoulders with them, and sipping champagne.

Not tonight. Back home after a long workday, he'd called Rob to say he couldn't make it out to Bergen County tonight. Predictably, Rob insisted that he come, and said he was sending his chauffeur. There is no arguing with the man.

As Smitty comes around to open the back door for him, Barnes quickly sends his text, tucks the phone into his cashmere overcoat.

"Do let me know when you're ready to return to the city. Mr. Owens has instructed me to await your call."

"It won't be long, I'll tell you that."

Inside, a member of the catering staff relieves him of his coat and another hands him a flute of champagne. The host and hostess greet him with hugs. Rob is dashing in a tux, Paulette lovely in blue velvet.

"I'm so glad you came! Now all we need is Kurtis,"

she says, scanning the crowd of new arrivals. "He promised he'd be here."

"Well, how many promises has he kept lately?" Rob asks.

Paulette glares at him, then turns to greet a newcomer with a bright smile and a gracious, "So nice to see you!"

"Everything okay with Kurtis?" Barnes asks Rob.

"He and I are on the outs again."

"Again? I didn't realize you two had been on the *ins* lately."

Rob and his oldest son have never seen eye to eye, but their relationship has grown increasingly fractured over Kurtis's inability to settle into a career despite his privileged background and Ivy League degree. He's bounced from one industry to another, living off his father's money while refusing his father's attempts to bring him on board at the record label, or even connect him with influential people in other industries.

Ongoing financial support, in Barnes's opinion, is where his friend went wrong, though he wouldn't dare criticize another man's parenting. If Rob cut off the bottomless cash flow, Kurtis might straighten out and settle down.

What do you know? You're not a father.

Barnes should probably update Rob, one of the few people in this world who knows about Charisse. But before he can, an R & B legend comes over to introduce his fiancée, a rising Instagram model. Barnes didn't know that was a thing, but Rob does, as do his daughters, who rush over with starstruck squeals.

Dodging the selfie session, Barnes heads for a quiet corner and reaches into his pocket for his own phone.

Not there. Wrong pocket, wrong jacket. Damn. He'd checked it with his overcoat.

"Lose something?"

Barnes turns to see Rob and Paulette's second-born son—Barnes's own godson and namesake. Blessed with his parents' good looks, confidence, and success, he's an internal medicine resident at New York-Presbyterian.

"Hey, you haven't seen Kurtis around, have you, Uncle Stockton?"

"No, but your parents were keeping an eye out for him."

"I hope he shows up. They haven't seen him since Christmas, and he and my father spent the whole time fighting."

"The usual?"

"Worse. They're opposite sides of the same coin."

"I disagree."

Rob is a vibrant person who embraces many passions with fervor bordering on obsession. Kurtis—at least in recent years—is moody and apathetic.

"But they're both addictive personalities, Uncle Stockton. Only my father doesn't dabble in dangerous stuff anymore."

"I don't know about that. Seems like he's always hanging from the side of a mountain lately. Upside down. No harness."

"Yeah, but who knows what my brother's doing these days? I hate to say he's a lost cause, but—"

"Don't say it."

"It's the truth."

"Plenty of people said that about me, too, once upon a time. I turned myself around. So will Kurtis."

Though Barnes had been a lot younger when he'd

reformed himself, and he couldn't have done it without Wash. Maybe Kurtis, too, would benefit from an older, wiser mentor. Barnes makes a mental note to reach out to him, maybe invite him to lunch over the weekend.

He spends the next couple of hours eating exquisite food, listening to world-class jazz, mingling with other guests, and trying to get his mind off his own troubles. But every time he manages to forget, his subconscious nudges him that something's wrong, just as Amelia had described.

"Everything seems fine but you have this feeling that things are off, and then—bam. It hits you again."

This isn't a death, but it feels like one.

At last, he makes his escape, summoning Smitty, thanking Rob and Paulette, and reclaiming his coat. In the car, he checks his phone and sees a missed call from Marissa Gomez, the colleague he'd texted on the way over.

"Damn," he says under his breath, dialing. It rings just enough times for him to think he's missed her for the night, but she picks up.

"Good, you're there. It's Barnes."

"I know it is and I'm always here. What, did you think I have a life, or something? Listen, sorry it took me so long to get back to you about that DB you were asking about, but it's been a crazy week, and I wanted to double-check a few things."

His pulse quickens. "Did you find something?"

"Sure did. I found her."

"You mean . . . Delia Montague? Where?"

"Morgue. Records, anyway. Jane Doe, Black, five foot seven, 115 pounds, in her late twenties, early thirties. Never identified. But I checked the postmortem photos against her mug shots, and it's her."

"How . . ."

"Medical examiner said it was an OD. She was found on a sidewalk outside a known crack house on . . ." He hears keys clacking. "December 4, 1990."

The small cottage had turned out to be charming, if no-frills, inside—dating back to the 1880s, Thelma had boasted. Jessie and her family live in an even older and far larger house that had once belonged to Silas Moss. As the two women discussed the charms of old architecture, Amelia had gazed out the window facing the Second Baptist Church, hearing Bettina's voice in her head. *"When I was a young'un in Georgia, we woke up bright and early on Sunday mornings, shiny clean from our Saturday night baths, so excited to put on our best dresses and walk on down the road to worship."*

She and her sisters had only bathed once a week, with water that had to be heated on the stove. Their Sunday clothes were threadbare hand-me-downs, and Bettina's feet were often blistered from outgrown shoes.

"But we never complained, child. Never, ever. We had everything that mattered, until our daddy died."

Her smile would fade then. Sometimes she talked about his funeral in the church next door. He and Bettina's mother are buried in the little graveyard out behind it. She'd married Calvin in the church, too, on September 8, 1956. Amelia has been planning to visit to see what she can piece together in the family tree. Church records and cemeteries are valuable genealogical resources. But now that she's here, remembering Bettina, and her stories . . .

I need to pay my respects.

She and Jessie had unpacked their bags and then walked right on over to Amelia's cousin Lucky's house, just a quarter mile down the road from the cottage.

"I have a good feeling about this," Jessie said. "It's Friday the thirteenth, you know."

"Then why do you have a good feeling?"

"Because her name is Lucky. It's a sign!"

No one answered their knock. They'd have to return later.

They drove back to the interstate and headed south, looking for a more populated area where they could eat dinner. They settled on a chain restaurant just off the last exit before the Florida State Line, too hungry to drive on in search of a place with homegrown appeal.

They decide to take the local roads back to Marshboro. Jessie's the designated driver, as Amelia had ordered Cabernet with dinner to calm her jittery nerves. It hadn't worked.

"Mimi, look!" Jessie says as they set out, and points at a green sign that lists mileage and arrows for nearby destinations. Jacksonville is to the west, Savannah to the north, and to the south . . .

"*Amelia* Island, Florida?" she reads.

"That must be where your name comes from."

"Maybe." Her heart is pounding. After all these years, another clue.

Half an hour later, they approach Lucky's front door again. This time, lamplight spills from the windows. Amelia is about to knock when her phone vibrates with a terse text from Barnes.

Delia OD'd 12/4/90.

Amelia closes her eyes, digesting it. So it had happened exactly as the family, and Cynthia, and even Amelia herself had suspected. But Delia Montague, Charisse, the Harrison murders, and even Stockton Barnes seem far away and far less significant than they had before she arrived in Marshboro.

"Mimi! Come on!" Jessie pokes her. "Knock, before you lose your nerve."

Text unanswered, she turns off the phone. Tonight is about her own past.

Again, she lifts her fist toward the door. It opens before she can make contact.

A woman stands there, looking out at her with Great Aunt Birdie's dark eyes, unsurprised and expectant.

Amelia steps forward. "Lucky? I'm—"

"Lucky! Well." The woman offers a faint smile and shakes her head. "It's been a long, long time since anyone called me that."

"Sorry, it's—I, uh . . . I know you're my mother's first cousin—her Aunt Birdie's daughter—and I'm . . . uh, I'm Bettina's daughter."

"No, you aren't."

Amelia's jaw drops. Jessie is, for once, at a loss for words.

"I heard you were in town," Lucky says. "Been waiting for you. Let me get my coat, and we'll go."

"Go where?"

"It's time you learned the truth. But it's not mine to tell."

Chapter Fourteen

Approaching Manhattan's glittering skyline with Smitty behind the wheel, Barnes dials Bobby Montague's number. It goes into voice mail, and he leaves a brief message asking the man to get in touch.

Wondering how likely it is that Bobby will call back, he decides to reach out to James and Regina Harrison. It's well past ten o'clock, and the news isn't urgent, but the family should know, for closure's sake, whether they actively seek it or not.

And, selfishly, Barnes is looking forward to finally getting some sleep without Delia keeping him awake or haunting his dreams.

"It's Stockton Barnes," he says when Regina picks up. "I'm sorry to call so late, but I just wanted to update you on some information I've received."

He tells her about Delia Montague's death in 1990. She murmurs that it's a shame, but takes the news in stride. He asks if she knows how he can get in touch with Bobby and is told he's working the night shift.

"I left a message for him. If you see him, though, let him know what happened."

"He always said Delia was dead. He won't be surprised. What about Alma and Brandy?"

He clears his throat. "Ma'am?"

"You said you were investigating the murder. Do you have any updates on that?"

"Oh . . . no, not yet," he says, with a bit of remorse that finding out who killed their loved ones is no longer a top priority for him. But Sumaira El Idrissi is a top-notch investigator. She'll solve it . . .

Or not. Probably not. Eventually, without leads or suspects, it won't be a priority for Homicide, either.

"What about Charisse?"

"Charisse?"

"You were looking for her. Now that Delia is dead . . . are you still looking for her daughter?"

"Delia's been dead a long time, Regina, and Charisse is an adult."

"You were all fired up to find her last time we talked."

"Well, I've been hitting dead ends," he tells Regina. "It's not easy to find someone who disappeared thirty years ago when you've got nothing to go on."

"I'm sure it isn't. But if she were *your* daughter, Detective Barnes, you'd still be looking."

It's not the first time a family member has made a comment like that when he's searching for their lost loved one. But it's always in an abstract "put yourself in my shoes" way. Regina Harrison's tone strikes him as pointed. As if she knows.

Does she? He and Amelia had sensed that the Harrisons might have been withholding details. But not that. Regina can't know *that.*

Anyway, he wouldn't have made any more progress uncovering her current identity if he still believed she's his own flesh and blood.

You just keep telling yourself that . . . Gloss.

"I'm still looking," he assures her, and hangs up with a promise to keep her posted.

Ten minutes later, he's in his apartment, shivering out

of his clothes and into layers of thermal and fleece after finally, finally calling the super about fixing the heat.

"Can it wait till tomorrow morning?"

Even more bone-tired than he is bone-chilled, Barnes tells him that it can, and the super tells him to make sure he's home between ten and noon.

He texts Amelia that he's going to bed and they can talk in the morning. Then he texts Kurtis to see if he can get together over the weekend and talk, saying he'd like to try to help him.

Brushing his teeth in the frigid bathroom, he continues to think about the case, reconsidering it from an outsider's perspective. Take away any personal connection, everything he'd ever known or assumed about Charisse, Perry Wayland and Gypsy Colt, and the victims . . .

What does pure logic tell him?

Alma and Brandy lived in a dangerous part of the city. They weren't insulated from the neighborhood's criminal activity and violent characters. Anything could have happened. He'd jumped to illogical conclusions based on what?

Guilt, over the money from Wayland?

That, yes, and gut instinct.

But it isn't foolproof. Especially when emotion comes into play.

Had Barnes been trying too hard to make sense of the past, haunted by the threats Wayland had made about his daughter on that Baracoa beach?

Barnes never even *had* a daughter.

If Wash were here, he'd advise him to stop licking his own wounds and start focusing on the unsolved murder.

Not my case. I'm Missing Persons, not Homicide.

Just because there was a vase of flowers at the scene . . .

Lilies, to most people, don't symbolize Cuba.

Brandy had used the pseudonym Lily Tucker when she visited Amelia with the baby ring. Maybe lilies are her favorite flower, and her new boyfriend knew that.

The fact that he was wealthy doesn't mean that he was Perry Wayland. Maybe he was a legitimate businessman. Maybe the murder had nothing to do with the boyfriend at all. Or maybe it did, and he's in a gang or a drug dealer or involved in organized crime . . .

There are countless reasons why getting involved with the wrong man could have led to a professional hit on the Harrison women.

But Sumaira and her team aren't investigating a possible connection, however unlikely, to Perry Wayland and Gypsy Colt.

He *had* looked into Wayland and Colt's whereabouts. He'd found no evidence that they'd survived the catastrophic storm in Baracoa, and no evidence that they did not. Certainly no evidence that they're in New York City.

"You're getting colder, son . . ."

Damn. It's time to confess the whole story, including the bribe money he'd accepted from Stef. Time to deal with the consequences, whatever they are. It's the right thing to do.

Now, before he loses his resolve. In person. He returns to the bedroom to get dressed again, turns on the light, and spots something he'd missed earlier in his haste to change into warm clothing.

An envelope is propped on the pillows. It bears a printed label addressed *Detective Barnes.*

He stares at it long and hard before looking around, heart pumping.

What the hell?

Barnes conducts a quick search of the apartment. No sign of forced entry. He grabs his gloves and a letter opener, returns to the bedroom, and uses his cell phone to snap photos of the envelope. Then he puts on the gloves, picks it up, and slits it open.

It contains a note folded around a four-by-six photo. It's grainy, snapped at night, showing a woman silhouetted in a backlit window.

The note is on printer paper, all in caps.

I WARNED YOU NOT TO SNOOP INTO MY PAST. NOW I'VE SNOOPED INTO YOURS. FINDERS KEEPERS.

Westport

HEARING A SNOWPLOW rumbling up the street, Liliana peers out the window, checking for headlights following along in the cleared swath behind the truck. But it passes, leaving the street deserted, snow swirling in the streetlights' glow. No sign of Bryant yet, and no sign of the shadowy figure she'd glimpsed a few times before.

Now, knowing what she knows, her theory seems ludicrous. To think that for weeks now, she's been imagining a stalker out there, watching her.

Not just a stalker, but her birth father, the volatile, violent man she remembers, the one with the scar by his mouth, the one who didn't want her. He'd been popping up in her nightmares again lately, triggered by the colored Christmas lights. No wonder she'd imagined that he was lurking during her waking hours.

Liliana turns away from the window and returns to the couch, where Briana had roused herself, expecting her master's return. "Not yet." She sits beside the dog and resumes petting her. "Soon, though."

Bryant had texted at around eight o'clock to say his client meeting in Norwalk was running late, and it would be a slow drive home afterward in the snow. He told her to eat without him, and she remembered she'd promised to make a homemade meal since she was working from home today.

But neither of those things had happened. Not the cooking, and not the working. After he left, she settled in to check her email and found something that had changed her plans for the day. Changed everything she'd ever assumed about who she is and where she came from.

She'd called her mother in Florida. Emily Tucker had gasped when Liliana told her. "Well, that's not what we were expecting, is it? How do you feel about it?"

"I don't know what to think."

"Are you going to—"

"I'm not going to do anything until I tell Bry, Mom."

"Good. The two of you can sort through this together. But whatever you decide, I want you to remember one thing, Lily my love. You are still the person you've always been."

Yes. She's the same person, and the loving couple who'd adopted her and raised her are, and will always be, her parents. But—

She hears another vehicle coming up the street. This time when she peeks out the window, she sees her husband's SUV. Briana follows her to the door, tail wagging.

Liliana pats her head, watching her husband climb out of the driver's seat and go around to the passenger's side to grab a bag of takeout he'd picked up on the way home after learning she hadn't cooked. She can see that it's Chinese food, and he hadn't asked her what to order. She always gets chicken and broccoli with brown rice, hot and sour soup, and a spring roll.

Once, early on, Bryant had theorized that she craves familiarity because she's an adoptee. He'd started asking questions; she'd said she doesn't like to talk about it. Her husband, never one to resurrect a dropped subject, had never asked about it again.

She watches him stride toward the house in his navy wool walking coat, a gray plaid scarf at his neck. There's a bounce in his step. He must have had a good day. He's one of the top reps on his team, receiving an award at his company's sales conference in San Diego this week. Bred for success, he's the son of a doctor and a college professor, grandson of one of the country's first Black airline pilots. So much pride in that family, and rightfully so.

Her parents are also prominent and successful. They, too, had raised her with high expectations, taught her to set lofty goals and achieve them.

But they're white.

Bryant greets her with a kiss, then points to the walk and driveway. "Babe, I don't want you shoveling on days when you don't have to go anywhere! I can do it when I get home."

"I used that service that left a flyer in the mailbox a few days ago offering a free trial. I thought they wouldn't even show up, but the guy came twice, and he said he'll be back tomorrow."

"Good, then I don't have to worry about you while I'm gone." Bryant hangs his coat on a hook, stomps his feet on the mat and heads for the kitchen with the food. "Let's eat, and then I have to pack."

She follows him. Now isn't a good time. He's had a long day, and his airport car service will be here at four in the morning, and he's leaving for a week . . .

And I can't keep this to myself for a week.

"Bry."

"Hmm?" He's unpacking the food, lining up white cartons on the counter.

"I need to tell you something. Can you sit down for a second?"

"Can we eat while you're telling me? Because it's late and I'm starved and—" He turns and catches sight of her face. He sits. "What happened?"

She takes a deep breath and sinks into the opposite chair, opening the laptop she'd left on the kitchen table. "You know I was adopted. But I never told you I was abandoned."

His eyes widen and then fill with tears as she tells him about her earliest memories of a grim life, and how she'd been found at the Chapel Square Mall as a toddler. He takes her hands in both of his as she tells the story leading up to finding a forever home with the Tuckers.

"I can't believe you never told me you had such a traumatic childhood."

"It wasn't, after I was adopted. I've never liked to talk about it, or even think about how I was abandoned. I mean, maybe a part of me always wondered, but the rest of me didn't want to know. Only lately . . . I guess the wondering part took over, and I didn't just want to know. I needed to know. Because of you, and how we're going to have children, and . . . you know, I kept thinking that my birth parents were not good people. Terrible people who are out there somewhere, and they might walk back into my life someday, into our lives. So . . ."

She tells him about the DNA test she'd taken.

About the results that had come back today with a match to a man with whom she shares 3,448 centimorgans across eight-two DNA segments.

"What does that even mean?"

"It means the higher those numbers are, the closer the relationship is. And one hundred percent of the time two people share that amount of DNA, they are parent and child."

"So you've found your birth father."

"Yes."

"The man who slapped you around and—"

"No."

Liliana takes a deep breath, turning the laptop to show him the match, accompanied by biographical information and a photo of a man who doesn't have a scar and hasn't been haunting her dim memories and recent nightmares. "This is my father, Bry. He's a detective in New York City, and his name is Stockton Barnes, and he's been looking for me."

There are still plenty of troopers monitoring the southbound interstate with radar guns, but Amelia's cousin is in no danger of a speeding ticket. Lucky drives a good fifteen miles per hour below the speed limit. Amelia, seated in the front passenger seat, can feel Jessie's impatience in the back. She knows Jessie's right foot is gunning an imaginary gas pedal as her mouth rattles at full speed, asking questions about the town, passing landmarks, Lucky's life . . .

Everything except where they're going. She'd already tried that, back at the house, and the woman had shaken her head.

"You'll see."

"But does it have something to do with—"

"Like I said, this truth isn't mine to reveal. So I'm taking you to meet someone who's been waiting a long time to tell it. Half a lifetime—and all of yours," she'd added with a glance at Amelia.

"But how did *you* know we were coming tonight?" Jessie asks. "Because when we showed up at your house, it was like you were expecting us."

"Marshboro is a small town. Folks know everything about everything."

Lucky is a lovely woman, not just for her age, which Amelia would guess is mid to late seventies. She's not roly-poly as Bettina had been, but there's a resemblance.

Back in October, Amelia's DNA test had turned up Lucky's daughter, Quinnlynn, as a first or second cousin. She'd sent a message through the private website. Waiting for a response that never came, Amelia had studied the genealogical profile. Based on DNA—she and Quinnlynn share 286 centimorgans across twenty segments—and three decades' worth of molecular biology research, she'd concluded that Quinnlynn's mother and her own birth mother had been first cousins.

Bettina.

There's always room for error, but . . .

What in the world is going on here? Amelia's brain darts along a path of possibilities as they exit the interstate just north of the state line.

Lucky heads east on a two-lane highway that's being widened to four, past new home construction and modern strip malls, with a smattering of shabby houses and small businesses in the mix.

They make several turns, with a steady stream of taillights in front of them and headlights behind.

"Lotta traffic, this bein' a holiday weekend and all," Lucky comments, squinting as if the glare bothers her. "Lotta traffic all the time, lately."

Most of the other vehicles are luxury cars and SUVs—couples with kids and dogs, coolers and surfboards.

"Barrow Island," Jessie reads aloud as they follow a sign toward a causeway. "That's where we're going?"

"It is."

Barrow Island . . .

Has someone mentioned it to Amelia? Not recently.

Barrow Island . . .

She can hear it, drawn out in a distinct Southern drawl. But the voice in her head isn't Bettina's.

They pass an old wooden bridge stretching out over the water, lit only by a lamppost on this shore and a distant one across the Intracoastal. On the near end, a marker designates it a historical landmark, for pedestrians only, according to Jessie the sign reader.

"Nowadays it is. Used to be for cars, too. Only way to the island till the causeway was built."

"When was that?"

"Let's see . . . early '70s. Now they're fixing it up and they want to build a second one, 'cause of all the traffic." She grips the wheel as she navigates between orange cones and concrete construction barriers. On the island, the rest of the traffic bears right toward the new vacation home developments on the island's south end.

Lucky goes left. "Nothing but the salt marsh and a few houses up this way—used to be outbuildings on a rice plantation. But they're talking about turning the main house into an inn. Then I s'pose the fancy folks will be up here, too, and they'll want to pave the road. Everything's changing. Old-timers don't go for that, but there aren't many left, so I s'pose it's a good thing . . ."

"What?" Jessie prods when she falls silent, but she shakes her head.

The road is hard-packed sandy dirt, bordered on both sides with dense foliage and live oaks draped in Spanish moss. In the headlights' distant glow, Amelia sees a herd of animals on the road.

"Look out! There are deer!" Jessie warns from the backseat. "I almost hit one last night, and—"

"Those aren't deer," Lucky says. "They're feral horses. Used to roam the whole island, but now they stick to this end, like the old-timers."

The animals move to the shoulder as they pass, and Amelia turns to watch them, hearing that same voice in her head—the drawl from the past, telling her about an exotic island where horses run free.

Maybe it was Bettina.

Lucky turns into a long lane leading to an antebellum cottage. It's low and wide, with a porch, and painted blue. Alongside the steps, blue bottles adorn the branches of a tall shrub.

Amelia's heart quakes. She remembers . . .

Not Bettina.

"Before we go in, child . . . I have something to give you." Lucky reaches up to flick on the car's interior light and hands Amelia a lumpy envelope. "It's from my mother."

"Auntie Birdie?"

"Mmm-hmm."

She opens the envelope, takes out a small rounded strip of plastic and holds it up to the light.

"What is it?" Jessie asks, leaning forward and then gasping. "Oh! Oh, Mimi!"

"What is it?" Amelia echoes, turning it over in her hands, seeing that something is printed on it. The words are in Courier font, slightly smudged letters and numbers pecked out on a typewriter like so many old records she's perused over the years, only . . .

This one pertains to her. The strip of plastic is a tiny hospital bracelet.

Martina Eleanor Hunter 4/25/68

"Who is . . ."

"You are," Lucky says simply.

"Oh, Mimi! No more maybe birthday," Jessie whispers, pressing her forehead to Amelia's shoulder.

I was born on April 25, 1968.

I'm Martina Eleanor Hunter.

Lucky opens her car door. "Let's go on in, then."

Martina.

Not Amelia.

April.

Not May.

She just sits there, clutching the little bracelet.

Then Jessie is there, outside, reaching into the car to hug her. "Come on, Mimi. Let's do this. I'm with you."

Clasping the bracelet with one hand and Jessie's arm with the other, she follows Lucky toward the house, feet crunching on gravel.

In the moonlight, horses graze beneath live oak branches that could shade a city block. A pale orange kitten sits on the step. As they climb past, it rolls onto its back, paws belly up, vulnerable. A tabby cat sits at the door like a sentry, fixing them with a green-eyed glare.

Lucky knocks, and a plump Black woman answers, flashing a gap-toothed smile. "What in the world are you doing here at this hour? Is everything all right?"

"Everything's fine, Tandy. Just fine. How is Auntie?"

Auntie . . .

For an illogical moment, Amelia's shell-shocked brain assumes she's talking about Bettina.

Bettina, who'd been Lucky's aunt. Bettina, alive here, after all these years later.

But no. No, Amelia had seen her lying cold and dead in a Harlem hospital decades ago.

"She's alert. Restless. Guess she knew you were coming."

Lucky introduces Tandy as her aunt's caregiver.

"This here is Jessie, and this . . ." Lucky pauses. "This is *Amelia.*"

"Well. Well, well. Praise the Lord you finally decided to—"

"I didn't, Tandy. You know I been praying on it ever since she called me in October, but I didn't have an answer, and then she just showed up in Marshboro today."

"Guess the good Lord took matters into His own hands, then." She holds the door wide-open and invites them inside. The front room is cluttered and pleasant, with a low beadboard ceiling and wide-planked floor. The television and stereo are from the last century and the furniture is even older.

"I'll take you to her." Tandy leads the way through a small kitchen. A familiar savory scent hangs in the air.

"*Supshun,*" a voice croons across the years, and Amelia squeezes her eyes closed, trying to capture a face, a place, a time . . .

She opens her eyes and finds herself staring at a produce-filled basket on the counter. It's made from sweetgrass, woven in tight coils, with an intricate pattern and distinct shape. Almost identical to the one in her living room. And to the one she'd seen an old friend carrying the last time they'd met.

She remembers the voice, the one that had mentioned Barrow Island so long ago . . .

And the blue bottles on the tree . . .

But it's impossible. Amelia counts backward over the decades as Tandy moves toward a closed door and opens it to a small bedroom.

An ancient woman lies propped on pillows, wide-awake, alert eyes set in a shriveled face. Familiar eyes.

"Auntie," Lucky tells Marceline LeBlanc. "I've brought Cyril's daughter. Your granddaughter. Amelia."

Part VI

1968

Chapter Fifteen

Saturday, April 27, 1968
Jacksonville

"Hello again, Mrs. Hunter!"

Melody opens her eyes. Yvonne breezes into the room, carrying a familiar pink bundle.

Ah, Martina.

Anxious to hold her daughter, Melody grips the bed rails to pull herself into a sitting position without waiting for the nurse to raise the top half of the bed.

Yvonne notes her wince. "Oh, my. It looks like your pain medication wore off again."

"Just a little sore still."

Understatement of the year. Two days after delivery, every inch of her body between her neck and her knees feels battered, torn, or bruised. Her throat is raw, not from screaming, but from the general anesthesia tube. Fortunately, she can only imagine the ordeal of childbirth itself, though there's a part of her that feels wistful, as though she'd missed out on a magical experience.

When she'd voiced that thought to Honeybee, however, her mother had gaped in horror. "Magical experience? Now why would you even say such a thing?"

"I don't know, it just seems like it would have been nice to welcome my baby into the world."

"You did just that."

"But not when she was born."

"Well, you wouldn't want her first sight of her mama to be screaming and carrying on like a heathen like folks did in the olden days. Just thank your lucky stars for modern medicine and doctors who can put you to sleep."

Melody supposes she's right, and she's also thankful for nurses who bring pain pills in little white fluted cups, provide cold compresses for her aching breasts, and administer lactation suppression medication along with advice on caring for both newborn and new mother.

She dutifully swallows the medication, aware that it won't just take away the pain, but will make her drowsy and a little woozy.

She holds out her arms, and Yvonne places Martina in them. The baby turns her face toward Melody's swollen bosom as if she instinctively wants to nurse, despite the tight binding and lactation suppression drugs.

"You enjoy your time together," she says, turning the bedside crank so that the top half rises. "Someone will be back soon to get the baby and bring you your supper tray."

"You're leaving?"

"My shift is over, but I'll see you tomorrow."

Melody is sorry to see her go. A rotating staff of nurses cares for her. The others are all white. Yvonne, with her Gullah patois and sly sense of humor, is Melody's favorite.

"Oh, and be sure you get your supshun before visiting hours. Something tells me your mama will be back here right on schedule!"

Melody had been grateful when three o'clock came and the staff went up and down the corridor ordering all visitors to leave the premises—no exceptions, even for Honeybee Beauregard Abernathy, who'd already tested the boundaries.

"How did you get in here?" Melody had asked when her mother popped up an hour before visitors were allowed, with an armload of gift-wrapped boxes.

"Why, through the front entrance!" She'd been indignant, as though Melody had suggested she'd helicoptered to the roof and rappelled down the building.

"Didn't anyone stop you?"

"Of course not. It's a hospital, not a bank vault. Now open these presents and see what I brought for our little princess."

More dresses—all pink, Honeybee's favorite color. But at the bottom of the stack, older and more delicate than the others and wrapped in layers of tissue paper, she found a pastel blue one with a Best & Co. Layette label.

"Was this mine?"

"Ellie's," Honeybee said softly. "This child looks just like her."

They'd swapped the baby's white hospital bunting for the blue dress.

"You look a little like her," Melody tells her drowsy daughter.

She appears white, just as Yvonne had said. No one, not even Travis's own mother, would guess that she doesn't belong to him.

"Big blue eyes, just like her daddy!" Doris had told Melody last night.

Fairly certain that all babies are born blue-eyed,

Melody had agreed. But those eyes, when they're open, radiate Cyril's intense awareness.

"All the pretty little horses . . ." Melody sings, rocking Martina in her arms, remembering how Honeybee's mellifluous soprano had lulled her back to sleep with the same song when she was very young and had awakened from a nightmare.

"Well, now, isn't that sweet," a male voice drawls from the doorway.

Startled, Melody looks up to see Rodney Lee Midget in his white milkman coveralls and cap.

"Don't stop singin' on my account. You always did have a voice like an angel. All those solos in the school choir, and whatnot."

Melody instinctively clutches her daughter close. "What are you doing here? It's not visiting hours."

Honeybee's words echo in her head. *"It's a hospital, not a bank vault."*

"Not for the public, but see, I work here. Just came by with the milk delivery and thought I'd pay a friendly visit to meet the baby." He looks over his shoulder and then steps into the room. "Little girl, is it? What's her name?"

"Martina Eleanor."

"That's unusual, ain't it? She named after someone special?"

"My sister."

"Dead, ain't she? Guess I forgot all about her. But her name wasn't Martina."

Melody had chosen the baby's first name in memory of Martin Luther King, though she'd told her parents and in-laws that she'd come across it in an old book and thought it was pretty.

Doris clearly didn't agree. "What about Travis?"

Melody forced a smile and an attempt at humor. "Travis is a good name for a boy, but not for a little girl."

Her own parents, and her father-in-law, too, had gotten a laugh out of that. But Doris pursed her lips and asked if Melody thought she should have waited for Travis's approval. Her father, bless his heart, had answered before she could.

"There's no telling when he'll be in touch, and a baby's got to have a name. I think Martina Eleanor is a fine one."

Rodney Lee crosses to Melody's bed. He's so close she can smell his breath, and he's been drinking something a lot stronger than milk.

"Come on, now, let's have a look."

She recoils, shielding the baby against her tender breasts.

"She's sleeping."

"That so? Looks to me like you're trying to smother her."

Melody thrusts her back in alarm. But Martina is breathing, awake now, wide-eyed and staring.

Rodney Lee laughs, peers at the baby, and gives a low whistle. "Guess your mother-in-law was right. This here little girl looks exactly like her daddy."

Melody is relieved. For a moment, there, she'd been worried he might—

"'Course . . ." He turns his head and looks her in the eye. "Like you said, a woman only sees what she wants to see."

"What are you talking about?"

"Don't tell me you don't remember that book you were tellin' me about, by that Lee fellow."

It takes her a moment to realize he's referring to the passage she'd shared with him from *To Kill a Mockingbird.* Rodney Lee has always struck her as barely literate, yet here he is paraphrasing the quote and recalling the author's name.

"Harper Lee is a woman."

"With a man's name? Lee?"

Ah . . . *Lee.* No wonder the name stayed with him.

"That can be either a man's name or a woman's name."

"Let's see, you got me, Lee Marvin, Lee Harvey Oswald . . . all men," he tells her with a triumphant nod. "So you can see why I'd think that."

"What Harper Lee *said* was, 'people generally see what they look for, and hear what they listen for.'"

"That's what I said."

"Not quite."

"You want to nitpick, do you?"

She does not.

"You were talking about Travis's mother? You saw her?"

"She called me to tell me the baby was born, like I asked her to. Travis and me been friends since we were tiny little kids. His wife havin' a baby and me not knowin' would be like . . . well, I wanted to know. And when she said the baby looks just like her daddy, I thought I should come on over and have a look-see for myself. After all, she's never actually met the man."

Melody's heart stops. "I . . . I don't know what you're talking about."

"Oh, I'd be willing to wager that you do." Rodney Lee straightens and starts for the door, then turns back. "You know, for a minute there when I thought you were tryin' to smother her, I didn't blame you. I imagine a lot of women would do the same thing in your place."

White-hot rage sweeps through her.

"That sure would make your troubles disappear in a jiffy. You don't have much time, see? 'Cause the way I understand it, every day, her skin's gonna get a little bit blacker, and you're gonna start to panic, 'cause people will be able to take one look at her and they'll know. Travis, he'll be back, and he'll—"

"Get *out.*"

He laughs. "I'm goin'. Need me to mail anything on my way?"

"What are you talking about?"

"I know you like to write nice long letters to Travis, but . . . oh, wait. I guess there's no need to tell him the baby was born, huh? Shame you can't share the news with her real daddy. I surely don't approve of what y'all did, but I'm guessin' he would'a been tickled pink over daddy's little gal. Well, maybe not *pink.*" He laughs, a staccato sound that reverberates like a gunshot, and Melody recoils.

A petite blonde wisp of a nurse appears in the doorway behind him, dwarfed by his bulk. "Excuse me, sir! Are you—"

"I was just paying a friendly visit, but I'll be getting back to work now." Rodney Lee tips his narrow white cap at her, then at Melody. "Be sure and take good care of that baby now, Mrs. Hunter. You just try and keep her safe, you hear?"

He disappears, and his words echoing like an ominous challenge.

You just try.

Greenwich Village

Yesterday was payday. After cashing his check and paying the most pressing bills, Oran was left with nothing but loose change in his pocket, a knot in his stomach, and a weekend to get his hands on more cash.

"You can't even support me . . ."

Gypsy's words propel him to the subway Saturday evening. He rides downtown and gets off at Christopher Street, then walks four blocks to a familiar century-old tavern near the river.

It all began here, at Fergie's Inn.

The place had never operated as an inn, according to its owner, though it had been a private residence, brothel, and speakeasy before finding its groove as a haunt for the beat generation's shining literary stars.

Oran had been tending bar here one night in '51 when Linda walked in. She was wearing a full-skirted pink dress, looking like the Nebraska farmer's daughter she'd been until she ran off to New York City. She'd come to Fergie's that night to hear a fellow former Midwesterner read from his novel in progress, but the morphine-addled Billy Burroughs hadn't shown up.

Linda sat at the bar ordering one sloe gin fizz after another. Oran couldn't decide whether she was a sore thumb or a breath of fresh air among the beatnik crowd, but they'd had immediate chemistry. She was open to his teachings and recruited other followers.

For a while, they'd all lived in harmonious kinship, Oran's women working various jobs to keep the household going so he could focus on his sidewalk sermons. But his new family grew restless waiting for the promised apocalypse. One by one, they showed their weaknesses, and he cast them away.

Linda got to stay, not because he cared about her, but because she was pregnant.

Even then, before Gypsy was born, Oran sensed that his child, unlike her mother, unlike the others, would be strong and loyal. She would never betray him.

And now, he has two more children on the way. Tara Sheeran is pregnant, and he'd confirmed that Christina Myers is as well. Soon, Margaret, too, will be carrying his child. His earthly family is blossoming, and he needs to take care of them as they await their eternal paradise.

He steps into a dingy room with a low tin ceiling and scarred plank floors. The place looks exactly the same as it had in Oran's day, but the poets and writers who'd frequented the place are long gone. At the moment there are only two patrons, middle-aged men hunched over beers.

"Well, there's a sight my eyes ain't seen in donkey's years!" the owner booms, spotting him in the doorway. "If it isn't my old pal O'Matty!"

Fergus Ferguson's copper hair has gone gray, but he has the same brogue, same beer belly, same jowly florid face, same Celtic knot tattooed on his forearm.

"Got any Irish blood, do you?" he'd asked Oran before hiring him.

"Sure. Real name's O'Matthews," Oran had quipped.

Fergus roared with laughter, and he, along with his patrons, called Oran "O'Matty" from that day on.

Fergus beckons him to the bar and pumps his hand. "How are you, mate? How's the wife?"

"Haven't seen her in a while. Guess you haven't,

either?" Oran remembers to ask, as if he doesn't know better.

"Not in years. You two split up, then?"

"Long time ago." Oran pulls a couple of coins from his pocket. "Whatever you've got on draft."

Fergus tosses the coins into a cash drawer and fills a mug as Oran looks at the spot where the open mic once stood. He'd watched from behind the bar as other men enthralled rapt audiences with magnetism and profound words, just as he'd always longed to do. But his own dream transformed. What good was being a movie star if you couldn't experience hero worship firsthand, in the moment?

Oran had come to Fergie's an aspiring actor and left a preacher and prophet, with a mesmerized Linda as his first disciple.

As Fergus sets the beer in front of him, Oran notices his gold wristwatch. "Fancy. Guess the bar's doing well, man."

"Nah, my grandfather died a few years back and left it to me."

"Must be worth a bundle."

Fergus shrugs. "I'd never sell it. Sentimental value, you know?"

Oran thinks of his mother, who left him nothing but heartache.

"Just stopping in for old times' sake?" Fergus asks.

"That, and I could use a job."

"Out of work?"

"Out of bread. I've got a day job, but I need another one."

"Sorry, I've got more bartenders than customers these days."

Oran sips his beer. Piss-warm, with too much foam.

"Hey, I hear the US Army's hiring," one of the guys down the bar says with a smirk. He's got a patchy red beard and military ink on his bicep.

"Don't think so, man."

"Country needs your service."

"I need you to stay out of my business."

"Cool it, there, O'Matty," Fergus says.

Oran glowers. "Clientele's gone downhill since I was here, man."

"Can't think of much that hasn't. Whole damned world's falling apart. Assassination, riots, war . . ."

" 'Then another horse came out, a fiery red one,' " Oran booms, glaring at Red Beard. "'Its rider was given power to take peace from the earth and to make men slay each other. To him was given a large sword—'"

"What the hell's wrong with your friend, Fergus?" Red Beard asks.

"Yeah, if I want church, I'll go on Sunday when my old lady makes me," his friend says, getting up.

" 'Before me was a black horse! Its rider was holding a pair of scales in his hand. Then I heard—'"

"Hey!" Fergus puts a hand on his arm. "Stop. They don't need your BS."

Oran shakes him off. "They need enlightenment. You all need—"

"I need to get out of here." Red Beard slaps a bill on the bar, and his friend follows suit.

"Suit yourselves," Oran calls after them as they amble out into the dusk. "Don't come to me to save your souls from eternal damnation!"

Scowling, Fergus grabs the money. "Take a hike, man. You're crazy."

"Crazy? I'll tell you what's crazy, man. I come in here, a paying customer, an old friend, looking for a job, and this is how you treat me?"

Oran swipes a hand across the bar, knocking the beer so that it spills warm suds all over the floor.

"Get out, Matthews, or I call the cops."

Oran strides to the door and reaches not for the knob, but for the lock. He flips it.

"No one's going anywhere," he tells Fergus. "Including you."

A WOMAN IN a white uniform enters Melody's room. She isn't Yvonne. Nor is she Darlene, the little blonde who'd curtailed Rodney Lee's visit earlier. And she's not Kathy, who'd sent Honeybee home when visiting hours ended.

She introduces herself as Louise, and says she's on the overnight shift. Tall, stocky and almost masculine in appearance, she's older than the others and not nearly as nurturing.

Under ordinary circumstances, Melody might find her intimidating. Tonight, however, she welcomes the no-nonsense attitude. Her nerves have been on edge since Rodney Lee Midget's visit, and she suspects Louise wouldn't hesitate to wrangle with him if he returns to cause any trouble.

The nurse checks Melody's vital signs and administers a dose of pain pills. None too soon, as the soreness is creeping in again. But no medication can ebb the current of fear chasing fury through her veins.

I know you like to write nice long letters to Travis . . .

Now she knows what happened to the one she'd written back in February. Rodney Lee had broken into her house, stolen it . . . mailed it? No wonder she hasn't heard from Travis ever since.

But there's nothing she can do about it from here, helpless in a hospital bed, other than confide her secret in someone—a nurse? Her parents? The police?

And then what?

Her innocent, vulnerable newborn will become tangible evidence of an illicit, illegal affair. Will the staff continue to care for Martina? Will the grandparents—maternal, anyway—view her as a treasured family member, or pariah? Travis's parents would certainly turn their backs, at the very least.

"You just try and keep her safe."

She stares at the painting of the duck and ducklings on a bucolic pond, and she thinks of the scars on Cyril's face, and the hate-fueled violence that's tearing apart the world beyond this hospital.

No. She can't reveal anything to anyone. She isn't yet strong enough to single-handedly protect Martina, and she has no way of reaching the only other person who'd lay down his life for this child.

"It's time for the baby to go back to the nursery now, Mrs. Hunter." Louise reaches for her.

"Please, not yet!" She clutches the swaddled baby to her shoulder and turns away, hearing a faint warble from her daughter. "Oh, no, don't cry."

"She's just hungry for her bottle."

Or maybe she's just protesting that her mother is gripping her as a toddler would a toy kept from a playmate's greedy grasp.

"I'd like to keep her here with me a little while longer."

"I'm sorry, but we keep a strict schedule in the

nursery, Mrs. Hunter. You'll thank us for it when you get her home next week."

"Louise . . . do you have children?"

"Me? No. No husband, no children. Never had them, never will," she adds without an ounce of regret. "Some women just aren't cut out to be mothers."

And some women are. Melody strokes her daughter's precious face with a gentle fingertip. This is what she'd been born to do.

"I know it must be lonely for you here. I understand your husband is in Vietnam." She clears her throat and shifts her weight. "But Mrs. Hunter—"

"I'm sorry," Melody says softly. "I know it's time for her feeding, and I don't want her to go hungry."

And I know you don't understand how I feel every time she's taken away, and I know that it's not as if I'm never going to see her again, but that's how it feels right now. I'm scared, so scared for her . . .

Fighting tears, she looks up, prepared to hand over the baby.

"Do you want to give her the bottle?" Louise asks.

"Me?"

"Ever fed a baby before?"

"No, I . . . no."

"I can show you how. We're supposed to wait another day or two for the mothers to get their strength back, but if you want to try it—"

"Oh, I do. And thank you, Louise. Thank you so much."

The corners of the woman's mouth bend into what might be a smile before she leaves the room, saying, "I'll finish my rounds down the hall and come back with the formula."

Melody leans into the pillows and looks down at her daughter. "Well, how about that? I'm going to learn how to feed you! I'm sure I'll be right good at it, once I get the hang of things."

Martina responds with a solemn gaze, as if she's certain she'll be in capable hands.

Yes. And the sooner Melody can take care of her baby's basic needs, the sooner they can get out of here and find Cyril.

In the meantime, we're sitting ducks, she thinks, gazing at the painting opposite her bed.

"Shame you can't share the news with her real daddy . . ."

Martina's little pink mouth quavers and she lets out a faint wail.

"Oh, sweetheart . . ." Melody holds her close, rocking her, and she quiets, but her little body is trembling.

Just hungry? Or is she picking up on Melody's apprehension?

"It's going to be okay," she whispers, to the baby and to herself.

Being Travis's friend doesn't make Rodney Lee guilty of Travis's sins. He's all talk, a bully all his life. Bullies take pleasure in taunting others, but inside, they're cowards.

Melody Hunter is anything but.

If Rodney Lee comes back here, she'll stand up to him.

The baby yawns in her arms, and Melody yawns, too. The pain medication is kicking in. She struggles to stay awake, feeling her eyelids flutter.

They drift closed. She forces them open. They close again.

The next time she opens them, feeling as though

she'd drifted off for a bit, a Negro nurse is by the bed. She's middle-aged, with a coil of cornrows beneath her white cap. Melody can't think of her name, but she's seen her before.

"I need to take the baby now."

"But . . . Louise said I could give her a bottle."

"No."

"I thought . . ." Had she dreamed it?

Is she dreaming *this*? The new nurse sounds like Cyril. So does Yvonne, but she doesn't look like him. This nurse does.

Melody closes her eyes, opens them again. The woman is still there.

"Come, now. I need to take her back to the nursery, but don't you worry none. I promise I'll take good care of her," she says in her thick patois.

"All right." Melody sighs, relieved to place her daughter in the nurse's outstretched, capable arms. She really is feeling weary.

Her eyes close again as the woman scurries out of the room with a muttered, "T'engky."

The Bronx

THE TROUBLE WITH night is that you can't tell, just by glancing at the sky, whether a storm is coming.

Gypsy hears the first rumble of thunder five minutes after leaving the apartment without her rain bonnet. She keeps going, fists deep in the pockets of an ancient spring coat that has never repelled water. Nor is it thick enough for a wind that feels more like early March than the brink of May, even with her violet cardigan layered beneath it.

She's wearing the sweater not for warmth, but because the shoulder seam has frayed into a gaping hole, and she needs thread in precisely the right shade so that the sweater will be wearable by Monday.

She'd been planning to wear it on her date with Greg tonight, but he'd canceled it yesterday.

"My grandmother's coming over for dinner," he'd told her during last period.

"I didn't know you had a grandmother."

"I do. And she's coming over."

For a moment she'd thought he might invite her to join them. But he'd just said to have a great weekend, as if she's the kind of girl who might spend it browsing Alexander's or at Loew's with a gaggle of friends, or having family dinners of her own.

The first few raindrops fall as she reaches the Grand Concourse and quickly becomes a torrent, stoplights and headlights and neon setting the rain-glossed boulevard aglow. Couples are everywhere, holding hands, splashing in and out of restaurants and stores. Gallant men hold umbrellas above women's stylish outfits and perfect coifs as Gypsy's jacket weighs limp and sodden and her hair weeps into her face.

At last, she reaches the Rexall. She smells the deep fryer and hears laughter coming from the back of the store as she browses spools of thread in the notions aisle, looking for just the right shade that matches her sweater. And the spring crocuses that had faded in the garden patch across from school.

"And your eyes," she hears Greg telling her, as he had

just weeks ago. *"Has anyone ever told you that you look like Elizabeth Taylor?"*

There's only one shade of purplish thread, and it's not close enough to the violet she needs. She should have just gone to a sewing store. But this is where Greg was planning to take her tonight and being here, even alone, makes her miss him a little less.

She starts toward the cash register with it and then, impulsively, walks in the opposite direction. She can't afford to buy the thread *and* an egg cream, though it's what she craves. But maybe a soda. She reaches into her pocket to see how much money she has. It's all in small coins, and a few have fallen through a hole in the lining. Her hand tears the hole even bigger digging them out from along the hem, but it's worth it when she counts forty-one cents total. Enough for a soda and the thread, with a penny to spare.

The back booths are filled, as always, with teenagers. She sits in an empty stool at the counter between a college-aged couple and a pair of junior high school girls. All are drinking chocolate egg creams.

She wants one, too.

One chocolate egg cream, two straws, across a booth from Greg.

And somehow, when she opens her mouth to order a Coke, that's what her mouth says. "Chocolate egg cream, please."

The counter man nods and walks away before she can take it back. She clenches the spool of thread, and then her hand, like her mouth, moves of its own accord to her pocket. Her fingers push the thread in, through the hole in the lining, and it drops to the hem. Glancing down, she sees the rounded outline and hurriedly rearranges the coat so that the telltale bulge is tucked beneath her.

Behind her, she hears a familiar shriek of laughter, and her heart sinks.

Leave it to Carol-Ann Ellis to witness Gypsy here, now, drenched and alone and shoplifting on a Saturday night.

She swivels her head to fix the girl with a dirty look. But as she scans the booth crowd for the trendy blond haircut, she recognizes someone else.

Someone who said his grandmother was coming for dinner.

Stunned, Gypsy turns back to face the counter.

Maybe Greg had confused the night of his grandmother's visit. Maybe she'd gotten sick and stayed home. Maybe she'd died suddenly.

Please let his grandmother be dead. Please don't let him be a liar.

She's jostled by the couple sitting next to her. They're joking around, taking turns holding an open, overturned glass bottle over their hamburgers in an effort to pour ketchup.

"Oops, sorry," the girl tells Gypsy, who barely registers her.

If there had been a death in Greg's family, would he be here in a booth with . . .

She turns her head again.

Carol-Ann.

But they're not alone, so it isn't a date, right? They're with a group—Sharon and her boyfriend, Vinnie, and Ricky Pflueger who's draped all over . . . is that Connie Barbero?

"Here, let me try again," the girl sitting next to

Gypsy tells her boyfriend, reaching for the ketchup bottle and jostling Gypsy again. "Oops, sorry."

Connie and Ricky look like a couple. They all, Gypsy realizes, look like couples. Everyone at Greg's table. Like maybe they're on a triple date or something, and—

"Roger! Cut it out and give it to me! I keep bumping this poor girl!"

"Fine, here! But it's not going to come out!"

"You just have to hit it, like—oh, no! Sorry!"

Something red and sticky splatters Gypsy's hand.

The girl plucks a handful of napkins from the silver holder on the counter and thrusts them at her. "I'm so sorry! My boyfriend is a jerk!"

Gypsy dabs at the ketchup in silence, staring at the frothy beverage in a tall glass with two straws that sits on the table between Greg and Carol-Ann. Carol-Ann is wearing a daffodil-colored bow in her hair.

My boyfriend is . . . so much worse than a jerk. My boyfriend is . . .

The girl next to her taps her arm. "Need more napkins?"

"What? Oh . . . no."

"Chocolate egg cream." The counterman sets a tall glass in front of her. There's only one straw, and a long silver spoon.

She looks back again. Greg and Carol-Ann lean forward and sip from their straws. Their noses bump, and they smile at each other.

She hears Oran's voice, reading from the book of John.

"When he speaketh a lie, he speaketh of his own: for he is a liar."

Gypsy reaches for her own glass. She'll march over to that booth and pour it over Greg's head. Both their heads.

She takes out the spoon, hand trembling. She imagines brown goo spattering into Carol-Ann's blond hair and yolk-colored bow and fake eyelashes.

No. It wouldn't be punishment enough for either of them. She closes her eyes and the spoon clenched in her hand becomes a knife, and the brown goo spatters become red. It isn't ketchup.

Yes. Much better.

She opens her eyes, puts down the spoon, leans into the straw, and drinks the egg cream. She leaves her money on the counter, and walks out into the night.

The street is awash in puddles and high ledges and sills are dripping. The storm has passed.

"Mrs. Hunter!"

Melody opens her eyes to see Louise holding a glass baby bottle.

"Sorry, I had a little problem down the hall, and it took me a little longer than I'd planned. Are you ready to . . . Where is your baby?"

"The nurse took her. She said they needed her back in the nursery."

"I told them you were going to feed her here," Louise grumbles, already on her way out the door. "I'll go find out what's what."

Melody closes her eyes again, feeling drowsiness slip back over her like a warm hug.

"Mrs. Hunter!" Louise is back. "Where is your daughter?"

"What do you mean?"

"She isn't in the nursery, and we're not sure why you would think she would be," a second nurse informs her.

Dazed, Melody sees a third nurse looking around the room as if she's misplaced her pocketbook.

"I told you, a nurse took her."

"Which nurse?" Louise asks.

"The one who sounds like Yvonne."

Cyril.

"You mean a Negro?" Louise shakes her head. "There are no other Negro nurses in this hospital, and Yvonne isn't on this shift."

"But a nurse came in while I was waiting for you, and I gave her the baby, and . . ."

"You were sleeping, Mrs. Hunter. Maybe you dreamed about a Negro nurse, but if you think you gave the baby to someone, we need to know who it was."

"I don't *think* I gave her to someone, I *know* I did. And I wouldn't have given her to anyone but a nurse, because I was worried after—"

She sees the painting opposite the bed.

Sitting ducks . . .

Panic sucker punches her.

"Someone kidnapped my baby!"

"Kidnapped?" She hears Louise tell one of the nurses to call the police, and she feels the world tilting, spinning, spinning . . .

Someone is screaming, and this time, she knows that it's her own voice.

Chapter Sixteen

Sunday, April 28, 1968
Marshboro, Georgia

Marshboro sits five miles east of US 17, coastal Camden County's north-south thoroughfare. About midway between the two, construction is underway to extend Interstate 95 to the Florida state line. When that major north-south route is completed, folks say, little old Marshboro will find itself on the map at last.

For now, it's a sleepy town populated by fewer than three hundred people, many of whom are related to Marceline. Two of her three surviving sisters live here. Her middle sister is buried in the Baptist churchyard alongside their parents and generations past.

The town proper is clumped along the east-west state road that becomes Main Street for a mile marked by a historic firehouse on one end and a memorial park at the other—a patch of grass barely big enough to hold a Civil War cannon and a flagpole. Between the two landmarks, the road meanders through the business district, past a service station, a laundromat, a bank, three churches, a five-and-dime, a small grocery, and Aunt Beulah's luncheonette.

As far as anyone knows, Aunt Beulah isn't related to anyone in Marshboro. Around these parts, the locals will flock to an establishment as long as you give it a homey, folksy name, hang blue-and-white-checkered curtains, and fry up good Southern cooking.

Aunt Beulah's doubles as the bus station, with a wooden bench to accommodate after-hours passengers and an awning to protect it from the elements. Marceline and her sister Birdie wait on the bench with the precious sweetgrass basket between them and Marceline's red satchel at their feet. Before leaving home, she'd emptied it of her late husband's belongings, packing them away in drawers now vacated by her own. Uncertain when—whether—she'll return to Barrow, she'd filled the bag with every stitch of her own clothing and a few sentimental keepsakes.

"You got the address?" Birdie asks.

Marceline pats the pocket of her traveling coat. "I got it right here . . . and right here." She taps her temple. "In case I lose the paper. I cannot take chances."

"You sure you don't want to wait a spell? I've got plenty of room for you to stay. That way, we can write a letter and see if—"

"Like I told you, and like Cyril, Sr., keeps telling me, no chances. He wants me to be gone right away."

Birdie says nothing to that, but she does give her head a little shake, as if she doesn't believe it.

Ah, dead folks never did go boddun' Birdie the way they did Marceline and their middle sisters, Wanda, Florence, and Alice. Maybe the world was just spinning too fast for spirits to stick by the time Birdie came along back in '18, after the war.

Or maybe it was Birdie who never stuck long enough to listen. From the time she was a young'un she was always flitting around, chirping about one thing or another, surrounded by a flock of friends—that's what their mother used to say, and it's how Birdie had gotten her nickname.

Marceline keeps an eye trained on the highway to the east, watching for headlights. Not a car has gone past them in the fifteen minutes they've been sitting here, but the Savannah-bound bus should be coming along anytime now.

"I wish I could go with you," her sister comments. "I don't like you travelin' so far all by yourself."

"Not by myself. Cyril, Sr., he's always with me."

"Just like Papa?" Birdie's tone is both wistful and doubtful.

"'Xactly like that."

Daddy had come to Marceline the night after he'd passed, telling her to look out for her mother and sisters, 'specially the baby. He stayed around for years, making sure they were all right, but he seemed to rest easier once the girls were grown and Mama and Florence had joined him on the other side.

If her husband has reunited with their son in the great beyond, he hasn't mentioned it. He's been busy guiding Marceline through the nightmare that's unfolded ever since Cyril, Jr., went missing out on Barrow sometime Thursday night or Friday morning.

She'd rounded up some menfolk to follow a trail of broken branches out in back of Cyril's property. They'd gone deep into the gator-infested marsh without question or qualm, and brought back only a filthy shred of fabric stained with what they didn't have to tell her was her son's blood.

"You goin' to call the law, Marceline?"

"Too late for the law."

"But they can chase down whoever—"

"You think they goin' to do any chasin'? For what? My boy is dead."

That brought silence all around. Two of those men, the Davis twins, had grown up with Cyril—once island boys, barefoot and carefree in the sunshine. Now they're somber men in a grim new world, Jimmy Davis with twin sons of his own. Those young boys tend to Otis every day while Cyril's at work, and they'll continue to do so, she knows. Especially now. The dog, and his property and hers, will be in good hands. They're family, her island neighbors, even those who don't share a drop of her blood. Now there's no telling when their paths will cross again; no telling what the future will bring.

She'd told no one on Barrow of her plan. If anyone comes looking for her, it'll be safer for everyone involved if they don't have to lie.

With the race wars heating up and Cyril's executioners on the loose, she'd looked over her shoulder all the way to the Jacksonville bus station, not just for men in pointy white hoods, but for the law. No one had followed her, though. Nor had anyone paid any attention to her when she got on and made her way to the colored seats in back.

She was the only passenger who sat there, and the only one to disembark here in Marshboro. She'd quickly covered the quarter mile out to her sister's concrete block house just south of town. Birdie was off working one of her jobs, so Marceline sat on her steps and waited.

She prayed for a while, and she sang softly.

"To everything there is a season . . ."

Cyril's song, with the biblical lyrics she'd learned as a child in Sunday school.

When Birdie came walking up at last, Marceline almost didn't recognize her.

At fifty, she's the youngest and prettiest of Marceline's sisters, with three others born in the decade between them.

People always said they look the most like each other, but in the few years since they last met, Birdie has changed. Today, she was wearing makeup—even false eyelashes, by the looks of it. And her skirt was short. Not as short as the young girls wear them, but above her knees. Most shockingly, she's cut her long cornrows clean off and coaxed her hair into a short bouffant with bangs, all glossy black without a hint of gray.

"Look at you, all fancy," Marceline had said when she'd seen her, before she'd told her why she was here. "You goin' to a beauty salon and colorin' your hair now?"

"You like it? Lucky thought I was gettin' frumpy. Now she says I look just like Diana Ross."

"Who?"

"Lucky! You know, Penelope. That's what we been callin' her."

Well aware of her niece's nickname, Marceline had said, "I mean Diana Ross?"

"You don't know her?"

"She must be new in town. I never heard'a her."

"In town?" Birdie threw her glossy black head back and laughed. "She's a celebrity. You must have heard of the Supremes? That's her singing group."

Marceline hadn't heard of them, either. She reckoned Cyril would probably know, and then she'd remembered that Cyril was gone, and grief had tried to engulf her all over again. She hadn't allowed it, not even when she'd shared the news with her sister.

Never one to rein in her emotions, poor Birdie, laughing one minute, had been leaking bitter tears on Marceline's shoulder the next. "I've been hearin' about violence and such, but I never thought it would take one of our own. Oh, Marceline . . ."

"Hush now, or you'll make me start wailin', too." She picked up the basket and nodded at the house. "Let's go inside. I have to show you something, and I need you to promise you'll never tell anyone, not even Lucky. I know how close she and Bettina are."

Birdie's daughter and their niece had been born just weeks apart, and been raised like sisters.

"They write from time to time, but they ain't seen each other in a dozen or so years now, since Bettina moved up to New York City."

"Still, Birdie . . . please don't tell Lucky."

"Don't you worry. You know I won't."

She does know that. In a large family where there are few secrets, Birdie is surprisingly good at keeping them—particularly her own. At eighteen, she'd delivered a baby girl, and never told anyone who the father was—not even her daughter, when Lucky was old enough to ask.

That's how it will be with Cyril's child, Marceline had thought when she'd crossed paths with the young, pregnant buckruh woman that day on the street in Fernandina. Even then, she'd been boddun' that her grandchild would likely never know anything about her daddy—who he was, and where he'd come from.

Now that he's gone, though his blood pumps life through that little girl's veins, his daughter won't likely hear his voice talkin' in her head. Too much going on in the modern mainland world, with all the noise and confusion, for a body to just be still and listen—especially for someone growing up without a clue to her Gullah heritage, with its spiritual beliefs.

And so, in those first awful hours when Marceline had realized what she'd lost, she'd known what she had to do. Every which way she'd looked at the situation, there was only one option. Some folks might not agree, but they don't know what it's like to lose a husband and then a son, neither one ever coming home to bury in a proper grave.

Yes, she feels a little bit guilty about the buckruh woman, who may not have been so crookety after all. But it can't be helped.

Marceline LeBlanc cannot—will not—lose another family member to violence.

You know where you need to go now, Cyril, Sr.'s voice had whispered from the Other Side on Friday morning. *You best start packing.*

"I don't want to leave. This is home."

Not anymore. Not without him.

That was true. But how would her trembling, grief-burdened bones carry her through the day, let alone on such a monumental and sorrowful journey?

Come, it's time to go. You just keep your head high and march on out of here. You'll be all right. Go on, get my mama's satchel.

"Isn't this just like you. You always did like travelin'."

And you never did. But you'll do what needs to be done now, and when you get up to Marshboro, Birdie will help you.

He was right on all counts.

Birdie had enough money stashed away for a bus ticket, and within an hour's time, scraped up enough from family and friends to keep Marceline going for a while in a new place. True to her word, she hadn't told anyone who or what the money was for—and true to tradition in their close-knit, bighearted family that didn't have much to spare, they gave whatever they could.

One day, Marceline would like to think, they might be able to be told that they'd saved a precious life. One day, perhaps the child will be able to thank them herself.

It's a lovely vision, though not likely to come to pass.

"It's comin'," Birdie says, and Marceline looks up to see distant headlights swinging toward them on the dark highway.

They stand. Marceline puts her heavy satchel over her shoulder and reaches for the basket.

"Wait, Marceline? One last look, please?"

"I don't want to wake her. She was fussin' all the way here on the bus."

"She misses her mama."

Marceline's mouth tightened. "I'm takin' her to find her mama. She won't even remember the other one."

Her sister gives a little shake of her sleek new hairdo.

"Don't go lookin' at me that way, Birdie. You know I'm savin' her life. They came for my boy, and they'd'a come for her if I left her be."

"I know. I just think of that buckruh woman and what she must be goin' through, losin' her child."

Marceline has also lost a child, dragged from his bed in the night and dead in the swamp because of that woman. Bettina, too, has lost a son. A year or two after she and Calvin were married, they'd buried their only child. The Lord hadn't seen fit to bless them with another, but Marceline will.

"You can't go boddun' 'bout buckruh, Birdie. You just think of this innocent child. Only one way to be sure she'll grow up."

"I know. Just let me say goodbye proper." Birdie pulls back a corner of the blanket draped over the opening. "Why you leavin' this on her?" She points to the plastic hospital bracelet on the baby's wrist.

Marceline hadn't realized it was there. She slips it over the tiny fist and hands it to her sister.

"Get rid of it, Birdie."

"Says here her name is Martina Eleanor Hunter. Why, the mama went and named her after you and Bettina! I thought you said—"

"What in tarnation are you talking about?"

"Marceline, Bettina . . . *Mar-tina.*"

Marceline stares. She'd missed that.

But the buckruh mother wouldn't have known, couldn't have known . . .

It's a sign. From Cyril, Sr., or Cyril, Jr., that she's doing the right thing.

Birdie pockets the bracelet before bending to bestow a gentle kiss on the baby's forehead. "Safe journey, child. Someday, I pray, we'll meet again. You won't remember me, but I'll never forget you."

Marceline swallows hard and looks away, at the big old magnolia tree down the road by the church. Oh, how her boy had loved that tire swing. She can hear him giggling, see those chubby fists clinging to the rope, little legs outstretched as he soared up to the clear blue Southern sky.

Tonight it hangs thick and black, starless and moonless.

The bus rattles up and the driver cranks open the doors. Marceline can see only a handful of passengers, and all appear to be sound asleep.

"T'engky for all you did for me, Birdie."

Her sister nods, tears running down her cheeks in a river of mascara, giving her one last hug before she climbs on the bus, and calling, "I love you."

Those words follow Marceline down the aisle. Maybe it's the last time she'll ever hear anyone say them on this earth, now that Cyril's gone.

She sits down alone in back with the basket on her lap and lifts the folds of blanket.

"Don't s'pose you'll ever say it to me," she whispers to his daughter. "That's all right, child. I'd raise you if I could, but you got a mama waitin', and she's lost her boy, too, and she's just achin' to fill her empty arms. You'll see, when we get to New York City."

Almost twenty-four hours after Melody had handed her daughter to the stranger who'd stolen her, the staff moved her off the maternity ward. Someone—a nurse, or her mother?—said it was for her own sake, that surely she was disturbed by the other mothers bonding with their babies just beyond her door.

Melody suspected it was for the other patients' sake. Surely *they* were disturbed by a bereft mother's hysteria, even if those traumatic waking moments were few and far between.

She'd slept through the transition and awakens now to find herself in a smaller room. No pastel walls or sweet duckling paintings here. Just dingy off-white paint. Her mother is seated beside her bed. She wears no makeup or jewelry, her hair is pulled straight back, and she has on a simple black sweater.

"Melody? You're awake."

"Yes."

She doesn't ask for an update. Honeybee's pale, drawn face confirms that the baby is still missing.

"Where's Daddy?"

"I sent him down to get me some coffee. I don't want it, but he needs something to do."

She looks ravaged, as she had the summer Ellie died, but older. Her blond hair is touched with gray that hadn't been there a few days earlier.

At least she seems to be keeping her composure this time. No fainting, nor histrionics. Just a sorrowful ghost of the vibrant, beaming woman who just yesterday had showered her new granddaughter with affection and gifts.

How much does she know?

"What time is it, Mother?"

"One fifteen."

"In the afternoon?"

"In the morning."

"Which day?"

"Monday."

"Monday?" She'd lost a day. "Can you . . . do you mind cranking my bed so that I can sit up? I need to stay awake for a bit, but all that pain medication knocks me out."

"They've been sedating you," Honeybee says,

raising the top half of the bed for her. "You were bleeding badly . . . probably from the stress. Don't you remember?"

"No."

"You were unconscious when Daddy and I got here. They said you'd fainted dead away. There, is the bed up enough for you?"

"Yes."

Honeybee fidgets with the blanket, untucking it along the edge of the mattress and then tucking it in again as she talks. "Doc Krebbs is keeping a real close eye on you. Been in and out every few hours to make sure you're all right."

"*All right?*" She turns away and stares at the ceiling.

Her mother should know that a mother who's lost a child is anything but all right. A mother who's lost a child collapses beneath the weight of her own grief.

You fainted dead away . . .

But Martina isn't . . . it's not like with Ellie. Martina is still alive. She has to be.

"Duke Mason came back a little while ago."

Debbie's father, the police officer. He'd been here earlier, too—or yesterday, wasn't it? He and Scotty came right after the baby disappeared.

"He wanted to talk to you again, but we couldn't get you to wake up. He should be back soon."

"Did he find Rodney Lee?"

"Yes, but it wasn't . . . Duke said he wasn't hard to find, wasn't hiding or anything. He was at home, in bed, sound asleep when they got over there. Ruth Midget said he'd been there all night, and she had a . . . gentleman there with her, and he said the same thing. None of them knew anything about the baby being kidnapped, so Duke says Rodney Lee's not the one who took—"

"I *know* he's not the one who *took* her, Mother. It was a nurse. But they say there is no such nurse working here, so she was an imposter."

"I just don't understand what Rodney Lee Midget has to do with any of this. Bob and Doris told us that he's always been a respectable young man, and a good friend to Travis."

"Well, there's another side to him. He was here right before the baby disappeared, and he told me to keep her safe."

Honeybee frowns. "I don't know how that—"

"What he said was, 'just try and keep her safe.'"

She sees her mother's lips tighten. Of course the words sound innocuous to Honeybee, and to anyone who doesn't know the whole story.

"It's not *what* he said. It's the *way* he said it. I just knew right away . . . he was up to something . . . and now . . . Mother, you have to believe me. Rodney Lee and that woman are in this together."

Yet it sounds far-fetched even to her own ears—like the plot of a bad movie.

"Think about what you're saying, Melody. Rodney Lee Midget might be jealous of you and Travis and all, but why in the world would he hire a Negro woman to kidnap your baby?"

Melody's brain fumbles with layers of drawn blackout curtains.

A Negro woman . . .

Clarity. Why would a racist send a *Black* woman to kidnap her child?

"He wouldn't, Mother. You're right," she says slowly.

Rodney Lee is no hero. She doesn't trust him. She's convinced he stole the letter she'd written to Travis. She remembers how uncomfortable he'd made her when he was here. And yet . . .

Could his words possibly have been a warning, because *he* knew the baby was in danger?

"You've been through so much." Honeybee glances over her shoulder into the hall, and lowers her voice. "Melody, honey, you were so exhausted, and on so much medication . . . is there any way you might have . . . I don't know, got up out of bed with Martina, maybe, and then put her down somewhere and forgot about it? Something like that?"

"Put her down?" Melody is incredulous. "*Forgotten* her? You think I would just leave my baby lying around like . . . like . . ."

"Shh! Or something else. You were on so much medication, and maybe you weren't, you know, in your right mind, and you might have just . . ."

Melody gapes at her mother, realizing what she's implying. The shock jars Rodney Lee's other words, terrible words, from her memory.

"I thought you were tryin' to smother her . . ."

She clenches the bed rails and pulls herself upright. "Mother, are you . . . do you actually believe that I would . . ."

"No! No, of course I don't."

"Does Duke Mason think . . . Is that why he wants to talk to me? Does he want to arrest me?"

"Of course not. He's just trying to find the baby, and they've searched every inch of this hospital, and they didn't find any trace of her."

"Because the nurse took her! But I would lay down my life for that little girl, Mother!"

She can't hold herself in an upright position. Her arms give out and she sinks back against the pillow, depleted, defeated.

But she'll be all right. Hadn't Cyril told her she's the strongest woman he knows, next to his mama?

"She doesn't wait around for someone else to fix things for her. Not many women are like that. She is. You are."

Yes, and one thing is certain: Melody hadn't carried their daughter off to some forgotten storage closet like a creature from *The Plague of the Zombies.* The white-uniformed woman who'd come into her room may not have been a nurse, but she'd been real.

Still . . .

If she wasn't a nurse, why had Melody recognized her?

Had she? Or was it just that she seemed familiar because she sounded so like Yvonne . . .

So like Cyril.

"T'engky," she'd said when Melody had handed her the baby, pronouncing the word with precisely the same inflection he uses—slightly different from the way Yvonne says it.

And she'd looked like Cyril, too, hadn't she?

"A woman only sees what she wants to see . . ."

Who had said that?

Harper Lee? Rodney Lee?

Never in her wildest imagination could she have foreseen confusing the two.

"Don't you worry none. I promise I'll take good care of her."

The nurse had said that, she remembers, when she wanted Melody to give her the baby.

Or had she?

Does a woman only *hear* what she wants to *hear*?

"Melody?"

Honeybee's voice is coming from farther away than it should be, and Melody is floating away on an icy current.

"Are you all right?"

"Just . . . so . . . t . . ."

Tired . . .

Dizzy . . .

The words are swept beyond her reach.

She needs to preserve her energy to recall what had happened in those precious last moments with Martina.

Had she conjured a nurse who looked like Cyril because she'd longed to see him?

Or could he have been here, and taken the baby?

"Melody!" Honeybee's voice is urgent.

She's leaning over Melody, blurry now, as if Melody is looking up at her from underwater.

". . . bleeding!. . . . Help!"

Honeybee is in trouble.

Something's wrong with her. She's bleeding.

She reaches for her mother but grasps emptiness, Honeybee and the room spinning slowly away as Melody swirls down, around and around, until silent, murky depths swallow her.

GYPSY HAD BEEN alone in the apartment when she finally fell asleep sometime after three in the morning, and was alone again when she awakened at ten.

In between, Oran had come and gone, leaving behind a pile of newspapers fat with extra sections and advertisements. A few are coffee-stained, many are crumpled, and all are damp. He steals them from stoops or scrounges trash cans, subways, and bus stops—not just the three daily papers but borough weeklies and smaller presses like *Co-op City Times* and Harlem's *Amsterdam News.*

He spends Sundays preaching sidewalk sermons and she's expected to spend hers combing the news for plagues, locusts, and various other Armageddon harbingers. She has to cut out relevant articles and glue them into a scrapbook for Oran's perusal. It sits open beside the stack of schoolbooks awaiting her attention. She likes to get her father's assignment out of the way early and move on to her homework.

But today, the papers are full of repetitive coverage on Martin Luther King's legacy and funeral, the hunt for his killer, the riots and violence sweeping the country. And instead of searching for other significant items, she's been toying with the scissors, staring at acres of newsprint without registering a word, thinking about last night.

Then she hears footsteps out in the hall. Oran, already?

She flips a page and peers at the newspaper, relieved when the footsteps move on past the door. Not Oran. But, checking the time, she knows he really will be here any minute, wanting to go over the articles she's found for him. He's always fired up on Sundays, doomsday sermons fresh in his mind, feeding off the crowd's energy.

She reads about a rash of Upper East Side burglaries,

a serial arsonist in Queens, a murdered bartender in Greenwich Village. As she moves past that one, about to turn the page, the victim's name jumps out at her. Fergus Ferguson—found dead last night in the pub he owned. No witnesses . . . motive was likely robbery . . . police seeking anyone who might have information . . .

The alliterative name seems vaguely familiar, but Gypsy can't place it. She goes back to fretting about how she's going to address Greg's lie when she sees him at school tomorrow.

"When he lies, he speaks out of his own character, for he is a liar and the father of lies."

But what if his family plans really had been canceled? It's not like he could have called Gypsy to tell her the date was back on, because she doesn't have a telephone and he doesn't know exactly where she lives.

Why, though, would he go out with his ex-girlfriend instead?

"He's just using you, you know . . ."

"Shut up, Carol-Ann," she mutters.

Maybe they weren't on a date. Maybe Greg had gone out with his buddies and run into Carol-Ann and the girls.

Chocolate egg cream, two straws.

Gypsy snaps the newspaper page, tearing it, as Carol-Ann's words echo in her brain.

"He's seeing how far you'll let him go. That's all he wants."

She's just jealous. She has no idea what Greg wants.

But how does she know about Gypsy's tattoo?

Again, she hears footsteps in the hall. This time, they stop at her door.

She inserts the scissors into the tear as if she's cutting out an important article.

Oran bursts into the apartment, hair standing on end, eyes manic. He's wearing a brown robe sashed with a frayed piece of rope. "Gypsy, baby! Check it out!"

"Hmm?" She continues cutting out the newspaper as if she's too busy for distraction.

"I've got a present for you."

No. Oh, no. She braces herself for chocolates, another tattoo. But he holds out his hand, and there's money in it.

"What's that for?"

"Bread. Buy yourself something."

She sets aside the scissors and meaningless clipping to accept the small stack of bills. Fanning it, she sees a bunch of ones, a five, more ones . . .

Nearly twenty dollars. Impressive. *Disturbing.*

"Where'd you get this?"

"Are you ready for this? Very truly I tell you . . . I found a new gig."

"For . . . what? Why would anyone pay you for . . . a gig? You're not a singer or a dancer or—"

"You don't know what I am!" he shouts in her face, a bead of spittle landing on her cheek.

You are of your father the devil . . .

She winces but holds his gaze, clutching the money.

"You don't want my present, man, I'll take it back." He reaches for it, and she sees a glint of gold on his wrist.

"I didn't say that. Thank you."

"All right, then."

As soon as he turns his back, she shoves the last clipping into her school binder and picks up the scissors.

"You got yourself a present, too, huh?" The question is an afterthought. She hadn't meant to ask it, stopping him in his tracks.

Slowly, he pivots. She points at his watch.

"Yeah. You like it? It's real old. Not broke-down old. Fancy old. What do you call it?"

"Antique?"

"That's right." He nods at his new watch, then up at her, grinning widely. "It's *antique*."

". . . SECONDARY POSTPARTUM HEMORRHAGE," Doc Krebbs is saying, sitting on a stool pulled up to Melody's bed in the surgical recovery room. He's wearing scrubs, with a mask dangling around his neck, his eyes somber behind his glasses.

She knows that he's talking to her and about her, telling her that she's had serious complications, and an operation. None of it matters. She needs to go back to drifting on the sunlit sea with Cyril and their daughter.

"Melody?"

She opens her eyes. There's Doc Krebbs, still talking.

". . . very lucky young woman . . ."

Lucky? Every inch of her body aches here, her heart worse than anything else.

". . . if your mother hadn't . . ."

Her mother.

She's supposed to remember something. About her mother . . .

She wants to ask, but her throat hurts almost as badly as her heart.

"From the tube . . . anesthesia . . ." Yvonne says in Mel-

ody's head, on a day when she'd awakened to find that she'd delivered a beautiful baby girl.

"... and I'm so sorry to have to tell you this..."

Her eyes jerk open. Doc Krebbs looks so sad. He isn't talking about Martina, because Martina is with Cyril.

But Honeybee...

Something about Honeybee...

Melody tries to remember what it is.

"... to stop the bleeding, and we..."

Bleeding?

Clarity: her mother, shouting that she was bleeding. She'd needed help, and Melody had been trying to get to her right before she found herself drowning...

"... I did everything I could, but..."

Oh, no.

No, no, no...

Rodney Lee came back for Melody, and he...

"Mother!" Melody rasps.

Doc Krebbs nods. "She and your daddy are in the waiting room. I've already told them."

"What...?"

"She'll come in to see you in a little while, when you're feeling up to it. She'll help you get through this."

"She'll help... *me*."

He nods.

Secondary postpartum hemorrhage...

Melody is the one who'd been bleeding. Not her mother. Honeybee had been calling for someone to help Melody.

She tries to focus on the doctor, forcing words past the fog in her brain and rawness in her throat. "I almost d..."

"Died? Yes. You almost did. Do you have any recollection?"

She'd been about to say *drown.* She'd been spiraling toward the ocean floor.

"I was dizzy. Cold . . . couldn't breathe."

"Your blood pressure dropped and you lost a lot of blood. Your mother saved your life."

No. Melody had almost drowned in a swirling storm, but it was Cyril who'd saved her.

And when the storm was over, he'd stayed with her, just floating, and Martina, too. She couldn't see them, couldn't hear their voices, but she could feel them with her, and everything was all right until the tide came in and swept her back to the world without them.

"I'm going to let you get some rest," Doc Krebbs says, and touches her arm. "Again, honey, I'm so sorry."

But why?

Her mother had saved her.

Cyril had saved her, too, and their daughter.

He's with Martina right now.

Ah, but the doctor wouldn't know that. He's sorry because he thinks her baby is still missing. Melody wants to tell him, but she can't. She can never tell anyone, not even her mother, that Rodney Lee hadn't sent that woman to take the baby away.

Cyril had.

"T'engky . . ."

The nurse with the patois and Cyril's face had been his mother.

"Don't you worry none . . ."

The baby is safe, with her grandma and her daddy . . .

In the sea?

No, that part had been a dream. But the rest is true. Martina is on Barrow with Cyril and his mother, who'd promised she'd take good care of her. She and Cyril will protect that child from Rodney Lee and Travis and anyone else who would dare try to get to her.

"I'll leave you be for now, Melody, honey," Doc Krebbs says, and she opens her eyes to see him pushing back his stool and standing. "I know this is a terrible blow, but you're one strong little lady and you'll get through it."

He's gone before she can ask him what he's talking about. But at least she knows it isn't her parents or her daughter, and he doesn't even know about Cyril. Nothing else really matters to her anymore, so whatever has him apologizing can't be as terrible as he thinks.

Melody closes her eyes and drifts back to the sea at last.

Part VII

2017

Chapter seventeen

Friday, January 13, 2017
Barrow Island

"Marceline," Amelia whispers, recognizing the old woman in the bed.

"Marceline?" Jessie echoes. "You mean . . . the Gullah priestess?"

Amelia whirls to Lucky, who nods. "Marceline's son, Cyril, was your daddy, honey."

"Not . . . not Calvin?"

She'd lost him once when he'd told her he'd found her in that church, and again when he'd passed away. When her DNA linked to Bettina's in October, she wondered if he was her biological father after all. Now she's lost him all over again—and Bettina, too.

The old woman speaks. Her voice, once resonant and forthright, quavers and the tone has thinned, but the distinct dialect is intact. "Calvin was a good man. He raised you, after Cyril . . ."

Her voice frays. Her eyes flutter closed.

Lucky touches Marceline's shoulder. "You can rest, Auntie. You don't have to do this now."

"She won't rest till it's done," Tandy comments, watching from the doorway. "I keep sayin' there's a reason she ain't goin' anywhere just yet. One hundred and eight years old, and she's just hangin' on and hangin' on no matter what the doctor says. Her body's ready, but her heart is strong and her mind is sharp, and so is her memory. She's a stubborn old gal. Ain't you, Miz LeBlanc?"

The eyelids snap open. "Y'all get on out of here and leave me to talk to Amelia. I got something to say, and I ain't wastin' a lick of energy on a bunch of folks that got nothing to do with this."

"All right, Auntie. Amelia, you have a seat, and speak up nice and strong so she can hear you. We'll be in the kitchen. Come on, Tandy, you can pour us some sweet tea."

"Mimi?" Jessie asks. "Are you okay if I . . ."

"Yes. Go ahead."

The others leave the room, closing the door after them, and Amelia sits in the chair beside the bed. Marceline appears to have fallen asleep. She wants to take the old woman's hand, but it looks fragile.

And you never were much for affection, were you? But you showed it other ways.

Marceline's eyes open, and they're sharp, focused on Amelia. "You look like him. Always did. Just like my son, Cyril."

"Cyril . . . Hunter?"

"Hunter! No! Cyril LeBlanc."

"Cyril LeBlanc."

Yet she was born Martina Eleanor Hunter.

"Where is he now, Marceline? My . . . your son."

"Died the night you were born, child. Buckruh murdered him."

Amelia pushes words past the lump in her throat. "But . . . why?"

"He was a Black man." Marceline's eyes close. Is

she remembering, or has she drifted off to sleep for real this time?

She's well over a hundred years old, Tandy had said, and clinging to life.

"Marceline, years ago, you told me you were outside the church when Calvin found me."

Her eyes open again. "I saw him come out of there that day with a baby."

Amelia's brain sorts the familiar, peculiar dialect, with *there* and *day* pronounced exactly the same.

"Did you see who left me?"

"*I* left you."

"Why?"

"Only way to save you. It was 1968 . . ."

"Terrible times for the Black man." Calvin had once told her the same thing. "But what about my mother? Where—"

"I brought you up to New York City on the bus," Marceline goes on, not hearing the question, or maybe just pretending. "I left you for Calvin to find, because I knew he'd take you right home to Bettina."

"But if you were my grandmother, why didn't you just take care of me yourself? And where was my—"

"A child needs a mama and a daddy. Bettina and Calvin needed to *be* a mama and a daddy. Bettina lost a child. She couldn't have another one."

"Bettina was your niece?"

"My sister Florence's girl."

Marceline's memory is remarkable. But they're running out of time. She's fading. Not just from this conversation.

"Calvin knew all of this?"

"That man went to his grave knowing none of this.

Bettina let him think you were a gift from the good Lord above. But she never spoke to me, never looked at me, again. Not another word."

"Why did you stay, then?"

"Didn't plan on it. I reckoned I'd go home to Georgia, but without Cyril . . ." She trails off sadly. "So I stayed. Keepin' an eye on things, makin' sure you was all right."

"When Bettina died, you came to pay a condolence call."

"She died young just like her mama."

"Why didn't you tell me the truth then?"

"And break Calvin's heart, when it was already broken?" She shakes her head. "You were going to be just fine. So I left."

"Did you follow me to Ithaca?"

Marceline offers a nod and a faint smile. "I surely did. There I was in the Port Authority waitin' for my bus, and who do I see? I thought, what in tarnation is that child doing? Runnin' away from home?"

"That's exactly what I was doing."

"I know that. Knew it then. I got on that bus and I made sure you were okay."

"Did you pay for my lunch?"

"I did," Marceline admits, looking pleased with herself. "But I let you be when I saw that you were going to be okay. Found a friend. Kept her, too. Good for you, child." She waves a hand at the closed door to the kitchen, where Amelia imagines Jessie is interrogating the older women.

"Marceline, what about the ring? A baby ring, with a *C* engraved on it. Calvin said I had it when he found me."

"Used to be your daddy's, and his daddy's before that." She closes her eyes. "I am tired."

"Tell me about my mother . . . please. And then you can sleep."

"I'm sorry, child."

"Please! Please tell me."

"Sorry for you. Sorry for her. Sorry . . ." She murmurs something that sounds like ". . . for what I did to her."

"Marceline, you said my father was murdered the night I was born, *because* I was born, and because he was Black."

"And because your mother was buckruh."

White? Her mother was *white*?

"And she was killed, too? By . . ."

Please don't say it, Marceline. Please don't tell me you killed my mother.

"She was not."

"Then why . . . why are you sorry?"

"Because she never knew . . ." She swallows with difficulty, then lifts her chin. "It was the only way to save you."

"What did you do, Marceline?"

"I took you. From the hospital. From her arms."

"You *took* me? From my mother?"

"She was young. She trusted me. I took you away. To New York. To *my* family."

"But . . ." Amelia's voice is choked. "What about my mother?"

"I am sorry every day, all these years. I wished I could have told her, but . . . terrible times."

"So she didn't know where I was? Who I was?"

"Never."

"Oh, Marceline. How could you do that to her?"

To me?

"She was married to a bad man."

"She was *married*? Not to . . . my father?"

"Her husband was a dangerous criminal. But she was a good woman."

A good woman . . .

A white married woman having an affair with a Black man. Pregnant with a Black man's child. 1968. The Deep South.

Terrible times.

"My Cyril was a good man. He wanted to change the world." A tear slips down her withered cheek.

Amelia bows her head. Her father had been killed because she'd been born. She'd been stolen from her mother's arms because her grandmother feared for her life.

No wonder. Oh, God, no wonder.

"Open this."

She looks up to see Marceline gesturing at the nightstand. Amelia wipes her eyes and leans toward it, pulling open the only drawer.

Marceline says something.

"Right day?" she asks, confused. "What?"

"He is right there! My Cyril."

Peering into the drawer, she sees a picture frame. "Do you want me to . . ."

"Take it."

She stares down at an old snapshot of a lanky young Black man with huge, serious eyes. He isn't smiling at the camera. He looks like he's thinking about the woman he loves, and a baby on the way, and changing the world.

"You look like him, you see?"

"I do. Do you have any other pictures of him?"

"No, child. Just that one. I found it with his things, after he was gone. You keep it, now."

"But if it's the only one you have . . ."

"Soon I will have my boy again." She closes her eyes.

"Marceline?"

"I'm tired, child. So tired . . . You go on, now. I need to rest."

"All right. I'll come see you again tomorrow." She stands, holding the framed photo and the little bracelet. She bends over the bed and presses a kiss to the old woman's forehead. "Thank you. For what you did. I understand."

Marceline lets out a little sigh.

Amelia walks slowly to the door. As she opens it, the old woman says, "When you see your mama, you show her that picture."

Amelia turns back. "When I . . ."

"Ask her to forgive me."

"My mother? She's . . ."

"My niece can tell you."

"Then she's . . ."

Marceline doesn't answer, breathing slowly, as if she's drifted off.

"She lives on Amelia Island," a voice says, and she looks up to see Lucky standing on the other side of the threshold.

"*Amelia* Island?" Jessie echoes in the kitchen. "I knew it, Mimi! I knew it!"

"Auntie changed your birth name when she brought you up north. It was her way of giving you a piece of your mother to carry all your life. She still lives there."

"She lives there. My mother is alive? And she doesn't know . . ."

"No. I can take y'all there to meet her if you don't mind waiting till later on tomorrow night."

"Tomorrow . . . night?" Amelia echoes in dismay.

"It's our annual church fundraiser. I'm the committee chairman, so I have to be there, otherwise, I'd—"

"But Mimi's been waiting her whole life for this!" Jessie protests. "Please don't make her go through another entire day!"

"Tell you what. I can give y'all the address and you can drive yourselves down in the morning."

Amelia offers a grateful smile and manages to say, "That would be . . . perfect. Just perfect. Thank you."

Chapter Eighteen

Saturday, January 14, 2017
Camden County, Georgia

Gypsy hadn't wasted time leaving Marshboro after insulting Aunt Beulah's fried chicken. She'd driven out to a budget chain hotel on the coastal highway, adjacent to a car rental agency and a large marina. She grabbed a lobby brochure for year-round fishing charters and called from her room to arrange one. Then, leaving her own rental car in the hotel lot, she walked next door and rented another.

"Daily, weekend, or weekly?" asked the man behind the counter.

She hesitated only a moment. "Weekly."

"You want to buy a tank of gas up front so that you can bring it back empty?"

"Sure, that would be great, thanks," she said, as if she did, indeed, intend to return it.

"I can upgrade you to a nice convertible. Cherry red. No extra charge."

"No, thanks."

"Really? You sure?"

Was it more conspicuous to turn down an upgrade than it would be to drive the damned red convertible? He might remember her. But if he does, and if anyone asks, she'll be long gone.

She chose the black compact car and drove it to a waterfront community of luxury homes, many of which are unoccupied at this time of year. She left the car in a secluded grove near garbage dumpsters at the edge of the development. From there, it was an easy walk back to a strip mall that contains several lively restaurants. She used the phone app to summon a ride back to the hotel.

The driver was a chatty older woman with a gray ponytail. "Have a nice dinner?"

"Yes."

"Visiting from New York, huh?"

It took Gypsy a moment to realize she knew that from the phone app. But of course, it isn't linked to her real name, or any other factual details. Before the weekend is over the phone, and all its data, will have vanished into the void along with Gypsy herself.

Now, long before daybreak, she arrives at the marina, bundled into a hooded parka against a cold sea breeze. The place is deserted, closed at this hour.

But out on the pier, a jovial man who calls himself Cappy Todd is waiting for her, untying the ropes that lash his forty-foot bowrider to the pier. It's called the *Reel Gent.* Fitting. He tips his woolen cap as she approaches and greets her with a warm handshake.

"Right on time. Ready to head out? The black sea bass have been biting offshore the last couple of days."

"Sounds good."

"Little nippy at this hour." He pulls his hat low over his weathered, smiling eyes. "There's a thermos of coffee under the stern seat. You just make yourself comfortable in there while I take us out."

"Will do. Mind if I smoke?"

"Not at all."

She lights a cigarette and stares at the black water as the boat leaves the marina.

On the same body of water a thousand miles north of here, another boat is being readied. She'd made a call this morning and made it very clear what will happen if anything goes wrong.

"Nothing will," he said. *"You can trust me. You should know that by now."*

Yes, but today's the day, and the endgame is crucial.

The first light of dawn appears on the horizon.

She remembers the long-ago voyage to Cuba with Perry at the helm. He'd grown up in New England, rowing at boarding school, sailing and yachting off coastal islands—yet another reason she'd chosen him. And he'd been perfect.

But now isn't the time to look back.

Now is the time to look ahead.

Fifteen minutes later, she's at the wheel of the *Reel Gent*, leaving Cappy Todd, his throat slit, bobbing in its bloody wake.

Washington Heights

THE PHOTOGRAPH BARNES found in his bedroom could have been anyone, any female figure silhouetted in a window anywhere in the world. But his instinct says that the woman in that photo is Charisse Montague, and that her life is in danger because someone believes she's Barnes's daughter and wants to hurt him by hurting her.

Only three people have a key to his place.

His mother was at sea last night.

Rob was at the party.

Barring emergency, the super can't—and wouldn't—cross the threshold without proper notification, and would have mentioned it.

Barnes stayed up with his pistol in hand, door dead-bolted and chained, windows securely locked. He pored over hard copies of his old files about the Wayland case until sleep finally overtook him at dawn.

Now he awakens to a ringing cell phone and morning light filtering in through the airshaft. He fumbles for the phone, sees an unidentified local number on caller ID, and answers with a wary, "Hello?"

"Is this Detective Stockton Barnes?"

"Yes, it is."

"My name is Kendra, and my aunt asked me to get in touch with you right away."

"Your aunt . . ."

"Regina Harrison. She said you need to talk to me about my cousins."

He sits up in bed, remembering. "That's right, I have some questions . . . are you free to meet this morning?"

She is. And she happens to live right here in Washington Heights.

Tawafuq. Again.

Barnes arranges to meet her and her husband at a coffee shop in an hour.

Amelia hasn't yet responded to last night's texts, so he dials her number.

Her phone goes into voice mail. Damn. He knows she's traveling down south with a friend to meet her mother's relatives and see if she can find information about the baby ring.

He leaves a message asking her to call him as soon as possible, then takes a long, hot shower. When he gets out and opens the bathroom door, the apartment's chill slams him, and he remembers something.

Glancing at the clock, he sees that it's ten to ten.

"Damn." Clad in a towel, he shivers his way back to the bedroom and hits Redial on his phone.

"Hi, Kendra, it's Stockton Barnes again. Listen, can you and your husband meet me at my apartment instead?"

"At . . . your apartment?"

"Yes, sorry. I only live a block from the coffee shop, but I have to be here to let my super in with a repairman."

Her silence doesn't surprise him. She and her husband are witnesses in an unsolved double homicide.

"I know what you're thinking, but I'm legit. NYPD. I'll show you my badge. Unless you want to wait until after twelve?"

"Jeremy and I have plans this afternoon. I'd rather just get it over with this morning. As long as you have ID . . ."

He assures her that he does, gives her his address, and she says they'll be here at ten thirty.

Barnes looks around. The kitchen garbage is full and there are dirty dishes in the sink. A bag of clothes for the dry cleaner sits beside the ever-mounting stack of unopened mail. Holiday cards still line the shelves. Though he'd taken down the Christmas tree last week, boxes of decorations and gifts remain stacked on the floor where it had stood, strewn with pine needles and curled poinsettia foliage. A lone petal clings to the plant, faded to a sickly pink.

He throws on jeans and his heaviest sweatshirt, intending to spend the next forty minutes making the apartment presentable. But as soon as he plugs in the vacuum cleaner, the super arrives with a maintenance man. Half an hour later, they're on their way out, heat hissing through the vents again, and someone buzzing from downstairs.

"You got company," the super says.

Yeah, no kidding. Barnes presses the button to unlock the main door.

"Hey, Tony? You didn't by any chance let anyone into my apartment yesterday, did you?"

Tony stops in the hallway and looks back at him. "What do you mean?"

"I'm just making sure no one was here while I was gone."

"Who would be here?"

"No one should have been. And I guess no one was."

"If you're trying to say I should'a had the heat fixed sooner, then—"

"No, it's not about that. I just . . . never mind. Thanks, Tony."

He watches Tony catch up with the coveralls-clad man at the door to the stairwell just as a young couple steps out.

Tony jerks a thumb over his shoulder. "If you're looking for Barnes, he's right there."

"A super, a repairman, and you're Barnes? That's pretty reassuring," Jeremy comments as they approach.

"But we'd still like to see your ID," Kendra adds.

"Of course." Barnes produces his badge. They take turns examining it closely, nod at each other, and accept his invitation to come in.

"Excuse the mess. I'd offer to take your coats, but it's still pretty cold in here, so I'll wait until the heat cranks up. But I can offer coffee. I was just about to make a pot."

They decline politely.

"You don't mind if I make it anyway?" he asks around a yawn. "Late night."

"On the case? My aunt said you have new information."

"About Delia Montague. Yes."

"Not about the murders?"

"Not directly." He measures coffee grounds into a filter.

"But my aunt said you're working with Detective El Idrissi on the case?"

"Not directly. I'm working another angle, and I have some questions about Brandy and Alma."

"We've told Detective El Idrissi everything we know," Jeremy says. "It's hard for us—especially for my wife—to keep rehashing it."

Barnes dumps water into the coffee maker and presses the button. "Why don't we go into the living room? I'll explain."

He moves a stack of magazines and a basket of folded laundry off the couch and invites them to sit down, belatedly noticing the Wayland case file lying open on the coffee table. But he can't move it with his hands full.

"Again, sorry about the"—brushing past the shelf with the magazines and laundry, he knocks several holiday cards to the floor—"mess. I'm just going to find a place to put this . . ."

He hurries into the bedroom, drops the heap on his unmade bed, and hears Kendra cry out.

"What the hell?" Jeremy exclaims.

Barnes rushes back to the living room and they whirl to face him. Jeremy takes a step, putting himself between his wife and Barnes, as if he's a threat.

"What's going—"

"Why do you have a picture of him?" Kendra demands in a high-pitched voice, waving something at him.

"A picture of who?"

"Brandy's new boyfriend!"

Westport

LILIANA HAD BARELY stirred when Bryant kissed her goodbye in the predawn darkness, whispering, "See you Friday morning, about this time."

He's taking a red-eye home so that they can spend the weekend together. He hates red-eyes.

But he loves me.

And she loves him. Any other morning, she'd have gotten up to make him coffee and see him off, even at that hour.

But she'd finally fallen asleep just an hour before he left, having lain awake most of the night, thinking about her birth father and trying to decide if she wants to let him into her life.

A thumping sound startles her from sleep. She opens her eyes and listens. Silence. The dog is sound asleep at the foot of the bed.

The thumping must have been part of her dream. It's fuzzy, but it had involved her father.

What time is it? She reaches for her phone to check

and finds several texts from her husband, whose flight was delayed out of JFK due to weather.

Looks like it might be canceled, the last one reads. Will keep you posted.

She gets out of bed and peers through the shade. There's weather, all right. It's snowing like crazy . . . and there's that thumping sound again, coming from downstairs. This time, even Briana stirs.

"It's okay," she tells the dog. "Someone's at the door."

It must be Bryant, back from the airport. She shoves her feet into her slippers, and hurries down the stairs.

Throwing open the door, she sees a familiar young Black man, not her husband, smiling at her.

"Morning," he says, shovel in hand. "Just wanted to let you know, I'm here to clear the walks and driveway, but I'm not sure where you want me to dump the snow out back by the deck. You want to come out and see what I mean?"

"Oh! Um, I'm sure it's fine."

He hesitates, looking over his shoulder. "Please, Mrs. Ford. Come on out and show me."

"What? But I—"

She sees the gun.

"WHY THE HELL are you calling me this early the morning after my party?" Rob's voice grumbles.

"Because you didn't answer my text, and it's urgent." Barnes clenches his phone hard against his ear. "Come on, Rob, wake up. Are you awake?"

"No."

"This is really important. I need you to listen to me. Something's happened, and I need—"

"What? What happened?" His friend sounds alert now. Alarmed.

"I'm looking for—" Barnes breaks off as his phone vibrates. It's an incoming call.

Kurtis.

"Rob—never mind. I just found it."

Rob mutters a reply and hangs up as Barnes answers the other line.

"Uncle Stockton?"

"Yes." He braces himself, nausea pumping through his gut.

"I'm sorry to bother you, but I saw your text last night, and I . . . I really would like to meet you. Thank you for offering to help me, because I'm kind of in trouble here, and I don't know what to do, and if you can possibly come . . ."

Barnes hesitates. He takes a deep breath. He has no choice. None at all.

"Anything you need, son. Where are you?"

"Up in Connecticut. Westport."

GYPSY RETURNS TO Marshboro in the rental car she'd parked last night near the waterfront development. The *Reel Gent* waits there, tied up to an empty private pier behind an unoccupied mansion.

She'd been prepared for small town bustle on this Saturday morning, and the main drag is thick with parked cars, but even Aunt Beulah's appears deserted. It doesn't take her long to realize that everyone is at the Baptist church, where a Martin Luther King fundraiser is underway.

She pulls into the cottage driveway behind Jessie's rental car, thinking about Kurtis Owens. He was wealthy enough to deliver her from the ruins of her life in Cuba, but he's so young, and he isn't a billionaire tycoon, and even if he were, she'll never grow fond of him the way she had Perry. Never love him, the way she'd loved Perry.

Yes, *loved* him, a fact she hadn't realized until it was too late.

She closes her eyes, remembering the last day in Baracoa.

Perry, looking back at her, blue eyes full of hope and trust. He was the only man she'd ever loved who hadn't betrayed her. No, he'd followed her command, and led the group into the tempest.

She'd promised them eternal salvation, just as her father had promised her. But they, like Oran Matthews, had turned out to be mere mortals, and she'd condemned them, lambs to the slaughter.

"And he said, Go forth, and stand upon the mount before the LORD. *And, behold, the* LORD *passed by, and a great and strong wind rent the mountains, and brake in pieces the rocks before the* LORD; *but the* LORD *was not in the wind . . ."*

After the hurricane blew north, she emerged from the depths of her cave high above the sea to find her island paradise reduced to rubble. The local population that had ridden out the hurricane in government shelters had survived, but her followers—her family—had not.

Gone. Perry. All of them.

Perry . . .

Sorrow washed over her as she stood staring into the wreckage-strewn waves lapping what was left of the beach.

She should have been more careful. She *would* have

been more careful, had an unwelcome visitor from the past not invaded her sanctuary at that crucial time.

In sorrow's wake came vengeful fury.

Stockton Barnes has to pay. He, and his daughter, and Amelia Crenshaw, and Margaret's daughter—they will die today, all of them, just as Perry had, swallowed by the sea.

BEHIND THE WHEEL, racing up the snowy highway toward Connecticut, Stockton calls Amelia.

This time she answers, with an apology. "I meant to get back to you last night, but you wouldn't believe what—"

"Where are you?"

"Hang on a second."

He hears a voice in the background calling, "Mimi?"

"I'm on the phone!" Amelia calls back and then, to Barnes, "Sorry."

"Who is that?"

"Just Jessie. That's her nickname for me. We're going—"

"Where are you?" Barnes asks again, urgently.

"What? We're at the house, getting ready to—"

"Okay, listen closely. It's important, Amelia. Really important. You and Jessie might be in danger."

"What?"

He explains quickly, telling her as much as he knows, and hears her gasp when he mentions the Brooklyn Butcher.

"Do you remember the copycat crimes in 1987, Barnes?"

"I worked that case, and I know the killer wound up in Ithaca, and that's why I wanted you to—"

"That was me!" She lowers her voice to a near whisper. "I'm the one who stabbed the killer after she broke into Jessie's house. We were there."

"You . . . you and Jessie were the teenaged girls who—"

"Yes. Oh, God. I need to tell her about this, but I think . . ."

"Mimi!"

This time, Jessie's background voice is closer, and Amelia drops hers to a whisper.

"I've got to go, Barnes. Thanks for the warning."

"I could be wrong. I'm praying I am. But if not . . . just be on guard. And don't trust anyone. No matter who it is, no matter what they say . . ."

Marshboro

Be on guard . . .

Barnes's words ring in Amelia's ears, phone and a dish towel trembling in her hands.

She'd been drying dishes when he called.

"I'll throw together an omelet while you get ready, Mimi," Jessie had said earlier. *"And then you can clean up the kitchen while I get ready."*

Amelia had grumbled good-naturedly about always getting the raw end of that familiar deal. Sure enough, her friend had left a mess—eggshells in the sink, crumbs and coffee grounds on the counter, a cutting board littered with onion skins and green pepper stems.

Cleanup had taken much longer than she'd anticipated, and as she greeted Barnes on the phone, she'd heard someone knocking at the cottage door. Jessie had called out to her from the bedroom, and then gone to open it.

By the times Barnes passed along the warning, Amelia could hear conversation in the next room.

Don't trust anyone, he'd said.

Too late.

Someone is in the house. A stranger's voice mingles with Jessie's.

The conversation sounds pleasant enough.

But Amelia whirls to the drainboard, that terrible Ithaca night thirty years ago blazing vividly in her memory.

The copycat killer had broken into Jessie's house after killing five of the Butcher's survivors.

"Where is she?" she'd demanded, and then Amelia had—

"Mimi!"

She whirls as Jessie appears in the doorway. An attractive older woman is with her. She's tanned and dressed all in black, with long black hair parted in a pronounced widow's peak.

Jessie, too, has a widow's peak.

"This is Gitana. She's a friend of your birth mom's. Your cousin Lucky asked her to drive us down to Amelia Island to meet your mom. Isn't that sweet?"

Amelia murmurs that it is, and thanks the woman. She smells of stale cigarette smoke.

Gitana . . .

She's smiling.

Jessie is smiling, too.

She and the stranger have the same dimples. The same smile.

Only Gitana's smile isn't reflected in her eyes. They're hard. Dangerous . . .

Purple.

Just as Barnes had described.

And *gitana* means "gypsy" in Spanish.

"Are you ready to go, Mimi?"

"Ready."

Amelia follows them out the door, pausing to swap the dish towel for the jacket she'd left draped over the chair, the kitchen knife she'd grabbed from the drainboard concealed beneath it.

WHEN BARNES ARRIVES at the waterfront address Kurtis had provided, he finds a deserted marina and a lone car in the parking lot. Kurtis is behind the wheel, engine idling. He rolls down his window. He looks gaunt, Barnes thinks. And he doesn't make eye contact.

"Thanks for coming, Uncle Stockton. Hop in. I need to talk to you." Seeing Barnes's expression, he holds up a paper cup. "I got you a coffee. Extra extra large, 'cause I know you."

Barnes forces a smile. "You sure do."

But I don't know you at all, son.

Barnes reminds himself that he has the edge here. Kurtis has no idea he's even suspicious. He thinks good old Uncle Stockton is here to lend a hand and an ear and maybe a couple of bucks. When Barnes reached out last night, that had been his intention. Now . . .

If he weren't armed, he would never have gotten out of his car and into the passenger seat of Kurtis's. But he is, so he does, though there's no way he's going to use his gun on Kurtis.

You will do what you have to do, Stockton.

I don't know if I can, Wash. Not this time.

"Hope it's still hot enough for you." Kurtis hands him the coffee.

"It's fine." Barnes sets it into the console cup holder. "Give it to me straight. What's going on with you?"

"I . . . I got myself into trouble."

Barnes hears the uncertainty, and he reminds himself that this is Kurtis. His best friend's son, born the same day as Charisse.

But then he thinks of the surly, troubled young man who'd accompanied him and Rob to Baracoa. Of Perry Wayland's warning, and of the ominous letter he'd found on his pillow.

Who had access to his apartment?

Rob.

Kurtis could easily have borrowed his key, duplicated it . . .

He could have . . . but . . .

It has to be a mistake. Kurtis would never, could never . . .

"Aren't you going to drink your coffee, Uncle Stockton? It's going to get cold."

Barnes looks down at the cup, then up at Kurtis's face. His jaw is tense.

He's trying too damned hard.

Did he put something in it?

That, more than anything else, is impossible to believe.

Then he hears a thump in the car trunk.

Part VIII

1968

Chapter Nineteen

Friday, May 10, 1968
Fernandina Beach

Home sweet home," Honeybee says, pulling up at the curb and looking at Melody in the passenger's seat. "Feeling all right?"

Nothing has changed since her mother asked the question five minutes ago—nor since the previous inquiry five minutes before that. But Melody nods. She can't fault Honeybee for being concerned, or for insisting that Melody stay here with her and Daddy while she recuperates.

"You can't come home from the hospital to an empty house," she'd told Melody, just as she had back in April.

This time, Melody didn't argue. She has no desire to return to the house she'd shared with Travis, even to get her clothes. Her mother had done that before her release. The woman has been an efficient and selfless stanchion of maternal valor throughout this ordeal.

The sun is high and the warm salt breeze is scented with southern magnolia and the sweet confederate jasmine that spills from every trellis and picket fence. Pedestrians stroll along, greeting neighbors tending to their gardens or perched on porch swings. Melody sees every head turn in her direction as she emerges from the car. Honeybee takes her arm gently, as if she's an elderly visitor or a young child.

"After we get you settled, we'll have some sweet tea out on the porch or in the garden. The fresh air will do you a world of good."

Melody keeps her gaze fixed on the front door as they walk toward the porch, her mother pointing out a hummingbird nosing a showy scarlet bloom along the border.

"Look! Look! See it? Right over there in the red buckeye tree. You're not looking, dear!"

"I'm sorry, Mother, I . . ." She lowers her voice. "*They're* looking. At me."

"Who . . . ?" Honeybee swivels her head as they climb the front steps. "Oh. Yes. I suppose they are, but we can't blame them. They've been so concerned. Mrs. Brady dropped by with vegetable soup for you just last night, and Bev Leonard said she'll—"

"Mother! Have you told *everyone* about this? About the baby, and . . . me?"

Honeybee pauses with her hand on the doorknob. "They already knew about the baby, Melody. It was in the papers."

Of course a kidnapping would make headlines. Melody stares at her feet, still too swollen for anything but tennis shoes, and at the welcome mat with its bright pink daisies.

Honeybee opens the door. "Doesn't it smell divine in here? I had Raelene make two pineapple upside down cakes, one for dessert, and the other in case of company, or . . ."

Something to celebrate.

She's thinking the baby might come home after all.

Raelene rushes from the kitchen to embrace Melody.

"Careful, careful," Honeybee says. "She's fragile right now."

"I'm just so relieved. Now we can take care of you and help you heal. Whenever y'all are ready for lunch, I've got hot biscuits and honey ham."

"Thank you. I think I'll just go up and take a nap."

"Your room is all made up for you," Honeybee says. "I'll just help you—"

"I'm just fine on my own. But thank you both, for . . . everything."

"You just holler if you need me," Honeybee calls after her as she heads up the polished wooden flight.

"Or me," Raelene chimes in.

On the second floor, Melody exhales for what might be the first time since she'd left the hospital. She continues down the hall, past her parents' bedroom at the front of the house and four doors along the wide hallway leading to her own. Linen closet, bathroom, guest room, Ellie's . . .

She stops. The door, so rarely opened, is slightly ajar and she peeks through the crack.

Frozen in time, Ellie's bedroom is pastel pink with ruffled linens. Stuffed animals—all dogs—mingle with pinup posters of Elvis and Frankie Avalon torn from *16* magazine. On the bookshelves, Dr. Seuss shares space with nine Beany Malone novels Melody had passed her sister's way, ignoring Honeybee's protests that Ellie was too young.

Melody crosses the threshold, running her fingertips along the row of neatly organized books.

Poor Ellie, perpetually trying to catch up with

Melody and wrench herself from her mother's overprotective grasp.

Poor Honeybee, trying to hold on long before any of them could have known . . .

The ninth Beany book is aptly titled *A Bright Star Falls*, about a terminally ill teenaged girl. Melody and Ellie had cried over it together back in 1959, never imagining that the plot would play out in their own lives a year later.

"Am I going to die like Rosellen did in the book?" Ellie asked when she got her own diagnosis.

"Of course not!" Honeybee glared at Melody.

"I told you she was too young."

Melody has long since come to regret sharing *A Bright Star Falls* with Ellie, and Lenora Mattingly Weber has since published four more Beany books that Melody couldn't bear to read.

She turns away from the bookshelf.

The February 1960 issue of *Teen World* lies on the bedside table, its cover featuring Kookie Byrnes and an article headlined "For Girls Who Will Marry Young."

"This is us, Melly!" Ellie had said. *"We'll get married when we're eighteen and be each other's maids of honor and live next door to each other and have lots of children and Mother will babysit when we go dancing with our husbands."*

Poor bright star Ellie . . .

As she turns away, Melody spots the one thing in the room that had never been part of the frozen-in-time shrine.

She's only seen the bassinet in an old album filled with photos of her and Ellie as infants back in the '40s. Now it's trying to hide in a shadowy corner, stashed between the bed and the wall. White wicker, with a pink organza skirt Honeybee had made for her first grandchild.

Nearly two weeks ago, the emergency hysterectomy that had saved Melody's life had stolen her fertility. On top of losing a child, and their only grandchild, her parents have lost the promise of any others.

How can they lose me, too?

Melody closes the door.

She can't bear to see them suffer, but she can't tell them that she's certain Martina is alive out on Barrow. Maybe one day, but she'd promised Cyril she wouldn't confide in her mother.

At the end of the hall, she retreats into her own room.

Nothing has changed since she last woke up here, on her wedding day. In fact, little has changed since she'd left for college back in 1964. Same Beatles posters; same snapshots stuck into the mirror frame along with programs from a decade of musical performances. Her favorite albums are stacked beside the record player. Travis had talked her out of transporting them to their new place.

"We don't have room for all that stuff, and it's not like housewives lounge around listening to music all day," he'd said, and kissed her before she could protest.

The comment hadn't thrilled her, but kissing him certainly had, back then. Now her stomach churns at the thought of it, of him.

She sits on the bed, with its lilac-sprigged bedspread that matches the curtains, accented by pastel lavender walls.

"Pink for Ellie, purple for Melly . . ."

Honeybee, doting on her precious, pretty pair of color-coded daughters.

Honeybee, red-eyed at Melody's bedside in the surgical recovery room.

"I'm so sorry. I know this is unbearable, but your life will go on. It will. I promise. And I'll be right by your side, darling."

"What do you mean? Why is everyone so sorry?"

Her mother faltered. "Doc Krebbs said he told you."

"Told me what?"

"Oh, Melody . . ." Honeybee had wept as she'd delivered news that would have destroyed any other young woman after having her newborn firstborn abducted from her arms.

Melody had listened, dry-eyed. Her pregnancy had traumatized and jeopardized so many lives, but her heart no longer ached.

She leans back and closes her eyes, thinking of Cyril and Martina waiting for her on Barrow as she drifts off.

Someone knocks. "Melody?"

She sighs. "Yes, Mother?"

"Duke Mason and Scotty Jackson are here, and they're insisting on talking to you."

The Bronx

GREG WASN'T IN school the Monday morning after Gypsy saw him in the drugstore. Nor was he there Tuesday, or Wednesday.

Gypsy speculated that his grandmother really had died, and that she'd hallucinated seeing him sharing an egg cream with Carol-Ann Saturday night.

When he finally showed up yesterday morning, he was on crutches.

"Broke my ankle playing baseball over the weekend," he explained, wincing as he shifted his weight and reached for a book on the top shelf of his locker.

She couldn't possibly ask him, in that moment, if he'd also gone out with his ex-girlfriend over the weekend. So she just helped him with his books and listened as he grumbled about having to sit out the rest of the season. He didn't comment on the new spring shift she'd bought with the money Oran had given her. It was yellow, his favorite color, but he barely looked at her before his friends came along and he hobbled off to class.

The rest of the week passed uneventfully, and he didn't ask her out for Friday or Saturday.

Only because he could barely walk, she told herself. And she certainly didn't see him talking to Carol-Ann. Every time their paths crossed, he was glum and appeared to be in pain.

This week brought more of the same, with the prospect of another dateless weekend for Gypsy. Greg wasn't even in last period this afternoon, having left school early for a doctor's appointment he hadn't mentioned to her.

Which means nothing, Gypsy assures herself, shuffling toward the exit after the last bell. Rounding the corner, she collides with a senior guy barreling from the opposite direction. She manages to keep her balance, but her books go flying. A binder snaps open as it falls, scattering paper like a ticker tape parade.

"Sorry," the guy says, and keeps going.

The corridor is crowded with students heading for

propped open doors, and a breeze scatters Gypsy's notes beneath their trampling feet. No one offers to help as she bends to gather the papers. Hearing a wolf whistle, she sees Greg's friends Vinnie and Ricky leaning against the trophy case behind her, leering.

"Great legs," Ricky comments.

"Nice ass, too," Vinnie says.

Gypsy's temper flares. She stoops again in an awkward pose, holding her short hem against her bare legs as they chatter on.

"Wonder why Martinez dumped her?"

"Because Carol-Ann's got great legs and a nice ass, too, and she's not—"

"What are you talking about?" Gypsy is upright again, and furious.

"Yeah, but this chick has great legs, a nice ass, *and* supersonic hearing."

They snicker.

"Hey, what's going on?" Connie appears, wedging herself under Ricky's lanky arm and fixing Gypsy with a stare.

"We were just talking about Greg and Linda's breakup."

"Breakup?"

For an illogical moment, Gypsy believes she's going to set them straight. But Connie says, "You can't break up if you weren't going steady."

Vinnie grins, tapping his temple. "She's smart, this one."

"She's an idiot," Gypsy snaps, hand trembling as she reaches for a sheet of paper covered in her own handwriting and a grimy shoe print.

Her reaction is, predictably, fuel for their commentary.

She hears Connie saying something about having to cover for Carol-Ann Saturday night. "She's telling her parents we're having a slumber party at my house."

"More like a slumber party for two at Greg's," Ricky says, and they laugh.

They don't know what they're talking about. Don't listen to them.

She swoops the rest of her notes into her binder and escapes into pale spring sunlight that radiates no warmth. In the miniscule garden patch across the street, someone has trampled the pink tulip buds she'd seen this morning. Shredded petals are strewn amid broken stems, cruel footprints stamped in the dirt. Gypsy imagines the little old lady huddled inside, weeping.

She, too, wants to weep, clutching her ruined notebook to her chest as she walks on home, Carol-Ann's voice taunting her . . . with the truth.

"He's just using you, you know."

Well, she's not going to cry about it, that's for damned sure. She's stronger than that, better than that, smarter than that. Smarter than anyone.

She has to study hard and get a scholarship to a good college, like Mr. Dixon said. Then she can live the kind of life where no one bullies you for what you don't have, and who you aren't.

She sits on the floor, opens her binder, and begins laying the pages of notes out before her, putting them back in order.

Mixed in, she finds a newspaper clipping. She assumes she'd scooped it up by accident, but then sees that it's the meaningless news clipping she'd cut out on that awful Sunday after Greg betrayed her.

Fergus Ferguson . . .

Again, the name stirs a memory, but it wriggles away like an exposed earthworm burrowing deeper into the soil.

She rereads the article. *Greenwich village . . . bartender . . . murder . . . robbery . . .*

This time, she notices a detail that hadn't meant anything before.

The contents of the pub's cash drawer had been stolen, along with the antique gold watch Fergus Ferguson had worn every day of his life.

"I SURE AM glad to see you looking like the picture of health," Duke Mason says, seated across the dining room table from Melody.

"I'm feeling much better, thank you kindly."

"A miraculous recovery from the brink of death. We wanted to talk to you at the hospital, but Doc Krebbs said you were too *ill*." Scotty Jackson emphasizes the last word as if it's in quotation marks.

Honeybee bristles, flanking Melody like a bodyguard or defense attorney. "She had a life-threatening condition and major surgery!"

Duke nods. "That's what Doc Krebbs said. Real protective of his patients."

"As he should be. He delivered Melody and her sister into this world."

"Same with my daughter, and I reckon he was there when Scotty was born as well."

"Sure was."

Raelene pours coffee and offers a plate of store-bought cookies. No pineapple upside down cake for these unwelcome visitors. After she retreats to the kitchen, Scotty says, "We'd like to update y'all on the kidnapping case."

"Has there been a development?"

"Not per se, Mrs. Abernathy, but we've been following up on a few leads."

He looks at Duke, who bites into a Lorna Doone with a nod for Scotty to continue.

"We haven't been able to track down your Negro nurse, but Rodney Lee Midget did give us some information before he left for Georgia."

"Georgia!"

"Yes, ma'am, Mrs. Hunter. Basic training at Fort Benning. I guess y'all didn't know Rodney Lee was drafted?"

"We didn't know," Honeybee says. "But we wish him well, don't we, Melody?"

She ignores the question, asking Scotty, "Are you sure about this?"

"Saw him off on the bus last Monday morning. Whole mess of local boys were headed to basic training that day. Duke was there, too, saying goodbye to his daughter's husband."

"Fiancé," Duke amends. "Debbie's been carrying on ever since he got that draft notice. She fell apart down there by the bus and got him started, too. Well, soon as I saw that, me being a World War Two veteran, I took him aside and I said, 'Son, you'd better pull yourself together. When this country calls you to serve, you don't cry.' And he wasn't the only one." He shrugs. "Oh, well. This war'll make 'em into men real fast."

"If it doesn't kill 'em first," Scotty mutters.

"Y'all might want to remember that Travis is over there," Honeybee announces pointedly, protectively. As if in this moment, with all that's going on, her fragile daughter might be undone by the reminder that soldiers die.

"Oh, I know, ma'am. Travis Hunter is one of my closest friends in this world. I was there to see him off last spring with all y'all, remember?"

Melody nods, recalling the throng of well-wishers watching Travis and several other draftees climb onto that bus a year ago. If Rodney Lee had done the same thing last Monday, then he's in the army for real. It isn't just a ruse to skip town.

"What information did Rodney Lee have, Scotty?" she asks, arms folded across her saggy stomach.

"I thought you were tryin' to smother her . . ."

"First off, ma'am, under the circumstances, you should call me Officer Jackson."

She offers a clenched, "Sorry. Officer Jackson. You were saying?"

"When Rodney Lee was leaving the hospital after delivering milk the night the baby was stolen, he saw a gang of Negro women sitting in a car out front of the hospital."

"A *gang*?"

"Yes, ma'am. Said they were suspicious looking."

"Mercy!" Honeybee looks as though she might faint.

"Suspicious looking . . . how?" Melody asks.

"Well, now, let me think on that." Scotty stares at her for a moment longer than necessary before turning to Duke. "Maybe he said suspicious acting?"

"Could be." Duke helps himself to another cookie.

"I didn't talk to him myself. You took down the report."

"I don't have it here, but as I recall now, Rodney Lee said they were suspicious acting. He went right over to the car and asked the women what they were up to. They did not take kindly to that."

"Did they threaten him?" Honeybee asks.

"Mother! Why would they threaten him?"

"Scotty said they were sinister."

"What Scotty *said* was that they were Negro, and it sounds like he—both of you—then jumped to the conclusion that—"

"It's Officer Jackson, if y'all can just call me by my proper name?"

"Only right," Duke agrees, brushing crumbs from his mustache. "Out'a respect."

Honeybee apologizes.

Melody does not. "What happened after Rodney Lee confronted this . . . gang, you said, Officer Jackson?"

"They claimed they were at the hospital to visit a sick friend, but see, that can't be right, because I did some investigating and there were only a couple of colored patients that night, and none of 'em had any visitors, and . . . why are you shaking your head, Melody?"

"Shouldn't you be calling me Mrs. Hunter? Out of respect, and all. Only right."

Scotty flashes a tight smile. "Sorry, I just got a little worked up there, thinking about these professional baby thieves parked right there brazen as you please, fixin' to make their move."

"Professional baby thieves!" Honeybee echoes in alarm.

"You look awfully thoughtful, there, Mrs. Hunter," Scotty comments. "I know this is hard for you, but at least we know you weren't the one who—"

Duke cuts him off, clearing his throat loudly. "Now, Officer Jackson, no one ever said this little lady had anything to do with her baby's disappearance."

"No, but when I asked Doc Krebbs if a woman who's just given birth might be capable of . . . you know, doing something she didn't mean to do, well, he did admit it's possible."

"That he did, Scotty. That he did."

"That sure would make your troubles disappear in a jiffy."

Had Rodney Lee planted that scenario with the police?

"'Course, Doc Krebbs was speaking hypothetically," Duke points out. "Wanted to make sure we knew he didn't believe someone like Mrs. Hunter would do such a thing—living right here all her life, a banker's daughter from such a respectable local family, married to a fine fellow serving his country." He allows that to sit for a moment. "We're glad we don't have any reason to pursue that because of what Rodney Lee saw."

Message received, loud and clear.

We're throwing you a lifeline, and if you know what's good for you, you'll take it.

Melody can tell Scotty doesn't believe in her innocence, sitting there rubbing his chin.

Neither does Duke, going on about a kidnapping ring that's been working up and down the East Coast, stealing babies from hospitals.

"Now, I don't know about it myself, but Scotty here says he's heard tell. Isn't that right, Sc—Officer Jackson?"

He nods. "Been seein' it in the newspapers and whatnot. Remember that big FBI investigation a few years back, lookin' for the baby who was kidnapped from that hospital in Chicago? Turned up alive a few years later? His mother handed him to a Black woman who said she was a nurse, too."

"Four years to the day Martina disappeared, wasn't it?"

"It was, Duke. It was. That's why it was in the newspapers again."

"About a ring of Black baby thieves?" Melody asks, hands clasped tightly under the table.

"About that one case, but there were others."

She nods, piecing it together in a way that almost makes sense. Rodney Lee, or more likely Scotty, could have stumbled across an article marking the anniversary of that 1964 Chicago kidnapping. It sounds conveniently similar to the scenario Melody had described.

"Is the FBI working on the case?" Honeybee asks, wringing her hands, her voice bordering on shrill.

"There's no evidence of interstate travel at this point," Scotty says. "And the Supreme Court ruled in that case just a few weeks ago that kidnapping isn't a capital offense."

"That's a fact," Duke agrees.

Maybe so, but there's another reason they don't want the FBI getting involved in this.

They believe Melody is guilty of harming her baby.

They're doing what they think is right, to avoid the shame and scandal that would accompany such a heinous crime. Or, if not to save Melody herself, then to spare her parents and in-laws, pillars in their beloved community, and yes, above all, to spare her fine husband.

Travis, Scotty Jackson's close friend, the dutiful soldier who hadn't gone weeping off to war.

The scenario seems far-fetched, and maybe it would be, beyond this small Southern town. But Melody has lived here all her life. She knows how things are and always will be here, and in a thousand other small Southern towns. That's why she and Cyril have to get away.

Duke Mason pushes back his chair and snags one more cookie for the road. "We'd best go on our way. But rest assured, Mrs. Hunter, Mrs. Abernathy, that we're going to do everything in our power to find that baby girl."

No, you aren't. For you, and for me, this case is as good as closed.

Harlem

"Hush now," Marceline tells the bundle in the basket when she spots a familiar figure rounding the corner onto Lexington Avenue. "There's your new mama comin'."

It isn't her first glimpse of her niece since she'd arrived in New York City. So far, she hasn't let Bettina see her, but every time she spots Bettina, her heart clenches.

That young woman works so hard, always looks so weary.

Today, as every weekday, she's wearing the black housekeeper's uniform with a white apron, and a frilly white band in her dark hair. She works for a wealthy family that lives fifty blocks south of here, headed home to change and probably gobble a quick supper before she goes to her other job, as a token booth clerk at the 116th Street subway station. Calvin has already returned from his day job and departed for his night job, from bus driver to busboy.

As Bettina approaches the alleyway, Marceline steps into her path. Her niece gasps, instinctively clutching her black vinyl pocketbook. Then her eyes widen with recognition, and she gasps again.

"Hello, child."

"Auntie . . . ?"

Marceline nods, noticing how very much the younger woman looks like Florence. Oh, how she misses Florence. She was always the most level-headed of the sisters, the peacemaker, the one who could cook and sew even better than their mama. She'd been a good wife to a fine man who'd died young. Now her daughter is a good wife to a fine man, and God willing, they'll live to a ripe old age . . . as parents.

"What are you doing here?"

"Come to visit."

"Well, that's . . . that's just . . ." She looks down, and then up again, eyes filled with tears.

"What's the matter, child?"

"We have a funeral to attend tomorrow. Calvin's friend died, and . . ." She shakes her head, anger flaring. "Well, Ernie didn't *die.* He was *murdered.* Because of the color of his skin."

Marceline's throat goes dry.

"We're broken up about it, me and Calvin," Bettina

goes on. "Everyone is. A gang of young white men ran him down. You just can't imagine—"

"Oh, but I can. I can, indeed."

"So you're welcome to stay with us, but I just wanted you to know—"

"I don't need to stay with you, child. I got a place of my own."

"What?"

"Three blocks up and around the corner, with a tree right outside the window."

"You're going to live *here*?"

"For now."

"But . . . what about Cyril? Is he here, too?"

"Cyril," she says, lifting her chin, "is gone. Murdered."

"Our Cyril . . . *gone*? How? Why?"

"Because his daughter has a buckruh mama, and she is married, and her husband is in the Ku Klux Klan. So I brought her here, to live with you and your husband. You can keep her safe."

"You want us to harbor a white woman whose husband *kills* Black people?" Bettina asks, darting a glance around to make sure no one is listening. "In times like these? In a place like this? Auntie, that's just—"

"Not the woman. The baby! Her name is Amelia, and—"

"No. No!"

"But—"

"You can't put our lives in danger!" She takes a step closer, hissing, "I just *told* you, our friend was *murdered*! What do you think is going to happen to us with a white baby under our roof?"

"She'll look Black. No one will ever know that she—"

"No! Auntie, I'm sorry. I love you, and I loved my cousin Cyril. But Ernie Fields was dragged through the streets, dead. His wife is *destroyed.* She can barely stand. She and her girls are terrified for their own lives. I can't risk Calvin's life. Or my own."

"What about the baby?"

"*You* raise her!"

Marceline shakes her head. "She needs a mama *and* a daddy."

"Then find them for her. But it can't be Calvin and me."

Bettina turns and walks away.

Marceline looks down at the basket. "Don't you worry, child. One way or another, I'll get you home, with them."

Oran whistles his way to his door Friday evening with a brown paper bag tucked under his arm, eager to present it to his Gypsy. But when he steps inside, the lights are off and the place feels empty.

"Where the hell did she go?" he mutters, feeling around for a switch.

"I'm here," his daughter's voice says in the dark.

"What, sleeping? It's not even—" He finds the switch and flips it.

Gypsy isn't sleeping. She's sitting on the couch. Just sitting.

"Hey! What happened?"

She says nothing.

Oran scowls. "Answer me when I speak."

"It works both ways."

"What?"

"I answer your questions, and you answer mine."

He fixes her with narrowed eyes, waiting for her to squirm. She doesn't. Not his Gypsy. She stares right back at him, chin lifted in defiance.

His fingers loosen around the paper bag, prepared to drop it and turn into a swinging fist.

No. Not now. Not with her.

Later. In Brooklyn. Tonight, that's all that matters. He has to keep her in line, so she doesn't get in the way.

"You been marching around with those women's liberation freaks?"

"No. You been to any pubs lately?"

He laughs. "Guess you been marching around with the Women's Temperance, then. You don't have to worry about me. I went to work, and I came home. Not straight home—stopped off along the way, but not for a drink. I got you a little present."

She eyes the bag. "Money?"

"Listen to you. *Money?*" he mimics in a falsetto. "*Money?* That the only thing that matters to you?"

"No, it isn't. Where'd you get your watch?"

He looks down at his empty wrist, then back at her. "What?"

"The gold one. The antique."

Oh, that watch. He'd worn it to work last Monday, and a couple of deadbeats spotted it and followed him to the subway. He knew they were about to mug him, but a beat cop came along. Oran jumped on the subway, came home, and put the watch away in a drawer. He'll sell it someday, when the heat dies down on Fergus Ferguson.

Lousy SOB deserved what he got. All Oran wanted was a job, to provide for his Gypsy.

Now she's acting like a spoiled brat, asking nosy questions . . . making him uneasy.

"Why are you asking me about the watch?"

She shrugs.

She doesn't know. She can't know.

Yet she's looking at him as if she does. As if she's weighing whether to answer his question, and how.

"No reason."

Oran studies her another moment.

Forget it. Brooklyn. Tonight. Do what you need to do.

He tosses her the paper bag. "Here."

The bag lands on the couch beside her. She doesn't touch it, or even look at it.

"I got you a present. Open it."

She picks up the bag, dangling it from two fingers like a dead rat.

His jaw clenches. "Look inside."

"Later."

"I *said* look inside." He can feel his eyes bulging, muscles straining, fists itching. He will do whatever it takes to make sure tonight happens. His prophecy must be fulfilled.

But at what cost?

Gypsy obeys his command.

She opens the bag. Gives a little nod. Looks up at him, wearing a strange smile. "Chocolates."

Chapter Twenty

Mother's Day
Sunday, May 12, 1968
Fernandina Beach, Florida

"Melody, dear?" Honeybee knocks on her bedroom door.

"Come in."

The door opens. Her mother is there in a dainty dress the color of lemon icebox pie, with matching shoes and hat.

"Are you feeling any better?"

"Not really."

She can feel Honeybee watching her, as she has been for two days now—watching Melody as if she's afraid to turn her back, lest she, too, might disappear.

"Are you sure you don't need me to stay here with you?"

"No. You go on to church with Daddy. I'll be all right for an hour. Truly, Mother. I need you to go to church and pray, like we said."

"I will. I'll pray for you, and for our dear little Martina."

"Pray for all of us. Yourself, and Daddy . . ."

Y'all are going to need all the prayers you can get. You're going to be just devastated when I vanish.

"I'll pray, darling. And I'll be home before you know it."

"Happy Mother's Day," she manages to say, and Honeybee smiles.

"Thank you. And, Melody, dear . . ."

Please don't, Mother. Don't talk about what we've lost, and how we have to stay strong, and we can get through this together.

"I want you to know that you've done me proud, holding your head high through the worst ordeal a woman can face."

"Well, I . . . I've had a good role model, now haven't I?"

"Wherever she is, Martina's got a guardian angel watchin' over her."

Ellie.

"Oh, Mother . . ." she chokes out, and rolls over, staring bleakly at the wall, hot tears stinging her eyes as Honeybee leaves the room, closing the door behind her.

Her heels tap down the hall, down the stairs. Moments later, the front door slams. A car engine starts. The tires roll away, carrying her parents away to church, away, away . . .

Melody stays still, eyes closed, fists clenched.

Are you a mother, or a daughter? You have to choose.

But she's already made her choice.

She throws back the coverlet. She's fully dressed beneath, wearing her turquoise dress with the Peter Pan collar and bow at the neckline.

You look purty as a picture, Cyril will say when he sees her, and the thought of that, of him, propels her out of her room, down the stairs, and out of her parents' home. She's halfway down the block before she remembers she won't be coming back here.

She turns to take one last look, but the view is obscured by a magnolia tree in full bloom, and tears.

GYPSY WAKES UP before dawn remembering a morning years ago, when she'd stirred from sleep expecting to see her mother.

Linda had been there the night before, been staying with them for a week, at least, maybe two by that time.

Then one morning she was gone, and their mod shag carpet was gone, too. Yet she'd left behind her shabby orange-and-brown-patchwork bag filled with worldly possessions.

"Why would she steal our rug and leave her stuff?" Gypsy had asked her father.

"Because she's crazy, man."

"Where'd she go?"

He shrugged. "She just split."

"Do you think she'll come back to get her bag?"

"I don't think she'll ever come back again."

"Why not?"

"I'm a prophet, you dig? You won't miss her, right?"

"Right. She's a drag. We don't need anyone around but us."

That's how it's been, ever since. She's never longed for a mother, certainly not *her* mother—

Until now.

But she has only Oran, and there's something wrong with him. Terribly, terrifyingly wrong.

Friday night, she'd pretended she'd eaten the chocolates he gave her and feigned a deep sleep. Because she didn't know what else to do. Because she knew, she *knew* . . .

No, you didn't know. Not yet. Not then.

Not even when he'd leaned over her and whispered her name.

"Gypsy. Hey, man, you awake?"

She forced her breathing to stay calm, willed her closed eyelids not to twitch, and even managed to not flinch when he poked at her.

Convinced she was out cold, he'd left.

Just before dawn, he returned and immediately ran a bath. She heard him vigorously scrubbing, muttering to himself. She heard the water drain, heard him scouring the tub. She smelled bleach.

She'd spent yesterday at the library with a pile of schoolbooks, avoiding him. When the library closed and she had no choice, she trudged home. Passing a newsstand, she'd seen a headline.

BUTCHER STRIKES AGAIN:
FAMILY SLAIN IN BENSONHURST

She hadn't bought the paper. She hadn't found somewhere else to go. She hadn't called the police.

All of those things had occurred to her.

But she'd continued home as if nothing had happened. Wanting, needing, to believe nothing had happened.

The apartment was empty. Oran hadn't left a note.

She dug out the chocolates she'd hidden the night before.

She'd examined them, chipping with her fingernail

wherever she could see that he'd tampered with the coating, and finding a grainy white substance mixed with the fillings.

She ate them. All of them, methodically, forcing slick, medicated goo down her throat as tears ran down her face. Then she lay down, praying she'd never wake up.

Now she has.

She drags herself out of bed, wrapped in a blanket.

"You up already?" Oran calls from the next room.

"Yes."

He appears in the doorway, dressed in his priest collar, wearing a trench coat and fedora she's never seen before.

"Do your Bible reading and then get busy. Lotta news today." He touches the tip of a long umbrella to a stack of Sunday papers. A faint smirk slithers across his face, as if he has a secret.

"What do you mean by that?"

"Just . . . things are going on. And if you go out, be careful crossing the street. There was another hit and run a few days ago, and—" He pauses to peer at her. "You listening to me, man?"

She clears her throat. "Where do you think she is?"

"What?"

"It's Mother's Day. I'm wondering why she never came back."

"Who?"

"Who do you think?"

"How would I know?"

They lock eyes.

"Don't waste time thinking about your mother, man.

I never think about mine. You have all the family you need." He taps his chest, just below the clerical collar.

"*You?* You're one person! Maybe I need—"

"Not *just* me."

"What are you talking about?"

"Psalm 127." He walks to the door, opens it, and slams it closed behind him.

His footsteps retreat down the hallway. She grabs the Bible. It falls open to John.

"He was a murderer from the beginning, and has nothing to do with the truth, because there is no truth in him. When he lies, he speaks out of his own character, for he is a liar and the father of lies."

She flips back to the psalm.

"As arrows are in the hand of a mighty man; so are children of the youth. Happy is the man that hath his quiver full of them: they shall not be ashamed, but they shall speak with the enemies in the gate."

She tosses aside the Bible and turns to the stack of newspapers.

The one on top, the *Amsterdam News*, has a front page story about a Negro bellhop being killed in that hit and run Oran had mentioned. She tosses it aside.

There it is—headline news in the *New York Times.* The Brooklyn Butcher struck Friday night in Bensonhurst, slaughtering four family members in their beds: Joe and Rose Costello, their twelve-year-old son, Danny, and Rose's mother, Margarita, who lived with them.

He'd allowed the teenaged daughter to live. Raped her.

"What are you doing?" Gypsy whispers. "What have you *done?*"

She has to get out of here. Before he comes back. Before she loses her nerve.

She dresses quickly, pulling on galoshes and the water-repellant coat she'd bought last week with the money her father had stolen from a tavern owner before he killed him.

Fergus Ferguson.

Friday night, lying awake after Oran left, she'd remembered why the name had been familiar. Her father had met her mother at Fergie's Inn years ago.

Still, her mind attempted to expel the possibility.

"None of this matters. Paradise is waiting for us, Gypsy."

Now she shuts out his voice because she can no longer deny the truth—about Fergus Ferguson. About what her father had done Friday night, and twice before, to two other families. Other girls, around her age . . .

Sisters . . .

"No."

She whirls, looking around the apartment. She needs something, some kind of proof. If only she hadn't eaten the chocolates.

She goes to the next room and digs through his top drawer. The watch isn't there. He isn't stupid. The press mentioned it had been stolen from the murder scene. Of course he'd gotten rid of it, only—

She opens another drawer and there it is.

Not even hidden.

He isn't stupid. Nor is he careless.

"You and me, we're the chosen ones, Gypsy, baby. No one else matters. They'll be gone, just like that . . ."

Hands trembling, she turns over the watch. The letters *FF* are emblazoned on the back.

She squeezes her eyes shut and sees the image of a horse etched in her own flesh. Oran's words sear her brain.

"In case one of us forgets and loses her way."

She almost had.

"But I'm about to find it back, you son of a bitch."

Gypsy pockets the watch, ties a plastic rain bonnet beneath her chin, and walks out the door.

THROUGH THE RAIN-SPATTERED windshield, Melody spots the weathered bridge that will take her across the Intracoastal at last. She glances in the rearview mirror to make sure, once more, that she isn't being followed. The puddle-cratered road stretches empty behind her.

Even back in town, the streets had been Sunday-quiet as she scurried away from her parents' house on foot. Folks were staying indoors out of the drenching downpour, most likely in church or celebrating Mother's Day with their families.

Such a cruel twist, Melody breaking Honeybee's heart on this day of all days, turning her back on the woman who gave her life and raised her right and has stood by her throughout this ordeal.

But Melody is a mother now, too, and she needs to hold her child again like she needs to breathe.

Crossing the threshold into the home she'd shared with Travis, she expected to feel something. Not guilt, necessarily, or even regret. Perhaps just nostalgia for the belongings she was leaving behind. But she seemed to have used up all her emotions, and had no desire to linger. She grabbed the keys to Travis's car.

Time to stop looking back, and start looking ahead.

Making the turn onto the bridge, she doesn't see the two young boys and their fishing poles. Perhaps the weather's kept them home today, or they're with their mama.

Mother's Day, and Melody will soon be cradling her baby girl in her arms. But not soon enough. It's always slow going, bumping along the wide road that bisects the island. Today is worse with the rain, but she's heedless of the potholes, no longer worried about Travis's precious car.

Later, she and Cyril will have to decide how to get rid of it. Maybe sink it in the Intracoastal after dark, or deep in the marsh behind his house. They can't keep it, and they can't sell it. She can't risk being traced back here.

The car is just one of the logistics she's been trying to think through. There are others. Cyril will have it all sorted out, or it'll sort itself out.

Had he been watching her, or the hospital? Or did the plan come later? Had he gotten wind of Rodney Lee's visit somehow, and realized they couldn't take any chances with their precious daughter?

He couldn't risk being seen at the hospital, and he certainly couldn't pose as a nurse himself. And his mother . . .

As much as Melody looks forward to hugging that woman and thanking her for the bold risk she'd taken, there's a part of her that bears resentment.

Toward her, and toward Cyril.

How could he, why would he, have put Melody, and her family, too, through such trauma?

Every time she feels that awful ache, she reminds

herself that this was the only way. He'd spared her the agony of planning, of having to cover their tracks with lies.

Couldn't his mother have whispered something to Melody at the hospital, though, to let her know who she was and what she was up to? Let her in on the plan?

But no, of course she couldn't do that. What mother immediately, instinctively trusts a stranger to carry her newborn child out of her life? If Melody had cried out or protested or tried to stop her, there would have been an uproar.

"Don't you worry none. I promise I'll take good care of her."

Whenever Melody recalls those words now, she's grateful for the heartfelt message, likely at her son's behest.

Cyril would never hurt you if he had a choice.

She's reached his house. His car is parked out front.

She pulls up behind it and jumps out of the Camaro. The flats she'd wedged onto her feet this morning sink into the mud.

Inside the house, Otis starts barking wildly.

He doesn't know it's me.

She hurries toward the porch, splashing through puddles without a care.

The front door opens.

"Cyr—"

The two young boys from the bridge stare out at her. Twins, she realizes. Not identical, but close. One has shy eyes and stands a step behind his brother, whose sturdier arms hold Otis back as he barks and snarls at Melody.

"It's okay, Otis! You know me," she says, and the

dog goes still at the sound of his name or her voice, or maybe her scent reaching his twitching nostrils.

The boy releases Otis from his grasp. Melody expects him to trot toward her, but he sinks onto the porch floor with his nose on his paws, sorrowful eyes fixed on her.

She just stands there in the pouring rain as the boys look at the red Camaro, exchange a glance, and then shift their attention back to her, wary. No, afraid. Terrified.

"I'm . . . a friend of Cyril's. Is he here?"

They look at each other and shake their heads.

Otis whimpers. The sound chills her.

"He's not here? Is he at work?"

Again, they shake their heads.

"Oh, right . . . it's Sunday," she says, as if that's it. As if nothing is wrong here. As if her voice doesn't sound high-pitched and unnatural to her own ears, and she's steady on her feet, and nothing terrible is going to happen, or . . .

Has already happened.

She glances again at Otis. His gaze is mournful, and a dark truth takes hold somewhere deep in her soul.

She snaps her head back to the boys and delivers questions, rapid fire to keep them from answering. "Do you know where Cyril is, then? Maybe at his mother's place? She lives right down the road, doesn't she? On the other side of the old plantation house? The one that's boarded up?"

She's run out of things to ask, other than the thing that's nudging its way to her consciousness.

The boy who'd held Otis steps forward. "Ma'am."

She swallows, tilts her face to the gray sky, raindrops dripping on her cheeks like tears, like blood.

"Ma'am?"

She whispers, "Yes."

"I'm right sorry to tell you, but they's both . . ." He breaks off and looks back at his brother.

"Gone," the other boy says, and his brother nods.

"Yeah. Gone."

"For how long?"

"Couple'a weeks now. First Cyril, our daddy said, and they came back to get his mama a few days later, and we's just been takin' care o' things here, tryin' to figure out what to do 'bout their places and Otis here, 'cause our mama says we can't 'ford another mouth to feed even if it's just a dog, and . . ."

"Wait, wait, I'm sorry, I'm just trying to . . . Who came? For Cyril and his mother?"

"Buckruh."

"You mean . . . the police? They arrested them?"

The boys look at each other and shake their heads.

"No, ma'am, it ain't like that. Bad buckruh. Cyril and his mama—they dead."

BENEATH THE BLACK umbrella, Oran walks briskly through the rain toward the subway, mulling what had happened upstairs.

It's natural, he supposes, that a girl Gypsy's age would be thinking about her mother on Mother's Day, but . . .

Any other girl, with any other mother.

Not his Gypsy. She'd always seen her mother for what she was. He'd allowed the wretched waste case to drift in and out of their lives. He didn't want Gypsy tempted to go searching for Linda one day as Oran had his own father, who'd turned out to be even more pathetic than his mother and stepfather.

Reaching the subway stairs, Oran lowers the umbrella and enters, brushing raindrops from the trench coat he'd snatched from the Costello house the other night. It fits him pretty well, though Joe had a larger build.

Oran had thought of Eddie as he'd plunged the knife into the man, though he bore no resemblance to his stepfather. By the time Oran was finished with them, Joe Costello and his family didn't resemble human beings.

He drops a token into the slot, pushes through the turnstile, and heads for the platform. The station is quiet. It's early.

Waiting for the downtown D train, he thinks about Linda.

About her last visit.

She'd been toying with the idea of going back to Nebraska to see her parents. They were getting older. Didn't they deserve to know their daughter was alive? That she had a child?

No, Oran told her. They did not. He didn't need strangers—narrow-minded squares—showing up to rescue their granddaughter from her bohemian father.

Linda wouldn't listen to reason.

That night was the first time he'd ever given his daughter sedative-laced chocolates. When she was asleep, he came up behind Linda with a butcher knife as she stood in the kitchen running a bath. He quietly slit her throat and she slumped into the tub, tinting the bathtub water pink as she bled out. Gypsy had slept peacefully through that, and through Oran's soft grunts as he rolled Linda in the rug.

He dragged it down the stairs and along the street to the new site for the Bruckner Expressway.

"Hey, you done with that, man? Give it here," a strung out vagrant told him.

"Sorry, man, I just found it."

"Right on." He flashed the peace sign and rolled over on his filthy blanket.

Oran dumped Linda in a bulldozed construction pit, kicking enough dirt to cover her. He dragged the rug a few more blocks and left it by an underpass populated by junkies who'd never notice the bloodstains.

Then, to be on the safe side, he'd circled back over to the vagrant, who never even opened his eyes when Oran leaned over and strangled him.

Things had been different that night than they are now. The families in Brooklyn hadn't gone quietly. The daughters hadn't submitted.

The train pulls in. He boards, and settles in for the long ride to the end of the line, where he'll visit Margaret Costello in Coney Island Hospital.

She'll never even know he was there. Like the others, Tara and Christina, she'll be heavily medicated and recovering from cuts and bruises she'd received in the struggle with her rapist. But he wants to see her, has to see her, because she belongs to him now, and so does the child he'd planted inside her.

GYPSY WALKS QUICKLY toward the police station, keeping an eye and ear out for Oran, though she can hear nothing but traffic and the sirens that are now pervasive in the city. If he's preaching nearby and sees her before she sees him, she'll make up a story. She can tell him she had to run to the supermarket.

At this hour on a Sunday?

Well, she'll say she's meeting a friend.

You have friends?

She thinks of Greg. Why, in all of this, is his betrayal as hard to accept as her father's?

Because it's impossible. How can an innocent person simultaneously lose the only two men—the only two people—she's ever loved and trusted?

Maybe she was wrong . . .

The gold watch weighs heavy in her pocket. She wasn't wrong about Oran.

But maybe somehow, Greg . . .

If she makes a right at the next corner, she can walk down the street where he lives.

It's too late for second chances, even if he hadn't lied to her. But maybe she'll catch one last glimpse of him before she goes to the police. When they arrest Oran, social services will take her away and her life will be destroyed.

She tries to focus on all the other lives she'll save in not saving her father's, and her own. She tries to ignore Oran's oft-spoken words echoing in her head.

"No one else matters."

She'd believed that, hadn't she? Until she'd discovered that innocent people are suffering, *dying* at his hands. Husbands and wives, children and grandmothers . . .

But not the daughters. The daughters are living. He wants them to live. To become Gypsy's sisters, and to bear his children.

No. *No.*

She walks along Greg's street, wondering which of the identical brick buildings is his, and what he's doing right now. Sleeping, most likely. He'd mentioned that his mother works a double overnight shift most weekends.

When she's off, she insists that he accompany her to early mass.

He isn't among the pedestrians Gypsy can see—someone walking a dog, a man in coveralls with a lunch box, a family in Sunday clothes waiting at the busy intersection ahead.

A young woman emerges from a building. Her legs are bare beneath the hem of her short coat. She's wearing white go-go boots and pulling a daffodil-colored scarf over her short blond hair. She ties it under her chin and cups her hand to a deep yawn.

"A slumber party for two at Greg's."

Gypsy follows her toward the avenue. Carol-Ann's pace is unhurried. She seems languid and preoccupied.

A voice whispers in Gypsy's head, louder, somehow, than the sirens screaming on the avenue.

"Ye are of your father the devil . . ."

Oran's voice.

Carol-Ann arrives at the intersection and stops, yawning again, staring almost trancelike at the traffic passing full speed, just inches from the curb—cars, cabs, a bus.

She seems unaware of Gypsy behind her, just inches from her back. Close enough to touch her.

They're the only two people waiting to cross.

"Ye are of your father the devil . . ."

She's alone in the world from here on in. She has to take care of herself now.

An ambulance wails toward the intersection, chased by a fire truck, and the whisper explodes into a scream. Not in Oran's voice, but in her own.

Do it! Do it now!

Her arms move.

Her hands land on Carol-Ann's back.

One push and the girl falls forward, into the streaming gutter, right in front of the fire truck.

Gypsy sees it hit her like a speeding train. Blood stains the yellow scarf. Brakes squeal.

She turns and runs as fast as she can, away from Carol-Ann's broken body, away from the police station, away from the terrible thing she just did and the far worse thing she was about to do.

It's going to be okay. It is. Because she is her father's daughter, and he's crooning in her ear.

You and me, we're the chosen ones, Gypsy, baby. No one else matters . . .

DRIVING BACK TO the mainland, Melody notices a splintered wooden rail halfway across the bridge.

She clenches the steering wheel.

If she jerks it hard in that direction, what's left of the rail will snap like a toothpick. The Camaro will sail over the edge into the air, into the water. It will float for a bit, won't it? Like a boat, bobbing along. But then it'll start to sink, slowly spinning toward the bottom.

She'll drown.

Maybe that's supposed to happen, like in the nightmare that had turned into that beautiful dream about floating on the sea with Cyril and Martina after he'd saved her.

If she drives off the bridge, will he be there waiting for her?

Maybe one day, she'll be brave enough, or coward enough, to fly over the edge. One day, when she's alone in the car.

"Don't worry," she says, glancing over her shoulder. "Not today."

She keeps on driving, past the splintered rail, onto the mainland, toward the place she'd thought she'd left behind forever just a couple of hours ago. Instead, it's Barrow that's disappearing for the last time in the rearview mirror. She'll never return, never have a reason or the heart to.

She'd collapsed onto Cyril's front steps when she realized what the boys were trying to tell her. One of them had run into the house and returned with a glass of water, as his brother, the one with the shy eyes, sat quietly beside her. Otis came and rested his head on her lap, and she stroked his fur as the boys shared the tragic tale they'd heard secondhand.

Buckruh came in the night, they said, and took Cyril from his bed. The next day, Cyril's mama sent the boys' daddy and uncle out into the swamp to look for his body.

"Did they . . . did they find him?" she'd managed to ask.

The shy brother looked away, staring in silence at the ground as his brother said, "Enough to know, Daddy told us."

She shuddered, and Otis whimpered. She hugged the dog close, buried her face in his soft fur as the boy went on, "Miz Marceline disappeared just the same way a few days later. They ain't found her yet, but they know the buckruh dunnit, too. They been comin' around here in that fancy car for a while now."

"Fancy car?" She looked up at the Camaro.

"Not like yours. This one is blue."

"It ain't, either," the shy brother spoke up. "It's green-blue, same as that there dress."

Turquoise.

Rodney Lee.

The rain lets up as she drives into town. She rolls down the window, taking deep breaths of fresh air.

So much of it makes sense now.

So much does not.

Why hadn't Cyril's grief-stricken mother told Melody what had happened to him, and that she feared Martina was in danger?

"If Marceline LeBlanc sets her mind to something, she doesn't let anything get in her way . . ."

Maybe she hadn't trusted Melody to protect her baby. Given her condition at the time, is it any wonder?

Or maybe she didn't think the buckruh would come looking for the baby out on Barrow.

Maybe they wouldn't have, if Melody hadn't told Duke and Scotty about the Negro nurse who'd taken Martina.

And so, Rodney Lee had returned to Barrow to destroy the child he believed would destroy Travis. He'd found her with her grandmother, and he'd killed them both.

What did he have to lose? He'd been drafted. He was leaving town. He knew Scotty would cover his tracks, although . . .

Melody had been so certain those police officers believed she was the guilty party, and were protecting her—well, protecting Travis.

In the end, that's exactly what they'd done, though, isn't it? Protected Travis. Punished her. Destroyed her; murdered the man she loved, and her only child, and the woman who'd lost her own life trying to save her.

Cyril had tried to warn her. He'd seen firsthand what deep-seated hatred can do.

She pulls up in front of her parents' house beneath a glistening pink and green magnolia canopy. The door bangs open. She's only been gone a few hours, but that had been more than enough time to send Honeybee Beauregard Abernathy into a tailspin.

"Oh, thank heavens! John, she's here!" Arms outstretched, her mother descends the porch steps as Melody opens the car door. "Where have you been? We've been so worried!"

"I went to find a friend."

"A friend!"

She flinches as her mother reaches to hug her.

Honeybee stops, almost close enough to touch Melody but not quite, keeping her at arm's length.

"A friend? But . . . you weren't feeling well."

"I'm sorry, Mother, I . . ."

"You've been crying."

Has she? She touches her face. Her cheeks feel tacky and her eyes burn as if she'd rubbed them with wet sand.

"So have you," she says, noticing Honeybee's smudged eye makeup and reddened skin. "You've been crying—oh, Mother, you're crying."

"Because I thought . . . I wasn't sure that you'd . . ." She wipes at her eyes. "But of course you'd come home. Where else would you go? That's what I said to Daddy, didn't I, John?"

She looks toward the porch, and Melody sees her father standing there in his Sunday suit.

"You did say that, Honeybee. And I told you that Poppet would never leave without telling us where she was going if she wasn't coming back soon."

"No, I know she wouldn't. You wouldn't." Her mother forces a smile. "Especially on Mother's Day."

Melody can't find words to tell her parents that they're right, or that they're wrong. Or that she'd been forced to choose whether to be a mother or a daughter because she couldn't be both, and now . . .

And now, there is no choice.

"All right, then . . . let's go inside," Honeybee says.

"Mother? It's just . . . I . . . I didn't come home alone, is all."

Honeybee follows her gaze to the car. Her eyes widen. "Is that . . ."

"If you don't want him here, I understand, and we can go back to my house until I find a place to—"

"That won't be necessary, will it, Honeybee?" Her father walks over and puts an arm on his wife's shoulders. "She went to find a *friend*."

Honeybee meets Melody's gaze with a nod and a tremulous smile. "I'd say it looks like she found one."

"Oh, Mother . . . I know how you feel about dogs."

"I'm not sure you know how I feel about a lot of things, Melody."

"I'm sorry. I—"

"Hush. I'm sorry, too."

Melody lets Otis out of the car. He gives a little yap, pauses to lick her hand, and then bounds into the muddy yard and looks back at her. His eyes are still mournful but his tail is wagging.

Honeybee, eyes shiny, tilts her face to the heavens. "Well, would you look at that."

Melody follows her gaze. High overhead, a patch of blue smears the murky sky, the same shade as the beautiful dress her daughter had worn the last time she'd held her.

Harlem

"HAINT BLUE," BETTINA Crenshaw murmurs, when Calvin lays the baby on their bed and she gets a good look at the dress.

"What's that?" He looks up, still stroking the little forehead with a gentle, work-calloused forefinger.

"Nothing, I . . . I . . ."

"It's okay. I was speechless, too, when I found her. Just sit down and let your heart settle, Bettina. Just say a prayer of thanksgiving that the good Lord has finally answered our prayers."

If it weren't for the dress, she'd almost believe it. It's Sunday, and Mother's Day, and the world has been especially treacherous lately. And her Auntie Marceline would never, ever, put Bettina and Calvin's lives in danger.

But now that she sees the dress, and the sweet-grass basket he'd set on the floor just inside the door, there's no denying the truth.

This child didn't come from heaven. She came from low country, down south. She's Cyril's daughter.

Cyril is dead. Murdered, just like Ernie Fields,

and the Reverend King, and countless Black men and women all over this violence-torn country.

"There but for the grace of God . . ." the famous writer James Baldwin had begun yesterday's eulogy for Ernie.

Every Black resident in Harlem—in the country—is a target in these turbulent times. And a Black couple harboring a child whose mother is buckruh and married to a Klansman . . .

"We need to take her to the police," Bettina tells Calvin. "Or, I don't know, turn her in to an orphanage, or—"

"Listen to yourself, woman!"

"We can't keep her!"

"No, don't listen to yourself! Listen to me! You know what will happen to her if we turn her over to the system! How can we do that to her?"

What's going to happen to us if we don't?

She needs to tell him—about Cyril, and Auntie Marceline . . .

She was going to mention Friday's encounter anyway, but with five jobs between them, and the funeral yesterday, she hasn't had a chance.

She opens her mouth, but before she can say a word, the baby lets out a warbling cry.

"Hungry," Calvin says.

Bettina, too, recognizes the sound. They'd had a son, lost him, a decade ago.

And now you've found a daughter, her auntie croons in her ear, as if it's that simple.

If Bettina and Calvin go to the police, they'll track down Marceline. Arrest her. The child will be returned to the mother, and the mother's husband will . . .

"Go down the street," Bettina tells her husband, "and buy a can of formula. I still have bottles put away from . . . Just hurry!"

He jumps into action, grabbing his coat and hat and hurrying out the door without another word.

Bettina looks down at the baby. Wide blue eyes stare up into hers. Then she scrunches her face, kicks her little legs, fists balled, and lets out another cry.

"Hush, now . . ."

"Her name is Amelia."

Bettina shakes her head. Her aunt's reckless actions have endangered Bettina and Calvin, and the child, and Marceline herself.

A grieving mother's actions aren't rooted in logic, but in a primal place that only another bereft woman can possibly comprehend.

Even Calvin, if Bettina shares the truth, might not find forgiveness in his heart, or the courage to risk their own lives after what had happened to his friend Ernie.

The baby cries—not just hungry, but needing her mother.

Bettina's hands tremble as she reaches for her.

You spend years trying to forget how it feels to cradle a newborn, arms gently swaying to soothe pitiful cries; how you press your face into downy hair, breathing in all that sweetness and promise; how nothing matters but this.

You try to forget, and your heart remembers in an instant.

Tears pool in Bettina's eyes. "Hello there, Amelia. Hello. It's going to be all right. I'm going to take care of you. I won't let anything happen to you. I promise."

The baby quiets, settling into her embrace, and Bettina offers a finger for her to grasp. Something glints on the tiny hand.

"Well, looky there. You have yourself a fine ring," she says, seeing the little gold sapphire-studded band etched with a haint-blue initial. "Your daddy's name starts with a *C*, did you know that? One day, you will. His name . . ." She takes a deep breath. "His name is Calvin."

Part IX

2017

Chapter Twenty-One

Saturday, January 14, 2017

Amelia follows Jessie and the woman who'd introduced herself as Gitana out into a crisp, sunny morning.

Yesterday, the area was crawling with police officers. Today, Amelia would give anything to see one.

Marshboro's main drag is quiet and lined with parked cars. The church parking lot next door is jammed. She can hear music coming from the large events hall out back, and someone speaking at a microphone.

Even if Amelia screams for help, there's a good chance no one will hear her. And even if they do, by the time help arrives, it might be too late.

Gitana opens the passenger's side door of a small car parked in the driveway for Jessie. "You sit in the front. Amelia in the back."

Amelia's heart pounds. If they get into this car, there's no telling what might happen.

She's tall, strong, and armed.

Yet this woman would be a formidable opponent, and very well might have a gun.

Jessie hops into the front seat. "Come on, Mimi! Aren't you dying to get there?"

She feels those violet eyes probing into her as she hesitates.

She smiles brightly at the woman as she climbs into the backseat, trying to keep her voice from warbling as she says, “Definitely! I can’t wait!”

Gitana closes the door after her, and it seems to reverberate like the slam of a dungeon’s iron gate.

“Jessie!” Amelia whispers urgently. “She’s not who she says. Trust me. Just don’t let on!”

Then Gitana is opening the driver’s door and climbing behind the wheel.

Amelia can’t tell whether her friend heard the warning as the woman lights a cigarette, backs out, and heads east out of town toward the coast.

AT THE MUFFLED thump from the car trunk, Barnes’s hand goes to his holster, and he sees Kurtis’s jaw go slack.

“Uncle Stockton . . .”

Barnes draws his weapon. “Hands in the air.”

Kurtis gasps. “What—”

“Hands in the air! Now!”

He raises his arms. “I’m sorry! I—”

“What the hell is going on here?”

“I’m in trouble! It’s bad!”

“What—who—is in the trunk of this car?”

Kurtis opens his mouth. His voice makes a strange, hoarse sound.

A sob. Like a terrified child.

Which he is not. He’s a grown man, and he’s involved in a double homicide, and it shouldn’t matter who his family is, or that Barnes loves him like a son.

Do the right thing, Stockton. Right now.

“Tell me!”

Tears in his eyes, Kurtis opens his mouth again. This time, he speaks. "A woman."

GYPSY SMOKES AS she drives, staring straight ahead, seeing not a sunny rural Georgia byway but a rainy New York City Street.

Mother's Day 1968.

That was the day everything had changed for her. The day she'd realized the truth about her father, and about herself. The day she'd started out to become a hero, and instead became a murderer.

Killing Carol-Ann Ellis was by far the most empowering thing she'd ever done. In an exhilarating split second, she eliminated her worst adversary and reclaimed control over her future.

Before she'd raced home, she stripped off her new raincoat like a snake shedding its skin and threw it in a trash can in front of the building Carol-Ann had exited only minutes before. The gold watch was still in the pocket. It no longer mattered.

She wasn't going to the police about Oran. Not after what she'd done.

They never even knew Carol-Ann Ellis had been murdered.

"Another pedestrian got mowed down," Oran commented the next morning, after reading the paper. "You be careful out there, Gypsy."

"Don't worry, I will. You be careful, too."

But he wasn't. Weeks later, the authorities caught up to him. But no one ever knew what the Butcher's daughter had done.

They won't know about this, either.

Her passengers have been silent since they left. Now the woman in the front seat asks, "How far is it?"

"What?"

"Amelia Island. How long until we get there?"

"Not long." Gypsy forces a casual tone and smiling glance, unnerved every time she looks at Jessamine.

It isn't just the faint resemblance to Oran, or even the strong one to Margaret Costello.

She looks like me.

Gypsy's grief over Perry's death has been a stark reminder that she's as alone in this world now as she was in 1968 when her father was taken away in handcuffs and she was placed in foster care.

She'd done so much reading about Professor Silas Moss, and Amelia's genealogy work, tormented by the knowledge that Jessie's DNA exists in every cell of Gypsy's body. All she could think about was exterminating her. She was unprepared to experience such an odd familiarity about her.

Familiarity.

She lights another cigarette and pockets the lighter as she makes the turnoff to the coastal road, considering the word.

Familiarity . . . family.

If only it didn't have to be this way.

Family.

What if Oran had been right all along? What if there really were a chosen few? What if Jessie is meant to join Gypsy in paradise? Maybe Oran is even waiting for them there. And Perry . . .

"Where are we?" the other woman, Amelia, asks from the backseat as Gypsy navigates the quiet streets of the coastal development.

"We're on our way to take a boat out to see your mother."

"A boat?"

"Yes, a *boat*! She lives on Amelia *Island*, remember? How do you think we're going to get there? Swim?"

She pulls to a stop beside the private pier where the *Reel Gent* waits, bobbing gently in the water.

"Let's go." She gets out of the car, puts out the cigarette in the sandy soil with her heel, and is about to close the door when she realizes that neither woman has moved.

She sees the look they exchange. Not just awareness, and fear, but fierce determination.

Rage surges to refill the vulnerable, hollow place in Gypsy's heart. She takes out her pistol and aims at Jessie's head.

"You have three seconds to get out," she says calmly, "before I pull the trigger. Both of you. Three . . . two . . ."

Jessie and Amelia get out of the car.

KURTIS DOESN'T RESIST as Barnes gets him out of the car, and a pat-down reveals only keys and a cell phone in his pockets. Barnes takes both.

"Down on the ground! Facedown!"

"Uncle Stockton, please . . ."

"Lie down on your stomach! Hands behind your back!"

Barnes cuffs him on the wet ground beside the open driver's side door. Weapon in hand, he scans the deserted parking lot, aware it might be a trap. He could open that trunk to an ambush—Wayland and Colt, guns blazing.

"Uncle St—"

"You put that letter in my apartment last night. You stole my damned *key* from your *father*, and you came into my *home*, and you—"

"I know!" His voice is a sob. "Please, let me just tell you . . ."

"Talk."

"I have something in the car to show you—"

"Stay where you are!"

"Can I just sit up? I told you I'm in trouble. There's a woman . . ."

"In the trunk."

"No, not her. It's—she's been . . . she—" Again the sob. "I didn't know what to do. I just didn't realize that she—and now it's too late. She's going to kill your friend Amelia, and her sister."

"Amelia doesn't have a sister."

"No, her friend is Gypsy's sister."

"Gypsy Colt."

"Yeah, and she thinks I'm going to kill you and Charisse, and this morning when I told her that I can't, she said that if I don't she'll go after my family and—"

"Where is she? Right now, where is she?"

"Down south. She's got Amelia and her friend in the car. I could see her—"

"See her how?"

"Her phone. There's a tracking app, Stealth Soldier. We have it on each other's phones, and on . . . yours."

Barnes swallows his fury. "Where is she taking them?"

"Out into the ocean. She's setting them on fire. That's what she said. That's what she told me to do to you."

"I need your damned thumb to open this phone right now." Clutching Kurtis's cell phone opened to the home screen, he bends over the cuffed hands. Kurtis flexes his thumb and Barnes presses it to the home button.

It opens to a GPS showing a dark blue dot against a light blue background. Barnes zooms out. The location signal is in the sea, just off the Georgia coast. He takes a screenshot. Then he zooms in until he can see the map coordinates and takes another screenshot.

Barnes calls the desk sergeant. He relays the information rapid fire, summoning backup here and sending the screenshots. He hangs up and tries Amelia's number. It rings into voice mail.

She's taking them out into the ocean and setting them on fire.

She's already out there. It might be too late.

You did what you could, Stockton. But you are here. You are here, right now.

He jabs the button in the car's door, gun trained on the trunk. He sees it pop up about an inch as the latch is released. Then it flies upward as if someone had kicked it from the inside.

"Freeze!" Barnes shouts, leaping toward it, taking aim.

"Help me!"

It's a woman's voice.

And then he sees her.

A young Black woman, disheveled, in pajamas.

He helps her out, steadying her in his strong arms. She blinks into daylight glare, and then her enormous dark eyes focus and fixate on him in recognition.

He's seen those eyes before. That face.

But she isn't Delia. She's her daughter. Charisse.

Before he can find his voice, she finds hers, breathless with wonder.

"It's you!"

A FRIGID SEA wind lashes Amelia's face as Gypsy Colt takes the bowrider into open water. She'd ordered her prisoners into the seats in front of the cockpit, their backs to her as she steers with the pistol in her hand.

"We're going to die, Mimi."

"No, we aren't. Just stay calm."

"She has a gun."

Amelia is almost certain their abductor can't hear their voices over the roaring engine, but she doesn't dare tell Jessie that she, too, is armed. A kitchen knife may be no match for a bullet, but the element of surprise is a key self-defense weapon.

"We can't panic," she murmurs to Jessie. "Be alert. Be ready."

"For what? You can't think we can overpower her when she's—"

"Trust me. Be ready!"

Jessie falls silent.

Amelia stares at the gray-blue sea and sky, thinking about her birth mother. She'd been about to discover that her long-lost daughter is alive after all these years.

I can't let her lose me twice in one lifetime. And I can't die without knowing her. I won't.

The boat slows. The engine putters.

Then Gypsy is there, in the bow, holding the gun in one hand and a gasoline can in the other.

She sets the can at her feet, puts a cigarette between her lips, and holds the lighter to the tip, looking at them over a flame she allows to flicker far longer than it takes to ignite the tobacco.

A lighter. A can of gasoline. A gun, and she's using it to gesture at Jessie.

"You first," she says. "Jump."

"What?"

"Jump into the water."

Jessie's wild gaze meets Amelia's.

"If you don't jump, I'll shoot you. Either way, you're going into the water."

Amelia clutches the knife's handle beneath a fold of her coat and watches Jessie weigh her options, her body shaking violently, her eyes on Amelia, pleading for her to do something.

This isn't the moment.

"Jump, Jessie," she hears herself say.

"What?"

"Jump!"

Jessie turns away from her. With an anguished cry, she throws herself over the bow.

This is the moment.

As Gypsy turns her head to watch her fall, Amelia lunges with the knife and sinks the blade into the side of the woman's neck. She staggers, her hand lifting to the wound, and bright red blood pours over her fingers.

The gun! Get the gun!

Amelia grabs for it and loses her footing. She flails. Her hand claws, snagging Gypsy's long hair. Now they're both falling, over the edge, into the sea.

Enveloped in shockingly cold water, Amelia surfaces to gulp air before strong arms pull her under again like a predator's jaws. Her lungs burn and she fights to escape the woman's grip, writhing and kicking herself free. Again she surfaces, gasping a deep breath and then another, braced for another frenzied struggle.

The attack doesn't come. Treading water, numb limbs weighted by clothing and cold, she sees that the boat is a good distance away, and there's no sign of Gypsy Colt.

Nor, she realizes, is there any sign of Jessie.

But not far away, she spots a churning beneath the surface skimmed with red foam.

She thinks of Gypsy's wound, all that blood in the water, sharks. A hand pops up, clawing in the air, and then disappears.

"Jessie! Jessie, no!" She paddles toward the spot.

Again, the hand breaks the surface, and then Jessie's head emerges with a mighty thrust and an anguished scream.

"Jessie!"

"Mimi!" She sputters, swimming toward her. "She was trying to . . ."

"I know."

"I kicked her." Jessie's teeth are chattering, lips blue. "Do you think she's . . ."

"Gone." The blood has dissolved. The corpse is out there somewhere, unless she swam away, somehow, and got to the boat.

It's distant now, pulled by the current. Alone, she'd attempt to reach it. But Jessie, for all her vigorous energy and personal presence, is physically smaller and weaker. She'd never make it, and waste precious energy trying.

"My m-mother . . ."

"No! Jessie, she's not! Half sister."

"How—"

"Shh. I'll explain later."

They can't afford to expend effort on conversation.

"We won't have later, Mimi. We're g-going to d-die."

"We're not!"

"Yes. So t-tired."

"We'll lie on our backs."

"No one knows we're here. Mimi. S-swim. You can—"

"I'm not going anywhere."

"But we'll die of exposure. We'll drown. You can save yourself if—"

"Shh. Here, grab my hand."

They float, shoulder to shoulder, hand in hand.

Amelia shifts her gaze to the wide swath of sky so she won't have to watch the boat drift away, stranding them in the vast, empty sea.

"It's you," the young woman whispers again, staring up at Barnes.

Well look at that, Wash says in his head. *She knows you, Stockton.*

But that would be scientifically impossible. Even if her newborn eyes had seen him clearly when she'd gazed up at him, she can't possibly have retained the memory of that fleeting encounter—a stranger, a face that's aged thirty years. He wouldn't even recognize hers if she didn't look so much like her mother.

He hears sirens in the distance. Backup, on the way. He looks at Kurtis lying on the ground, facedown.

This will destroy Rob. He needs to hear it from Barnes.

Beside him, the young woman sways. He steadies her with an arm around her shoulder. She's staring up at him in wonder.

"I can't believe you're the one who found me. You're my father, and you—"

"No, I found you, but I'm not your father. I knew your mother when you were born, but—"

"Wait, aren't you Stockton Barnes?"

He stares at her, and there's Wash, as always, in his head.

She knows your name. Listen to her, Stockton. Listen to your instincts.

"I am Stockton Barnes, but I'm not . . . Why do you think that I'm . . . ?"

"Because we match."

Look at her, Stockton. Take a good, long look. She doesn't just have Delia's features. She has yours.

"Because we look alike?"

"No, we *match.* DNA."

"DNA!"

"Yes, I just got my results."

There must be some mistake.

Bobby said he was Charisse's father.

So did his family, and Cynthia . . .

Based on what? Delia's word? She was looking for child support, for money. Desperate, an addict . . .

Delia was a proven liar, but DNA . . .

DNA doesn't lie.

"I was going to find you . . ." Tears fill her eyes. She draws a ragged breath. "And then this man came and he—"

"I know."

"And then you found me. You saved me."

She buries her face in his shoulder, and he holds her steady as sirens close in.

AMELIA STARES AT the sky, numb with cold and exhaustion, clinging tightly to Jessie's hand.

It's fitting, she supposes, that two lives that had begun under such bizarre and similar circumstances would end the same way . . .

Only this time, we're together.

There is, she's concluded, peculiar comfort in leaving this world with a soul mate to accompany you on the journey.

Years ago, Calvin and Amelia had tag-teamed Bettina's deathbed vigil. He'd been aghast when Bettina slipped away in the short window when Amelia left her alone. Three years later, she'd held his hand when he drew his last breath, with him and yet not. He was isolated, trapped in the dying, and she in the grieving.

It's different now. Today. She and Jessie are going hand in hand.

She closes her eyes, shutting out the sky, salty tears meeting salty sea.

I'm not ready. I don't want to go. I want to know my mother. I want her to know me.

All those years searching, wondering, longing . . .

Wasted years.

"Mimi . . ." Jessie tugs her hand. She's moving in the water. Slipping from Amelia's grasp. "Listen! Look!"

"Shh, Jess, stay calm."

If you struggle, you drown.

But you're both going to drown regardless. It's over.

"Mimi!" Jessie is thrashing wildly, waving her arms above her head.

But she isn't drowning or struggling or dying. She's staring at the sky.

Mimi looks up, and she, too, sees it.

A coast guard chopper, flying low over the water, right toward them.

Chapter Twenty-Two

Amelia Island

On Saturday nights, Melody sings with a live band at the Ritz-Carlton. They get a nice crowd—families, business conventions, wedding parties, couples. People come to sip cocktails, and to dance, and a few locals come to see her.

One, in particular.

As a Manhattan physician, Grant had come to Amelia Island with his wife for medical conferences long before he retired here and became a regular. Melody remembers him—them—requesting "At Last."

Silver-haired and deeply tanned with kind eyes, Grant has been widowed for a few years. He always sits at a window table, intent on Melody's performance even when he's joined by his golf buddies and their wives. Afterward, he'll come over to chat and often asks if she can stay for a drink. Sometimes, she says yes. She likes talking to him. They have a lot in common, beyond being single.

Melody, too, is a widow—not just because Travis was killed in action on Hamburger Hill in May 1969. She got the news nearly a year to the day she'd learned that Cyril and Martina weren't alive and waiting for her on Barrow Island. Travis's death did eventually bring some measure of closure, though she hadn't heard from him in over a year. She would never grieve him, rarely allowing herself to think of him at all. Nor did she think of Rodney Lee. He'd returned from Vietnam, one of nearly three hundred thousand veterans who'd been physically shattered as well as emotionally. For a long time, she worried that he might come back for her. But in the late 1970s, she heard he'd died in a VA home, limbless and alone.

Closure . . .

About a year after Grant lost his wife, he'd asked her how long it had taken her to put away her wedding band. He still wore his.

She'd managed not to answer, preferring not to tell him that she'd never married her own true love, the one she still mourns, along with their child. She doesn't want pity, nor anything more than friendship from him or any man. She's lost much, but she's been surrounded by love all her life.

Grant is waiting for her after the last song, as people linger to chat on the dance floor and the musicians pack up their instruments.

"I loved that encore."

She smiles. "I figured you would."

"You sing it better than Etta James ever did."

Her smile wobbles, and she looks down at her phone. Even now, after all these years, she still hears Cyril's voice.

But it's Grant's that asks, "Nightcap?"

"I can't. Sorry. I have a couple of texts . . ."

"I know, I know . . . sitter on the clock and wondering where you are, right?"

Melody nods, texting Hannah that she's on her way. It's not like her to check in on the timing more than once on a Saturday evening. But she's probably eager to meet her friends at the Green Turtle Tavern, where the live music is more raucous and goes far later than it does here.

Grant stands waiting to walk Melody to her car as she swaps her glittery heeled sandals for sneakers with arch support and pulls a cardigan over her slinky black dress.

"It's not easy singing for your supper when you're my age," she tells him with a laugh as they wait for the valet to bring their cars to the entrance.

"*Our* age. And you look two decades younger."

"After performing, I feel two decades older."

The night is starlit and chilly, and she can hear the waves crashing out on the beach as they say good-night. As always, his headlights follow her the few miles back along Amelia Parkway to town, over a mile past the turnoff to his condo. He flashes his high beams as she pulls into the driveway, and waits, idling, as she climbs the front steps and unlocks the door. Then he's gone, and she's crossing the threshold into the grand old house where she's lived all her life, with the exception of one terrible year.

Hannah meets her by the door. One of Melody's longtime voice students, she's now a music major at Jacksonville University. Oh, to be young, blonde, effortlessly lovely, and blissfully unencumbered. At her age, Melody had been a married housewife pregnant with another man's child, on the verge of violent loss in a war-torn hate-filled era.

"Everything okay?" she asks.

"Yes, I think she's finally asleep. We had some excitement here earlier. Someone rang the bell, and the puppies weren't in their crate yet and they went crazy, and when I opened the door one of them got out."

"I bet I can guess which one."

"Yep, but I got him back right away. It was a lot of commotion, though, and she could hear it from upstairs, and it took her a while to settle down again."

"Who rang the bell?"

"A woman. She said she had to talk to you, no matter what time you got back. She wanted to wait on the porch, but I didn't think that was a good idea."

"Was she selling something?" Melody asks, digging through her pocketbook for cash.

"No, not like that. She was super nice, and nervous. It was kind of . . ."

"Kind of . . . ?"

"Sweet."

"Sweet?"

Hannah laughs and shrugs. "Never mind. I'm sure she'll be back tomorrow or something."

Melody pays Hannah, thanks her, and locks the door after her. She can hear the puppies scuffling and yapping, crated in the kitchen. She'll go see them after she goes upstairs to peek in and make sure everything is okay.

She's just reached the top of the flight when the doorbell rings.

Hannah must have forgotten something.

But when she returns to the door and peers through the glass, she sees a stranger. At this hour? Really?

She's Black, and attractive, and her eyes . . .

She has Cyril's eyes. After all these years, Cyril's eyes.

Melody throws open the door, heart pounding, thoughts racing.

For a moment, the woman just stares back at her, as though she, too, is bewildered.

But then her eyes fill with tears and when she speaks, her voice is thick with emotion. "Melody? Melody Abernathy?"

"Yes . . ."

"I'm . . ." She falters. Her hand trembles as she holds it out, offering something.

Melody takes it. Sees that it's a tiny plastic bracelet, the kind they put on people—babies—at the hospital.

"I'm . . ."

She points at the name typed on the narrow, yellowed band, as if she can't say it.

Melody can't, either.

Martina Eleanor Hunter 4/25/68

BARNES STAYS WITH Rob and Paulette until nearly eleven o'clock, then leaves them with the local detectives.

Rob stands and clasps his hand, not a handshake, but a man grasping for a lifeline. "Barnes, I . . ." He dissolves into sobs, collapsing against Barnes.

Holding him steady in a hard embrace, fighting tears himself, Barnes says, "I'm so sorry."

Not for what he did—he will not apologize for that—but for the anguish from which his friends will never fully recover.

On the job, he often deals with grieving parents, some whose children are still alive, like Kurtis, yet lost to them just the same. This is different, though. He shares their excruciating grief, and he can't compartmentalize it.

Paulette sits with her head buried in her hands as he touches her shoulder and walks out. Still in shock, maybe, or just refusing to acknowledge the man who'd had their son taken into custody.

Barnes doesn't break down until he gets into the car.

He cries for Rob and Paulette, and for the young man who'd strayed just as Gloss had years ago. Barnes had hoped to save Kurtis as Wash had saved him, but he'd been far too late for that.

Brainwashed, Kurtis did it all for Gypsy Colt.

"She said she had a hitman on the way to execute both of us, just like the Harrisons, if I didn't do what she said," Kurtis told the detectives when they arrived on the scene. "And she was going to kill my family."

Another lost soul vulnerable to a charismatic cult leader. Barnes has seen it on the job, many times. Maybe he should have suspected it was what was going on with Kurtis, before it was too late.

Despite having everything money can buy, Rob's son was as restless and unhappy as Perry Wayland had been when Gypsy met him on an Ivy League campus in the early 1970s. Like Perry, Kurtis was easily seduced, followed her commands without question, and was willing to turn his back on his family and friends. He'd brought Gypsy to the States under an assumed identity and put her up in a posh hotel. He'd been dating Brandy Harrison in an effort to find Charisse so that Gypsy could use her as a pawn against Barnes.

It's over at last—the reign of terror that had begun with the Brooklyn Butcher's first murder decades ago.

Gypsy Colt is missing at sea off the Georgia coast and presumed dead. So is Perry Wayland, back in Baracoa, along with the rest of Gypsy's followers.

The gold initial ring—Barnes's ring, Charisse's ring, Amelia's ring—had been in the glove compartment of Kurtis's car. He'd stolen it from Brandy right before Christmas. She was carrying it around in her pocketbook, thinking about revisiting Amelia Crenshaw, she'd said.

The ring was how she'd found her way to Amelia in the first place, having found the necklace tucked away in her mother's apartment with the newspaper clippings. In need of cash, she'd googled to see how much the ring was worth, just as they'd speculated. She came across Amelia's story, and came up with a plot to claim the reward. She'd always known that Delia's daughter was the Connecticut foundling. She remembered hearing the older relatives talking about how she'd been adopted by a fancy family and given a new name.

"Lily Tucker," she'd told Kurtis. *"Something like that."*

He shared the information with Gypsy, and that Brandy was thinking of going back to Amelia. Gypsy told him to bring Brandy white ginger mariposa lilies, so he did, no questions asked, same as everything else . . . until she told him to kill the Harrison women. He said he convinced her it would be an unnecessary risk, so she hired a professional.

If his story is true—and Barnes's gut tells him it is—he hadn't murdered anyone. But he'd financed his homicidal mistress, and he'd been an accessory, and he hadn't gone to the police after the double murder. And he'd abducted a young woman at gunpoint.

Barnes wipes his eyes on a linen handkerchief, takes some deep breaths, and starts the engine. Consulting a folded slip of paper from his pocket, he enters the address into his phone's navigation app. Five minutes away.

He calls Amelia as he pulls onto a local road, heading south. Her phone rings into voice mail.

"Me again," he says. "I'm still thinking about you. Thought you might still be sitting in your car waiting for her to show up. Maybe you gave up and went to bed? Or maybe you're with her now. I hope so, Amelia. I really do. Let me know."

He hangs up.

If not for Kurtis and that tracking software, Amelia and Jessie would have drowned out there in the Atlantic. The coast guard chopper had tracked the GPS signal to the missing boat, and spotted the women nearby. Two tiny dots in the open sea.

"A miracle," Amelia had said earlier. "You saved our lives, Barnes."

"How is Jessie?"

"They're keeping her overnight, but she'll be fine. I'm being released soon, and I'm, uh . . . I'm going to meet my mother."

"Sure you don't want to wait and do that tomorrow, after you've had a chance to rest?"

"I've waited most of my life, Barnes. I'm doing it today. Right now."

Barnes, too, has been waiting—not most of his life, but much of it—to meet his daughter.

At the police station, he'd checked his email and found that a DNA match had, indeed, come in. Liliana Tucker Ford is Charisse Montague—and Barnes's biological daughter.

His phone's robotic voice announces that he has arrived at his destination.

He parks in front of a small shingled colonial with a front porch and a brick chimney puffing smoke into the night sky. It's the kind of home he'd hoped Charisse was living in years ago, when he'd learned she and Delia had left the housing project a month before he came looking for them. A month. Mere weeks. Things would have been different if he'd been sooner.

He thinks of that little girl, all alone in a cavernous mall on a cold December night.

Of Amelia, left in a Harlem church.

Of her friend Jessie, abandoned in a snow swept Ithaca gorge.

Regardless, all had been raised by loving parents. They'd been lucky.

So am I.

Barnes picks up his phone and sends a text.

I'm here. Too late?

He climbs out of the car, clutching his phone, waiting for wobbly dots to appear, indicating that she's writing back.

The screen remains empty.

Barnes exhales heavily, breath frosty white in the damp night air. It's okay. It's late. She must have gone to bed. He'll just have to wait a little longer.

But as he turns to get into the car, the porch light

flicks on and the door opens. She's there, with her husband's protective arm encircling her shoulder.

"Come on in," his daughter calls. "You're not too late at all."

Standing before her mother, Amelia finds that her lungs have forgotten how to breathe, and her brain has shed its vocabulary, and her legs are barely, just barely, supporting her.

The woman, Melody, is just staring down at the bracelet in her hand. She's beautiful—so beautiful, tall and slender, with wideset green eyes and blond hair pulled back in a chignon. Her face is fully made up, complexion luminous despite her age and a fine network of wrinkles around her mouth and eyes.

At last, she looks up, dazed. "Where did you get this?"

"From . . . Lucky. She had it . . . I don't . . . I guess . . ."

"Who?"

"Lucky. My mother's cousin . . ."

Melody is shaking her head, holding up the bracelet. "She died."

"What? No, she lives up in Marshboro."

At the last word, Melody gasps. "Marshboro."

"Yes. She's Birdie's daughter, and Marceline's . . ."

Another gasp.

". . . niece."

Melody's head jerks up, and she stares hard at Amelia. "My daughter . . . my *daughter* died. She was kidnapped from my arms, and she was murdered, with her father and her grandmother. My daughter is dead."

"No. She—I—*was* kidnapped. By Marceline, but . . ."

"*Marceline.* Yes . . ."

"But she's alive, and . . ." She reaches into her bag and pulls out the framed photograph. "She wanted me to show you this."

Melody cries out, pressing a fist to her mouth.

"My father. Cyril. Marceline gave it to me, and she told me how she brought me to New York City after he died. She—I, I was raised by his cousin Bettina and—"

She's still shaking her head. "I lost Martina. I lost her . . ."

"You didn't." Amelia draws in a ragged breath. "I've been looking for you all my life, and I can't believe . . . I can't believe . . ."

"You're . . ." Melody is sobbing. "You're . . ."

"Yes . . . I'm . . . I'm—"

Melody lunges at her, and the rest of the halting sentence, whatever it was going to be, is sacrificed to a savage embrace.

I'm . . .

"Melody?" a voice calls from above, and a dog is barking. "Land sakes!"

At last, she loosens her grip, not letting go, but allowing Amelia to see a large black Labrador bounding down the stairs toward them.

"That's my mother's dog, Otis. We, uh, name them all after . . ." Melody clears her throat, wiping tears on her shoulders, as though unable to let go of her daughter for even a moment. "It keeps him alive, you know?"

She doesn't know. But she laughs as the dog nudges their legs with his wet nose, tail wagging.

"Melody? What in the world is going on down there?"

I'm . . .

Alive . . .

"Who . . ." she asks Melody. "Who's upstairs?"

"That's Honeybee. Come on." Suddenly urgent, she grabs Amelia's hand and pulls her toward the stairway. "She always said we'd find you again, even though—and I always said she was crazy. I mean, she is . . . she's crazy all right, but good crazy."

She's laughing, and they're walking up the stairs, past framed photos. A family. Melody's family. Amelia's family.

I'm . . .

Back . . .

"Melody!"

"Mother! Oh, Mother! You were right! Martina came home."

Yes.

I'm home.

Epilogue

Mother's Day
Sunday, May 14, 2017
Amelia Island

It had taken some maneuvering to score an ocean view table for ten at the Ritz-Carlton's lavish brunch, let alone changing it to eleven at the last minute. But Melody had accomplished it, and now here they are, a big happy group on a sunny spring Sunday.

"What are we celebrating, folks?" the waiter asks, arriving with a tray of crystal flutes. Ten mimosas, one straight orange juice for the youngest member. "Mother's Day?"

Melody looks at her daughter, seated to her right. Amelia beams at her, but she, too, has tears in her eyes and neither of them manages to speak.

Amelia's friend Jessie has no such problem—now, or ever. "We're celebrating *everything*!" she tells the waiter. "Including Mimi's belated maybe birthday!"

"But we already celebrated my maybe birthday Friday night, on the actual date," Amelia points out. "And my real one back in April."

"That doesn't count, because I wasn't there," Jessie informs her.

Melody was. She'd flown to New York for the occasion with a special birthday gift—a little black Lab puppy, part of the latest litter she was raising, and descended from Cyril's beloved dog.

Amelia named him Otis, of course.

She showed Melody around the city that week. Not just the tourist attractions, but the places that matter to her—her office, the block where she'd grown up, and of course, Park Baptist Church. It had been her week to sing at Sunday services. Melody sat in the front pew, her own voice raised with the choir. Afterward, they visited the cemetery where the Crenshaws are buried with their infant son between them.

"I found comfort when they died, knowing they were reunited with their child," Amelia said.

Melody nodded. "I felt the same way years ago when we laid my daddy to rest beside my sister."

She placed an enormous bouquet of lilacs on the grave and then stood arm in arm with the daughter Calvin and Bettina had raised, mascara trickling down her face and Amelia's.

There have been so many tears these last few months, but few are the bitter, sorrowful kind. Melody only sheds those when she's alone, pining for what might have been or realizing how close she'd come to losing her precious daughter forever.

"Keep the champagne coming!" Grant tells the waiter.

Melody had been surprised when he walked into the lounge last night just before she and the band started their last set. He was supposed to be spending the weekend up north with his daughters and their families.

"My flight was canceled," he said. "Thunderstorms. Good thing your group wasn't flying in today."

Yes. A very good thing. Melody has been longing all her life for a Mother's Day like this. It almost—*almost*—makes up for the one that had ended so tragically. Here she is, incredibly, celebrating with her mother *and* her daughter.

Honeybee's "I told you so's" haven't worn thin . . . yet.

In the decades that passed after Melody confided the tragic story about her lost child, Cyril, and Marceline, Honeybee had inexplicably believed it might still end happily.

"You never know, Melody, honey. You just never know."

I do know, Mother. I do know.

Still, shocked and relieved by her mother's acceptance of a Black granddaughter, she'd allowed the aging woman to cling to futile hope.

"We didn't get our miracle last time around," Honeybee would tell Melody over the years.

"This time, we will. That child will come back to us."

As if it were that simple. As if the angels in heaven above could wave celestial magic wands and make things right.

Now Honeybee believes that's precisely what happened.

Maybe, on this glorious spring Sunday morning, Melody almost believes it herself.

Amelia had arrived last weekend and the rest of the group on Friday—Amelia's friend Jessie, Jessie's husband, Billy, and their three children. The older two, Chip and Petty, are college students—blissfully unencumbered, Melody thought when she met them. Just like Lucky's daughter, Quinnlynn. As it should be. Though they're separated by more than a decade, the three of them have their heads together, talking about a podcast their elders have never heard of and the youngest, Theodore, dismissed as "sheer drivel."

He's an awkward adolescent with a gifted mind.

"He has special needs," Amelia had told Melody and Honeybee before they arrived.

"Don't we all, my dear," Honeybee said. "Don't we all."

She and Lucky have both taken a shine to young Theodore, seated between them. The two women are having a grand time regaling him with tales of the good old days, and he doesn't seem to mind a bit.

"I'd like to propose a toast," Grant says, lifting his champagne flute.

"Please don't make my wife start crying again," Billy warns him, and Jessie swats his arm.

"No more tears! I just want to say thank you for including me, and lift a glass to family and friends, new and old, young and old."

"I don't know who you're calling old. I'm only ninety," Honeybee says, and the group dissolves in laughter.

"Your mom is quite a pistol," Grant tells Melody, clinking his glass against hers.

"Isn't she just."

She smiles, glad she'd impulsively invited him to brunch when he showed up last night. "We'd love to have you. I'll just change the reservation and add another person."

"It's not that easy," he protested. "I can't even get a table for one tomorrow."

"You just have to know someone," Melody assured

him, and sent him off to sit with Honeybee and Jessie's family as she stepped into the spotlight.

"I've been solo all these years," she told the crowd. "But tonight, I'm doing a duet. Let me tell you a little story . . ."

By the time Amelia joined her to sing "At Last," there wasn't a dry eye in the house.

"Mom?"

Melody hears the word, but doesn't realize it's meant for her until Amelia touches her hand.

"I have something for you."

She stares at the small gift box wrapped in lavender sprigged paper.

Purple for Melly . . .

"Oh, honey, you didn't have to get me a present."

"Trust me. It's something you need to have."

"Trust *me.* I have everything I need." Melody squeezes her hand.

"You should open it."

She tears off the paper, the group around her occupied in their own conversations. Only Amelia is focused on her as she lifts the cover.

Inside the box is a tiny gold ring, encrusted with sapphires, etched with a blue letter *C.*

Melody closes her eyes and sees it against Cyril's bare chest, dangling on a gold chain, glinting in early morning sunlight. Hears his voice, rich as pecan pie, saying, *"Dayclean—a fresh start, with yesterday left behind."*

You'd be so proud, Cyril. We didn't get to raise her, but she's grown up to be a brave, strong woman just like you said.

She opens her eyes and looks at her daughter.

"See? I told you it was something you needed."

"I did. I surely did. Thank you, my love," Melody says aloud, and her heart whispers, *Thank you, Cyril.*

AMELIA STANDS ON the beach, barefoot in warm, shallow surf, gazing at the water.

In January, the ocean had been a dark, blood-tainted death trap. Today, it's translucent, a lovely shade Melody calls *haint* blue.

"I don't care if it's rainbow-sprinkled with surfing unicorns," Jessie said yesterday on the beach, before the rain rolled in. "I'm not going near it."

Her daughter rolled her eyes. "Then why are we even here? I could be back on campus, studying for finals."

"You mean doing shots with your suite mates," Jessie shot back. "And we're here because it's Mother's Day weekend, and I get to choose!"

"You're impossible!" Petty stormed away.

Jessie sighed and looked at Melody. "You dodged a bullet, believe me."

"Pardon?"

"Diane—she's my mom—always said raising a daughter is no picnic until they're all grown up. You got the good part with Mimi."

"Jessie!" Amelia and Billy scolded in unison.

"My mother would probably say the same thing," Melody said, and if she was stung, she hid it behind a good-natured laugh.

Amelia knows that Jessie, too, is hiding an ache behind her usual buoyant, acerbic facade. She'd given up on finding her biological family decades ago, deciding she was content with the one she'd grown up in and the one she was raising.

She should have been spared the terrible truth—that her mother was a teenaged rape victim, her father one of the most notorious serial killers in history, her half-sister a delusional murderess.

"They're all dead, though, Mimi," she'd said. "Thank God I never have to deal with them, you know?"

"You're the most resilient person I've ever known, Jess."

"Oh, it sucks. And believe me, I'm going to need a hell of a lot of therapy after this. But I'm going to focus on the good things, and I feel lucky to be alive."

Rob Owens hired the country's most powerful criminal defense attorneys to defend his son.

Stockton Barnes predicts a lesser conviction or case dismissal.

"Sometimes, for better or worse, the punishment doesn't fit the crime," he said. "And sometimes, the penance a person gives himself is worse than anything the justice system could hand him."

Back in January, he'd told Amelia about Stef and the bribe from Wayland. And then he'd told the bureau chief.

He'd been prepared to turn over his badge, serve time, make restitution . . .

Nothing happened.

There was an investigation, but when Stef was questioned, he said he'd made up the story about Wayland. The money had been his own. A gambling windfall.

"Maybe it's the truth," Amelia told Barnes.

"It isn't. It's the code of silence."

"Well, there's nothing you can do about it now, is there? I mean, you tried to go back, and undo, and redo, and . . . you can't. Sometimes, you just have to move on, Barnes."

Amelia stares out at the ocean, thinking about Cyril, and about his mother. She'd never had the chance to see Marceline again. She passed away in early February.

"She was just hangin' on all these years 'cause she needed to make things right, child," Lucky told Amelia when she flew down for the funeral. "Now she's at peace."

We all are.

She paid her respects to Marceline, and a month later, to Silas Moss. She and Jessie delivered a joint eulogy, and then they drank an entire bottle of wine in the spot where it all began, on the steps of a yellow mansion that had once belonged to Si, and now belonged to Jessie.

"Just like old times, Mimi," Jessie said as they passed the bottle back and forth. "Who needs stemware?"

"Or coats?" Amelia said, shivering a little in the cold March night.

"Jess, have you seen my uniform pants?" Billy called from inside the house.

"Nope!" she called back, then hissed at Amelia, "And who needs men? Or pants?"

They were drunk, and silly. Just like old times.

Back at home in New York, Amelia ended her marriage.

"I'm sorry I wasn't always present . . . in the present," she told Aaron.

"And I'm sorry I didn't understand where you were coming from. I'm glad you found what you were looking for."

She certainly has.

Her phone buzzes with a text.

Hope you had a great brunch with your mom.

She smiles.

Yes. Hope you did, too.

Great? Clearly, you haven't met my mom yet.

No, but she will next week. He's taking them both to dinner. He says it's time. She agrees. He'd met Melody when she came to New York.

"I'm so happy you have such a wonderful man in your life, Amelia," she'd said.

"We're taking it slow. I'm not sure where it's going . . ."

"Life is too short to take anything slow."

"You're right, Mom. Remember that when you get back to Florida, and Grant."

Her mother had protested that they were just friends. Maybe. But they'll get there.

Amelia texts, I hope you have a better dinner with your daughter tonight.

The response comes quickly—a thumbs-up and a heart emoji. Counting down the hours. Did you give your mom the ring?

She smiles. Yes! It was perfect. Thanks again.

He responds with the same words he said in person, when he gave it to her after the police released it as evidence.

It was always yours.

The screen vibrates with ellipses, indicating he's typing again.

Just fed Clancy and Otis.

The text is accompanied by a photo of a kitten and puppy snuggled together on Amelia's bed.

Aw! I miss them!

A new message whooshes in.

I miss you.

A moment later, a selfie pops up.

Barnes again, making an exaggerated sad face.

She laughs.

I miss you, too, she writes back. She turns her phone around and snaps a shot of herself making an equally ridiculous sad face with the ocean in the background. About to hit Send, she notices something in the photo.

Behind her, on the horizon, a single dolphin arcs against the blue sky as if dancing in midair above the water.

Amelia whirls to look, but it's disappeared. She sees nothing on the haint-blue horizon now but a glowing sun, rays falling in a golden band across the shimmering sea.

***NEW YORK TIMES* BESTSELLING AUTHOR**

WENDY CORSI STAUB

THE GOOD SISTER

978-0-06-222237-4

Jen Archer hoped her daughter, Carley, would thrive at Sacred Sisters Catholic girls' school. Instead, shy, studious Carley becomes the target of vicious bullies. The only person Carley can talk to is "Angel," a kindred spirit she met online. When a schoolgirl is found dead, Jen's unease grows, as every instinct tells her Carley is the next target.

THE PERFECT STRANGER

978-0-06-222240-4

During the darkest period of her life, Landry Wells found solace in a group of bloggers. She shared things with her online friends that even her husband doesn't know. Now, one of the bloggers is dead, victim of a random crime—or was it? At the funeral, Landry is about to come face to face with the others—and one of them might be a cold-blooded killer …

THE BLACK WIDOW

978-0-06-222243-5

Newly divorced Gaby Duran isn't expecting to find her soul mate on a dating site like InTune. She just needs a distraction from pining over the happy marriage she once had. But Gaby soon discovers there is more at stake than her lonely heart. Local singles are going missing after making online connections. And a predator is again searching for a perfect match.

SPINE-TINGLING SUSPENSE FROM
***NEW YORK TIMES* BESTSELLING AUTHOR**

WENDY CORSI STAUB

NIGHTWATCHER

978-0-06-207028-9

Allison Taylor adores her adopted city, New York. But on a bright and clear September morning in 2001, the familiar landscape around her is savagely altered—and in the midst of widespread chaos and fear, a woman living upstairs from her is found, brutally slaughtered and mutilated. Now a different kind of terror has entered Allison's life . . . and it's coming to claim her as its next victim.

SLEEPWALKER

978-0-06-207030-2

The nightmare of 9/11 is a distant but still painful memory for Allison Taylor MacKenna—now married and living in a quiet Westchester suburb. She has moved on with her life ten years after barely escaping death at the hands of New York's Nightwatcher serial killer. But now here, north of the city, more women are being savagely murdered, their bodies bearing the Nightwatcher's unmistakable signature.

SHADOWKILLER

978-0-06-207032-6

Nestled in the warm, domestic cocoon of loving husband and family, Allison finally feels safe—unaware that a stranger's brutal murder on a Caribbean island is the first step in an intricate plan to destroy everything in her life.

WCS1 0416